Bethan Roberts was born in Oxford and brought up in nearby Abingdon. She has MAs from Sussex and Chichester universities and teaches creative writing at Chichester and for the Open University. She was awarded a Jerwood/Arvon Young Writers' Prize for *The Pools*. *The Good Plain Cook* is her second novel.

Praise for *The Good Plain Cook*

'Delicious… Gorgeously written, full of teasing observations about love, class and cookery' Kate Saunders, *The Times*

'Vividly drawn and affecting… fine touches of subtlety and humour' Sophie Davies, *Financial Times*

'Roberts judiciously balances Ellen's delicious outré flamboyance with a beautifully observed portrait of her tolerant, bemused cook. Roberts has said it was her intention to "put the below-stairs girl centre stage". She has succeeded admirably' Eithne Farry, *Daily Mail*

'A subtly witty study of class tensions and general human folly… Roberts writes an understated, suggestive prose that achieves maximum comic impact with deceptively slight materials… One of the novel's greatest strengths is the way in which the surface comedy is underpinned by a darker narrative seam' Elizabeth Lowry, *Guardian*

‘One of this summer’s purest pleasures… Bethan Roberts is a clever, confident young writer who enjoys herself hugely, producing a perfectly proportioned story of love, inadequate cooking, cultural confusion and complex characters in domestic difficulties’ Iain Finlayson, *Saga*

‘Excellent... Has plenty to say about sex and class and says it with subtle wit and concision’ John O’Connell, *Time Out* Books of the Year

Praise for *The Pools*

‘A complex anatomy of a murder, *The Pools* brilliantly evokes the sickening recognition of a wasteful death. Bethan Roberts is a fearless writer whose first novel raises questions about fate and responsibility that remain with the reader long after the last page has been turned. A compelling debut’ Louise Welsh

‘A wonderfully self-assured debut… There is a forbidding feeling throughout the novel – an almost audible hum of misgiving coming off the pages. Superb’ Ruth Atkins, Booksellers’ Choice, *The Bookseller*

‘An unsettling and disturbing tale of awakening sexuality and predatory parents’ Patricia Duncker

Bonus material

Turn to page 312 for Bethan Roberts’ account of researching *The Good Plain Cook*, on being published for the first time, and for the two opening chapters of her critically acclaimed debut novel, *The Pools*.

... The Good Plain Cook ...

Bethan Roberts

A complete catalogue record for this book can be obtained from the British Library on request

First published in this edition in 2009 by Serpent's Tail
First published in 2008 by Serpent's Tail,
an imprint of Profile Books Ltd
3A Exmouth House
Pine Street
London EC1R 0JH
website: www.serpentstail.com

ISBN 978 1 84668 670 2

Designed and typeset by Sue Lamble

Printed in the UK by CPI Bookmarque, Croydon, CR0 4TD

10 9 8 7 6 5 4 3 2 1

For the good, lovely Hugh
and in memory of Evelyn Dix

Surely there could be no more fitting medium of individual expression for women than fashioning something of loveliness.

The Big Book of Needlecraft (c.1935)

... Sussex, 1936 ...

... One ...

WANTED – *Good plain cook to perform domestic duties for artistic household. Room and board included. Broad outlook essential. Apply Mrs E. Steinberg, Willow Cottage, Harting.*

It was the third time since breakfast that Kitty had read the notice she'd cut from the *Hants and Sussex Herald*. Folding the slip of paper back into the pocket of her raincoat, which she'd belted tightly because her waist – as her sister Lou often pointed out – was her best feature, she walked along the slippery grass verge towards her interview at Willow Cottage. Beneath her blue beret, the ends of her hair were beginning to kink in the mist of spring drizzle.

Lou had told her that the cottage was now in the ownership of an American woman, and that she lived with a man who was, apparently, a poet – not that you'd think it to look at him; he was quite young, and didn't have a beard. No one was sure if the poet was the American woman's husband or not. 'No one else will answer that advert, knowing who *she* is,' Lou had said. 'And I'll bet they want one person to do it all: cooking and skivvying both.' But Kitty had had enough of living with her sister, despite all the modern comforts laid on at 60 Woodbury Avenue, and so she'd written, not mentioning that she'd no experience as a cook. At the last minute, she'd added the words, *I have a broad outlook.*

She turned into the lane which led to the gravel driveway. The cottage was just off the main road out of Harting and was the largest in the village. Through the dripping beech hedge, she caught glimpses of the place. It was red brick, and had exposed beams, like many in the village, but the front door was crimson, with a long stained-glass panel of all colours, much brighter and swirlier than anything Kitty had seen in church, and obviously new. There was a large garage at the end of the drive, from which a loud *chuck-chuck* noise was coming. Kitty recognised the sound: there'd been an electricity generator at the Macklows' too, where she'd worked as a kitchen maid after leaving school.

As she approached the house, Kitty noticed a woman's round-toed shoe on the front lawn, its high heel skewed in the mud. Bending down, she tugged it free. It was quite large for a woman's shoe, and the sole was shiny with wear. The inside was soft cream leather, the outside brilliant green and scuffed. She tapped it on the stones to remove some of the mud, then walked around to the back of the house.

Squinting through the rain, Kitty could see a stream and a line of willow trees at the end of the garden, before which was some kind of building that looked like a tiny house. Plants seemed to be everywhere, spilling over the paths without any apparent order; the large lawn needed a cut. Amongst the daffodils, Kitty caught a glimpse of a woman's rain-streaked backside, sculpted in stone.

She adjusted her beret, tried to comb out the ends of her hair with her fingers, and knocked at the back door.

Immediately there was a series of high yaps, and when the door opened, a little grey dog with large ears, a straggly beard and black eyes jumped at Kitty's legs. Kitty stooped to scratch its head. When she was very young, her father had owned a docile Jack Russell, who'd never minded the sisters dressing him up in bonnet and bootees. The grey dog caught hold of Kitty's cuff and gently licked the rain from its edge.

'Don't mind Blotto, he gets excited with strangers.' A tall girl of about twelve stood in the doorway, chewing a piece of her long blonde hair. 'Who are you and why didn't you knock on the front door?'

Kitty straightened up and held the shoe behind her back, suddenly worried that the girl would think she was stealing. The rain was coming down harder and she hadn't brought her umbrella. Her beret must look flat and ridiculous by now, like a wet lily pad on her head.

'I've come about the position, Miss.'

'Position?'

'Is your mother – is Madam in?'

'Who?'

'Madam – Mrs Steinberg, Miss.'

The girl frowned and chewed. 'I don't know,' she said, not letting the strand of hair drop from her mouth. 'What have you got behind your back?'

Kitty glanced down at the girl's dirty knees. She was wearing a very short and ill-fitting tulle skirt with an orange cardigan.

'I found it on the front lawn, Miss.' Kitty held the shoe out to the girl, who shrugged.

'That's been there for ages,' she said.

Kitty let her arm drop. 'Have I come to the right place?'

'*I* don't know.' The girl bent down and scooped up the dog, which buried itself in her hair and began licking her ear.

'There was a notice, in the *Herald*. For a plain cook, Miss.'

Rain was dripping into Kitty's collar now. She tried to see into the kitchen, but the girl shifted and blocked Kitty's view.

'Ellen never said anything to me.'

'Perhaps I'd better be going.'

The girl stared at Kitty for a moment. Her eyes were startlingly blue.

'But then, she never tells us anything, does she, Blotto?' She kissed the dog on his nose and was licked right up her forehead. 'My name's Regina, but that's horrible so everyone calls me Geenie, and this is Blotto, he's a miniature schnauzer, which is a very good breed of dog.'

'I think I've made a mistake.'

She'd be dripping all the way back on the bus by the time it came.

'Geenie! Who's there?'

So she *was* American.

'She won't tell me her name and she's got your shoe.'

A tall woman came to the door. She was wearing an embroidered red jacket and wide-legged mauve slacks. Her hair waved above her high forehead and was the colour of brown bread. She wore no jewellery. Her nose was huge; the end of it looked like a large radish. She blinked at Kitty.

'What's your name, please?'

'Allen, Madam, Kate – Kitty – Allen. I've come about…'

The woman stuck out a hand and Kitty met it with the shoe.

'What's that?'

'It's been on the lawn for ages,' said Geenie. 'I wear it when I'm being Dietrich.'

The woman ignored this. 'Is it Kate or Kitty?'

At the Macklows' she'd been plain 'Allen'.

'Kitty, Madam, please.'

'I'm Ellen Steinberg. Do come in. You could have used the front door, you know, this isn't London, and it's only a cottage.'

'Yes, Madam.'

'Get out of the way, Geenie, and let the girl through.'

Geenie ducked under Mrs Steinberg's arm and fled, taking the dog with her.

'You'll have to excuse my daughter. I'm afraid she's always been highly strung.'

Kitty followed the woman into the cottage, still gripping the sodden shoe in one hand.

.....

There was no fire in the sitting-room grate. Ashes floated in the air as Mrs Steinberg walked past the enormous fireplace, dropped into a velvet armchair, and drew a fur rug across her knees. 'Take a seat, please, Kitty.'

Kitty sat on the sofa, which was covered in a tapestry-like fabric, threaded with gold. She thought about putting the shoe on the floor, but changed her mind and folded her hands around it in her lap. Then she looked up and noticed, above the armchair where Mrs Steinberg was sitting, a hole in the wall. It was as big as the woman's head, and its edges were ragged.

Mrs Steinberg twisted around and looked at the hole too, but said nothing.

Kitty let her eyes wander over the rest of the room. The walls were all white, except for one which was covered in wooden racks filled with records. The floorboards were bare, apart from a red rug in front of the hearth. The curtains were pink and green chintz, lined with purple satin. On the mantelpiece was a large bunch of irises and daffodils, stuffed into a blue ceramic jug. The flowers were interspersed with long blades of grass.

'Mr Crane loves grass,' said Mrs Steinberg.

Kitty dropped her eyes.

'He says the grass of Sussex is the best in the world. He's worked wonders with this place; it's really all his doing. He's an absolute whiz with interiors. We're both very keen on modernisation. But it's still damned icy, don't you think? And the rooms are ridiculously small.'

The woman's voice was strange – not as American as Kitty had imagined, and high-pitched, like a girl's. Kitty shifted her feet. Mrs Steinberg had hung her raincoat and hat to dry in the kitchen, but her shoes were soaked.

'However. We *have* got gas *and* electricity, Kitty! A very recent addition out here in the wilderness. So it will be easy for you – in the kitchen. And music. We've got plenty of music. I hope you like music?'

'Yes, Madam,' said Kitty, wondering what music had to do with anything.

'Excellent. Geenie's never been musical and Mr Crane is hopeless. He thinks brass bands are a good thing! So, you see, I need an ally.' She adjusted the fur rug and stretched out her feet. Her shoes were made of a soft material, gathered in a visible seam around the sole; to Kitty, they looked like a pair of man's slippers.

'Every woman needs an ally in the house, don't you think? It's no good just having men and children. You must have dogs, too, and other women.'

Kitty plucked at her skirt. She'd worn her best – blue boiled wool with a pleat at the side – and now it had a damp patch on the front from the wet shoe.

'How old are you, Kitty?'

'Nineteen, Madam.'

Mrs Steinberg frowned. Kitty wasn't sure if she was too young, or too old, for the job. At the Macklows', all the girls had complained about this problem: when you were young they didn't want you because you'd no experience, but as you got older they were reluctant to promote you for fear you'd go off and get married.

'And what was it you did before?'

'I'm a cleaner in the school, Madam, at the moment. But before that I did a bit of cooking for a lady in Petersfield.' In reality, she'd scrubbed the zinc, laid out the cook's knives, and fetched, cleaned or carried anything she was told.

'Are the schools here awful? The ones in London were really dreadful. Geenie was very unhappy in all of them. The English seem to believe children can learn only through punishment.'

Kitty thought of her school, of the hours spent copying words and numbers from a blackboard, the dust that gathered in the grooves of her desk, the teacher who used to pick the boys up by their collars and shake them. 'I – wouldn't like to say, Madam.'

'Can you brush hair?'

'Yes, Madam.'

'Because Geenie's hair needs a lot of brushing and although I don't expect you to be her nanny there will be times when I may need help—'

'Oh.' Kitty grasped her knees. 'I hadn't realised…'

'Our old nanny, Dora, left us recently. Geenie was far too attached to her, so in the end it was all to the good.'

Mrs Steinberg fixed Kitty with her grey eyes, which seemed to be smiling, even though her mouth was not. 'So.

Tell me. What can you do?'

Kitty wanted to ask about the times when Mrs Steinberg would need help with the girl, but she'd been rehearsing her answer to this question, so she replied, 'I'm schooled in domestic science.'

It was what Lou had told her to say, insisting it had enough meaning without having too much. She'd read about it in one of her magazines.

'Whatever does that mean?'

A sharp heat rose up Kitty's neck. Her mouth jumped into a smile, as it always did when she was nervous.

Mrs Steinberg laughed. 'Do you mean you can cook and clean?'

Kitty nodded, but couldn't seem to find enough breath for words. Her feet were numb with cold now, and she was beginning to feel awfully hungry.

Mrs Steinberg waved a hand in the air. 'So what can you cook?'

Kitty had prepared an answer to this as well. She'd always cooked for Mother, and had seen enough, she felt, in the year she'd spent in the Macklow house to know what the job was. The most important thing seemed to be always to have a stockpot on the go.

'Meat and vegetables both, Madam. Savouries and sweets.'

Mrs Steinberg seemed to be waiting for more.

'I can do meat cakes, beef olives, faggots… And castle pudding, bread and butter pudding, and all of that, puddings are what I do best, Madam.' She could eat some bread and butter pudding now, with cold custard on it.

Mrs Steinberg's face was blank. 'Anything else?'

Perhaps they were vegetarians. Lou's husband Bob said that some of these bohemians were. 'Fruit fritters… and, um…'

'Nothing more... continental, Kitty?'

'I can do cheese puffs, Madam.'

Mrs Steinberg laughed. 'Well. Never mind. I hope you won't mind doing some housework, too. I'm not very fussy about it, but there'll be a bit of sweeping and dusting now and then, keeping the place looking generally presentable.' She twisted round in her seat and looked again at the hole above her head. 'It will be easier for you when Mr Crane and Arthur have finished knocking these two rooms together, of course. One large, light, all-purpose room, that's what we want. I don't believe in all this *compartmentalisation*, do you?'

'Yes, Madam. I mean, no, Madam.'

'Stop calling me that. It makes me sound like a brothel-keeper. You can call me Mrs Steinberg.' The woman's long fingers rummaged at her scalp as she spoke. 'Now. Would you like to ask me anything?' She perched on the edge of the armchair and held the wave of her hair back from her forehead with both hands. 'Anything at all.'

Kitty looked at the woman's clear forehead for a moment.

'Anything at all, Kitty.'

'Are there any other staff here, Mrs Steinberg?'

'Just Arthur, the gardener and... handyman, I suppose you'd call him. He doesn't live with us, but he's here most days.'

Kitty shifted in her seat. 'There's no housemaid or parlour-maid?'

'You won't be expected to wait on us, Kitty, if that's what you're worrying about. We don't go in for all that.'

'No, Madam.'

There was a pause. Kitty squeezed the green shoe in her hands.

'Are we settled, then? Could you start next week?'

She must ask it. 'Will I be expected to – what you said about when you're not here... your daughter...' She mustn't be the nanny. That was not what the notice said. 'What I mean is, what will I be doing, exactly?'

'Kitty, I'm probably the only bohemian in the country who likes order.' Mrs Steinberg smiled and widened her eyes. 'Let's see. Start with the bedrooms. There are four rooms, one for myself, one for Geenie... And one for Mr Crane, of course.' She paused. 'Then a guest room. And, downstairs, sitting and dining room – soon to be one – bathroom, a cubby-hole that's supposed to be a library, but you don't have to bother with that: only I go in there. So it's not very much. A little cleaning and polishing, fires swept and laid when it's cold, which it is all the damn time, isn't it? And the cooking, of course, but we quite often have a cold plate for lunch, and only two courses for dinner, unless we've got company. Geenie eats with us; we don't believe in that nonsense of hiding children away for meals. And we don't go in for any fuss at breakfast time, either. Toast will do for me, but Mr Crane does like his porridge.'

Kitty blinked.

'He has a little writing studio in the garden, you probably noticed – it's where he works. But, if you'll take my advice, you won't go in there. The place is always a mess, anyway, and he hates to be disturbed. He's a poet, but at the moment he's working on a novel.' Here she paused and smiled so brilliantly that Kitty had to smile back. 'I'm encouraging him all I can. That's why he's living here, you see; it's a vocational thing, really; if one has artistic friends, one must help them out.'

Kitty looked about the room for a clock but couldn't find one. How long had she been here? Her stomach felt hollow. She thought of sausage rolls, of biting into the greasy pastry, the deep salty taste of the meat.

'And then there's Geenie. Well, of course, I would really appreciate it if you could keep an eye on her occasionally but she's my responsibility now.'

If Kitty didn't move, her stomach might not growl.

'Children need their mothers first and foremost, don't they?'

Kitty nodded, relieved. 'Oh yes, Mrs Steinberg.'

There was a pause. The growl was building in Kitty's stomach, pressing against her insides as if some creature were crawling around the pit of her.

'So. Can you start next week?'

As she nodded, Kitty's stomach gave a long, loud rumble. Mrs Steinberg raised an eyebrow and smiled. 'It's lunchtime, isn't it? Yes. I must let you go.' She clapped her hands together. 'Kitty, I think you'll do nicely. Forty pounds a year, and two afternoons off a week, all right?'

'Thank you, Mrs Steinberg.'

The woman stood, and Kitty followed.

'Are you still holding that shoe?' Mrs Steinberg laughed. 'Why don't you keep it? As a welcome gift. We might even be able to find the other.'

Kitty looked at the sodden shoe. It was at least two sizes too big for her. 'Thank you, Mrs Steinberg,' she repeated.

... Two ...

Geenie walked into a sitting room full of dust. Her shoes made a strange scrunching noise on the floor-boards and she could taste something in the air: a cloud of powder, like the stuff Ellen threw about her face every evening.

Her palms were still smarting from gripping the willow tree in the back garden. It was a new game: holding on to the ridged bark with all her strength, digging her nails in, seeing how much matter would lodge beneath her finger-tips, then going in the house and telling Ellen that she'd fallen. Showing the marks on her palms, she usually got a frown from her mother. Just occasionally, though, she was rewarded with a short spell on her lap, which, although not wide, was always warm, and she could run her hands along the smooth skin of Ellen's knees and listen as she breathed close to her ear. 'You're too old for this sort of thing,' her mother would say. 'Girls of eleven shouldn't be sitting in their mothers' laps.'

Blotto trotted behind as she walked into the sitting room. 'Ellen!' she yelled. 'Ellen!'

The dust fell. Blotto sniffed the air.

Then she saw it. A hole right through to the next room.

Pressing her palms together, she approached, and Blotto followed. She stood for a minute, examining the gap where wall had once been. The dog sniffed the pile of rubble at her feet and gave an interested half-bark. Geenie ignored him and pushed a finger into the damaged brick. A few crumbs fell on her shoes and she smiled. Now they would be scuffed, but it wasn't really her fault, because there was a hole in the wall. She pulled a loose bit of plaster away and a cascade of brick dust covered both shoes. Again, not her fault, and more interesting, even, than the willow tree game. Brick made a greater imprint than bark, and the sound of it falling around her bare legs distracted her from the familiar afternoon noises that had begun to seep from her mother's bedroom.

Blotto sniffed at the new pile of debris, whimpered, then retreated.

After a bit more working, her knuckles scraping on the rough brick until they were peppered with blood, the hole was big enough for Geenie to put a leg through, so one patent T-bar shoe touched the floorboards in the dining room, whilst the other remained in the sitting room. The broken brick dug into her inner thigh as she shifted her leg until her foot was planted firmly on the floor. She tried to imagine what it would be like to live between two rooms like this: one foot always in the sitting room, the other in the dining room. If the hole were large enough to walk through, they could have their dinner and Blotto need not be shut in the other room, because there would be no other room. That would be good. But it would also be bad, because she wouldn't be able to shut herself in the dining room as tightly as she liked. There was a particularly useful cupboard in the corner of the dining room, which smelled of sherry and dust, whose door made a lovely clunkety-click noise when opened or closed. The bottom shelf was big enough for Geenie to curl into, and if she hooked her finger round the knot of wood by the handle in the right way, she could hold the door almost closed and breathe its dark sherry air and no one would know she was there. Then she could listen to George and Ellen as they argued or kissed, and she could think of the times when Jimmy, who was gone now, had read to her whilst they sat together in the cupboard under the stairs in their London house, eating sherbet.

The familiar noises from her mother's bedroom had become more drawn out. Geenie called for Blotto. If the dog came back, they could howl together, and then she wouldn't have to listen to the bedroom noises. She called him again, and waited for the tick-tick of his claws on the floor. But the dog did not come.

She looked at the pile of rubble by her sitting-room foot and noticed the wooden handle of the lump hammer amongst the destroyed brick. She reached down, her dining-room leg catching on the teeth of the hole, and ran a finger along the hammer's cool head. Bringing her finger to her face, she considered the dust there. It had lodged in all the ridges of her skin. If she were to pick the hammer up and then drop it on her shoe, she would probably break her toes, like the Chinese women who had their feet smashed and bound so they could wear small shoes. Ellen often said she wished a kindly aunt had broken and bound her own nose when she was younger than Geenie, so that one marvellous day she might have unravelled the bandages to reveal a tiny nose, *tip-tilted like a flower*, which is what it said in the Tennyson poem, and what Geenie's nose was like.

If she dropped the hammer, it would make a noise so loud that Ellen and George might run downstairs. They might stop kissing, or arguing, and rush to her aid, because they would hear a loud noise and not know what it was, and a loud noise meant trouble.

Geenie twisted her body so that she faced the sitting room. She picked up the hammer and held it in both hands. She lifted her arms above her head. Breathing out, feeling the stretch in her muscles as her dining-room leg struggled to remain planted on the floorboards, she stayed still for at least a minute, focusing on the middle pane of the front window. This was necessary in order to concentrate on the banging coming from above. It was becoming more insistent, and there was now a low grunt accompanying every bang. Still Geenie held the hammer above her head and waited. Her arms began to ache. Then it came, familiar and awful: her mother's long 'yes'.

As the 'yes' grew louder, Geenie swung her body round and slammed the hammer to the wall with all her strength.

... Three ...

Mrs Steinberg had told her to make herself at home, and said they would like lunch at half past twelve, if she could manage it. She hadn't said what they would like for lunch or how Kitty was to prepare it. They'd walked through the kitchen – they had to, to reach Kitty's room – but the American woman hadn't mentioned anything useful, such as where the pans were kept, where an apron might be, or what was in the larder. She'd just waved a hand and said, 'Isn't that lantern absolutely beautiful? My first husband brought it back from China. But everything else is brand new.' The lantern, hanging over the central table, was made of red silk; a greasy yellow tassel trailed from its base. The tassel was so long that it almost brushed the tabletop, which couldn't be hygienic.

Mrs Steinberg had been very generous, though, Kitty reminded herself as she looked around her new room: forty pounds a year was more than she'd ever been paid before, and the room wasn't bad, either. There were a couple of small multi-coloured woollen rugs for the tiled floor; a chest of drawers; and a wardrobe, so Kitty didn't have to hang her clothes on the back of the door. Mrs Steinberg had also provided a picture above Kitty's bed of a naked woman beside a waterfall, at which Kitty now stood and stared. She hadn't liked to look at it too closely when the other woman was in the room, but her initial impression had been right: the woman's flesh had a greenish tint, and was full to bursting. Her neck seemed unnaturally long, and her head twisted to the side as if she'd just heard a stranger approaching through the ferns. Kitty imagined the woman was thinking about plunging in, but had first to pluck up enough courage to submerge herself in cold water.

The first thing Kitty did was place the framed photograph of her mother and father, sitting very upright, on the chest of drawers. Her mother's gaze was steady, her mouth fixed; her father looked off to the side, as if he were about to move. They must have been quite young when it was taken, as her father had died in his early thirties, when Kitty was five, but to Kitty they already looked unreachably old. Perhaps it was something to do with her mother's high lace collars, which she would sew on to make an old dress new. Kitty had mended those collars herself during her mother's illness, spending hours darning them with her finest needle.

Opening the wardrobe, she was surprised to smell not mothballs but perfume: something powdery and sweet, like cinnamon. Onto the top shelf she bundled her cloth bag of scraps. Then she took up her wooden work-box, sat on the narrow bed, and opened the lid.

Now she was going to live in this new place, it was important to see that everything was there, all the things she'd carefully collected together over the years. She brought out the odd pink suspender clasp (had it been Mother's?); the paper packets of sharp and between needles; the dirty lump of beeswax, deeply scored; the scissors with the tortoiseshell handles which she saved for her embroidery; her other, sharper scissors, for cutting out; her star-shaped cushion, studded with steel and ribbon pins; her woollen strawberry, for cleaning needles; several reels of cotton of differing thicknesses; a card of hooks and eyes; a smooth copper thimble, which she hated using but kept anyway; and buttons of various shapes and sizes. The buttons were the most precious items in Kitty's work-box. Her favourite had always been the large lilac one with the wooden surround, but she'd recently come into a set of four tiny mother-of-pearl buttons which Lou had cut from a nightie before shredding it for dusters, and it was one of these that she now rubbed along her bottom lip, relishing its smoothness.

There was a knock on the door.

It was too late to put the sewing things away in the work-box, so she stood in front of the bed, hoping to conceal them.

'Come in.'

Geenie loomed in the doorway. She was wearing a long white cotton robe with wide sleeves and a square neck, together with a thick gold necklace. Her large eyes were rimmed with black kohl. 'What's for lunch today?'

Kitty stared at the girl, trying to make sense of her appearance. The girl stared back.

'I – don't know, Miss.'

'I hope it's not salad.'

The kohl had left a black smudge in the corner of the girl's eye, like a piece of soot. Why was the child dressed like that, at half past ten on a Monday morning?

'I need to speak with your mother,' said Kitty. 'It's up to her, Miss.'

'Dora used to decide for herself, and she always made me plain omelettes.'

'Well. I'll ask your mother what she thinks…'

Why wasn't that girl at school?

Geenie stepped into the room. Pointing to the bed, she asked, 'What's that?'

'It's my work-box. I was just looking at it. Sorting it, I mean.' Kitty started gathering up the sewing things and putting them back in the box.

'Let me see.'

The girl was close to her now; she had an earthy scent. It was what Kitty had noticed about the children at the school where she'd cleaned – the smell of them, warm and yeasty, like the scent of excited terriers. But this girl smelled fresher than that.

Geenie sat on the bed. Her white robe rustled as she bent over the box and peered inside. She picked out a large cardigan button. 'What sort of wood is this?'

'I don't know, Miss.'

The girl tossed the button back into the box. Then she rummaged again and found the cut-glass button from Lou's wedding dress. Bob had paid for everything, even tea at the White Hart Hotel, and he hadn't allowed his bride to have a home-made dress run up by her sister.

'This one's pretty.'

'Yes.' Kitty smiled. 'It's from my sister's wedding dress.'

Geenie ignored this. 'Is it the kind of thing Cleopatra would wear?'

'I don't know, Miss. Possibly.'

'I'm Cleopatra today.'

'Are you, Miss?'

'Do you think I make a good one?'

Kitty hesitated. She knew she should say yes, but she wasn't really sure what a good Cleopatra should look like.

'You look very pretty, Miss.'

Geenie looked at Kitty. 'Do you like pretty things?'

'Yes Miss,' said Kitty. 'Everybody likes pretty things, don't they?'

The girl lay back on the bed. 'My mother says pretty's not enough. Things ought to be beautiful.'

There was another knock at the door. Before she could answer, Mrs Steinberg was standing on the rug.

'What are you doing here?' she asked Geenie.

The girl did not sit up or reply.

Mrs Steinberg straightened her navy blue jacket and stepped towards the bed. 'I suggest you stop bothering the cook. She's got a lot to get on with.' She pulled her daughter up by one arm. Geenie dangled before Kitty, her feet hardly touching the floor.

'May I show you to Mr Crane before lunch, Kitty? He's got a gap in his writing schedule and has asked to meet you.'

Kitty closed the work-box.

.....

'The writing studio,' said Mrs Steinberg, opening the door to the little house at the bottom of the garden. 'Kitty, this is Mr Crane.'

The room smelled of flowers, gas and dog. On the windowsill, a row of hyacinths bloomed in glass bowls, their flowers stiff and bright, like the coral Kitty had seen once, in the aquarium at Bognor. The curtains were flame yellow, and in the corner of the room a gas burner sputtered. Beneath the window, there was a desk strewn with papers, amongst which was an old typewriter. Under the desk was a pile of dirty blankets.

'Pleased to meet you, Kitty.'

He was tall and his nose was long and straight, but his

left eye drooped a bit, making his face seem slightly lop-sided. His clothes were too large for him, his long green cardigan patched at the elbows. As Lou had said, he didn't look like a poet. Not that Kitty knew what poets were supposed to look like. The only picture she'd seen was a painting of Byron in a schoolbook, and he wore a very white shirt and had lots of unruly hair. Mr Crane's hair was dark and quite neat.

For a brief moment, Kitty thought she should bob, but Mr Crane's firm handshake kept her upright.

'Kitty's going to be our new help, George. She's a plain cook.'

He touched his forehead, as if considering the situation. His sleeves were pushed up his forearms and Kitty saw lines of flat dark hair and an ink stain on his wrist. It was an elegant wrist, with a prominent, rounded bone.

'Isn't it wonderful? She's been cleaning at the school until now, but she loves music and she's got a broad outlook, haven't you, Kitty?'

'Yes, Madam.'

'I've told her not to call me that, George. And I've told her there's no need to come in here.' Mrs Steinberg walked across to the desk, trailed her fingers along the typewriter keys and leaned back on Mr Crane's chair, one leg crossed over the other. 'He *hates* to be disturbed, don't you, George?'

Mr Crane didn't reply. He was still holding his forehead and looking at Kitty.

'He loathes it. Particularly if he's reading Karl Marx.'

Mr Crane gave a short laugh. 'Welcome to Willow Cottage, Kitty. I hope you'll be happy here.'

'Thank you, Sir.' She did bob, then, without meaning to; her knees bent and she cast her eyes to the floor.

He touched her elbow as she came back up. 'Don't,' he said. 'Don't do that, there's really no earthly need ever to do that, and please don't call me Sir.'

She looked at the place where his long fingers had been on her arm.

'Please. You can call me—'

'Mr Crane,' said Mrs Steinberg, showing Kitty the door.

.....

The kitchen smelled of coffee and Blotto, who was snoozing under the large table. She slipped the apron that was hanging on the back of the door over her head and buttoned the straps. She was already late getting on with the lunch, and she'd have to work fast if she was going to have anything ready on time.

Geenie skipped ahead and sat at the table to watch with her blackened eyes.

'Excuse me, Miss, but don't you go to school?' asked Kitty.

The girl shook her head. 'George says he could teach me at home but Ellen says he should be working on his book.'

She seemed to draw her lips inward as she gazed at Kitty, as if keeping something close.

'Your mother doesn't mind?'

The girl shook her head again. 'What are we having for lunch?'

Kitty walked to the larder without replying. Perhaps it would become clear what she was to prepare once she was inside. Mrs Steinberg may have left a note, or a particular set of ingredients might have been set aside. There was no need, no need at all, to panic. She closed the door behind her so the girl couldn't follow.

In the larder, she was greeted by bottles and bottles of wine, stacked all around the walls, beneath the lowest shelf. At least a quarter of them were empty. She brought one to her nose and sniffed. Vinegar. Raspberries. Something burny, like medicine. On the shelves were three bags of sugar, a sack of flour, and at least a dozen bottles of oil, all with labels that seemed to be in French; there were jars of lobster and cockle paste, and jam. One was open and had crumbs in it. There were two jars of something black that looked like Bovril but wasn't. In the corner, a refrigerator – bigger than the one Bob had recently bought for Lou – hummed. Kitty opened the door: a dozen eggs, a packet of butter and bottle of milk, but no cheese.

The larder door opened.

'Can I have an omelette?'

Kitty could scramble, poach and boil eggs with confidence, but her omelettes were always flat.

'Just a minute, Miss.'

She closed the door and stood biting the skin around her nails. What could she make from eggs and quarter of a loaf? Was Mrs Steinberg expecting her to go into Petersfield to fetch some groceries? Kitty hadn't asked about the time of the deliveries. It was already eleven o'clock, and even if she managed the eleven-thirty bus she wouldn't be back before one.

She did another circuit of the larder, opened a jar of the black stuff that looked like Bovril and sniffed. Sardines and mud.

If Lou were here, she'd have asked Mrs Steinberg outright, first thing. *What should I make for lunch, Madam?* It would have been easy to ask the question when the woman was showing Kitty her room; it would have been easy, if she hadn't been too busy not looking at the awful painting of the naked woman to think straight. Why hadn't she spoken up, then and there, and got it over with?

She opened the larder door, took a step back into the kitchen, and almost walked into him.

'Sorry to startle you,' the man said, looking her up and down. He stood firm, with his legs apart and his feet planted evenly on the floor, as if he'd been rooted there all the time she'd been in the larder. His mouth was set in a peculiar shape. Was he chewing on something?

Kitty held on to the door handle and tried to arrange her smile in the right way. She looked around the kitchen: no sign of the girl. She must have got bored of waiting and gone outside.

There was a clicking sound as the man rolled whatever was in his mouth from one side to the other, making his neatly trimmed moustache twitch. His cheeks looked weathered but his eyes were bright, the skin around them unlined. 'I do the garden and that.'

Kitty nodded, still holding on to the door handle.

'And look after the beast in the garage.'

'The beast?'

'Mrs S. asked me to fetch you these.'

He brought a bunch of carrots, already cleaned so they were gleaming yellow, from behind his back. His hands were large and tanned. Then he swallowed, and Kitty smelled aniseed.

'She said something about soup.'

Kitty looked at the trailing ends of the vegetables. 'But I haven't any stock.'

'And these.' He produced a bundle of onions. 'I keep all the veg in the shed.'

Kitty let go of the door handle. She walked past him, sat at the table and pressed a hand to her mouth. Crying was not what a new cook should do on her first day, not in front of this man with his big hands and his low voice.

The man placed the vegetables on the table. Then he produced a penknife from his pocket, divided the carrots into three piles, and deftly sliced the tops from them.

After a minute she heard the rustling of a paper bag. 'Want a sweet?'

She hated aniseed but she took one and held it. The man had left his boots at the door, and his thick sock had a hole in it, Kitty noticed. A long nail was pointing in her direction.

'Sorry,' she said, rolling the sweet between her finger and thumb. 'I'm not quite...' she took a breath. 'I'm Kitty.'

'Arthur.'

Kitty rose from her chair. 'I ought to get on – the stock-pot...'

'Sit down, don't bother yourself.'

She sat, and Arthur stood over her, stroking his moustache. How old was he? Probably not yet in his thirties, but that moustache made him look older.

'All right?'

She nodded.

'I'm making myself a cup of tea. I daresay you'd like one.'

Once he'd turned his back to her and was filling the kettle, Kitty slipped the aniseed twist into the pocket of her apron.

He wasn't tall and his shoulders were bulky, as if he had a lot of clothing bundled under his jacket. His wavy hair looked a bit like the woollen fur on a toy bear she'd had once.

She watched him as he fetched the pot and cups in silence. The pot was light green and strangely angular.

There was no cosy. He measured out the tea carefully, tapping the spoon on the side of the caddy to even it out before he tipped the contents into the pot. Then he went into the larder and Kitty rubbed at her cheeks and straightened her apron.

Arthur set the pot on the table. He'd poured the milk into a jug and found the sugar basin. 'Always have tea at eleven,' he said, pouring two cups.

Kitty looked at his face as he spoke. His teeth seemed set deep inside his mouth, a long way back from his lips.

'Where were you before?' he asked.

'At the school,' she said. 'And I was a – cook, a plain cook, for a lady in Petersfield.' She wasn't sure why she'd lied to him. He looked like you could tell him the truth and he wouldn't mind.

'You'll soon settle.'

Some tea had slopped over the edge of his cup and he scraped its bottom along the edge of his saucer before pouring the spill back. Then he took a slurp, swallowed, and sighed. He held his cup with both hands and stared into space for a long time before speaking again. 'The girl before you didn't stay long.'

'Dora?'

'That's her.'

'Why did she leave?'

'The usual.'

Kitty waited for more, but he was staring into space again.

'What are they like?' she asked, being careful not to look at him too closely.

'Mr Crane and Mrs S.?' He swilled his tea around the cup. 'He's all right. Bit wet, but not afraid to get his hands dirty.' He took another slurp.

'And her?'

He drained his tea. 'She's – all right.'

There was a silence. Arthur began to clean his fingernails with the end of his penknife.

'How long have you been here?'

'Since before they came, end of last summer. I worked for Mr Jacks, whose house it was. So I stayed with the house. Part of the furniture, you could say.' He frowned and studied his own hands, which he'd spread before her on the table. They were, Kitty noticed, completely hairless. The muscles at the base of his thumbs bulged as he formed, then released, fists. 'They wanted it all different, of course.'

Kitty tried a smile.

Arthur looked at the clock. 'Best get on.' He flicked the penknife closed and tucked it in his top pocket. 'The beast will need stroking.'

He stood up and flexed his fingers. 'Like I said, veg is in the shed. Help yourself.'

She watched him as he pulled on his boots, noticing the way he stooped over the laces and tightened them with some effort.

'Sorry,' she said, 'but where did you say the shed was?'

Without a word, he opened the back door, stepped outside, and motioned for her to follow him.

They walked along the gravel path at the back of the cottage, Kitty watching Arthur's broad back. He walked swiftly, swinging his hands by his sides. He pointed to the garage. 'Beast's in there. Useless thing, electricity, if you ask me. Lights go off all the time. Don't know why they don't have gas,' he said. 'And my shed's there.' He stopped and nodded at a one-windowed wooden hut, covered in ivy and almost hidden behind the garage.

Kitty looked from one to the other and swallowed. 'Right.'

'Leave you to it, then,' he said, disappearing into the garage.

When he was gone, Kitty stood for a moment, staring at the shed door, before hurrying back to the kitchen. It would have to be omelettes. They would have to be flat.

... Four ...

Come on, Flossy,' said her mother. 'Nothing really matters if you're naked. Remember what Jimmy used to say, darling? *Nudity is the magician of the genders*. He was right, wasn't he?'

Geenie's toes were cold, even now. It was Sunday afternoon, and it had begun to warm up outside, but she was still wearing her orange cardigan with the flower buttons, knitted by Nanny Dora. Now Dora was married and living with her husband in London. Ellen said it was for the best, because Dora had her life and they had theirs. But Kitty was not the same at all. She was not nearly so pretty. Everyone said that Dora was more like a Gaiety girl than a nurse, with her plump little figure and her budding lips. Kitty was short and wiry-haired, never took her apron off and hadn't shown any sign of knitting.

'What if someone sees?'

'Who's to see, apart from George? Kitty and Arthur are both off this afternoon. And who's to care, anyway?'

Ellen had already removed her own short-sleeved turquoise blouse. She rubbed the military-style shoulders together as if trying to get rid of a stain. 'Rather manly, isn't it? Better to take it off,' she said, opening her fingers and letting the blouse fall to the ground. The buttons clattered and, beneath the table, Blotto stirred. 'It's not as if you've got much to show, anyway. Nothing to make a fuss about. If I can do it, you can.'

Geenie looked down. It was true: nothing interrupted the view to her sandals. There was no bosom, stomach or thigh to upset the straight plane of space between her nose and her toes. But she knew that, underneath the orange cardigan and sundress, her body held secrets. The faint lines of a few pubic hairs, for instance, disturbing the smoothness of her own skin. When she was in bed at night she sometimes put a hand there and stroked them.

Her mother crouched down and looked into her face. 'When you've got something, I'll be the first to notice.' She paused and licked her lips. 'And then we can take action. It's no good being shy about these things.' She touched Geenie's cheek and lowered her voice. 'God knows, I thought of sex as the most awful ogre until I met your father. Can you imagine? I was twenty-three! A scandalous age to be a virgin. But he enlightened me. It was really nothing to worry about, nothing at all. In fact, he was more worried than I was, when I'd finished with him.'

Ellen straightened up and undid the buttons on her skirt, which shot to the floor, turquoise stripes concertinaing before Geenie's eyes.

'Is George going to sunbathe?'

'George is writing, darling. I'm sure he won't be interested in sunshine. Or, for that matter, in naked females.' As she spoke, her mother pulled her ivory petticoat over her head and her thick hair crackled. Geenie could see the brown strands standing up on the crown, like skinny twigs.

'Are you still in that damned dress? The sun will be gone by the time you get out there. This is England, Geenie. You have to make the most of these days of grace. Unhook this for me.'

She knelt down to allow her daughter to reach the hook of her bra. Geenie hesitated before facing the bunched-up skin around the straps of the device. She particularly hated the way it bulged over the hooks, and wondered how her mother could stand this cage of rubber, ribbons and gauzy cotton. It was something like the tents Dora used to use for spotted dick and other steamed puddings.

After a small struggle, she unhooked the bra, and felt the relief of her mother's flesh as it was released.

Ellen bent over and stepped out of her knickers. Geenie decided to stare at the sink.

'Still not ready?'

She shook her head.

'All right. But you'll regret it. It'll be wonderful out there. The sun on every part of you. There's nothing more natural than that, darling. Nothing more natural than the sun on your own skin.'

As Ellen opened the back door, Geenie caught the smell of her mother: something sharp but spicy, like dandelions.

When she'd gone, Geenie took off her cardigan and put her chin on the edge of the sink, letting the enamel cool her jaw. She could hear her mother humming and flapping out a towel. With one hand, she gathered up the hem of her sun-dress and hooked it beneath her chin. Then, staring at the taps, she circled a finger around the slight swelling of her nipples, first one, then the other. The skin there was like the lamb's ears Arthur grew in the garden, all velvet springiness. She raised her chin from the sink and pulled the dress over her head. Cupping a hand beneath each nipple, she hunched her shoulders and thrust the flesh on her chest upwards in an effort to make a cleavage. But Ellen was right: there was nothing to make a fuss about.

Clutching her sundress, Geenie tiptoed to the back door, which was still slightly ajar, and peeped out of the crack. Her mother was reclined on a white towel in the centre of the lawn. Apart from her sunglasses, she was totally naked, and she was tapping her nails on one thigh, bouncing them off the flesh.

The door to George's writing studio, Geenie noticed, remained closed. A few weeks ago, Geenie had peeked through the studio window and seen a piece of paper scrolled into George's typewriter with the words LOVE ON THE DOWNS typed at the top. When she'd peeped again yesterday, that piece of paper was still there, with nothing else added. But, as Ellen often pointed out, George was very busy. He was making the cottage into a modern home so they could be a real family. Which was why Geenie shouldn't go around knocking holes in walls, even if they were already broken and rubble was all over the rug, and why her mother had told her to stay in her room and miss supper last week. It hadn't been too bad, though, as she'd remembered the three Garibaldis stored in her sock drawer.

Blotto stretched and waddled from beneath the table. She patted him on the head and he began to lick her hand, pushing his long tongue between each of her fingers.

After a while, her mother shouted, 'You should come out here, Flossy. It's divine.'

Geenie wiped the dog's saliva down the back door and continued to watch through the crack.

George emerged from the studio. He stood on the step, shielding his eyes from the sun. He was wearing his writing cardigan, which Ellen said he should never wear out of the house. It was pale blue with a cream collar and big cream buttons, and was so long it almost reached his knees.

He didn't say anything for a long time.

'There you are. How's Karl, darling? Getting to the good bits yet?' Ellen hitched herself up on one elbow and smiled in George's direction. 'Surely it's too hot to be indoors, even for Marx?'

George stepped onto the lawn and frowned. He stared at Ellen for a long time, his eyes going up and down her body but never resting on her face.

'Ellen. What on earth are you doing?'

'I should've thought that was obvious.'

He ran a hand over his mouth. 'Where's your bathing suit?'

'I don't know, darling. I'm not going bathing.'

George's frown deepened. 'It's still only April…'

'Almost May. You should get some sun on those marvellous legs of yours,' said Ellen. 'It does the skin tone no end of good.'

He looked about. 'Won't the neighbours—'

'There are no neighbours. We're miles from anyone. We're practically in the wilderness. And you're still wearing that infernal cardigan.'

'I'd hardly call Harting a wilderness.'

They stared at each other for a moment. Then Ellen sat up and thrust her arms out towards him. 'Nudity,' she said in a loud voice, 'is the magician of the genders.'

George let out a laugh.

'It's not funny, darling. It's poetic. James told me.'

'What does it mean, I wonder?' asked George, walking towards her.

'It means,' said Ellen, settling back down on her towel, 'that you should get undressed immediately.'

George looked about again.

'It is rather hot, isn't it?'

'Blistering.'

He started to remove his cardigan. 'And no one's about.'

'Not a soul.'

From behind the back door, Geenie watched as George slipped his braces from his shoulders and began to unbutton his shirt.

'I suppose it wouldn't hurt.'

'How could your magnificent body possibly inflict pain on anyone or anything?'

George's chest was speckled with patches of black curly hair. He folded his shirt carefully and placed it on the grass. Then he removed his shoes and socks, unbuttoned his trousers and bent over to step out of them.

Geenie made her decision. With Blotto trotting behind, she strolled into the garden and stood before them with her hands on her naked hips. 'Is there room for me?'

'Good grief—'

Ellen sat up. 'Flossy! How wonderful! Now we can all be magicians together.'

George hopped about on one leg, trying to get his braces in place and his socks on at the same time.

'Don't be shy, darling. Lie down next to me. George is sunbathing, too.' Ellen held out a hand and her daughter took it. The sun was fierce on Geenie's shoulders, and her neck was hot beneath her pile of heavy hair. But Ellen was right: it was wonderful, the sun on every part of you: back, bottom, legs, belly.

'I've got rather a mound of work to get through, actually,' said George, still hopping. His sock seemed to have jammed on his toes. 'I think I'd better get back to it.'

'What's the hurry, darling?'

He gave up on the socks and finally snapped his braces into place. 'I've got to finish something. Lots to do before

Diana arrives.'

'But you said—'

'Second thoughts. You girls carry on.'

'Please stay,' said Geenie.

But he wouldn't look at her. He'd fixed his gaze over their heads, on the door of his studio. Plucking his shirt from the grass, he walked back inside and closed the door firmly behind him.

Geenie looked at her mother. Ellen's cheeks had swelled with laughter, which she managed to hold for half a minute before letting it out in a long, loud rush. Geenie flung herself down on the towel and laughed too. Their bodies shook together, Geenie curling her legs to her chest and rolling from side to side, Ellen clutching her own elbows and rocking back and forth. They laughed and laughed until they ran out of air and had to calm down. Then they laughed again. When they were exhausted, Geenie slotted into Ellen's side, her small hipbone curving into her mother's waist, and Ellen put an arm around her shoulders. Geenie closed her eyes and stayed still for as long as she could, savouring the warmth of her mother's flesh.

Eventually, Ellen sat up. 'Poor Crane,' she said, laughing again.

'Who's Diana?' asked Geenie.

'She's George's daughter, darling. She's coming to live here for a bit. Didn't I mention it?'

'When?'

'Soon.'

Geenie tried to nudge herself back into her mother's side, but Ellen gave a shiver and stood up, looking at the sky. The clouds were thickening.

'What's she like?'

'I don't know, darling. A bit like George, probably. But

a girl, and eleven years old.'

'Will she like me?' asked Geenie.

'What a ridiculous question.' Ellen frowned, still gazing upwards. 'Maybe I was a bit optimistic. We'd better go in.'

Geenie watched her mother's naked bottom wobble towards the house and wondered if Diana knocked holes in walls, too.

... Five ...

It was her second go at rolling out. Mrs Steinberg had asked for a savoury tart, 'a quiche – like the French eat, you know the sort of thing.'

Kitty did not know the sort of thing. She'd spent most of the morning looking for something like it in *Silvester's Sensible Cookery*. Egg and bacon pie sounded nearly right, an open flan with a cheesy filling, although Mrs Steinberg had mentioned artichokes, not knowing, probably, that the season hadn't yet begun. There were certainly no artichokes at the greengrocers' in Petersfield, and if she'd have telephoned to ask if she could add them to the order, Mr Bailey would have laughed. Cabbages aplenty, Kitty, he would have said, but whoever heard of artichokes in April? What's the matter with that American woman? Doesn't she even know the seasons?

Kitty wondered if she did. She had yet to see her in stockings, even though it had been a cold spring until now, the air licking around your calves and shrinking your feet inside your shoes. And there had been only one occasion on which she'd seen her in a hat, a terrible woollen beret that covered half her face, when it had suddenly hailed a week ago. You could just see that great nose sticking out, like a fat coat hook.

The marble rolling pin was heavy and Kitty was careful to place it behind the sugar jar so it wouldn't roll off the table and onto her foot. It was an awful rolling pin – flour slipped from its shiny surface, and now the pastry was sticking and tearing as she rolled. Mrs Steinberg had told her it had been Dora's pride and joy, and was quite the best thing for pastry. Kitty wondered how Mrs Steinberg would know this. She'd never seen her so much as put the kettle on to boil, let alone roll out shortcrust.

She gathered up the pieces of dough and pressed them together. She'd roll out one more time, then she'd have to start again. The sun glared through the kitchen window and sweat was blooming along her top lip. It was typical that the first really warm day should come while she was making shortcrust. Everyone knew heat was bad for pastry, and Kitty's hands were, for once, very warm.

She raised the rolling pin and smashed it down on the lump of pastry to get it going. It was easy, now, to flatten the greying wodge. She managed to roll it out into a ragged circle, almost thin enough, then a corner stuck on the pin and a flap ripped up, like a hangnail. Bugger. It would have to be patched up in the dish. She could force a lump of pastry into the hole and press it with her thumb. With a bit of egg it might stick.

Looking out of the window, she saw Mr Crane sitting on the step of his studio, rubbing his eye. He was handsome, with his slick of dark hair and strong chin, and younger than Mrs Steinberg, Kitty guessed, by at least five years. When Lou had caught a glimpse of him in town, she'd said he looked *intense*. It was a shame about his eye.

'Can I have a biscuit?'

That child had a habit of sneaking up on you. You'd just

be dusting the mantelpiece or scrubbing the rim of the lavatory, and there she'd be, asking for something. Now she was leaning on the stove, her chin tucked into her chest in the same way as her mother, sucking on a long strand of hair that looked like a wet worm hanging from her mouth.

'Go on, then,' said Kitty.

Here was the queer thing, though: Geenie took the Garibaldi from the barrel, but never seemed to eat it. Kitty knew this because she'd begun to find slightly chewed biscuits hidden behind cushions. Once she found three, all of them nibbled at the corners, stacked side by side in the sitting-room cupboard. It was a shocking waste, but Kitty told herself that she was not responsible for the child. It was her mother's look-out.

'What are you doing?'

'Making a French tart for your lunch. Bacon and egg.'

'A quiche.'

'That's it.'

Geenie pretended to examine her biscuit for a few moments. Then she said, 'Can I help?'

This was another thing the child did: offer to help and then get in the way.

'No. Thank you, Miss.'

'Please.'

'There's nothing for you to do, Miss.'

'I'm bored.'

Kitty sighed. 'You can grate the cheese, if you like.'

Geenie screwed up her nose. 'I hate cheese.'

'You could measure out the milk, then.'

'Cheese smells like sick.'

Kitty floured the pastry dish. 'You're a rum sort of a girl, aren't you?'

'What are you doing that for?'

'So it won't stick, Miss.'

'It always sticks, doesn't it?'

She mustn't blush, not in front of the child.

Kitty gathered the pastry around the pin and prepared to lift. She'd have to be careful not to let anything brush the tassel of that greasy lantern. If she could just transport the thing without a rip...

'Can I have another biscuit?'

The pastry gave up; a large strip fell in folds on the table. 'Bother!'

Geenie stuck a finger into the crumpled mess. 'Can't you roll it out again?'

Kitty stared at the table. 'It's too far gone. It's got too warm.'

'What difference does that make?'

Now Kitty felt the blood stinging her cheeks. 'I don't know, Miss; it's just ruined, is all. I'll have to start over.' It would be impossible with the child here, asking questions, and she only had – what? an hour left, at most.

'Here.' She held out the grey ball to Geenie. 'Have this to play with. It's yours.'

Geenie pressed a finger into it with such force that Kitty's hand dipped.

'You could make something with it, couldn't you, Miss?'

Geenie prodded the dough again, gently this time. 'I could try,' she said.

Kitty placed the tacky pastry firmly in the girl's hand. 'I'm sure you could make something out of that, with all your talents,' she said. Geenie was always drawing something, or drawing on something. Last week she'd done a scribble which she claimed was a map of the world on the kitchen table. Luckily it was only in pencil, and Kitty had been able to scrub the thing off. She thought Geenie's efforts a bit slow for a girl of eleven, but she said nothing.

'I could try,' Geenie said again, smiling.

'I'm sure you could, Miss. You could make something lovely. A real work of art.'

The child took the pastry and walked out of the kitchen, swinging her blonde hair.

'Or you could hide it somewhere,' Kitty muttered under her breath.

.....

Arthur was batting at a wasp. With the patched-up egg and bacon pie in the oven at last, Kitty watched him from the sitting-room window. His arms windmilled around his head. The movement had caught her eye whilst she was dusting and she'd nearly dropped Mrs Steinberg's African mask, the one that looked a bit like Bob. Of all the things in the room, she sensed this would be the worst to drop. She held it tight in both arms now as she watched Arthur jogging on the spot, his limbs bouncing like those of a puppet jolted from above. He seemed to be moving to the rhythm of the thumping noise coming from the library: Mrs Steinberg's typewriter. The woman was always in there, banging out something or other on those keys. Arthur swatted the air again, his mouth opening in horror. But he made no sound. He simply danced on the grass, batting the air around him.

Later she could say to him, the still, controlled Arthur with the straight moustache: *I know your weakness*.

She wouldn't say that, of course. It was the sort of thing Mae West would say, with a hearty wink. Kitty would ask, instead, if he had room in his bag for the piece of egg and bacon pie she'd put by. She'd ask him if he could squeeze it in, this piece of pie so carefully cut, and wrapped in waxed paper, twice, so the grease wouldn't leak, because she knew Arthur worried about things being clean and neat: when she went to his shed to fetch vegetables, she'd seen the numbered rows of tools, the swept corners of his tool box. And she worried about the pie being crushed in his bag by his flask and his book as he cycled home.

Arthur always had a Western with him. At the kitchen table he held it with one hand and ate with the other, keeping the book at arm's length, as though frightened of smearing the pages. His eyes rarely strayed from the words, making her wonder how the bread arrived at his mouth, how he bit into his boiled egg without chomping his fingers. He'd a different book every week. Kitty guessed he got them from the twopenny library in town. Or perhaps he had someone who bought them for him? He'd yet to mention any girl. She'd seen him at the Savoy on his own last week, which must mean there was no girl. She'd been there with Lou, and had spotted Arthur leaning by the ticket booth, scrutinising the poster for next week's performance of *Come Out of the Pantry*. It was strange, seeing him away from Willow Cottage, in his smart clothes. She'd noticed how white his collar was. They stood under the lights of the foyer, and he'd looked at her and said, 'Lovely here, isn't it?'

Kitty gazed through the window again. Arthur had stopped windmilling his arms. The child was talking to him, holding the lump of dough in the air. Arthur crouched down and took the dough in his hands. He rolled the lump around his palm, weighing it as though it were something precious.

That was her dough and the child had given it away. And now Arthur would know that she, Kitty, had ruined the pastry and wasted a whole batch.

She opened the kitchen window. 'Miss Geenie!'

She hadn't meant to shout, but now they were both looking towards her. She'd have to follow through, as Lou would put it. *That's the trouble with you, Kitty,* her sister always said. *You never follow through.*

'Lunch is almost ready, Miss. Come in and wash your hands.'

The girl stared at Kitty in silence, her mouth slightly open. Arthur straightened up and nodded to Kitty. 'You'd best go in, Miss.' He gestured towards the door.

'It's too early for lunch,' grumbled Geenie. 'Where's Ellen?'

Kitty couldn't lie. 'I'm not sure. But lunch is nearly ready.'

'Can't I come in when Ellen says?'

Kitty couldn't get used to Geenie calling Mrs Steinberg by her first name; it gave her a start every time she heard it. *Ellen.* It just wasn't who she was, just as *Mary* was not who her own mother had been.

'I – I think you should come in now, please, Miss.' Her voice wasn't as steady as she'd have liked.

Arthur was looking at the ground, the lump of dough still in his hand.

Geenie folded her arms. 'In a minute,' she said.

'I should get on,' said Arthur, with a half wave at Kitty. 'Lots to do.'

She tried a smile, but he was already walking back to his shed, gripping the dough in his fist.

... Six ...

It was red, with white handle grips and chipped lettering on the crossbar. George wheeled it through the back garden, whistling.

Geenie had never heard him whistle before. It reminded her of Dora, who'd whistled though it was unladylike. When she was washing up, or ironing, Dora had whistled, and Geenie had tried to whistle, too, but her lips were too soft to get the shape, somehow.

They watched him from the library window, mother and daughter leaning together on Ellen's desk, stretching their necks. George's shirt sleeves were folded up close to his armpits, the way Arthur's often were.

'It's broken,' said Ellen. 'He's brought a broken bicycle home.'

The brake cables clattered against the spokes, raining ticks across the garden.

Ellen marched out of the house, and, after giving it a second or two, Geenie followed behind, quietly. She knew that if she stayed in the shadow of her mother's skirt, she wouldn't get in much trouble. There was a certain position she could take behind her mother which usually meant that people didn't seem to notice her.

'What are you doing with that?'

George had leant the bike against the wall of his studio and stepped back to admire it. He didn't look at Ellen. Instead, he ran a hand over the saddle.

'Lovely, isn't she?'

'Broken, Crane. *It* is broken.'

Geenie noticed that her mother was pronouncing all her words very clearly.

He shrugged. 'Not for long.'

Geenie grabbed one of the trailing cables in her fist and gave it a tug. 'What's this, George?'

'That's a broken bit,' muttered her mother, prising the cable from her.

George took the cable from Ellen. 'It's fixable, though.' He crouched down and held the end of the cable before Geenie's face. 'Perfectly fixable.'

'Really, Crane, you look quite proletarian.'

George bit his lip. 'Ellen—'

'I'm joking. You couldn't look proletarian if you tried.'

He bit his lip again. Then he said, 'I happen to like bikes.'

'How many do you need? You already have one, which you never use, and I've offered you a car of your own. Besides which, there's the Lanchester, which you're free to use any time.'

George smiled at Geenie. 'But I like bikes,' he said again, sending a pedal spinning with one hand. 'And anyway. It's not for me.'

He looked up at Ellen, who was standing with her hands on her hips. 'Can Geenie ride?' he asked. 'Diana can. And since she'll be here soon, I thought it only fair that Geenie has her own bicycle. Then they can ride together.'

'Why would Geenie want to ride a bike? She doesn't need to. She can ride a horse. What good's a bike on the

Downs? A bike's only any good on a road, where a car's much better.'

George straightened up and folded his arms. He looked into Ellen's face and she looked back at him.

'And that thing is far too big for her. Really, Crane. For an intellectual you're awfully slow sometimes.'

'Why are you so set against this?'

Ellen shifted her gaze to the willows at the bottom of the garden. She tapped her foot. For a few moments, all three of them listened to the leaves swishing in the breeze, and waited.

'Ellen?'

'I'm not against it.'

'Oh?' George laughed. 'It sounded like you were. But if you're not...'

'Not entirely.' She traced a semicircle in the wet grass with her shoe.

'I could give you a backie.'

'What on earth is that?' Ellen smiled a little. 'It sounds slightly obscene. I might like it.'

'It means I cycle and you sit.'

'I'd much rather have a horse between my thighs.'

'Have you ever tried?'

'A horse?'

'A bicycle.'

Geenie stepped out from behind her mother. This was her chance. 'Ellen can't ride a bicycle.'

Ellen's hand landed on her daughter's shoulder and pressed down, hard. There was a long silence.

Geenie persisted. 'She's never learned to ride a bicycle. Have you, Ellen?'

George's eyes flickered towards Ellen. 'Really?'

'You can give *me* a backie, George,' said Geenie.

'Shut up, Geenie. That's enough.' Through her thin

cardigan, Geenie could feel her mother's nails.

George drew a hand slowly across his mouth. 'You can't ride a bike?'

Ellen let go of her daughter and threw her hands in the air. 'Not really.'

'Not really? Can you, or not?'

'No! All right? No! I cannot ride a bicycle. Who cares about riding a damn bicycle? There's more to life than pedalling along roads. More to my life, anyway.'

'I'm just a bit surprised. I thought everyone—'

'Everyone what?'

'Could cycle.'

'Well, I can't. It's just one of those useless things I never learned, like ancient Greek and cricket.'

'But, riding a bike. It's, ah, well…'

'It may have escaped your notice, Crane, but I was brought up by a family of New York millionaires. No one in my family rides a bicycle. NO ONE. It's just not something you do if you're a Steinberg.'

'All right, all right.' He reached out to touch her hand, but she pulled away. Geenie wondered if she should step into that place behind her mother which would make her invisible again.

'James never rode a bicycle.'

George didn't reply. Geenie tried to remember if she'd ever seen Jimmy on a bicycle. Cars were more his thing. She remembered him letting her rest her head on his thighs during long journeys, when she would gaze at his hands on the steering wheel, marvelling at how he could touch the sides quite lightly, it seemed, and the car would move this way or that.

'He never rode a bicycle. Ever.' Ellen's eyes were very wide, and her chin was jutting forward.

'No,' said George. 'Of course not.'

There was another long silence.

After a while, George said, 'Look. None of that means that Geenie shouldn't learn, does it?'

'It's not up for discussion.' Ellen turned and began to walk back to the house.

Geenie decided not to step into that place behind her mother. Instead, she stood beside George and watched Ellen stride away. George sighed and patted the saddle again, as if it were a faithful dog. Geenie gazed at his lop-sided face, and saw that his cheeks had hollowed.

'But I'm not a Steinberg.'

Ellen stopped. Very slowly, she turned around. 'What did you say?'

George covered his eyes. Geenie looked at her mother. Ellen's chin was tucked tightly into her chest, and she knew she may as well carry on. It would be as bad either way. 'My name's Floyd,' she said. 'Regina Eleanor Floyd and I want to ride a bike with Diana.'

Ellen charged towards her daughter and grabbed her by the upper arm. 'And where's Charles Floyd now? Do you see him?'

Geenie did what she always did when her mother got mad: she went silent.

'Do you see him?'

Geenie looked down at the grass and shook her head.

'No. That's because he's not here. He left. Charles Floyd, your illustrious father, abandoned us before you were two years old. But I am here, Ellen Steinberg, your mother, is here. And that makes you a Steinberg too, do you hear me?'

Geenie looked at George.

'I said, do you hear me?'

Geenie swallowed hard. If she kept her head completely still, if she concentrated on the individual blades of grass and the way some of them were curved and some of them were straight, the tears might not start.

George cleared his throat. 'Now then. Ah. Look. Might it not be a good thing if Geenie here were to have a little go? What harm can it do?'

Ellen let go of Geenie's arm.

Geenie held her breath. Some of the blades were twisted right round, so they looked like tiny tubes of grass.

'Come on, Ellen. It's just a bicycle. Geenie didn't mean what she said, did you, Geenie?'

Like hollow green tubes. A few of the tubes had water in them.

'She's sorry. She'll always be a Steinberg, won't you, Geenie?'

Geenie looked up at George. His eyes were brown and soft, and she knew she could say yes and not mean it, and it would still be all right.

She nodded.

After a minute, her mother said, 'She could fall off.'

'Ellen.'

'She could fall off and break a leg. Or an ankle. And whose fault would it be? Who'd be responsible?'

'I would,' said George. He put a hand on Geenie's hair, and breathed out. 'I'd be responsible.'

.....

The first time was terrible. The saddle was much harder than it looked, with lumps in the wrong places, and, just when she thought she'd got a good grip on them, the pedals kept whipping round and banging Geenie's ankles. Her socks would be stained with black, her shins stained with bruise. The handle grips were hard, too; they were cold beneath her fingers, and slippery to touch. Like the pedals they could escape without warning, causing the whole thing to swerve and topple beneath her.

Her mother watched silently from the window as Geenie grappled with the bike and George tried to steady her. Geenie could see Ellen's pale face beyond the glass. Her nose looked particularly large and pink that day. She said it reacted to the weather: any dampness caused a swell. The cottage was always damp, and the grass outside was wet after a thunderstorm in the night.

The wheel slipped again, and Geenie's feet skidded on the grass, but she managed to keep the thing upright by gripping the crossbar between her knees. She looked up at the window and caught her mother's eye, but Ellen did not move from her ringside position. She just stared out, nose glowing slightly, mouth drawn in a tight line.

Geenie realised her legs were shaking, and her fingers ached from gripping the handlebars. She stood still for a moment, allowing herself to breathe.

'I don't think I can,' she said, looking at George, who was holding the back of the saddle.

'You'll get it. Right foot on pedal and push off. I've got you, so you won't fall.'

'I can't.'

'No such word as can't. Only won't.'

He wasn't usually like this, his words coming fast and sounding like the truth. Normally he left gaps, sighed and hummed. But now he was telling her what to do, very clearly, and she found that she wanted to follow his instructions.

'Both hands on the handlebars?'

She took hold of the tough white rubber again and squeezed.

'Yes.'

'All right.' He paused. 'Remember what I told you?'

'Keep looking ahead.'

'Good. And?'

'Don't look down.'

'Good girl. And?'

'Keep pedalling.'

'Exactly.'

There was sweat on his forehead, and he had his sleeves rolled up again. His hair, usually greased back in place in a short wave, was sticking up in a peak above his forehead.

'All right?'

'Yes.'

She glanced at the library window, but her mother was gone.

'Off we go, then. And push!'

At his command, she pressed her right foot on the pedal and lifted her left from the floor. This was the worst moment: one foot in the air, the other groping for the flat surface of the pedal, the bicycle's balance depending on finding it. Everything wobbled as her foot floundered madly.

'Steady.'

She found it. Pushed down. And the bicycle moved forward.

'I've got you. Keep pedalling.'

She pushed down again and the spokes rattled. The grass sighed. The breeze was suddenly loud in her ears.

'Very good. Keep going.'

His footsteps were behind her as she pedalled. She pedalled right across the grass and along the side of the house, past the garage and to the front gate.

'Feel good?'

He sounded breathless, but she kept pedalling. If she kept pedalling, she could be on the road and away from the house and no one could stop her. She could pedal across the village and up the Downs, and over the top to the sea. She could keep going, her feet pushing down, pushing down, pushing down, her hands light on the handlebars, the saddle warm between her thighs. All she had to do was keep looking ahead.

She was out in the lane now. The may bushes were frothy with white and smelled of clean laundry. Cow parsley brushed her arms.

She pushed down. She looked ahead.

It wasn't far to the end of the lane, where the road began. Geenie sat up straight and pedalled, letting her legs go light as the wheels gathered momentum and the pedals seemed to push themselves around. It was like swimming, only better: she was dry and warm, and she could go faster, right to the end. But there was that same feeling of weightlessness, of being borne up, held above the path by rubber and air.

The end of the path was near now, and she looked back. Just to check if he was still there, because she'd have to turn the bicycle, or stop, and she wasn't sure how you did either of those things.

He was not holding on to the bike. He was not running behind her. Instead, he was standing at the beginning of the lane, and he was starting to clap. He was applauding her as if she had achieved this thing.

Then the bike swerved and there was cow parsley in her face and a branch scratching her arm in a long sharp line, but she kept pushing her feet down and looking ahead and somehow the bike straightened again and she was back on the path.

'Brake!' George was shouting. 'Brake, Geenie! Pull the brakes!'

She squeezed the brakes and crashed her feet to the floor at the same time, so her shoes dragged along the stones and her bottom came right off the seat. She kept braking and dragging until the bicycle came to a stop, and only then was she able to unlock her fingers from the handlebars. The whole frame crashed to the side, and so did she.

There were small stones in her cheek and the back wheel was on her leg.

'Good girl,' she heard him shout. 'What a journey!'

Geenie sat up. Brushing herself off, she gazed at the puffed clouds bubbling overhead, and she did not cry. When she got back to the cottage, she'd say nothing about this to her mother, she decided; she'd keep it all to herself.

··· Seven ···

All week, Kitty longed for her bath. At Lou's, she'd become used to taking a bath on whatever evening she liked, but here she had to take it on a Friday, between eight and ten o'clock. When the time finally came, she waited until nine, when Geenie was usually in bed, and Mrs Steinberg and Mr Crane were in the sitting room together. Venturing out of her room at any other time was just too risky: Mrs Steinberg might be wandering the house, looking for Mr Crane, and Geenie might be anywhere at all.

She gathered up her dressing gown, towel, and the copy of *Garden and Home* Lou had given her, and listened at the door. Kitty's room was only reachable through the kitchen, and it was unlikely anyone would be in there at this time. Occasionally she heard Mr Crane's steady footsteps on the flags at night; in the morning there would be crumbs on the table and butter left out by the sink.

She opened her door, walked across the kitchen floor, and then listened again to check no one was in the corridor.

In the kitchen, she could hear music coming from the sitting room: a man's deep voice, but not Bing Crosby or even Al Bowlly. Lou loved Bing, but Kitty found his songs too sleepy. This voice was much raspier, younger. *The things*

I do are never forgiven it sang. Then there was a bang, and Mr Crane's laugh.

Kitty imagined that Mrs Steinberg was dancing around that huge room. Now that the wall had come down, there was certainly plenty of space for it. Mr Crane would be sitting in his armchair, watching, perhaps with a book on his lap. The woman would be flinging her arms about, just like her daughter when she was dressed up and acting out those solo plays of hers on the lawn. And wearing no stockings.

It was probably safe to make a dash for it.

She opened the door. The hallway looked clear. It was impossible to see around that blasted corner, though, and she almost shrieked when she came across Blotto, sitting on the hall floorboards, waiting for some action. The dog looked up hopefully, then got down on his belly and shuffled along the floor like a huge hairy insect towards Kitty's feet. Deciding it wasn't safe to stop and pat, Kitty stepped past the creature and pressed along the hall, her stockinged feet rasping on the bare wood.

There was Mr Crane's laugh again: sudden and surprisingly loud.

She didn't run along the corridor, not exactly. But she must have taken the two steps up to the bathroom too fast, because now she was holding out her hands and the gown and towel were wrapping themselves around her legs as she went down. Her shin bone cracked against the step, but she didn't yelp; she went down silently, still clutching the magazine in one hand, then sprang up again, grabbing the gown and the towel with the other hand as she leapt inside.

Once in the bathroom, she leant against the door and tried to breathe normally. She couldn't hear any footsteps. Perhaps no one had heard her fall. If Mr Crane had heard, would he have come to see what was wrong? Or would he have shrugged and continued to watch Mrs Steinberg dance without stockings?

The bath was huge, with gnarled claw feet and brass taps which squealed as she twisted them. The geyser choked. It would take at least ten minutes to even half-fill the tub; sometimes she thought it would actually be simpler to use the public baths in Petersfield, as she'd done before Mother died. Whilst waiting, Kitty sat on the bath's edge and opened her magazine.

Are You the STAR in Your Husband's Life? she read. *Or have you allowed yourself to slide into a minor, supporting role?* Wasn't that what wives were supposed to do? Slide into supporting roles? Not that her own mother had done any of that. She was always the one who went to the pub whilst her father waited in. 'Once he looked at the clock when I came home,' she'd told her daughters. It was one of her many stories, meant to prove that they were all better off without him. 'I told him, don't you dare look at that clock.' She'd gripped the arms of her chair as she spoke. 'And he never did again.'

> *Remember your husband is human. What he really expects of you is that you should continue to be the leading lady in his life, the heroine of the domestic drama, and that every now and then you should spring on him a new act. In that light, look at the woman you see in the mirror and ask yourself today: 'Is she slipping or is she still a star?'*

Had Mrs Steinberg read this? Kitty had never seen the woman with a magazine. She was always carting big books by authors with foreign names about. Not that Kitty had ever seen her actually reading. It would be easy, Kitty thought, for Mrs Steinberg to become a leading lady, if she put a bit of effort in; that was what money was for, wasn't it? Money could put a shine on the ugliest of women, as Lou often pointed out, particularly when she saw a photograph of Mrs Sweeny in the *Daily Mail*.

She dipped her fingers in the bath. Still warm enough, although the water had started to run cold.

Unbuttoning her frock, she glimpsed her reflection in the full-length mirror which stood in the corner of the room, and she turned away to unhook her stays and roll down her stockings. Then she stepped in the bath quickly, so as not to catch sight of herself again. Kitty had yet to look at the whole of herself in that glass; it was the first full-length mirror she'd been confronted by. She'd seen parts of her body at Lou's house, of course, in the dressing-table glass: her shoulders, small and yet fleshy; her belly-button, like a comma in her rounded stomach; her breasts, which seemed alarmingly blue. Once, she'd even peered at the dark nest between her legs with a compact, but had been unable to see much with just the bedside lamp, which had been a bit of a relief. But never the whole thing together.

She slid into the water, turned over on her stomach, and rested her cheek on the enamel. It wasn't very comfortable this way but if she balanced right, she could pretend she was floating in the sea. She could still hear music coming from the sitting room, and she began to rock back and forth, the water rippling over her hands and thighs and backside as she pushed herself along the bottom of the bath. It was like the time she'd gone to Bognor Regis on the Sunday School outing and had spent hours letting the tide wash her up and down the sand, the whole length of her brushing the beach as the sea moved beneath. She closed her eyes and listened to the raspy young voice coming from downstairs. *I hear music, then I'm through!* It was full of – what? Something like movement. Sweetness, too.

There was no more laughter now, just the low gurgle of water in the pipes, and the ticking of the recovering geyser. Were they dancing together? Kitty herself had danced with a man only once. Her sister had set the whole thing up, introducing her to Frank, who'd worked at the bakery with Lou, at the Drill Hall dance. Kitty remembered the way he'd let his fingers wander from her shoulder to her neck, feeling the hairs that lay there like weeds – that's how she'd always thought of her hair, like a clump of weeds on a riverbank, thick and straight, fanning out in broken ends, no particular colour. She rinsed it in vinegar every week but it was still the brown-yellow shade of Oxo cubes. All night she'd felt that she was pushing against his steps, because he kept getting them wrong; she hadn't meant to do that, and told herself to stop, but he would keep standing on her feet when she'd polished her shoes specially, and he wasn't the lightest of men, so she'd had to try to take his hot hand and correct it. Eventually he'd barked, 'You're leading!' and she'd apologised over and over again but his hand was crushing hers by then; the bones in her fingers crunched together as he said, 'For Christ's sake, what's the matter with you?' She'd thought of her father looking at the clock and what her mother would have said to him to stop him dead, but she'd carried on dancing until the music stopped. Then she ran from the dance floor and out of the Drill Hall without her coat or hat, and Frank hadn't come after her.

But not all men would be like that, she thought. Dancing with Arthur, for example, would be different: Arthur left his boots at the door before walking on her kitchen floor; he rinsed out his own cup after tea; his fingers were nimble when they loaded his pipe with tobacco.

But dancing with Arthur would be nothing like dancing with Mr Crane.

She opened her eyes, rolled on to her back and took up the soap. After she'd scrubbed herself everywhere she could – soaping between each toe, along each leg, swishing the water about between her thighs without touching anything for too long, then sliding the bar up her stomach and across her breasts, round the back of her neck and down her arms – she heaved herself out of the bath.

Now was the time to look, before she could think about it too much, before she was cold and shivering and needed to put the dressing gown on.

She stood before the full-length mirror. At first, she looked only at her own face. She was not, she'd decided long ago, pretty: her nose was too wide, her chin too prominent. But if she turned and looked back over her shoulder – like those photos in *Film Pictorial* – she wasn't too bad. It was always better to look at her face when it was rosy from the heat, and viewed like this, all cheek and naked shoulder, her hair wet and dark and even a bit wavy, she looked not quite herself. It was strange how like another person she seemed, as she gazed at the length of her body in the mirror; strange how it all connected up, all the parts of herself she'd often thought separate: thighs to bottom, stomach to chest to neck and arms, and her head on top. She tried to take it all in, putting a hand on her hip and smiling. She blushed at herself in the pose, then giggled, leaning forward and putting her hand to her mouth so the tips of her breasts shook; she felt them beneath her arm, swaying. Taking her hand away, she watched her own fingers connect with her breast, and saw her nipple turn brown and wrinkled like a walnut. Was it normal for flesh to move of its own accord like that?

There was a noise from the sitting room: a shrieking laugh. It wouldn't be long, then, before the other noises began. She turned away from the mirror, pulled her dressing gown tightly around her, and sat on the rim of the bath to watch the water run away.

... Eight ...

The sunlight, striking through the large French windows, flooded the dining room with warmth. Ellen and Geenie were at George's sister Laura's house in the nearby village of Heyshott, waiting for the new girl. They sat together at the wide table, watching petals fall from the vase of bluebells at its centre. Ellen was wearing her best red jacket, the one she'd had made in Paris with the white collar and cuffs, and her red heels. The jacket made her neck itch and she thought about removing it, but she wanted to look respectable for this meeting. She should have put more powder on, too. She could feel that her cheeks were flushed and damp, like Kitty's always were at mealtimes.

Geenie kept rubbing at a knot in the wood, and Ellen clamped a hand on her daughter's arm to still her. Diana's mother, Lillian, was supposed to have dropped Diana in time for lunch. Now it was half past two, and there was no sign of Lillian, or of the girl. Ellen was, she told herself, ready to face the other woman in Crane's life. She did pride herself on her tolerance of ex-wives. It was, she felt, a necessary part of being a bohemian. After all, Rachel had actually married James while he was living with Ellen, and she'd never run on at him for that. Rachel had been a pathetic creature: lumpy ankles and nails bitten down to the flesh. She'd begged James to marry her, saying all she wanted was the title – *Mrs Holt*; she'd promised never to bother him again if he granted her this one last chance of respectability. Ellen felt it was the least she could do not to carp about it, seeing as she'd stolen James from under Rachel's (small) nose in the first place. And, in fact, Rachel had gone quiet after that. Whenever Ellen had thought of this other woman who was out there, legally bound to her lover, she'd always reminded herself that she was the one who had him in the flesh.

But Lillian was different. And not ex, even, not yet. What made it worse was that Crane wouldn't say a word about her. She'd asked him again, last night, after the usual. Running a finger down his stomach, she'd enquired how he and Lillian had got on in bed. He'd looked at the ceiling and considered. He always considered his replies. Then he'd said, 'Well enough.' She'd tried another tack. How had they met? This time she'd propped herself up on one elbow and smiled, pulling the sheets up over her breasts to help him concentrate. 'Through a friend,' was the considered reply. Why had they separated, then? At this, he'd winced. 'It just died,' he'd said, very quietly, and he turned onto his side and said he'd like to go to sleep.

'She's late,' said Ellen, squinting up at Laura. 'Just like her husband. Like her *estranged* husband, I should say.'

Laura was leaning back on the French windows, smoking. In shiny black riding boots and a man's green cotton over-shirt, dramatically back-lit by the sun, she looked like a film star in a girl's horse-riding adventure. Her legs, hugged tightly by tan jodhpurs, were long and thin, like Ellen's own, but, Ellen noted, Laura's thighs were rounded like risen loaves, and her knees had no hint of knobble. Her black hair, cut in a bob with a severe fringe, was as glossy as her boots. When they'd first met, Ellen had thought Laura exactly the kind of woman she herself would love to be: sophisticated, daring, unpredictable. Glamorous. Gradually, though, it had dawned on her that Laura could only live the life she did because her solid, intellectual and thoroughly tedious husband, Humphrey, was always waiting in their well-appointed parlour for his wife's return.

Laura narrowed her eyes, slid them sidelong, and drew on her cigarette.

'I suppose ballet dancers are always late,' Ellen continued. 'Artistic temperament and all that. I don't know why I don't start being late. It might help my bohemian credentials. What do you think, darling? Would your brother love me more if I were late?'

'*Is* she late?' Laura asked, exhaling a curl of smoke.

'Over two hours, darling.'

Laura nodded and slowly slid one hand over her rounded belly, first along the top of the little bump, then along the bottom. 'I don't have a watch.'

Ellen snorted. 'How romantic!'

'Not romantic. Practical. If you don't have a watch, you're never late, and you never expect anyone. Stands to reason.'

Ellen let out a hoot. 'Laura, you are a strange creature.'

Laura brought her cigarette to her mouth in a long sweep and sucked on it.

'Talking of expecting – when's this damn baby due, darling?' asked Ellen.

Unpeeling herself from the French windows, Laura walked over to the table. She walked slowly, her boots clacking on the polished floor like a swashbuckler's, the sun flashing behind her. She leant over Geenie so the tip of her bob pricked the girl's ear, and ground out her cigarette in the ashtray.

'Autumn, I think.'

'You're not sure? Not even of the month?'

'I told you, Ellen. I don't have a watch.' She leant her elbows on the table and blinked at Geenie. 'Don't go dragging on that cig end,' she said, fixing the girl with her bright green eyes. 'How old are you, anyway?'

'She's eleven,' said Ellen. 'Twelve in August.'

'Is that all?' Laura shook her head. 'Never mind. A couple of years and it will all be happening for you, with hair like that.'

'Won't it just?' Ellen agreed. 'She's like something from a fairy tale, isn't she, Laura? Men can't resist helpless blondes.'

Laura smiled. 'Neither can women.'

Bobbie, Laura's help, poked her head round the door. 'Mrs Crane and her daughter are arriving.'

'Christ, I'm off,' said Laura. 'Tell Lillian I'll see her some other time. I can't face her prissiness just now. And I promised to meet Humphrey in Petersfield at three. Got to keep the husband happy.'

She scooped up her riding hat and jacket from the top of the dresser. 'Don't go snaring any helpless men while I'm gone,' she said to Geenie.

Ellen watched her stride through the French windows and out into the garden, and – for just a second – wished she could straddle the back of Laura's horse and ride off over the Downs with her.

Bobbie cleared her throat. 'She'll be here most *imminently*, Mrs Steinberg—'

'All right, all right.' Ellen touched her hair, scraped back her chair and straightened her jacket. 'You stay put, Flossy.'

'Why can't I come?'

'I think I'll deal with this myself, darling.'

'I want to come.'

Ellen sighed. She bent down to look her daughter in the face. 'I'll bring her through in a minute, then we can all go home together. It'll only be a minute.'

.....

'This is—' Ellen stopped and stared.

She'd opened the door to the dining room with Diana in tow, only to find her daughter standing against the French windows, holding Laura's cig end. Geenie was leaning her head back on the glass and trailing the fingers of one hand across her stomach.

The new girl stepped from behind Ellen. 'Hello,' she said. 'I'm Diana.'

'I am a helpless blonde, darling,' declared Geenie, and she lifted the cig to her mouth and sucked, closing her eyes.

Ellen looked from one girl to the other, then burst out laughing. Diana smiled, showing a gap between her front teeth, and Geenie blew out a big breath.

.....

On the way home, Diana was quiet. She was even prettier than Ellen had expected. Her black hair shone like wet stone, and her eyelashes were as thick as a doll's. Ellen chattered as much as she could, occasionally looking over her shoulder for a response, but the girl just stared out of the car window.

'You'll love our cottage, Diana, I'm sure of it. It was a damp heap of ugliness when we first came, wasn't it,

Geenie? Now it's quite the palace. Albeit a small one. And very modern, too.'

They'd been in the cottage for less than a year, and already Crane and Arthur had dug new flower beds in the garden, knocked kitchen and scullery into one room, installed the chugging electricity generator and built the writing studio. Sometimes she felt all Crane wanted was to demolish the entire cottage and start again. But, she reasoned, it was better to let him get on with it. Let him knock down all the old stuff, if that's what he wanted. Much better to forget the past. Hadn't that been what she'd wished for, when they'd moved to Harting after James's death? She hadn't let Crane loose on the library, though. That was her place. It was where she worked every day, typing up James's letters. She'd collected enough now for a whole book. It was important work, and she wanted it finished by the end of the summer.

Ellen glanced over her shoulder again. Diana hooked her dark hair behind one ear and carried on staring out of the window.

Geenie was just as bad. After her little cigarette show, she was now sitting on the other side of the back seat, gazing at her knees.

'Your daddy's done wonders,' Ellen continued. 'He's really transformed the place. It's our country idyll, isn't it, Geenie? He's very clever with his hands.'

'I know,' Diana said, but still she didn't look round. For some reason, she reminded Ellen of Josephine Baker: perhaps it was those smooth cheeks and lively eyes. She could see Diana easily controlling a pair of cheetahs whilst dancing an exotic number.

'My mother says houses are his forte,' added Diana.

'And writing, darling, your daddy's a very clever writer,

isn't he?'

'But houses are his forte,' Diana insisted.

'What's forte?' asked Geenie.

'It's like a special talent, darling, like you and dressing up.'

'Or drawing,' said Geenie. 'That's my forte, isn't it, Ellen?'

She looked up then, hopefully, and Ellen conceded, 'That too.'

'My mother's forte is dancing,' said Diana. 'What's yours?'

'Mine?' Ellen asked. The may blossom flashed past as she bit her lip. She couldn't very well say sex. *My forte is fucking your daddy*.

'I should say it's helping people. Making them happy and comfortable.'

Diana looked confused. 'Isn't that what servants are for?'

Ellen turned into a slip road rather too fast and a man on a tractor shook his fist at her. 'Ellen's concentrating, darling.'

Of course, Diana's mother probably had lots of fortes. It had been a short meeting, for which Ellen was glad. Lillian had worn a mint green hat like a miniature meringue, and a green short jacket with mother-of-pearl buttons. Her eyebrows were heavily plucked. But, Ellen had noticed, she looked old for her twenty-eight years. Perhaps all that dancing took it out of you. And Lillian's legs – the part Ellen had glimpsed beneath her fish-tail calf-length skirt – looked no better than her own. She'd greeted her brightly enough, but had looked at her watch when Ellen suggested tea at Willow Cottage, which she'd done on a whim, really, suddenly interested to see how Crane would react to seeing the two women together.

And now here was this girl, thankfully much more like her father than her mother – big brown eyes, a straight, strong nose, prominent cheekbones – but when she closed her mouth, her lips were Lillian's: large and slightly bunched together, as if she had plenty to say, but couldn't quite bring herself to the bother of letting it out.

'What do you like?' Geenie asked Diana.

Ellen had almost forgotten Geenie was in the car. It was strange how her daughter did that, seemed to disappear under her cloud of blonde hair. She'd done it since she was small, her chin receding first, her eyes dropping to the ground, then her shoulders sagging forward, until her face was almost entirely covered by hair. It was what had made James call her 'Flossy'. When she decided to make her presence felt with a scream or a tantrum, it was all the more shocking. Ellen remembered the time she and James had been fighting, and neither of them had known that Geenie was under the table until James threw a dish of hot beans at Ellen, and they'd splashed Geenie's toes, making her yelp. They'd stopped, then, and spent the afternoon bathing the girl's feet in a jug of iced water in the garden. That was in the early days, when such an event was still enough to stop them rowing.

She turned into the drive of Willow Cottage.

'Do you like dancing?' Geenie asked the other girl.

Diana shifted in her seat. 'I'm still thinking,' she said.

'Thinking?'

'About what I like.'

Ellen stopped the car.

'What do you like?' Geenie asked again.

'Come on, then, time to get out.'

'What do you like?'

'Reading,' said Diana.

'Oh,' said Geenie.

Ellen got out of the car and opened the door for the girls.

'And dressing up,' said Diana. 'I like dressing up and being in plays.'

.....

Diana forked up her luncheon-meat salad with one hand. Unlike Geenie, who scattered crumbs and left mounds of lettuce untouched, Diana ate everything and left the plate clean. Then she went on to tackle Kitty's apple pie, using her spoon like a knife to cut the pudding into even chunks before slowly chewing each piece.

'Look at that, Flossy,' said Ellen. 'A good appetite, even for Kitty's food.'

Diana did not return Ellen's beam, but Ellen pressed on regardless. 'Good girl, Diana. Geenie picks at her food like I don't know what. You'd think she ate between meals, but she doesn't, do you, Flossy? No interest in food, is what I sometimes think. Like her father. Too wrapped up in her own thoughts to notice.'

'I liked Dora's pies,' said Geenie.

Ellen ignored this.

'I like food,' announced Diana. 'Pies included.'

'I dare say your mother's taught you that.'

Diana looked steadily at Ellen. 'No,' she said. 'My mother eats like a bird. She's a ballet dancer and they can't eat much or they get fat and lose their grace.'

'How miserable for her!'

Diana scooped another piece of pie.

'George eats a lot, doesn't he, Ellen?' Geenie pushed her own plate away and leant towards her mother. 'He eats like a horse, doesn't he? That means you've got a bird and a horse for parents, Diana.' She giggled.

'Maybe,' said Diana, clicking her nails together.

'George – your father – is totally indiscriminate when it comes to food. He'll consume anything that's edible. Or even inedible.' Ellen looked down at the remains of Geenie's luncheon meat. 'I think I'm going to have to get someone in to teach Kitty a thing or two about cuisine. How to use salt and pepper, that sort of thing.'

'Can we play now?' asked Geenie.

Ellen threw up her hands. 'Why not?' she asked. 'Games are so much more interesting than food.'

The girls scraped back their chairs and Ellen watched the two of them disappear.

... Nine ...

Lou looked like an oversized mermaid in the new dress. The shiny green fabric was clamped to her thighs. Her breasts were squashed into a loaf shape, and her waist had become a series of rolls. It was Macclesfield silk, crème de menthe green, she said, with three-quarter-length sleeves and a cowl neckline. The hem didn't quite touch the floor.

'It's bloody well shrunk.'

Lou had inherited their grandmother's ginger curls, which meant green was her colour.

'I'll murder that laundry woman.'

It was Saturday night, and Mrs Steinberg, Geenie, Mr Crane and the new girl had gone to his sister's for dinner, telling Kitty she may as well take the evening off. So here she was, in Lou and Bob's bedroom, kneeling on the Axminster, her fingertips beginning to sweat as she held the hem of the dress and looked up at her sister.

'Can you do anything at all?' asked Lou.

Kitty pulled the hem taut and examined it.

'You must be able to do something, Kit.'

She stood and took her sister by the shoulders, turning her round so she could see the back of the dress. 'Hmm.' She whipped the inch tape from around her neck and drew it across Lou's back. She wasn't sure why she did it, but it was what her sister would expect. Some sort of measuring and working out in order to reshape the garment to her size. Kitty knew she could do nothing to this dress to make it any better. But when she had a tape around her neck and pins in her mouth, her sister seemed to move easily in her hands.

She pinched a piece of fabric at Lou's waist.

'Ouch! That's me you're squeezing!'

'I might be able to let it out here…' She spoke from the corner of her mouth so as not to drop the pins. Turning her sister around again, she ran a hand over the neckline, trying to smooth it down over Lou's chest.

'How are things at the cottage? You haven't said much about it.'

'I could let it out at the back, maybe…'

'Could you?'

Kitty stabbed a pin into the shoulder of the dress.

'What's she like then, the American?'

'She's – unusual.'

'I knew that much. What does she do all day?'

'She types.'

'Types what?'

'I don't know. She wants me to call her Mrs Steinberg.'

Lou raised an eyebrow.

'The girl calls her Ellen.'

'She doesn't call her Mother?'

'Not as far as I've heard.'

'How peculiar.'

'Perhaps it's an American thing.'

'Don't be idiotic.'

'They've lived all over, Lou, in France and everything.'

'She *is* her mother, isn't she?'

Kitty hesitated. In a way, Mrs Steinberg didn't seem

much like Geenie's mother. She let the child play outside as she pleased, even when it was wet and cold. She didn't bother about her dirty knees. She'd paid no attention when Geenie had painted her eyes with kohl on Kitty's first day. She hadn't even insisted that the girl go to school, saying she wanted to find the right one in the autumn and let Geenie be a 'free spirit' all summer.

But they did have exactly the same chin, and, whenever the two of them were together, the girl was always looking at her.

'Of course she is.' Kitty pinned the dress from the shoulders so the whole thing shifted up and away from Lou's thighs. The waist was now under the bust, and the hem hung in the middle of Lou's shins.

'We might be able to add a waistband…'

'A waistband?'

'Give you some more room around the middle.'

'But that would completely ruin the look, Kit. It's supposed to be high-waisted, and fitted on the hips. It's long-line, see?'

'Hmm.'

'What about him, the poet?'

Kitty unpinned the shoulders and stood back from the dress. 'He doesn't seem like a poet.'

'What does he seem like, then?'

'I don't know. A teacher, or something.'

'Like Bob?'

Lou had met Bob when she'd worked in the bakery. Bob loved macaroons and, after his first wife died, always went to Warbington's for them. Lou told Kitty that he'd held her fingers, once, when she'd handed him his change; she'd known then that she would be his wife. On Lou's request, Bob had got Kitty the cleaning job at the school. He was a senior master there; he'd joined after Lou had left, but he'd taught Kitty. A huge picture of Queen Elizabeth was tacked on the wall of his classroom, and when he told the pupils about her *parsimony* he'd thumped the desk and his shirt had come free of his trousers.

Their mother had said it was a miracle, her daughter having the good fortune to marry a school teacher, even though Bob was forty-five and Lou only nineteen when they'd wed.

Kitty had trouble thinking of Bob as anything but Mr Purser. Living in his house, she'd been careful to keep her voice low and look just below his eye-line when he spoke to her.

'Not like Bob. Turn around.'

Lou did as she was asked.

'You're settling in, though?'

Kitty glanced at her sister's reflection. Lou was wearing a small smile, but her eyes were watching her sister's face.

Kitty held her gaze. 'Yes, I suppose.'

'That's good, isn't it? You're making yourself at home.'

'Hmm. Can you put your arms above your head?'

Rolling her eyes, Lou flung one arm in the air. There was a sharp crack as a seam snapped. She glared at Kitty in the dressing-table mirror. 'I told you. The bloody thing's shrunk.'

Kitty gathered up a handful of fabric from the back of the dress and examined it.

'I'm going to have to buy new, aren't I?' said Lou.

'I might be able to unpick it and make a skirt – a different shape, perhaps, but…'

'Don't be an idiot. I can't wear a skirt to the schoolmasters' summer dance.'

'But we should try to make something, Lou. It's such pretty stuff.'

Lou shrugged off Kitty's hands. She reached behind and tried to unzip herself. There was the sound of another seam breaking.

'Help me, then!'

Kitty pulled the puckering zip slowly, being careful not to catch her sister's skin in its teeth. Lou stepped from the pile of silk. Beneath her white French knickers, her thighs were flecked pink, like coconut ice.

'You might as well have it.'

'Lou, I couldn't.'

'Just take it, will you?'

Kitty gazed at her sister's face in the mirror. Lou set her mouth in a line. 'I'll get Bob to buy me another. God knows he owes me.'

.....

Lou had folded the dress in brown paper for Kitty to take home. In the car with Bob, Kitty kept the package flat on her lap, resting both hands on it, partly to steady the parcel as Bob took the winding lane back to Harting, and partly so she could move her fingers over it and hear the rustle of paper on silk. She could already picture the dress next to her own skin. The colour, perhaps, wasn't as suited to her, with her dull brown hair, as it was to Lou, but that didn't matter. That dress reflected all the light in a room. Even if she never wore it (and where would she?), even if no one ever saw her in it, it would still be hers; she could look at it hanging in her wardrobe that smelled of cinnamon, and she could touch it whenever she liked.

There was no car in the drive when Bob dropped her at the cottage. That was good. She might have time to put the dress on and creep to the bathroom to look at herself in the full-length mirror before they came back.

She was just about to let herself in the back door when the tiny window of Arthur's shed caught her eye. It was glowing in the darkness. She returned her key to her bag and, still holding the dress, squinted into the night. There was no breeze, and hardly any moon. Surely he couldn't still be in there, at this time on a Saturday evening?

If he'd left the paraffin lamp on by mistake, she'd have to go and put it out. It wouldn't be meddling, it would be what Mr Purser, Bob, used to say at school: safety first, children. Safety first. He'd said it at home once, when Lou had handed him a pair of scissors with the blades pointing in his direction, and Lou had told him not to speak to her like one of his pupils. He'd looked at the floor and received the scissors in silence. Kitty held that picture of Bob's downcast eyes in her mind whenever he rustled his newspaper in her direction.

As she walked to the shed, she became aware of the smell of the grass. It had been a warm day, and the earth seemed to have loosened in the sun. She'd left her coat unbuttoned all the way home. The brown paper crackled beneath her hands. The only other sound was the generator in the garage, which had slowed to a low chug.

She knew she should call his name, in case he was in there, to warn him, but something stopped her from speaking aloud as she reached out to pull the shed door open.

There were the rows of nails, numbered, each with the correct tool hanging from it. There was the shelf full of labelled tins, and the stack of terracotta pots in one corner. And there was Arthur, sitting in his deckchair, asleep.

In the low light of the lamp, Arthur's face seemed to flicker. His head had dropped forward and his mouth was slightly open. He was still holding his pipe and a book was open on his lap. An empty tin mug and a flask stood on top of an upturned flowerpot beside him.

He opened his eyes and looked directly at her. 'You're back,' he said.

Her mouth jumped into a smile. 'I saw the light – from your lamp – I was worried, in case you weren't here and you'd forgotten...'

'Why wouldn't I be here?'

She clasped the package to her chest.

He fixed his gaze somewhere above her right shoulder and stretched out his arms. 'Got a parcel?'

She smoothed the paper. 'A dress.'

He nodded.

On the wall next to him was a calendar with the days crossed off, each 'x' the same size and shape.

'A dress for dancing,' she said, and felt herself blush.

Then something beneath Arthur's deckchair caught her eye. On its side, with mud on the heel, was a round-toed shoe of brilliant green.

She almost pointed at the shoe, wanting to tell him that she had the other in her wardrobe. But when she looked at him, he kept his eyes on his book, and began to flick through its pages.

Kitty turned to go, wishing she'd ignored the glow from the window and got on with trying the dress. Mr Crane and Mrs Steinberg would be back soon, and then it would be too late for the bathroom mirror.

'I suppose you dance quite a bit, then?'

She stopped.

'Young girl like you. Should be dancing. Like Ginger Rogers, eh? I expect you've been dancing all night.'

She looked into the blackness of the garden and said, 'Yes. Yes, I have.'

'Drill Hall?'

'Yes. I danced all night. It was lovely.'

There was a silence. Then she heard him rise from the deckchair and walk towards her. The lamp's glow died, and she waited there, holding the dress to her chest and with her coat unbuttoned, until he'd closed the shed door and was standing next to her in the darkness. There was the smell of his pipe, and the flash of his large hands as he lit it. He sucked in, blew out, gave a series of small coughs, then said, 'Perhaps we'll go together one day. Dancing.'

All Kitty's nerves seemed to up-end themselves. 'Dancing?' Her voice came out shrill.

'I can dance, you know.' He gave a little laugh. 'You might not think it to look at me.'

Kitty put a hand to her hair. 'I didn't mean—'

'I daresay you're tired. I'm dead on my feet myself.' He cleared his throat. 'It was good of you to look in.'

She nodded.

'I'll say goodnight, then.'

'Goodnight.'

Arthur stayed where he was, feet evenly planted in front of his shed, smoking his pipe.

As she moved quickly towards the house, Kitty had a sudden thought: did he sometimes stand there all night and keep watch over the cottage? She was sure she could still hear him chewing on his pipe when she opened the back door and stepped inside. And it wasn't until she was in her room and had hung the emerald dress in the wardrobe that she heard the crunch of Arthur's bicycle wheels on the gravel.

... Ten ...

When they reached the landing, Geenie said, 'This is my room. And that's Ellen's. Your father sleeps in there, but he has his own room, too. And that one will be yours.'

'Aren't there any other rooms?' asked Diana.

'Only downstairs.'

'Hasn't your mother got an awful lot of money?'

'I think so, yes.'

'Then why hasn't she got a bigger house?'

The question had never occurred to Geenie, who'd lived in all sorts of houses, big and small, all over Europe. She'd presumed that most houses in the English countryside were cottages, which meant they were small.

'I don't know.'

'Does she like it here?'

'Not much.'

'Do you like it?'

Geenie didn't know the answer until the word came out of her mouth. 'Yes,' she said. 'I like it.'

.....

George had chosen the glazed chintz curtains with the peacock pattern and the eiderdown in matching greens and blues for her bedroom. Ellen had brought her old French furniture from their house in Paris. But Geenie herself had chosen the picture on the wall above her bed. It was an illustration from one of Jimmy's favourite books: *Jack the Giant Killer*. It showed the moment when Jack came upon the three princesses imprisoned by the giant, each one hanging from the ceiling by her own hair. Jimmy had always taken great pleasure in reading this scene aloud to Geenie, particularly the part about the ladies being kept for many days without food in order to encourage them to *feed upon the flesh of their murdered husbands*.

The two girls looked at the picture. The princesses looked quite happy to be hung up by their hair. Great swirls of it twirled and curled around metal hooks, as though the princesses' bondage were merely a matter of hair-styling. Their dainty shoes pointed downwards, like ballerinas' feet. George had some postcards on the wall of his writer's studio of the *Soviet People Enjoying a Healthy Lifestyle*, which he'd brought back from Russia. They all wore gym knickers and little cotton vests with belts and pointed their feet downwards in a manner similar to these princesses.

'That one looks like you,' said Diana, pointing to the fair-haired princess at the front of the picture. 'A helpless blonde.'

Geenie didn't say anything, but she'd always thought the blonde princess *was* a bit like her. Her face was round and her lips made a little red cross. Her nose was a mere line down the centre of her face – quite unlike Ellen's *dog-nose*, as Jimmy had once called it. She swung from her hook with grace and charm, unruffled by her fate. She was the only princess who looked the least bit impressed by Jack's appearance. A handbag dangled from her fingertips. Geenie made a silent vow to get one like it, with a jewelled clasp and the thinnest of straps.

'Do you think Jack marries one of them?' asked Diana.

'No,' said Geenie. 'It says in the story that he gives them their liberty then continues on his journey into Wales.'

'Perhaps they didn't want to marry him.'

'Why not?' said Geenie. 'He rescued them, didn't he?'

'They could have got off those hooks easily enough by themselves. All they had to do was untangle their hair. Or cut it off.'

'Maybe they didn't want to cut their hair. When my mother cut her hair off Jimmy cried.'

Diana shrugged. 'Let's dress up,' she said.

Geenie pulled the dressing-up things from the bottom of her wardrobe, where she kept them in a tangled heap. Plunging her wrists into the twists of fabric on the floor, she wrenched each item from the muddle. There was a long sable coat with gathered cuffs (once Jimmy's); a brocade waistcoat with tortoiseshell buttons; a blue French sailor's jacket; a slightly squashed hat made entirely of kittiwake feathers; and a long white nightie trimmed with pink lace. There was a short silk dress with a dropped waist, turquoise blue in the bodice, green in the skirt; a huge corset, camomile-lotion pink, which had once belonged to Geenie's grandmother; a pair of silk stockings, laddered; a fez; and an ivory fan showing scenes from Venice. There was a white Egyptian robe with gold trim and boxy neck, in the Tutankhamen style, which Ellen had bought on her honey-moon. There was a red and white checked Arab headdress; an electric blue feather boa; and a huge hooped petti-coat, which had been Ellen's when she was a little girl in New York. And there was a pair of jade Turkish slippers, studded with glass and turned up at the end like gondolas (which Geenie was forbidden to wear, in case she tripped over them on the stairs), and a matching long jade necklace.

Diana picked the necklace from the top of the pile. 'I'll have this,' she said. She ran the beads across her face, rubbing each one on her cheek.

'Then you'll have to wear the slippers.'

'Why?'

'Because they match.'

Diana frowned. 'I want to wear the white thing, though.'

'But that's Egyptian. It's what I wear when I'm being Cleopatra. And the beads aren't Egyptian.' Geenie twisted the feather boa around her neck. It was hot and scratchy against her skin.

'Show me, then,' said Diana. 'Show me your favourite outfit.'

Geenie thought for a moment. The corset was one of her favourites, but she didn't think that she should tell Diana that.

Just as she was reaching into the pile of clothes to find something more suitable, Diana caught her elbow. 'Tell you what!' she said, 'Let me guess what it is.'

'You won't guess.'

'I will.' Her eyes flashed and she clasped her hands together. 'I will guess.'

'Go on, then,' said Geenie, straightening up.

Diana's hand hovered over the bundle of silk and cotton, feathers and lace. 'Let's see. It's a process of deduction, like in a detective story.'

'I don't like those.'

'Nor do I. But my mother loves them. Dorothy Sayers.'

'My mother loves Dostoyevsky.'

Diana pulled out the ripped silk stockings. Pulling one

taut over her face, she breathed heavily and leant close to Geenie. 'Now I'm a robber.'

'That's not my favourite.'

'I know that.'

Diana dropped the stocking and picked up the brocade waistcoat. 'It's not this.'

'No.'

Diana held out the white nightie with the pink lace. 'Or this.'

'Of course not.'

Diana heaved the sable coat from the heap and hung it from her head, like a hooded cape. 'This smells,' she said, 'like a dead animal.'

'That's because it is a dead animal,' said Geenie, throwing herself back on her bed and stretching her arms above her head. 'It was Jimmy's.'

'Who's Jimmy?'

'He lived with us for ages after my father left. I don't remember my father, but I remember everything about Jimmy. He was a true bohemian.'

Diana peered out from her dark cave of fur. 'My Aunt Laura's one of them. But my father's a Communist.'

The girls looked at one another.

'What does that mean?' asked Geenie.

'He thinks the working classes should be – equal with us. Or like us. Something like that. He went to Russia a couple of years ago.'

'What for?'

'To see how they do communism there. He said the ballet was very good, and everything was clean and the people were happy.'

'Did *you* go with him?'

'No.'

Diana sat on the bed beside Geenie and let the coat drop to her shoulders. 'Did Jimmy really wear this?'

'He wore it on car journeys. He drove from our house in Paris to Nice in one go.'

'Did you go with him?'

Geenie shook her head.

'Where is he now?'

Geenie sat up. 'He's dead.'

Diana pulled the fur coat tighter around her and said nothing.

After a while, Geenie said, 'Can I wear it now?' and Diana shrugged the coat from her own shoulders and placed it around Geenie's. Then she stood back and frowned, as if concentrating very hard. 'It suits you,' she said, nodding.

Geenie wrapped the coat tightly around herself and smiled.

··· Eleven ···

Although Willow was a large cottage, the corridors were narrow. In the downstairs hallway, Kitty had to turn sideways to get along from the kitchen to the sitting room with the tray, due to a narrow bend that could catch elbows and was already covered in ancient dents and nicks where other trays and limbs had made their mark. It wasn't much better upstairs; by far the easiest way to fold sheets, as Kitty was doing now, was to hang them over the banister like sails and gather the corners together, tucking the sheet under her chin and widening her arms to their furthest stretch as she did so. You had to be a bit careful with this method, because Mrs Steinberg's sheets were surprisingly old. The cotton was thick and smooth, like the icing on Lou's Christmas cakes (her sister was marvellous at baking, and even understood the intricacies of icing), but there was the odd rip here and there which someone, probably Dora, had darned. The stitches were uneven, and they formed bumps on the sheets, like scar tissue. Kitty worried that these vulnerable points might catch on a picture hook or a sharp corner of banister as she flapped, and then the sheet would tear and she'd have to explain; she might even have to mention that Dora's darning really wasn't up to much in the first place, which would be awkward.

As she drew up the corners of the sheet, the scent of Lysol caught in her nostrils. Mrs Steinberg insisted a few drops were included with all the bedding when it was laundered by the woman in Petersfield. She came once a week to collect all their linen, and always rolled her eyes at the sight of the bottle of bleach.

Kitty had just got the last sheet tucked into a decent shape and was about to transport the whole pile into the airing cupboard when Mrs Steinberg called her name. She hadn't realised anyone else was upstairs. At this time in the afternoon, Mrs Steinberg was usually typing in the library, or sleeping. Once Kitty had walked into the sitting room at half past three and found her mistress splayed over the cushions, mouth open, eyes half closed. A long snort like a glugging sink came from her nose, and the whites of her eyes flickered.

'Kitty. I'm in the bedroom. Can you come in?'

What was she doing in there at this time of day? A cold queasiness crawled through Kitty's stomach. She had a sudden vision of Mrs Steinberg in bed with Mr Crane, both of them sitting up, naked to the waist. There could be no other explanation for the woman being in her bedroom in the middle of the afternoon.

'Kitty? That is you out there?'

Mrs Steinberg's breasts would probably be quite flat and long, what with childbearing, and three husbands, if you counted Mr Crane and the last man, who no one ever talked about, except the girl; Jimmy, that was his name—

'Kitty?'

And Mr Crane was very keen on tea in the afternoon; in fact, that was the next task on her list. Surely they wouldn't dare to ask for a tray to be brought up after *that*?

Kitty straightened her apron and faced the bedroom door, which was slightly ajar. A slit of light was all that was visible of the room beyond. 'Yes, Mrs Steinberg?'

'Come in here, please.'

Kitty's mouth jolted into a smile. 'What is it, Mrs Steinberg?'

'Come in here.'

That woman's voice had metal in it.

'I'm just folding the sheets—'

'Damn it, why won't you come in here?'

Kitty pushed open the door a little, being careful to keep her eyes focused on the doorframe. 'What is it, Mrs Steinberg?'

The curtains – green silk, decorated with Chinese boatmen in large hats with long poles, which Kitty had often admired – were open, she could tell that much by the light. Mr Crane's shoes weren't anywhere near the door. But perhaps he'd removed them and left them in his room before going to her. He had a room at the other end of the corridor, complete with a wardrobe full of clothes and a bed covered in a sea-blue eiderdown. But Kitty knew he never slept in there. His cream cotton pyjamas (she'd expected a poet to have silk, and was surprised by the practical choice of fabric) were never dirty. They were bundled under his pillow each morning. Kitty sent them off with the rest of the laundry, but she knew they hadn't been worn. They smelled too fresh.

'Come and sit down, Kitty.'

She didn't sound as if she'd just had relations, which was what Lou called it. 'You'll learn, Kitty, when you're married,' she'd said to her one day as they were sitting by Lou's fiery orange azaleas. 'Relations aren't always what you think. And a woman has to be flexible.' A little smile on her face and a flush on her cheek. The words rushing out in the warm spring afternoon.

'Kitty!'

She'd have to go in.

She took a step forward and let her eyes settle on the edge of the bed where Mrs Steinberg was sitting, fully clothed, holding a handkerchief in one hand. Her face *was* a little flushed. But her eyes were slightly pink, and there was no smile. And no Mr Crane.

'What is it, Mrs Steinberg?'

The woman seemed to be breathing oddly, unevenly, taking a little breath in and letting a big one out.

'Sit with me, Kitty.'

There was a notebook and a cardboard folder on the bed, full of what appeared to be letters.

'I was just doing the sheets—'

'They can wait.'

Kitty sat on the bed, being careful not to touch the folder or any of the papers. It was a wide bed – the widest she'd seen – with large acorn-shaped brass knobs on each corner of the frame. Sleeping alone in such a bed would be like having a whole house to yourself.

Mrs Steinberg placed her long fingers on Kitty's shoulder. 'I'd like to ask your advice.'

'My advice?'

Kitty couldn't remember anyone asking her for advice before. Certainly not Lou or her mother. Looking at Mrs Steinberg, she saw that the other woman's hair was even coarser than her own. It never stayed where it was put, and she always had her hands in it, pushing it this way and that. She ran her fingers through her fringe now, rubbing at it as vigorously as Blotto scratched his ear. Blotches of freckle the colour of toffee covered her large nose and her orange lipstick had dried out around the edges of her mouth.

'I hope you don't mind me speaking frankly to you, Kitty.'

Kitty shook her head.

'As you've no doubt gathered by now, I've lived a rather strange life. I've had so much fun, and I've seen lots of things. And I've tried to learn.'

In order to avoid the other woman's eyes, Kitty gazed at the silver ring which flashed on Mrs Steinberg's finger as she spoke. The woman had a habit of staring at you very intently whenever she said anything, as if she wanted to hold you in place with her cool eyes. Kitty wished this conversation were taking place somewhere else, somewhere away from the bed where Mrs Steinberg had relations with Mr Crane, and with something in the room to distract her, like Blotto, or even Geenie.

'And I've always chosen men who might teach me something. If you know what I mean. I've always thought that any fun must also be about learning something... James, my second and dearest husband – which he was in all but name – used to say that a life without learning was a wasted existence. I hope I've honoured that sentiment.' She stretched her legs in front of her. No stockings again, and sandals with the thinnest ankle straps. Her toenails were painted green, but, Kitty noticed, the colour didn't quite reach the ends of each nail. 'And I so want to learn. But I've never been very good on the domestic side of things.'

There was a pause. Kitty filled it by nodding.

Mrs Steinberg laughed. 'So you agree.'

'Agree with what, Mrs Steinberg?'

'Never mind.' She pressed her fingers into Kitty's shoulder. 'What I want to ask you, Kitty is... I want to ask for your help.'

Kitty couldn't think of any correct response to this statement.

'I'd like you to help me become a domesticated woman.'

'Domesticated?'

Kitty hadn't thought herself particularly domesticated. She wasn't like Lou, who their mother called a *tidy little homemaker*. At home Kitty had thrown her dirty clothes in a pile, never baked a cake and left the washing up to her mother. Domesticated was just her job. Before she came to Willow, she'd never made even rough-puff pastry.

'You see, the thing with Mr Crane is that he's really rather old fashioned, despite all his communist sympathies. And I think that's what he'd really like me to do, in his heart of hearts. Become a housewife. A really good one. His own mother's an absolute angel. And he adores you, of course, Kitty.'

Kitty felt a heat rise up her throat and spread across her cheeks. She looked down at Mrs Steinberg's ankles.

'You must have noticed it. I have. He really admires the work you do, for us and the girls. You've taken it all on, the cooking, the cleaning – the *domestic science* – with such aplomb.'

The metal had returned to her voice.

'Thank you, Mrs Steinberg.'

'So all I'm asking is that you show me, Kitty. Show me how to keep house.'

Kitty nodded, still staring at the brittle ankles.

'When you're ready, you could give me a few lessons in cookery. We could go through a book together.' She paused. 'And, from now on, I am going to take full responsibility for *both* girls. Diana will be a daughter to me.' Mrs Steinberg gripped her handkerchief and smiled. 'This is the beginning of my life as a true wife and mother.'

Kitty smiled back, wondering what the woman had thought herself to be up to this moment.

... Twelve ...

By day, Diana was calm. Her lips did not jabber; her nose did not twitch; her voice was level; her eyes were straight. She moved carefully around the house, sitting in chairs to read books rather than lying on rugs, joining her father to listen to the wireless in his studio rather than sprawling in the garden to sunbathe. And when her finger-tips touched Geenie's hand at dinnertime, while passing the salt or the water jug, they were cool and dry. Wherever she went, Diana seldom left a mark.

But one night Geenie heard a groaning quite different from her mother's usual nocturnal noises, and she knew it must be coming from Diana's room.

The noise sounded like a 'whoa', as if Diana were riding an out-of-control horse. Geenie imagined the creature bucking in Diana's bed, trampling the mattress so the girl flew in the air, rolling the sheets to rags at her feet.

When Geenie found her, Diana's room was lit a blue-grey by the moon, and she could see the sheet was stuck to the girl's stomach like a wet curtain. Diana's nightgown was wrapped around her thighs. A strip of dark hair clung to her forehead, and she made the noise again, a long and wavering *whoooah*.

Geenie stood in the doorway, watching the other girl's nightmare. Her own nightgown was dry and heavy, the lace prickly at her neck. Diana thrashed again. She was trying, Geenie realised, to speak: her mouth was working frantically, the muscles around her eyes quivering, but no sound – other than the *whoa* noise, which happened once more – would come out.

She'd have to go in and rescue her friend from this damp hell.

She stole into Diana's bedroom. Sitting on the edge of the bed, she put a hand on Diana's ankle. It was very hot, but not wet. The sweat had yet to reach all the way down there. Slowly, Geenie applied a gentle pressure to the ankle. She wasn't sure if this was the right thing to do, but she'd heard Jimmy say that waking sleepwalkers was dangerous, so she thought this careful, doctorly approach was best. Doctors always sat on the edge of a bed and applied gentle pressure. That's what they did when Jimmy broke his ankle falling from his horse, before his operation, and that's what they did when she herself had caught pneumonia after he'd died.

She decided she should work her way up: a touch on the ankle, the knee, the side, the wrist. There would be no sudden moves or noises.

Very slowly, she began to increase the pressure on Diana's ankle, staring at her damp face all the while. The girl's nose twitched and her arm swung out and above her head so suddenly that Geenie ducked. But there was no *whoa*. Geenie put a hand on Diana's other ankle and gently squeezed there, too. As she increased the pressure, the girl stopped thrashing and her face fell still. Diana's eyes half opened, showing flickering whites, which made Geenie start back and release her grip. She wondered how she could explain her presence on the edge of the other girl's bed. But then Diana turned, gave a long sigh, and began to breathe easily.

Geenie sat on the bed, looking at the side of Diana's calm face in the moonlight, until her toes felt frozen together and her back was stiff.

.....

Every night after that, Geenie lay awake in her own double bed waiting for the *whoa*. She'd never slept in a small bed (her mother didn't believe in them) and for as long as she could remember she'd spent hours trying out different positions on the wide mattress before sleep. There was room for four Geenies in that bed. The headboard was a complicated grid of iron, twisted and hammered into swirls, from which her mother had hung a few pairs of old earrings which rattled each time Geenie moved. The hoops clanked, the drops clacked. Her eiderdown was lilac silk and stained in one corner with a banana-shaped blob of ink. Geenie didn't remember where that had come from.

She thought of the mattress as something like the huge map of the world which Jimmy had kept on his study wall. Each of its corners, its dips and lumps, were countries in which she could try to sleep. The far left was rocky terrain, with good breezes: ideal for hot nights. The mid-right was flat and firm, comfortless but solid; it offered a long night if you managed to drift off there. And the very centre, where the mattress gave out and yielded to her every move, was deep water where dreams were guaranteed. Lying there was like rocking in a ship at sea; waves of sleep came up to meet you, then pitched you back into wakefulness.

When waiting for Diana's nightmares, Geenie favoured

the flat, unsurprising middle-right plane. Sleep was least likely to grasp her there.

She waited, thinking of how Jimmy had once come into her bedroom at night and looked over her. She was six years old, and had listened to another long row for what seemed like hours. She could never quite make out the thread of the argument, only occasional words, such as *your money* (Jimmy) or *not fair* (her mother), or, once, *better writer than you* (her mother again). It had been quiet for a while when the door handle shook and turned. She could smell him immediately: whisky, tobacco, glue, sandalwood talcum powder.

As Jimmy opened the door, and the light from the landing brightened her room, Geenie lifted her eyelids a fraction of an inch so she could spy on him. She wished she looked deeply, sweetly asleep, with her blonde waves chasing across the pillow, so Jimmy could stand and admire her and think about how much he'd lose if he left her mother. But instead she was curled in this tight ball, her fist clenching the sheet, her hair caught behind her neck, both feet tucked up below her bottom, and her eyelids fluttering with the effort of remaining slightly lifted.

She didn't move. She listened to Jimmy's breathing, which was slightly laboured, as if he'd run up the stairs. His hand would be on his hip, as it always was when he was watching something – her mother dancing on a tabletop, or Geenie riding her horse. He might be smiling his bright, sudden smile that made his cheeks wrinkle, the way he had when she'd shown him the drawings she'd done on the paving stones outside their London house. 'Ellen will never forgive you,' he'd said, smiling.

She waited for him to retreat. She thought perhaps he'd come to calm himself. She hoped the sight of his sleeping

Flossy – even in this strangled position – did that.

But instead he sat on the chair by her bed. She closed her eyes in case he saw her lids flickering. The smell of whisky grew warmer. His breathing was steadier now. Perhaps he would sleep there tonight. Perhaps Ellen had locked him out of their bedroom and he had nowhere else to go. Geenie's bedroom was the only place he could rest. That wasn't true of course. There were plenty of guest rooms and a huge chaise longue downstairs in his study.

Her limbs were stiff from staying in one position for so long, curled in this tight ball. Her toes started to itch with heat. How long would he sit there? She opened her eyes a crack. Jimmy had his face in his hands and was rubbing at his cheeks. Then he looked at her and she clamped her eyes shut again. Perhaps she should do heavy breathing to make her sleep more convincing.

'Geenie,' he said, in a soft voice. 'Are you awake?'

Her legs not moving, her arms not moving. Just the air in her lungs, out of her lungs, in her lungs, out of her lungs.

It was silent for a long moment before the sob. And even then, she couldn't be sure it was a sob, because she couldn't open her eyes again. Was that thin rasp of air the sound of Jimmy crying? That sudden rush of breath, was that the sound of Jimmy's sadness? She couldn't be sure. There was no way to be sure of that.

··· Thirteen ···

On Sunday afternoon, when she was free until Monday morning, Kitty prepared herself for tea with Lou. She put on her blue frock with the lily print, which was nipped in at the waist in just the right way, and took the bus from the village to Petersfield.

On the journey, she peered at the Downs through the dirty glass of the bus window. She'd overheard Mr Crane telling Arthur that this landscape was inspirational, and wondered what he'd meant, exactly. Did the mere sight of grass get him going on a poem? How did those ordinary hills, so bare and bald, inspire anyone? They made Kitty think of chapped hands and eyes streaming in the wind. The picture in Mr Crane's unused bedroom of rugged mountain tops and vast lakes – that was more the sort of thing, surely. Something you could really call a view.

Perhaps she should go up on the Downs again sometime, and look at them in more detail. Close-up things revealed a lot. She was working on an embroidery design she'd bought from Wells & Rush of Victorian girls rock-pooling on a beach, and that was all tiny details: the shine on the pebbles, the black beads of the crabs' eyes, the way the children's lines caught in the water. It was going to be lovely when it was finished. The Downs weren't like that. They were blankly green, empty of trees, and they seemed to hold the village captive, keeping the air from the streets.

Often she visited her parents' grave on the way to Lou's, pulled whatever weeds had sprung up around the base of the stone with her hands, and knelt before it to try to say a prayer. She knew it wasn't what Mother would have wanted: prayers weren't her thing. But what else were you supposed to do at gravesides?

Today, though, Kitty went straight to Lou's. Reaching Woodbury Avenue, she opened Lou's gate, which had *60* worked into the wood, and walked up the box-lined front path.

'It's you.' Lou opened the door and peered over Kitty's shoulder. 'I thought it might be Bob, coming back for his extra set of irons. He's always on that bloody golf course lately. Come in, then.'

Lou led Kitty through the house, with its familiar scent of Nettine and new paint, to the back garden: a square of lawn framed by forget-me-nots, delphiniums and white moon daisies. In the centre of the lawn was a deep red rose bush. Red, white and blue: they'd planted the garden for the Jubilee last year, not long after they'd first moved in. Lou said it was Bob's pride. But Kitty knew it was Lou who did the work: she'd seen the dirt beneath her fingernails, the calloused forefinger of her right hand, like Arthur's.

They sat on Lou's wicker garden chairs.

'What do you think of my new skirt, then?' Lou smoothed it over her thighs and twisted to the side, jutting out her chin and widening her eyes. It was calf-length, bright orange with two pleats at the knees, and tight enough to show the curve of her bottom. 'It's rayon. Dries like a dream but a bit scratchy. Bob says this is his favourite colour on me, but I'm not sure. Is it a bit much, do you think?'

Today Lou was wearing her red curls straightened and rolled at the ends so they rested on her shoulders and glinted as she moved. They reminded Kitty of the fox stole Mrs Steinberg kept hanging in her wardrobe but never wore.

'It's lovely.'

'I expect your American woman has dozens.'

'Not as many as you'd think,' Kitty began, reaching for an egg and cress sandwich from the little camp table Lou had placed on the lawn. 'I've seen her in the same outfit lots of times. She likes quite, well, boyish things. Buttons and military whatnot.'

'I thought that bohemian lot were all scarves and no underwear.'

Kitty giggled. 'Lou!'

'Well. That's what I've heard. And she is on her third husband.'

'He's not her husband.'

'Exactly.'

Kitty bit into her sandwich. The bread was a strange mixture of soggy and slightly crispy. Lou must have made them this morning. She'd always been very organised.

'It must be nice, to have anything you want,' Lou continued. 'If it was me, I'd have a new cashmere coat, plenty of Swiss lace petticoats and dozens of silk stockings. And a georgette swagger suit. I've seen just the one in Norman Burton's.'

'She doesn't wear stockings.'

Lou raised her eyebrows. 'What does she wear then?'

'Socks, sometimes.'

'Like a schoolgirl?'

'Short ones. I think it must be an American thing.'

Kitty looked at the back of her sister's house. The sparkling kitchen window reflected the scene back to her: two sisters sitting on a lawn, one in a rayon skirt and the other in an old frock. New garden furniture with blue cretonne cushions. The Jubilee garden. It was fortunate that the King had died in the winter, because a red, white and blue garden would have seemed inappropriate when the nation was supposed to be in mourning.

'What does *he* think of that?'

Kitty reached for another sandwich, then changed her mind. 'Is there cake, Lou?'

'Later. Marble. What does he think of that, the no-stockings thing?'

'Who?'

'The poet, you ninny. Handsome Henry. Crake.'

'Crane.' Kitty twisted her hands in her lap. 'I don't know what he thinks.'

'Are you blushing?'

Kitty took a sandwich and bit into it. 'No.' The yolks were powdery, too.

'He is handsome, though, isn't he?'

'Is he?'

Lou tutted. 'She's a lucky so-and-so. Fancy having all that and not even being married to it. I suppose she can afford it.'

Now Kitty did blush.

'And having you to cook and clean for him, too.' Lou stretched her neck to one side and closed her eyes. 'Sometimes I wish I had a char. Then I could go and do something else occasionally.'

Kitty said nothing.

'Not that Bob's very demanding. But it's a big house to

clean all on your own.'

'Easy, though. What with it being so square – modern, I mean.'

Lou shot her sister a sideways look. 'I suppose.' She sighed. 'I'm a lucky bugger, when you think of it.'

'Mother would have loved it.'

Lou picked up a sandwich, prised it open with one finger and studied the contents. 'It's you she would have been proud of, though.'

'Get off. What about you marrying a schoolmaster? She never stopped on about that.'

'But I don't actually *do* anything, though, do I? Not any more.'

When she was fourteen, Lou had begged their mother to let her stay at school so she could become a teacher, but their mother had said there was no way she could afford to support her until she was qualified. And, anyway, Lou was sure to meet some young man and change her mind before that, and then it would all be a waste. Kitty remembered the long nights of her sister's sobbing in their bed. She'd always tried to comfort Lou, if only in an attempt to get some sleep herself, and Lou had always resisted, turning away and crying all the harder at the slightest touch.

Lou dumped the sandwich back on the plate. 'The bakery wasn't much but it was something. Now I don't do anything that's of use to anyone. It's not as if I've even got any children to look after.'

'You will have, though, Lou.'

Lou shook her head and smiled. 'How do you know that? It's been two years already.'

'You keep house for Bob, and cook—'

'But like you said, that's easy.'

Kitty touched the ends of her hair and looked at her

sister. 'Not for Mrs Steinberg, it isn't. She's asked me to show her how to do it.'

Lou widened her eyes.

'She said she wanted to become *domesticated*. She's asked me to help her learn how to be a housewife. I don't know what to do about it.'

'*I* know what to do about it,' said Lou. 'I know exactly what you should do. You should show her how to scrub the floor and heave the bloody mangle round. You should get her on her hands and knees cleaning the lav. See how she likes it.'

'I don't think she wants to learn that bit.'

'I'm sure she doesn't.'

'I think it's more the cooking and things. And the children…'

'But you're not the nanny, Kitty, you've always said that. You're the cook. She should be looking after them already, shouldn't she?'

'Yes, but—'

'If a woman has children she should look after them herself. What's the point in it, otherwise?' Lou bit her bottom lip and stared at the rose bed.

'Thing is,' said Kitty, 'I was wondering, Lou, if you could help me.'

Lou's gaze snapped back to her sister.

'You're good at that sort of thing,' Kitty continued. 'You were always better than me.'

Lou waved a hand in the air. 'It's just getting a recipe from a book. Anyone can do it.'

'She can't.'

'But what does she want? I can't do anything fancy.'

'I don't know. The basics, I suppose…'

'You can do that. I've never heard anything like it, a lady

asking the staff for recipes. What's wrong with her?'

'Please, Lou. All you have to do is show me a few things. And then I can show her. What about that lovely omelette you made the other week, with the bacon in?'

'Savoyarde.'

'That would be the sort of thing. She likes French things.'

Lou ran a finger along her neckline. 'I suppose I could show you a couple of things. I did make a nice kedgeree last night. Bob was amazed that rice could be so edible.'

.....

On the way back to the cottage, Kitty decided to get off the bus a stop early. It was a lovely evening; the sky was streaked all kinds of pink. She was free until the morning, so why not walk back? Lou had Bob to drive her in their Ford. She, Kitty, would walk. She'd seen young couples on the hills by the cottage, both wearing shorts and carrying packs on their backs. Rambling, they called it. She wondered what it would be like to walk in shorts, baring your legs to the cows. Cold, probably. And what did they carry on their backs? Maps, compasses, treacle biscuits? Notebooks, perhaps, for moments of inspiration. That was probably what Mr Crane did, although she'd never seen him in shorts.

Smiling at the thought, she stood on the verge of the main road to Harting and looked about. There was a cut-through across the fields back to the cottage somewhere. Arthur had mentioned he walked home this way sometimes in the summer, 'to make the most of it'.

She couldn't find a gate, so she squeezed through a gap in the hedgerow, scratching her arm on a branch. A thin line of blood rose to the surface of her skin. She rubbed at it for a moment before making her way around the edge of the field. The wheat was almost to her waist, bristling green. Kitty couldn't remember ever walking in the fields like this before. When they were younger, she and Lou sometimes cycled from their house in Petersfield to Harting; they'd shared a bicycle between them, and would take it in turns to sit on the saddle whilst the other stood and pedalled. The picnic was always the bit Kitty liked the best – a piece of cheese and bread, perhaps a slice of apple cake if their mother had felt like baking. They always ate in the village churchyard, then cycled home along the road again. Kitty remembered feeling that the devil must be in that churchyard. The pointed wooden doors and mossy arches of the church were, she thought, where the devil was likely to lurk. If it was God's house, wouldn't the devil want to hang about outside? That way, he had more chance of getting in and causing havoc.

She reached a patch of trees which she thought she recognised, but she couldn't see the cottage from here. Leaves flicked in the wind. Her shoes were beginning to feel damp. The only way, she decided, was to go through the wood.

Although it had been a warm week, the ground was boggy, and mud crept over the edges of her shoes. As she went deeper into the wood, it was so quiet that she became aware of her own breath. She wished, now, that she'd accepted the piece of marble cake Lou had offered her to take home. She could have stopped for a bite then.

Did Arthur come this way? She couldn't see any track through the trees, which were getting denser. She'd have to go back. What had she been thinking? Even if she had reached the back of the garden, there was the stream to cross. She'd have to go back to the road and walk all the way round and through the village.

The sun was getting lower in the sky. If she still had a bicycle, she could get away from Willow on her free evenings without having to pay for the bus. Perhaps she could cycle up to the church and sit in the graveyard again, to see if the devil had made an appearance yet. When they were younger, Lou liked to stretch out on the graves and sunbathe, hitching her skirt above her knees and closing her eyes. Kitty herself kept upright. When Lou had asked her why she didn't lie down, Kitty told her, *you never know who'll come along*. 'Exactly,' Lou said, and smiled.

They'd waited long hours like that, some Sunday afternoons, Lou's legs going goose-pimply as shadows dragged across the graves, and Kitty's bottom turning to stone. The yew trees smelled of mould, and the grave they most often chose was dedicated to Mary Belcher, she remembered that. Mary Belcher had a headstone, which had fallen over and now lay flat in the grass, all to herself. Was it better to have room in the grave, or to have company? Would it be good to have someone else in there, waiting for you? Or better to be left in peace? She thought that her own mother would have preferred to have been left in peace, but she was in with their father, even though the two of them had hardly spoken when he was alive, so Lou said. What Kitty remembered most about him was the ripe smell of tea on his breath every evening when he kissed her goodnight. And how he used to go up the side passage of the house to fart, putting a finger to his lips. 'Don't tell, Kitty-Cat,' he'd say. Their mother said he'd been a fool to go to war when he was already too old, and even more of a fool to die of the flu when he got back.

She was at the road again now and her toes were rubbing together. Starlings clattered in the trees. She thought again of the marble cake she could have brought back in her bag. The hills were taking on their hunched appearance as the sun went down. All chalk and dust and wind.

She was almost at the edge of the village when a car drove up behind her. It was Mrs Steinberg's new vehicle: a yellow MG sports car with headlamps like moons.

'Can I offer you a lift?'

Mr Crane was squinting against the low sun, one arm reaching across to open the passenger door for her.

She hid her handbag behind her back and looked down at her damp shoes.

'I'd be pleased to drive you back, Kitty, if you'd like.'

He didn't smile, exactly, but he'd opened the door now and was holding out a hand. 'Do climb in.'

'Thank you, Mr Crane, sir, but I'm fine, really I am.'

He was wearing a dark green corduroy jacket and no driving gloves or hat. His hair had gone awry and was hanging down over his forehead, which seemed to make his lopsided eye squint all the more.

'I was hoping to put this blessed car to some sort of use.'

'Thank you so much, really, Mr Crane, but I was walking, you see—'

At this, he turned off the engine.

'Do you often walk?'

'Yes – no, I mean, I'd like to, but…' She twisted the strap of the handbag behind her back. 'I was thinking of getting a bicycle.'

She hadn't meant to say that.

He nodded. 'Cycling is enormous fun, isn't it? For me, though, walking is absolutely the best way to travel. But – well, Mrs Steinberg has bought me this car, so one really ought to use it.'

'Yes.'

'Lovely here, isn't it? For walking.'

'Yes. It is. Lovely.' She shifted from foot to foot.

'With the Downs just there.'

'Yes.'

That leather seat *would* be comfortable.

'You can cut through to the cottage across that field, you know.'

'Oh?'

'Quite wonderful now, with the wheat at full height.'

Kitty touched her hair.

'Of course, you have to cross the stream, but there's a narrow bit, where it's quite safe to jump.'

'I see.'

'Anyhow.' He started the engine again and reached across to close the door. 'I mustn't hold you up—'

'You weren't.'

He looked at her then, and she thought that he smiled.

'Glorious evening. Enjoy it.'

As he drove off, he lifted one hand and waved and said something that she didn't quite catch, but she nodded anyway, then stood looking after the disappearing car.

Lou would have got in with him, skirt hitched up to show her good knees, rounded and pale like curls of butter. *You never knew who might come along*, and here she was, still walking in her stiffening shoes, with no cake in her bag and at least another mile to go.

··· Fourteen ···

Ellen had always been the one who washed her daughter's hair, and now she washed Diana's too. Both girls had beautiful hair, and plenty of it: she hadn't cut Geenie's since the girl was four, and every year its cloud of blonde not only grew longer, but seemed to expand widthways, becoming thicker and fluffier. Diana was dark, like her father, and her hair slipped over her shoulders like a living thing, a muscled eel or a stretching cat, but she showed no sign, yet, of being aware of her own prettiness. She simply hooked the glossy eel behind one ear and carried on reading.

As a treat, Ellen was using her own shampoo for the girls, Rubenstein's *Ecstase*, jasmine scented, ordered from London. Its golden bottle glinted on the window ledge. She hated lilies, roses, violets and any other scent that reminded her of her own mother, who, she reasoned, probably never once washed her own hair, let alone anyone else's. Sandalwood, jasmine, bergamot, ylang-ylang – these were the perfumes worth wearing. Their muskiness was more honest, closer to the earth. She loved the smell of Crane's fingers when he'd been helping Arthur to cut the rosemary or when he brought her a sprig of thyme, saying she should make Kitty put it in with the bird.

The girls bathed together. Their long legs jostled for space in the tub, and they pretended to fight over the soap. Today Ellen made them sit back to back for the hair washing – that way she could kneel on a towel and scrub from head to head without too much stretching. She was still tired after last night's drinking, which had gone on till two in the morning (although she'd noticed that Crane himself had stopped at midnight), and knew that she should save any elasticity left in her body for Crane.

Scooping up a huge handful of blonde and black hair, she soaped both manes together, winding them in a kind of maypole until Geenie stopped giggling and protested at her scalp being pulled. 'Ellen! Stop it!'

Ellen dropped the hair and reached for the jug in silence.

She found her hands running through the black streaks down Diana's back for longer than was necessary, and became aware of her daughter's big blue eyes on her.

'It's my turn now. And I'm getting cold.'

'Diana's not complaining.'

Geenie swivelled round and pressed her big toe into Diana's thigh. 'Diana never complains, Ellen, you've said so yourself.'

Diana smiled. 'Don't I?'

'And don't start complaining, Diana, that's my advice. Men don't like it.' Ellen squeezed the moisture from the girl's hair, and then thought to add, 'And neither do other women.'

'I think she should complain more. I think it's unnatural not to complain.'

Ellen filled the jug with clean water from the tap.

'Who told you that? Put your head back.'

She poured water over her daughter's hair, digging her fingers into her scalp, chasing out the suds, until Geenie cried out again.

'Don't make a fuss.'

'George says that complaining can change things.'

'George says a lot of silly things.'

'Can I get out?' asked Diana, standing up suddenly and dripping water onto Ellen's shoulders. Unlike Geenie, whose hips had recently begun to fan out, Diana was thin as a stripling.

'There's a towel over there,' said Ellen.

Whilst Diana stood with the towel held up to her nose, Ellen filled the jug again. 'Head back, Flossy.'

She began to pour, but as she did so, Geenie went limp and slid herself into the bath until she was fully submerged in the water.

Ellen put the jug down and sat back on her heels. It was just a matter of waiting. She knew Geenie couldn't hold her breath for long. Behind her, Diana sighed, then came to kneel by the tub. Together they watched Geenie as she lay beneath the water. Ellen noticed the small swellings around the girl's nipples, magnified by the bathwater, but – she looked down – no real pubic hair yet. Her amphibian daughter. Any chance she got, she went under.

.....

'Why aren't you writing?'

Ellen had had a drink – just one, just a gin and it – and wandered outside into the warm evening. Only half an hour until supper. Soon she'd be preparing it herself, of course, something light and fresh and French; but for now, Kitty was perspiring over another roasted piece of pig.

She hovered in the doorway of Crane's studio, smiling. She knew she shouldn't be here when he was trying to work. Crane never disturbed her when she was typing, although she often wished he would. If only he would ask about the letters, just once; then she might let it all come out. But he hadn't shown the slightest interest in what she did in the library.

He did have the most charming taste, despite the messiness of his studio. On his desk was a beautiful red porcelain vase with orange dots painted up one side; it reminded Ellen of a woman's thigh, it was so rounded and yet so long and elegant, with a fluted, open neck. Beside it were the usual piles of poetry books, newspapers, dirty cups and sheaves of paper. James had always said that what Crane needed was a good editor, rather than a willing publisher. Someone to take a scalpel to all that self-indulgence. James could've done it himself, of course, if he'd have thought it worth his while. Not that she'd encouraged him, she remembered now. Something had made her want to limit any contact the two men had, and she'd always been rather glad when James had dismissed Crane in that icy way of his.

'You're not writing?'

Without looking at her, Crane stretched back in his chair and sighed. 'Reading.'

He said it as if it were just as good.

'Reading what?'

She was through the door now, putting her hands on the desk beside him.

Crane rose from his chair. 'Marx.'

'Of course.'

When he was this close, she could smell him. At first she'd loved the smell, that warm, leathery scent; but now that the hot weather seemed set in, his sweat was beginning to turn a little sharp. She'd have to say something soon.

'Do you object?' he asked.

'I never object to reading, you know that. But sometimes there are better things to do.'

'Like what, Ellen?'

'Like… writing.'

He moved closer to her. She closed her eyes.

'Crane,' she said, 'you've never kissed me here —'

Reaching past her, he ripped the sheet of paper from his typewriter. He paused to plant a light kiss on her cheek, then he folded the paper and put it in his pocket.

'What was that?'

'Writing,' he said. 'Or as close to writing as I've got today.'

'Is it your novel?'

He dropped into his armchair. 'I don't have a novel, Ellen.'

'Yes you do. You told me. You're writing a novel. It's inspired by the Sussex Downs.'

He'd said to her, when they first came here: 'You make me want to write stories again.' He'd said that. And she'd imagined herself in the pages of his book: the exciting foreign vamp, raising the English gent from his metaphorical grave. *Am I the woman in your book?* she'd ask, knowingly. How could she not appear in his book, after all she'd given him?

'What was the point in coming here, in giving up your job at the publishing house, if you're not writing?' She gave him a few moments, leaning on his desk and staring down at him, waiting for his reply.

Eventually, he dropped his eyes and said in a quiet voice, 'It was for you.'

She wished she had a cigarette, so she could exhale scornfully, like Laura.

'I gave it up for you,' he continued, swallowing. 'Had you forgotten?'

She tried to remember. True, she'd been the first to suggest that he didn't have to go to work. A gentleman shouldn't have to hold down a day job. Messing about in the offices of a publishing house wasn't what he should be doing with his life. Besides, London was such a long way away, and it was where Lillian was, with her kick-pleat skirts and her neat nose.

'I've bought you something,' she said.

She hadn't, but it was good to change the subject. She'd been thinking about buying him another typewriter, a newer one – it didn't feel right that hers was a more modern model than his – but she hadn't quite got around to it yet.

'I wish you'd stop.' His voice was still quiet, but steady.

'Stop what?'

'Buying things. For me.'

'Don't you like things?'

'Well. I—'

'You used to like things. New books. Pens. That cashmere coat. You liked them.'

'Of course I liked them, I loved them. It's just...'

She'd bought him a silk tie, that was the first thing; he'd looked pleased but had never worn it. Bottles of whisky didn't go down well, either. And there was the MG, of course; she'd had to nag him to take it out of the drive the other day. Blotto had been the best present, probably the only one he'd really liked: they'd bought him from a breeder in Midhurst, and in the car on the way home the dog had panted so heavily that Crane insisted they stop to give him a drink from a puddle. He was ten weeks old, small enough to fit in Crane's jacket, which was where he'd hidden for hours when they were back at the cottage. Finally they'd prised him out, and he'd trembled in the corner of the kitchen until Crane scooped him up and took him to the studio. Now the dog slept beneath Crane's desk every night.

'Look. I don't want to fight,' he said, his mouth working in a way she recognised: he was trying to make himself smile. It was how he always avoided a row. Side-stepping her just when she was working up to it.

He rubbed at his chin. 'Isn't it almost time for supper?'

'Another piece of pig.' She pulled a face.

He grinned a little then, his lopsided eyes creasing. 'What's wrong with that?'

'Nothing. It's going to change soon, though.' She hadn't meant to tell him, but he would push her to these things. These declarations. Sometimes they were the only way to get a real reaction from him.

'Things are going to change.' She spoke rapidly. 'I'm going to be cooking. And looking after the girls. I need *something* to do out here, don't I?' She felt the blood rising to her face. 'You're keen on the importance of work, and workers, darling, aren't you? Earning your place in the world and all that. I'm going to earn mine.'

He leant forward in his chair and opened his mouth to speak, but she cut him off.

'It's going to be wonderful, George. I'm going to be a domesticated woman. Can you imagine? Kitty's going to help me.'

She should have had another gin and it before she started this, but it was too late to stop now.

'That sounds – ah – intriguing—'

'All I need is another baby, and then I will be quite the little housewife.'

Now he was staring at her, his mouth open.

'Don't worry, darling. It won't hurt. Well. It won't hurt *you*, anyway.'

'Ellen.' His voice had lowered. It was the tone she'd

heard him use when Diana said something out of place. 'Are you – ah. Are you serious?'

She knelt by the side of his armchair and looked up at him. She waited for a while, hoping he would meet her gaze. But his eyes seemed fixed on his own knees. So she said, 'Yes, I am,' and took his hand in hers. It was a knobbly hand and a skinny wrist. But his skin was smooth. In her experience, most English gentlemen had skin like this: boyish, pale, easily marked. 'Don't you want us to have a child, George?' she asked, softly.

He gripped her fingers. 'Well – I suppose we've always said, haven't we, that we came here to be a family together…'

'That's what we said.'

'The thing is, though, I *am* still married to Lillian, officially, and—'

Ellen jumped up. 'What difference does that make? You live here with me. We're already a family, you and Diana, me and Geenie…'

He closed his eyes. He seemed to be counting breaths.

She really should have had another gin. She pushed her hair away from her forehead and held it for a few moments, pressing down on her own scalp while she tried not to shout. 'It's just – I want to be – you know, *proper* for you.'

'You *are* proper, Ellen.' He caught her fingers and brought them to his lips. 'You've always been that.'

She knelt by him again. It was a great effort, but she managed to keep her voice steady. 'You'll think about it, darling?'

With his eyes closed, he nodded, and, after a moment, he took her head in his hands and kissed her so hard it was all she could do not to flinch.

··· Fifteen ···

Sweat pooled in the crease at Kitty's waist as she scrubbed the kitchen flags. The soapy water in her bucket was almost scalding, and her hands and face felt as red as the tiles. It was better, though, to do the floor in the morning, while the kitchen was still shady, and before Arthur's tea at eleven. She could sit down, then, and watch him eat one of the walnut pyramids she'd made yesterday; he might even say something more about dancing. Every time they had tea together she expected him to bring it up again, but he hadn't said another word on the subject.

'What are you doing?'

Kitty knew, now, that it wasn't always necessary to answer Geenie's questions. If you waited long enough, pretending not to hear, or could look as though you were very, very busy, the girl might move on.

'Why are you doing that?'

Perhaps not today, though. 'It's my work, Miss.'

'It will only get dirty again, won't it?'

Kitty dropped her brush into the bucket and pulled it out again, slopping soap suds over her apron. 'Yes, Miss.'

'So wouldn't it be better to leave it?'

Kitty pushed her brush very close to Geenie's bare toes

and wondered how she could get the girl to go outside.

'Why do things have to be clean, anyway?'

'I think I heard Miss Diana calling for you earlier.'

Kitty had hardly heard the new girl speak since she'd arrived in the house a week ago. She was usually just behind Geenie, looking at you with her dark eyes, then looking away when you spoke, listening to Geenie's questions without asking any of her own.

Geenie cocked her head to one side. 'I didn't hear anything.'

Kitty tried another tack. Nodding towards the back door, she said, 'Don't step over there, Miss, will you? It's soaking—'

Before she could finish, Geenie was running towards the door. 'I won't slip,' she called over her shoulder. 'Look.'

Kitty sat back on her heels and watched the girl disappear into the garden.

Half an hour until Arthur's tea break. She began scrubbing again, concentrating on the sound of the bristles on the flags. A ragged rasp, rasp, rasp. It reminded Kitty of her mother's breath when she'd taken to her bed after Lou was married. At first, Kitty had thought it was just one of Mother's phases; a day or so in bed hadn't been uncommon after their father died. The two girls would make cups of beef tea and take them upstairs, then fetch them down again an hour later, cold and untouched. They played together then, Kitty remembered; she and her sister actually played together, quietly, on the kitchen rug, while they waited for their mother to appear. At any other time they squabbled and kept their games separate, but when Mother was in bed, Lou would show an interest in Kitty's tea-set, and Kitty would sit still as Lou read aloud from *The Girl's Book of Adventure Stories*.

But years later, when Lou had left for married life with Bob, Mother had taken to her bed for a week. After work Kitty sat on the counterpane and pretended to embroider whilst listening to her mother's thickening breath. The room began to smell of glue, no matter how long she left the window open. When Lou came she looked at Kitty, her face creased into odd angles, and said, 'Why haven't you fetched the doctor?' Kitty didn't like to say *it's just one of her phases, you remember them*, because now Lou was here that suddenly didn't seem true. Mother said all she wanted was a little Petroleum Compound and some rest, but when she saw Bob she'd murmured, 'The teacher'll see me right,' and Bob had rocked back and forth on his heels and declared he would telephone for the doctor from his house because this was *a most serious situation*.

There was a stubborn mark just here, beneath the table, where Geenie had spilled her paints. Kitty scrubbed and scrubbed until her eyes blurred.

'Diana's stuck.'

She hadn't heard the girl come in, but here she was again, her bare feet leaving prints on the wet flags, panting like Blotto.

'She's stuck!'

'Stuck?'

'In the tree!'

Kitty stopped scrubbing and took several breaths. 'Have you told Mr Crane, Miss?'

Geenie tucked her chin into her chest. 'He's not here. They've gone into town.'

'Your mother, too?'

'Yes. I told you.'

'What about Arthur?'

'What about him?'

Kitty threw her brush into the bucket. 'How long has she been stuck, Miss?'

'I don't know. Quarter of an hour. We were climbing and now she says she can't get down.'

Kitty stood and wiped her hands on her apron. 'You'd better show me.'

Outside, the sculpture of the naked bottom glared in the sunshine as Kitty followed Geenie to the end of the garden. Where was Arthur? Wasn't it a man's job to get children out of trees? If he really wanted her to go dancing with him, shouldn't he be coming to the rescue?

Geenie pointed to the sprawling willow by the stream. Blotto was racing around the base, barking.

'She's stuck,' the girl said again.

Shooing the dog away, Kitty stood looking up at a pair of bare feet. Inside the cavern of the tree's branches, the sunlight was fractured with green. Everything seemed to flicker as Diana's feet swayed high above.

'Are you all right, Miss?'

'She should jump, shouldn't she?' said Geenie.

'No!' Kitty covered her mouth with a hand. 'I mean, I don't think so, Miss.'

Geenie sauntered around the trunk, digging her toes into the soft dirt of the bank. 'She might fall in the stream.'

Kitty suddenly thought of the woman in the awful painting above her bed, summoning up the courage to plunge into the waterfall. The water would be deliciously cold on such a sunny day. It was really too hot for a vest. She should've gone without.

'Should I go up and fetch her?'

'I don't think so, Miss.'

'What shall we do then?'

Kitty looked around the garden, hoping to see the red

streak of Arthur's moustache. 'When will your mother be back?'

'How should I know?' Geenie was hanging on a low branch, her feet skimming the dirt below.

'It'd probably be better if you didn't do that, Miss. It's making the branches move.'

Kitty looked up into the tree. Surely if the girl got up there she could get down again.

'Do you think you could come down, Miss Diana?'

There was no reply.

Kitty glanced at Geenie, who was still hanging on the branch. 'How did she get up there?'

Geenie rolled her eyes. 'I told you. She climbed. She's like a cat. Her mother's a ballerina.'

Kitty touched her hair. So he'd been married to a dancer. She hadn't imagined that.

She cleared her throat and called again. 'Won't you try to come down, Miss? Please?'

There was a long silence. They watched the girl's feet swaying above.

Then there was a voice, surprisingly flat and calm. 'I don't think I can.'

Geenie grinned. 'What shall we do?' She skipped around the base of the tree, and began to chant. 'What shall we do? What shall we do? What shall we do?'

Kitty's hands were greasy with sweat as she ran them down the front of her apron. Where the devil was Arthur? Reading in his shed, probably. She knew that's what he did when Mr Crane and Mrs Steinberg weren't about. He stood his spade in the earth and disappeared, emerging only when a long farting sound announced the arrival of Mrs Steinberg's car.

Kitty took off her apron, folded it, and placed it on the

ground. As a girl, she'd never climbed trees. Lou had been the one who came home with holes in her stockings and grit in her knees. Once Kitty had managed to scale a slippery log in the school yard, but towards the end she'd fallen and twisted her wrist, and that was the end of that.

'What shall we do? What shall we do?' Geenie chanted.

Taking hold of the nearest branch with both hands, Kitty pulled herself upwards. The whole tree seemed to shake. She attempted to grip the trunk with her feet, but the soles of her shoes were slippery and she was soon back on the ground.

She unlaced her shoes and kicked them to one side. Reaching up beneath her skirt, she unhooked her stockings, rolled them down and folded them on top of her apron. Then she started again.

Geenie stopped chanting, sat on the bank, and watched.

Every time she reached for another branch, bark grazed Kitty's skin, but she was off the ground now and Diana's feet were dangling above, pale and arched. Is that what her mother's, what a ballerina's, feet looked like? She heaved herself up to another branch, clinging to a spindly twig that was piercing her side. Kitty knew she must not, at any point, look down.

Probably Mr Crane would return to find two females stuck in a tree, instead of one. She hadn't thought that poets would like dancers. It didn't seem very likely, somehow, that people who spent all day with words would like people who spent all day jigging about. She tried to grasp the trunk with her bare knees and hauled herself up another level. A piece of bark broke off under the pressure of her foot and fell to the ground. She mustn't think about the slipperiness of her hands in this heat. It was good, at any rate, to have her shoes and stockings off, even if it was up a willow tree in search of a silly girl.

Then she thought: what am I to do when I reach her? A child of eleven would be too heavy to carry even on the flat, and Kitty herself was small and slight. Diana was almost at her height already.

She reached for Diana's foot, but her fingers came just short. 'Do you think you can come down with me, Miss Diana?' She couldn't yet see the girl's face, only the long stretch of her legs and the mushroom-shape of her gathered skirt. 'Can you just get to where I am?' Kitty could feel the warm air on the backs of her knees. She must be at least twelve feet above the ground now. She peered through the branches over the garden. The cottage seemed a long way off.

'Is my father back yet?' asked Diana.

'No, Miss.' Kitty tried to grasp the girl's foot again, and wobbled so severely that her stomach leapt towards her lungs.

'He's not back?'

Kitty took a breath. 'Not yet, Miss.'

'I think I might stay here. Until he comes.'

Diana swung her foot away from Kitty's reaching hand.

'Is she coming down?' called Geenie.

Kitty tried to steady herself. Her fingers were beginning to feel numb from gripping the branch so hard. 'I think you should come down now, Miss Diana, please.'

'But my father might be here in a minute.'

The leaves flickered in the breeze.

'Please, Miss. He might be hours, mightn't he?'

'How do you know?'

Kitty closed her eyes. She must not look down. 'It will be all right, Miss.' Her voice was shaking. 'I'll help you.'

The branches shuddered again as Diana kicked out her

foot. 'But he might come! Don't you understand? My daddy might come!'

Kitty was sure she could hear her own knees creaking in time with the branches. She licked a bead of sweat from her lip. Then she reached for Diana's ankle again, caught it, and held fast. The girl let out a little yelp.

'You've got to come down.'

To her surprise, the girl gave a loud sob.

'Come on now,' said Kitty, softening her voice.

'You won't tell him I got stuck, will you?'

'Of course not.'

Diana sniffed. 'You're hurting my ankle.'

As Kitty let go of Diana's foot, the girl slipped from her branch and hung before Kitty for a moment, her plump lips open, her eyes wide and slightly red, her limbs stretched at impossible angles; then, before Kitty could say anything, Diana swung herself to a low branch, then a lower one, and finally launched to the ground, where she landed with a *whump*.

'Is she hurt?' Kitty called.

There was no reply, just the sound of running, and Blotto's high-pitched bark.

Kitty looked down. It didn't seem so far, after all. The dog was still standing there, yapping at her. For a moment she considered what would happen if she stayed in the tree. How long would it be before anyone noticed? Then she thought: Arthur *would* come. In the end. But she couldn't wait for that.

Her fingers seemed jammed with heat and her knees were shaking, but somehow her feet found their hold. Slowly, she lowered herself through the branches and to the ground. The girls had disappeared and there was still no sign of Arthur. The bloody floor could wait. Who would notice, anyway? Leaving her apron, stockings and shoes on the dirt, Kitty sat on the bank, dipped her bare toes into the stream and wondered if her cooling feet were anything like a ballerina's.

··· Sixteen ···

After Diana slid from the tree so gracefully – Geenie didn't hear a sound until the other girl's feet were on the ground – the two girls ran into the cottage together, stifling giggles. Geenie wasn't entirely sure what they were laughing about, but the sight of Diana's puffed-up cheeks and bunched lips was enough to build a laugh in her own belly. Once they reached the kitchen, they looked at one another and let go; Diana opened her mouth and howled, grabbing the handle of the stove to steady herself. Geenie collapsed on the damp tiles and, catching sight of Kitty's abandoned bucket, laughed harder. It wasn't until her ribs were aching and her cheeks felt as if they'd been stretched behind her ears that she noticed Diana had stopped laughing and was sitting at the table, staring at her own hands.

Geenie swallowed another giggle and got up from the floor. 'Are you all right?'

Diana's dark hair fell over her eyes as her head drooped forward.

'How did you manage it?' asked Geenie. 'You slipped right past her.' She stepped closer to her friend. 'Diana?'

'He didn't come.'

'Who didn't?'

Diana didn't reply, but Geenie knew the answer.

Then there was a rattle and a cough, and Arthur appeared. He stooped in the doorway, removing his boots. 'Hello there,' he said, heading for the tea kettle, not looking at the girls. 'Where's Kitty?'

'Let's go upstairs,' said Geenie.

.....

The box of watercolours was still open on the floor, the brushes stuffed in the jam jar of water. Geenie ignored the splodge of cobalt blue that had now dried on her bedroom rug.

Geenie's room felt damp with heat and was always gloomy, even in summer. Diana lay back on the bed, holding a copy of *The Arabian Nights* above her head.

Geenie frowned at the other girl's foot. 'Flowers?'

'We had flowers this morning,' said Diana, without looking up.

'How about swirls?'

'Whatever you like.'

Geenie licked her thumb and rubbed it along Diana's sole before beginning. It was good to have a slightly damp surface. Then she sucked on the end of her paintbrush. The wood was beginning to flake and tiny strips of it caught between her teeth.

'Burnt sienna?'

Diana shifted on the bed but said nothing.

'Or vermilion?'

'Either.'

'Vermilion, then.' Geenie wetted her brush and loaded it with so much paint that it dripped down the sides and trailed across her fingers.

'Hold still.' She clasped Diana's foot and brought the brush to her skin.

'That tickles.'

Geenie flicked the brush between Diana's toes.

'Stop it!' Diana threw her book to the floor.

Red paint had speckled the bedclothes. Both girls looked at the drops in silence.

'I'm sure George would have come, eventually,' said Geenie. 'And the way you leapt from your branch was absolutely amazing. Like a gazelle, or something.'

Diana laid her head on the pillow and sighed. Geenie waited, brush in hand. Should she begin again? A pattern of swirls was all worked out in her head. They would start small, right in the centre of Diana's foot, then get larger, spreading out to lasso each of her toes.

After a while, Diana said, 'Did I tell you about my mother's feet?'

Geenie had already heard all about Diana's mother's toes, and how Mrs Crane had found it hard to walk on normal shoes since she'd become a ballerina, but she said, 'Tell me.'

'Her toes are like claws. She has special muscles in them. She can stand on pointe for ages. When my father saw her in *Pulcinella* he was *intoxicated*.'

Geenie decided her swirls would have to wait for another day. She held out her brush. 'Do you want to do me instead? You can do whatever you like.'

'All right.' Diana sat up. 'Take off your blouse.'

Geenie did as she was asked, glad to be rid of the blue, heavily embroidered garment, which was slightly too small for her and was clinging to her armpits in the heat. Her nipples prickled in the air. She stood before Diana, who looked her up and down without smiling.

'Turn around.'

Geenie faced the door, scooping her hair away from her back with one hand. She could hear Diana rubbing the brush in the paint. Then she was jabbed, hard, between the shoulders, and Diana splurged paint right across her cooling skin.

'Don't get it everywhere. Ellen won't like it.'

'It's a bit late for that.'

The brush was prickly, and Diana pressed so hard that Geenie almost lost her balance. But she said nothing. She heard the other girl's breathing become heavier, and felt the outward rush of warm air on her left shoulder as Diana concentrated on covering her back with paint.

'You'll be like a Red Indian.'

Geenie's arm started to ache from holding her hair, and her skin felt tight where the paint was beginning to dry.

Diana's brush reached the bottom of her back. 'I'm going right down,' she said.

'*That* tickles.'

'Keep still.'

Geenie closed her eyes to keep from squirming. Cold paint was dribbling into her knickers.

Diana sat back on the bed. 'It's perfect. Look.'

Looking over her shoulder, Geenie saw her own reflection in the hand mirror Diana was holding up. The paint was already cracking as she moved. There were streaks of orange in the hair at the back of her neck, and the strokes on her lower back were sketchier than those on her shoulders, but the effect was dramatic.

'You look wild,' said Diana. 'We could do all of you. Like in a show. My mother wore an all-over sheath once. The newspapers said it was shocking and degenerate.'

Geenie studied her red back, thinking she looked like she

had some kind of disease. Then she said, 'I don't think we've got enough paint.'

'Suit yourself.' Diana dropped her brush into the jam jar and went back to her book.

.....

That night, after listening to the soft *whoas* for a while, Geenie let herself into Diana's bedroom, closed the door, and tried to still her breathing. The other girl wasn't rolling around, but a low whimper came from her lips, as if she were trying to speak.

Geenie sat on the end of the bed and watched. She thought of Diana sliding through the willow, of how the branches would have caught her arms and legs, grazed her knees and elbows. When she'd landed on the ground, had she turned an ankle, or bashed her toes? Was she hurting? Were there bruises she hadn't shown to anyone? All through dinner, she'd been silent. Geenie had known she shouldn't mention the tree incident, no matter how much she longed to blurt out the details to Ellen, especially the bit about Kitty taking off her stockings and climbing into the branches. So she'd been quiet too, occasionally scratching at the flaking paint on her back until her mother had snapped, 'Have you caught fleas from that dog?'

She moved up the bed, flicked on the bedside lamp, and looked into Diana's face. It was glowing, despite the crease between her eyebrows; her cheeks were plump and flushed, and saliva glistened on her open bottom lip. Geenie put a hand to Diana's forehead and held it there for a moment. Then, when she'd found the courage, she moved her fingers gently back and forth across Diana's brow. Her own feet were heavy with cold and her legs were beginning to go to sleep, but she kept stroking the other girl's skin.

Suddenly Diana took a big breath and opened her eyes wide. She stared at Geenie for a second, her pupils huge and black. 'I thought you were my mother.'

Geenie said nothing.

'I thought I was at home.' Groaning, Diana turned over in the bed.

The blankets muffled her movement, but Geenie could see Diana's shoulders heaving.

'Do you miss her?' Geenie whispered.

The blankets heaved again.

Standing up, Geenie pulled Diana's sheets back and climbed into bed beside her.

It was awkward at first: Diana's bed wasn't as large as Geenie's, and it was a squash just getting all her limbs onto the mattress. Their knees clashed, and she didn't know where to put her hands. 'I'm cold,' she said, moving closer, trying to burrow into Diana's warm fug.

When Diana opened her arms, Geenie was surprised by how small she was, despite her height; up close like this, the other girl's body seemed wispy, full of angles and protruding bones; even her chin was tiny and hard as she dug her face into Geenie's chest and wept. But eventually the two of them closed their eyes and found sleep.

... Seventeen ...

There was the snap of cotton being shaken out before she saw anything. The snap of cotton, followed by Geenie's voice: 'You be Clark Gable. I'm being Claudette Colbert.'

Kitty was on her way downstairs to clear away the breakfast things, having finished sweeping the landing, when she heard the sound, and noticed Mrs Steinberg's bedroom door was ajar.

'Draw a moustache on me, then.' Diana's voice came from Geenie's bedroom, and Kitty stopped, her soft broom in her hand, and glanced through the crack from where the snapping sound had come.

The blood seemed to thicken and slow in her veins as she stood in the gloom of the landing, holding her broom and watching Mr Crane dressing.

He was standing with his back to her, looking at himself in the mirror, his green shirt in his hand. He was naked to the waist. His shoulders were wider than they appeared when clothed, his waist slim, his spine straight, and at the very bottom of his back there was what looked like a large dimple, an indent of pale flesh just above where his braces hung down to his thighs. A soft place.

As he moved to slip an arm into a sleeve, the muscle on his shoulder jumped and stretched. He swung the shirt across his back, the fabric billowing out, and pushed the other arm in. With several shrugs, he eased himself into the shirt, smoothing it over his chest and belly with one hand, tucking it into his trousers with the other.

The girls laughed together and Kitty gave a start. But a quick glance over her shoulder confirmed that Geenie's door was still closed.

She was about to move away and get on, ready to pretend she hadn't been peeking; ready to pretend she hadn't seen Mr Crane's naked back and shoulders, hadn't felt any tingle along her neck and down her spine; ready to pretend she didn't now know that he chose not to wear a vest beneath his shirt. It was just a matter of getting her legs going and her heartbeat back to normal. But then he began the business of buttoning, and she knew she couldn't move. She would have to stay and watch.

He started at the bottom and worked his way up towards his throat, teasing each button into its hole with a little twist of his fingers whilst staring at his own hands in the mirror.

'*I* have to tell *you* what to do!' shrieked Diana. 'I'm Clark Gable!'

Kitty realised she was holding her breath.

Tugging his cuffs into place, he turned to the side, frowned at himself, then cupped his hands and wiped them over his hair, pressing it into shape. When he was satisfied, he pulled his braces up.

His eyes shifted then, and Kitty was sure he'd noticed her reflection in the mirror – the shadow of a girl in an apron, her hair unwashed since Friday, spying on him. She found, though, that she could not avert her gaze, and for a second it seemed as though they were staring directly at each other in the mirror. Blood was loud in her ears and a heat forced its way from her stomach to her chest to her head as his eyes remained, fixed and unblinking, seemingly on hers.

That's that then, she thought. It's back to Lou's.

But he looked towards the window, and a broad smile crept across his face as he reached across for something out of Kitty's view.

At last she managed to move. She walked downstairs as quickly and quietly as she could, clutching the soft broom to her chest, a pulse still pumping in her ears and belly.

.....

'What's this, then?'

'It's a French bun.'

'Is it now?' Arthur turned his plate around, watching the cake as if it might make a sudden move. 'Fancy.'

She'd made them yesterday, for Mr Crane's tea, using a recipe from Lou. Arthur had the one that was left over; the icing was a little cracked around the edges, but it didn't matter. Arthur ate everything quickly and neatly and always said, afterwards, 'That was good.'

Kitty sat and picked up her tea.

Arthur took a bite, then went back to reading his Western, glancing towards her just once to nod his approval.

'Did – did Geenie say anything to you, yesterday?'

He seemed to finish reading his sentence before answering. 'What about?'

Kitty swilled her tea round her cup. The back door was open and a warm breeze blew at her ankles. It was going to be another hot day. 'About the willow tree.'

He swallowed the last of the bun, licked his fingers and

shook his head. 'What would she say about it?'

'Nothing.' Kitty stood and began to clear the crockery.

'That was good,' said Arthur, still gripping the plate as she lifted it from the table. Their eyes met and she held his gaze until he looked down at his own fingers on the china. When he'd let go, he wiped his moustache with his hand. 'What about the willow, then?'

'Diana got stuck there yesterday morning.'

'Stuck in the tree?'

'She was up quite high.'

'I never heard nothing.'

That's because you'd disappeared, thought Kitty, crashing the crocks into the sink. You'd probably dozed off over one of your silly books.

'What happened?'

She wasn't sure, now, why she'd begun to tell Arthur this story. She kept thinking of Mr Crane's fingers on his shirt buttons, how he'd taken such care over each one, how he'd watched himself whilst he dressed. The flick of his muscle as the cotton sailed behind him.

She turned the hot tap. There was a belch and a spurt of water flew out.

'What happened, Kitty?'

'Diana was climbing the tree and she couldn't get down.' She looked out of the window towards the studio. The door was closed, but the windows were flung wide open and the curtains were shuddering back and forth.

'I had to go and get her.'

'Why didn't you ask me?'

Submerging her hands in the warm water, she began to scrub at the teacups. 'Because you weren't here.'

There was a pause. 'Can't think where I was.'

'Doesn't matter now.' She'd never understand why Mrs

Steinberg didn't buy a new, matching set of good white crockery. All her cups were different shapes and colours.

'Just a minute, though. You went up that tree?'

She turned to face him, her fingers dripping. 'Yes. I climbed the tree and I got the girl down.'

That hadn't been quite what had happened, but how could she explain to Arthur how Diana had slipped before her, springing to the ground like a damn monkey?

His moustache was twitching, as if he were holding in a laugh. 'You climbed the willow tree?'

'Yes. I said, didn't I?' With a damp hand, she wiped the hair away from her forehead.

His eyes were narrowed but bright. She noticed they had specks of yellow in them. As he continued to look at her, his moustache twisted in an odd shape, the yellow in his eyes sparking, she found herself shifting on the spot.

'Well!' he said. 'Well I never!' He let out a sudden laugh, so loud that Kitty jumped. It was more of a shout – or a kind of bark – than a laugh: gruff and low, as if it escaped him without his knowledge.

She tried not to smile.

'However did you manage it?'

'I don't know, I...'

'I don't think I could do it,' said Arthur, slapping the table. 'Get up that tree. There's not much to hold on to, is there? Spindly as hell.'

Kitty shook her head and laughed. 'It wasn't easy.'

'I bet it wasn't!'

'I didn't want to look down.'

'I'm certain of it!'

'I had to take my shoes and stockings off,' she said. 'I felt five years old again.'

At this, Arthur ducked his head and was silent. Kitty

covered her mouth with a hand.

'Well,' he said, quietly. 'To think of it. Kitty up a tree. I wish to heaven I'd seen it.' When he pushed back his chair, she saw his cheeks had coloured. He didn't look at her as he walked to the door and began putting on his boots.

She turned to the sink, rinsed out the last cup and placed it on the drainer. When she looked towards the door again, he was still standing there, and he was staring straight at her. Her eyes remained steady, and a moment of silence passed before he said, 'What I mentioned the other night—'

'Yes?'

'About dancing—'

'Yes?'

'Well. I just want you to know. If you think you'd like to, the offer still stands.' His forehead was shining with perspiration.

She found herself smiling. 'All right, then.'

He let out a breath. 'Friday?'

She nodded, once, quickly.

Beaming, Arthur walked through the door and out into the sunshine. Kitty could hear him whistling all the way back to his shed.

··· Eighteen ···

It was going to be a perfect evening. She'd asked Kitty for coq au vin, and the results hadn't been bad – the bird was a little stringy, and why did British mushrooms taste of nothing? – overall though, it was much more satisfactory than the usual boiled beef or rabbit pie, and had complemented the Beaujolais well. She'd changed, too, into her long cream silk with the drape sleeves; she didn't usually bother dressing for dinner, unless they had guests (and who came now they lived in the wilderness? Even Laura's visits were becoming rare), but after she'd blurted out the thing about the baby, she felt she should make an effort for Crane.

As if to avoid any mention of the subject over dinner, he'd lectured them on the three million unemployed, telling the girls how lucky they were to be living here, rather than in one of the 'distressed areas' of the country, where the miners couldn't feed their families. Diana had pointed out that it wouldn't matter if *she* lived in a distressed area; she'd still have a gentleman poet and a ballerina for parents, which Ellen had thought a fair assessment, but Crane had put down his knife and fork very definitely and said, 'Never, ever take your wealth for granted,' which had put Diana into a sulk.

Now the girls were in bed, and Ellen and Crane had retired to the sofa with a new bottle, she hoped to get him off politics. It wasn't that she found it boring, precisely; she was always willing to learn. It was just that she'd heard it all before: the misery of the unemployed, the suppression of the masses, how only revolution could bring true equality and an end to the class system that was tearing the country apart. And she agreed that it would be better if things were a bit more evenly spread, but wouldn't it be more pleasant – and perhaps, in the end, of greater importance – to discuss art and literature, as she had with James? Of course, when she'd made this point, Crane had insisted that art and literature should be the spouse, that's how he'd put it, the *spouse* of politics: the two could not be separated. Though she'd said nothing at the time, Ellen didn't quite see it. Wasn't the joy of great art the offer of escape, the opportunity to submerge oneself in personal, particular passions? Politics seemed slightly grubby, not much to do with her, and not nearly as much fun. And Crane always became so deadly serious whenever he started on about Marx and how *the world's future lay in the hands of the workers*.

'You really should join the party, Ellen, if you're – ah – serious about things, you know.'

He rolled his empty wine glass between his palms and looked at her squarely. Not a good opening. It wasn't the first time he'd said this, and she'd never liked being told what she *should* do. She thought perhaps this stemmed from her father, who'd done nothing he should, apart from make money. He'd spent most of his time travelling around Europe with his mistress, a woman named Valentina. Ellen had caught sight of her once over the glove display in McCreary's. Her nanny had nodded, and she'd known that the woman with the dark eyebrows and the chiselled nose was her father's lover.

'But I'm not a worker or an intellectual, darling. They wouldn't have me.' She held out the bottle to him, but he shook his head and placed his glass on the floor.

'I thought you were going to be a housewife.'

After topping up her own glass, she sat on the sofa beside him and swung one leg over the other, flashing her bare feet. Her toenail polish needed re-applying, she noted, but her ankle was as slim as ever.

'What of it?'

'That's work, isn't it?' He clasped one of her gold-beaded cushions before him, as if holding on to a lectern. 'You could tell them you have full-time employment, looking after two children and the cottage.'

'Oh, Crane,' she sighed. 'You really are a unique man.'

He smiled. 'So you'll do it, then?'

Laughing, she snatched the cushion from his hands and swiped him over the head, splashing his trousers with Beaujolais. 'If I do, what will you do for me?'

He wiped himself down, gave a theatrical sigh, and looked towards the ceiling. 'Well. Let me see. We could see what I could – ah – come up with…'

She grabbed his hand and pulled him to the door.

.....

She had a moment to prepare before he came upstairs: Crane always insisted on going outside to 'feel the air' before coming to bed. He was absolutely mad on fresh air. All the men she'd ever slept with were, even though they declared themselves intellectuals. She suddenly wondered what it would be like to sleep with a man who hated the outdoors. Or a man for whom the outdoors was a place of work, rather than worship.

Selecting a red silk negligee, she reflected that the sex had always been pretty good, just as she'd known it would be from the day they'd first met. James had invited Crane to the house in Paris. Dora was sick, she remembered, and Ellen had been standing in the kitchen, flicking the broom about, when Crane had taken over. Holding her elbow, he'd unpeeled her fingers from the broom handle and begun. It was like he was dancing with the broom, his long legs carrying him swiftly to each corner of the kitchen, his arms twirling the bristles round to reach the furthest, most dust-filled, locations. Bringing the dirt together in a hairy mound in the centre of the tiled floor, he'd negotiated the pile of wine bottles stacked by the stove without knocking a single one over. As he'd pushed the broom past her lace-up shoes, she wished she'd gone barefoot, so a bristle might have touched her toes.

When he'd finished, he turned to her, his cheeks slightly pink from the effort, his dark eyes shining. She'd noticed the squint, of course. Not an athlete, she'd thought, not like James; but there was something angular about him that she liked. He was straight-backed and long-limbed, but he did not look too strong for her.

Then he'd shown her how to sweep the dust onto opened sheets of newsprint, gathering each corner together and depositing the whole package in the waste basket without spilling anything. It was like a magician's trick, this disappearance of dirt in newspaper; she'd watched him as if he were producing a dove from his sleeve or a flower from behind her ear. She hadn't dared ask where he'd learned such a thing.

Back in London only a couple of weeks later (was it actually on the day James had told her he'd need the operation? – she shuddered to think), she'd met Crane in that pub in Fitzrovia. Was it the Wheatsheaf? Or the Bricklayer's Arms? He'd taken her to both, eventually, but before Crane she'd never been in a pub. Plenty of cafés and French bars, of course, but never an English pub like this, with men in caps, for God's sake, and stained raincoats, and a woman serving who had at least three teeth missing and hair the colour of Ellen's brightest Moroccan rug. The stools were incredibly small, the floor covered in cigarette stubs and spilled beer, but it was warm in there; everyone was very close together; it seemed there was hardly light or air: just smoke, and beer, and men. Someone was playing 'Hands Across the Sea' on the concertina. She'd loved it immediately.

He hadn't said much at all that time. He'd just kept kissing her, his lips tasting bitter-rich, like the beer he'd bought for them both. It was lunchtime and she'd been hungry – she would have suggested Taglioni's, if there'd been time – but she'd forgotten about that, because his hand touched her side, sliding in between her coat and her blouse and finding her waist, and they'd gone to Laura's place in town, a flat with dust an inch thick everywhere. And, she remembered, he'd been so *fluent*. He'd warmed his hands by the gas fire before he touched her, then undid the clasp of her coat, slipping it from her shoulders; he'd known how to free stockings from suspenders and roll them down without fuss. As he unbuttoned her blouse his fingers trembled and there was a very serious look in his eyes, and even when he was inside her he'd looked at her the whole time; he didn't close his eyes until his moment, when his neck arched and seemed impossibly long, and his throat contracted, just as it did when he was formulating a thought.

On her way home to Woburn Square, watching the glow in her cheeks fading in the glass of the cab window, Ellen had allowed herself to imagine – just for half a minute – how convenient it would be for James to die, suddenly and painlessly, so she would be free again, and blameless.

Now she surveyed the results of the scarlet negligee in the glass, and decided it was far too obvious; she'd do away with clothes altogether and go naked. She'd never had the knack for clothes, anyway, particularly anything frilly or chiffon. James had never minded, saying he preferred her straightforward approach, but she wondered if Crane, for all his Bolshevism, wouldn't rather see her in feathers and furs, like Lillian.

'It's a beautiful night.' Crane came into the room, smiling. 'The moon's beaming.'

Then she knew what she should do. Right now. Jumping out of bed, she cried, 'Outside!'

Crane looked her up and down.

'Let's. Please, let's go outside. Under the moon. We've never – have we?' She pulled her dressing gown around her. 'Come on!'

'I—'

'Back to nature, darling, close to the earth, isn't that how the proletariat procreate?'

He smiled. 'Ellen—'

But she was already on the landing, sprinting towards the stairs.

Strange, how they'd never performed outside before. James had been very keen on it, especially in the summers, by the lake at Heathstead Hall. In fact, she'd grown a little tired of grazing her shoulder blades on stony ground and inspecting her elbows for bruises in the morning. But Crane, despite his worship of the outdoors, had never suggested it, and for a while she'd been glad of a mattress beneath her back and a cover on top.

It was past midnight and there was, of course, no one about. Crane was right about the moon: it left a silver stain on the garden and, she was delighted to see, lit up the beautiful sculpture of female buttocks that she'd always loved. That had to be a good omen.

The gravel path crackled beneath her feet as she trotted along, giggling to herself. Kitty's window looked onto the garden, but she was no doubt fast asleep after grappling with that bird. The girl had looked quite worn out when she'd brought the plates through; Crane had advised her to get an early night, at which she'd blushed furiously, as if he'd suggested tucking her in bed himself.

Ellen looked over her shoulder. He was following her, albeit slowly and still in his trousers. 'Come on!' she hissed.

By the stream, beneath one of the willows, would be the best spot. Even though it was a warm night, the soil on the bank was sticky beneath her toes. It was all right for Crane – he still had his shoes and socks on. Unlike James, he wasn't a sandals man, and she was glad of it. She could never stand the sight of men's toes. They always seemed to be gripping something, usually the soles of their damned sandals; there was something simian about it.

'Here?' He looked around.

Leaning back on the gnarled trunk, she untied her dressing gown. There was the sour smell of stream water, and the click-click-click of leaves in the breeze. Here was as good a place as any, although her feet were tingling with cold and Crane's eyebrows seemed to have been raised since she'd made her suggestion in the bedroom.

Ellen closed her eyes and waited.

To her relief, he stepped forward and kissed her. It was

a dry, rather precise kiss, and she pulled him closer, trying to soften his lips with hers. When his mouth had warmed, she tugged down his braces and, twisting her arm between their two bodies, began to unbutton him. Her fingers knew exactly where to go, and she could feel the tautness in his stomach as she slid her hand into place.

Immediately his lips went to her neck, but, as she took him in her hand, she found he was still small and soft.

'George?'

He was sucking at her neck as though it were a segment of orange. Trying to squeeze out all the juice.

'George.'

He lifted his head but did not look at her. They were both breathing hard.

She mustn't say anything, she suddenly realised. If she wanted this baby she'd have to pretend it was her fault.

Giving a little shiver, she offered, 'Sorry, darling, it's just I'm feeling a bit cold all of a sudden. Shall we go inside, after all?'

She was about to step away from him, but he said her name, caught her by the shoulders and shoved her against the tree. His eyes were fierce, and when he began kissing her again, his lips and tongue were so forceful that her head was driven back into the trunk and the bark dug into her scalp. He pressed his whole body against hers, and for a moment she panicked, thinking he was going to push the breath right out of her, flatten her into nothing against the willow. But then she reached up and felt the dampness of the night in his hair, and she remembered who they were: Ellen Steinberg and her lover, outside, not caring who knew or who disapproved, and she let herself go with it.

Crane gathered her thighs in his hands and lifted her until she was in the right position. Ellen closed her eyes and told herself to hold on, to hold on and feel nothing but the pressure of her lover's body.

··· Nineteen ···

After some confusion over which button fastened to which strap, Mrs Steinberg had finally got her apron on the right way round. The sight of the woman clad in starched white cotton made Kitty take a step back. She looked strangely like the angel in the painting above the altar of her old Sunday School church in Petersfield: shining, determined, and stiff as a ship's sail.

'What are we starting with, Kitty? I'm terribly excited about this, aren't you?'

Kitty hadn't slept all night. On Sunday she'd asked Lou's advice about what to cook for the first 'lesson' with her mistress, and Lou had been very clear: 'Mutton cutlets. You can't go wrong. It's all in the presentation.' She'd presented Kitty with a set of cutlet frills – little paper collars for the bones – which would make the dish look 'just like it does in the White Hart Hotel'. The meat should be breadcrumbed, deep-fried, and served standing upright around a mound of peas, on top of a layer of piped mashed potato. Last night, every time she'd closed her eyes, Kitty had seen sheep wearing frilly white cuffs.

'Cutlets, Mrs Steinberg.'

It was eleven o'clock and they were standing on opposite

sides of the kitchen table, a pile of meat and the basin of breadcrumbs, which Kitty had risen at half past six this morning to make, between them. Kitty had been careful to place them away from the reach of the lantern's greasy tassel.

Mrs Steinberg put her hands on her hips. 'Cutlets?'

'Mutton cutlets, Mrs Steinberg. Mr Gander's boy brought them this morning. Best end of neck.' Kitty gestured towards the package on the table.

Mrs Steinberg peeled back the paper wrapper and peered at the red flesh. With her forefinger, she prodded each piece in the meatiest part. 'Just cutlets?'

'Oh no. There's a special way of serving them, you see, on a layer of mashed potato...'

'Don't take this the wrong way, Kitty dear,' Mrs Steinberg flashed a half smile, 'but don't you think we could attempt something a little more, well, adventurous?'

Kitty felt her lips tighten. She glanced towards the window. Outside, Mr Crane was doing his exercises, swaying his arms back and forth, his elegant hands white in the sun.

'What about something French, for example?'

Kitty made herself look back at her mistress. The woman's cheeks had a greyish tinge, and her eyes were a little bloodshot. But despite appearing tired, she was still constantly moving: touching her hair, tapping her foot, licking her bottom lip, which she did now, as if in a hurry to get somewhere.

'I've got a book,' Kitty ventured, knowing she could always cook the cutlets by herself, without Mrs Steinberg interfering. And if the woman chose the recipe, well, then it would be her responsibility.

She fetched *Silvester's Sensible Cookery* from the shelf by the sink, noticing that he was still striding about outside, his arms waving. Remembering the jump of his muscle as he'd pulled on his shirt, she held the book tightly to her chest.

'Let me see,' Mrs Steinberg snatched the book and thumbed through its pages, muttering under her breath. '*Oyster patties* – why mess with perfection? – *Beef à la Mode* – not more beef – *Kromesques of Veal* – have we any veal?'

Kitty shook her head.

'*Omelette Soufflé*. Well, that's French, I suppose. And I am very good at scrambled eggs, Kitty; did I ever tell you that? Now, let's see.' Mrs Steinberg tapped her foot and nodded to herself as she read the recipe through. 'Sounds simple enough. Take six eggs—' She looked up.

'In the larder, Madam.'

'Naturally.' Mrs Steinberg closed the book.

Whilst her mistress was in the larder, Kitty sat at the table and waited. Outside, there was a clunk as the door to the writing studio closed. That meant he wouldn't come out again for a while.

A voice floated through the larder door. 'Where, exactly?'

'Second shelf. On the left.'

'Damn.' Mrs Steinberg came back into the kitchen and circled the table. 'There's only four. Why have we only four eggs, Kitty?'

'I've ordered more for tomorrow morning, Mrs Steinberg.'

Then Kitty heard a stifled sound, something like a chirp, or a giggle. Behind her mistress, she saw Geenie and Diana peering through the doorway, hands over their mouths.

'What was that?' asked Mrs Steinberg, turning.

The girls ran off.

'I – don't know, Madam.'

Mrs Steinberg was tapping her foot and holding her hair away from her face, stretching her forehead in the most peculiar way. 'Right. Well. It looks like it'll have to be cutlets, then.'

Kitty looked at the clock. Half past eleven already, and no sign of Arthur. It would probably be better if he didn't come in for his morning tea today, what with the lesson and the invitation to the dance still hanging in the air. She still wasn't sure why she'd said yes, and had been trying to think of ways to take her answer back. It had been such a relief to hear him ask again, that the 'yes' had just popped out. Now she'd have to face a whole evening with him, and she'd have to try her hardest not to lead, like she had with Frank. Unless she could think of some excuse not to go.

'Where shall we start?'

'First we have to do the potatoes.'

'What do we have to do with them?'

'Peel them, Mrs Steinberg.'

'Right. Yes.'

'I can do it, though.' Kitty began spreading an old copy of the *Herald* on the table. 'The potatoes are in the shed—'

'I'll get them.'

Before she could protest, the woman had disappeared again, leaving Kitty standing, chewing on her forefinger, staring at the newsprint. This was going to take even longer than she'd imagined.

'Look,' said Mrs Steinberg, 'I carried them in on my apron! Isn't that what you do?' She tipped four small potatoes onto the newspaper, scattering the table, and Kitty's shoes, with dirt.

'Yes. That's what you do. Only—'

'What?'

'We might need a few more, eventually, for all of you…'

Mrs Steinberg looked at the vegetables. 'Oh. I hadn't thought.' The woman's hands dropped by her sides and she looked so downcast that, for a moment, Kitty considered consoling her. But then her mistress clapped her hands together. 'I know what we need! Music! Let's have some music!' And once more she disappeared.

Whilst the woman was out of the room, Kitty carried the potatoes to the sink and began to scrub them clean, staring through the window at the writing studio as she rubbed at the dirt. He'd opened and propped the door ajar, which was unusual. It must get warm in there, though, in this sunshine. He'd have to take his jacket off, and perhaps roll up his shirt sleeves. His bare wrists would be resting against the desk, rubbing against white paper.

'I thought you might need these.'

Kitty dropped her potato. She hadn't heard Arthur come in.

'I tried to tell her she'd need more but it was too late,' he said, standing close behind her and emptying a basin of potatoes into the sink. Muddy water splashed up her arms. 'Fetched you some peas, too.' There was the smell of aniseed and his breath warmed her ear as he whispered, 'You will come, won't you? On Friday.'

She squeezed a clump of mud between her fingers. 'I— I've got to see about the time off. Wednesdays and Sundays are my usual evenings.'

'Ask her today, then. Now's a good time.'

'Oh! Arthur! Duke Ellington or Glen Gray?' Mrs Steinberg was leaning on the doorframe.

'Duke Ellington, definitely, Mrs Steinberg.'

There were those yellow sparks in his eyes again, and he stroked at his moustache.

'I knew you'd be a fan of the Duke, Arthur, I just knew it!'

Arthur rolled his sweet around his mouth and grinned.

'Didn't you think so, Kitty? That Arthur would be a Duke man?'

Kitty said nothing.

'Best get on,' said Arthur, opening the back door.

'Don't you want your tea?' Kitty wiped her hair away from her brow.

Mrs Steinberg looked from Arthur to Kitty and back again.

'Later, maybe.'

'Music!' said Mrs Steinberg, heading back to the living room.

Kitty turned to the sink and watched Arthur walk to his shed.

'Don't you love this one, Kitty?' Mrs Steinberg was clicking her fingers in time with the beat. She twirled, her apron drawing a tight circle in the air. 'Divine. Hot and sweet.'

Kitty began to peel the potatoes while her mistress spun around the kitchen. 'Ah do-wap, do-wap, do-wap, do-wap – dah!' Her body, usually twitching and pulling this way and that, seemed loosened. There was no pattern to her movements – you couldn't say she'd mastered any particular dance – but Kitty couldn't stop watching her. The woman seemed changed by the music into a dipping, gliding thing.

'Hot and *sweet*.'

Kitty piled the potatoes into the pan and went to the sink to cover them with water, narrowly avoiding a collision with Mrs Steinberg.

'I danced on the tabletops in the Dôme, you know, Kitty. That's in Paris. Quite regularly. My first husband had to pull me to the floor to stop me.' She spun around, flinging her arms above her head and letting out a long hoot like an owl.

Kitty put the pan on the stove and started to smile.

'How can you stand there when there's music, Kitty? Dance with me.'

'I couldn't—'

'Come on.' Mrs Steinberg grabbed Kitty's wrists and pulled her away from the stove.

'The potatoes—'

Although she was smiling, the woman had a determined look on her face, and Kitty thought again of the angel in the church, its wings stretching and carrying it into the sky, and she started to move. She was suddenly sharply aware of her own body, of how the limbs joined together and creaked into life. If she wanted it to, would her left leg kick as high as Mrs Steinberg's? Would her bottom sway back and forth in that way?

'From the hips, Kitty dear, from the hips.' Mrs Steinberg grasped Kitty's waist and swung her from side to side. Laughing, Kitty allowed herself to move with her mistress. Mrs Steinberg pressed her thighs into the backs of Kitty's own and leaned back, taking Kitty with her.

'Now forward.'

With the other woman's arm around her waist, Kitty bent forward.

'Now hop.' They hopped on the spot. 'Now back. Now hop. You've got it!'

'Haven't you made lunch yet?' Geenie was standing in the doorway, her arms folded. 'It's almost twelve o'clock. Diana and I are hungry.'

The two women were panting; Kitty could feel Mrs Steinberg's chest rising and falling at her own back. Once her mistress had let her go, Kitty wiped her moist neck with her hankie, turned, and immediately fired the stove so she wouldn't have to look at Geenie while she was so flushed.

Her fingers slipped on the pan, causing it to crash onto the burner.

Mrs Steinberg laughed. 'Oh, Regina, you look so cross. How can you be cross when there's such music, darling?' She spun over to her daughter. The woman's face, Kitty noticed, was shining with perspiration, and her nose looked bigger than ever.

Geenie folded her arms across her chest. 'Where's lunch?'

'Honestly, darling, sometimes you're so conventional. Will the world end if we don't sit down for lunch at half past twelve on the dot?'

The record had finished, but Mrs Steinberg was still dancing, swaying back and forth before her daughter, bobbing at the knee and reaching up into the air.

'The potatoes aren't even boiling, are they?' Geenie tapped her foot.

Her mother stopped dancing. 'And what do you know about potatoes?'

The girl looked directly at Kitty. 'I watch Kitty. When you're not here. She lets me watch.'

Mrs Steinberg took Geenie by the shoulders. 'You can watch me now, then. You can watch your mother do it.' Her high voice was dangerously even and clear. Marching the girl to the stove, she pushed Kitty aside. 'I'll show you how to get them boiling.' With a flick of her wrist, she turned the gas as high as it would go. The flame sprung around the pan.

'What are we having with it?'

'Cutlets.'

Geenie pulled a face.

Kitty tried to make herself as invisible as possible by sliding past mother and daughter, sitting at the table and beginning to shell the peas.

'Look, Geenie, I'm doing it. Your mother's doing it.' Mrs Steinberg reached across Kitty, picked up a cutlet by the bone, and held it in front of her daughter's face. A drip of moisture fell through the air, landing on Geenie's bare toe.

'Ugh.'

'Don't be so silly. It's just meat. You want it juicy. Tell her, Kitty. You want meat juicy. It's got no flavour, no *life*, in it otherwise.'

'If it's dead, how can it have life?'

Eyes flashing, Mrs Steinberg held the meat out to her daughter. 'Why don't you touch it and see?'

Geenie stepped back.

Kitty had never liked touching meat herself, but she'd become used to it. Pulling the skin from anything was still a job she feared. She hated the way white fat would stick to the pink flesh beneath, trails of membrane stretching between the two parts of the animal like lengths of spittle.

'Go on. Touch it.'

With her eyes half closed, the girl held out her fingers.

'You'll have to come closer than that.'

But Geenie seemed to have frozen in position, her mouth skewed in disgust. Her bottom lip began to tremble.

Kitty stood up. 'I should get on—'

Mrs Steinberg was still staring at her daughter. 'Can't you even touch it?'

Kitty raised her voice. 'I should really get on with those now, Mrs Steinberg.'

The woman let out a long breath. Then she dropped the meat back onto the paper. 'You'll have to be more daring than that, Regina, if you're going to get on in life. If there's one thing I've learned, it's how to take a risk.' She turned on her heel and faced Kitty. 'We'll have lunch at half past one today.'

'Yes, Mrs Steinberg.'

'Our lesson has been ruined by my daughter, I'm afraid. We'll have to do it another time.' She unbuttoned her apron and hung it on the door.

'Mrs Steinberg?'

'Yes?'

Kitty hesitated. Her mistress's nose was inflamed, her mouth pulled tight, and Geenie was still standing by the stove, staring at the floor. But if she said it now, she might get the answer that would give her an excuse. 'Could I have my evening off on Friday this week?'

'Friday?' The woman sighed. 'I really need your help on Friday, dear. Mr Crane's sister is coming for dinner and I can't cope by myself.'

Kitty nodded.

'I hope it wasn't anything important?'

Kitty forced the last pea from its pod. 'Oh no. Nothing important.'

'Good. That's settled then.' Mrs Steinberg swept from the room with Geenie following close behind, her blonde head still drooping.

··· Twenty ···

It was the middle of the afternoon and the girls were bored. Geenie lay on the grass in the sun and Diana sat behind her in the shade of a willow. Bees droned in the air around them. Diana didn't flinch, but, no matter how hard she tried to remain calm, Geenie had to squeal when a bee seemed close enough to enter her ear. She was sure she could feel its prickly woolliness against her lobe.

Diana let out a loud tut. 'It won't hurt you unless you startle it.'

'Why not?'

'I don't know. It's what my father says.'

'Does he know about bees?'

'He's very knowledgeable on flora and fauna, as it happens.'

Geenie was silent. She wasn't entirely sure what *flora and fauna* meant. Another bee whirred past, and she flicked her fingers close to her ear again. A hot, rotten smell wafted over from Arthur's compost heap, and, in the distance, there was the regular thud of typewriter keys. Geenie knew this sound wasn't coming from George's writing studio. This sound was being made by her mother, who was typing in the library, as she did every afternoon until she went for her nap. Lately, Geenie had noticed that the door to George's writing studio remained closed during her mother's nap, and the only afternoon sounds that came from upstairs were Ellen's snores.

Both girls were wearing white cotton camisoles. After lunch they'd decided to dress up as Pierrot clowns, but, finding no pompoms, neck ruffs or pantaloons in Geenie's dressing-up pile, they'd had to settle for Ellen's old camisoles and lots of make-up. Diana had inherited some theatrical face paint from her Aunt Laura, who'd once been on the stage, and Geenie's face felt stiff beneath several layers of white pan-stick. She'd drawn a tear-drop on Diana's cheek, close to her eye – which had got smudged and now looked like a squashed currant – and a downward mouth around her own lips, which didn't look as tragic as she'd first imagined, since it had turned out lopsided.

The thump of the typewriter stopped and Geenie sat up. 'Do you want to know what my mother is writing?'

It took Diana a few moments to respond. '*Is* your mother writing?'

'She's typing.'

'Yes. But that's different.'

Geenie decided that Diana's squashed currant now looked more like a flattened fly. 'Do you want to know or not?'

Diana sighed. 'All right.'

'She's typing Jimmy's letters.' Geenie left what she felt was a dramatic pause. 'For a book.'

Diana gave Geenie a sideways look. 'What evidence do you have?'

'I've seen it. The front page says: *Collected Letters of James Holt, edited by Ellen Steinberg*.'

'Why would anyone want to read that?'

Geenie leaned close to Diana so her blonde hair brushed the other girl's camisole. 'Because Jimmy was very clever, and people like reading about clever men.'

Diana rolled her black-rimmed eyes.

'And,' Geenie continued, 'and, there are probably lots of romantic letters in there. Love letters. You know. *My darling I cannot live without you, I am dying of this amorous affliction…*'

Diana began to smile. 'Shall we go and look, then?'

.....

They crossed the crisp grass, padded through the kitchen, where Kitty was huffing over the washing-up, and stood outside the library. Geenie listened at the door, pulling Diana in so close behind that she could smell the waxy scent of her make-up. Geenie was sure her mother would be upstairs by now, taking a nap. But, to be certain, she pressed her eye to the keyhole. It was dark in the library, even today, and she had to squint, but she could make out the outline of the empty chair by the desk, which was enough to convince her to turn the door handle.

The door creaked, just like it did in stories where children went places they shouldn't. Geenie put a finger to her lips and hunched herself up on tiptoes. Diana clutched the top of her friend's arm. Their camisoles rustled together as they crept across the rug.

'Where are the letters?' hissed Diana.

'Ssh!'

It was a tiny room, not a quarter of the size of Jimmy's library in their London house. There was no shining globe, no coloured maps on the walls. There were just shelves of books along every wall, the desk and chair, and, in the corner, the stuffed fox in a pair of spectacles and a hunting outfit which had been left in the cottage by the previous owners. Ellen had wanted to burn the fox on the fire, but George had said they should keep it, so it had ended up here, dust covering its red jacket, the bugle in its paw tarnished and bent.

Geenie stopped. Diana froze behind her. 'What?'

'I thought I heard something.' Geenie narrowed her eyes and looked about, but nothing was stirring in the hot afternoon. As her heart slowed, she pictured the scene of her mother bursting in, discovering the two sleuthing girls. She would swoop down on them, label them snoops, send them to their rooms. Then, later, she would feel sorry, call her daughter into the sitting room, sit her on her lap and read aloud from *The Last Days of Pompeii*, and Geenie would imagine the grey cloud hanging over the Romans' heads like a terrible speech bubble.

'That's horrible.' Diana was looking at the stuffed fox.

'It was here when we moved in. Your father wanted to keep it. He said it would remind us that someone lived here before.'

'Shall we take his glasses off? He'd be better without his glasses.'

'We're supposed to be reading the letters.'

Leaving Diana squinting at the fox, Geenie opened the cardboard folder marked 'personal' on the desk and took a letter from the top of the pile. The paper was thin and soft, the writing long and slanting. *Herbert*, she read. *Eliot's latest is, as you say, a masterpiece. What a pity he is such a dullard.* She let the letter fall on the desk and reached for another. *Emily, Come as soon as you can.* More interesting. *We are having a party on the fifteenth, and everyone will be here, waiting for you to perform…*

'Do you think they're in love?' With the fox's glasses

balanced on the end of her nose, Diana was looking out of the window. Geenie peered over her shoulder. Outside, Arthur was saying something to Kitty. She was studying the ground, and he was looking at her hair. They didn't look to Geenie like two people in love. There wasn't any shine about them. Kitty's cheeks *were* flushed, but in a blotchy way, like a rash, rather than a glow.

'Why?'

'Housemaids are always falling in love with gardeners and errand boys and whatnot, aren't they? My mother says they're all flighty, and you have to watch them.' Diana sat on the rug, pulled the glasses from her nose, and wiped her face, leaving a black streak across her cheek. 'And it's so hot.' She flopped on her back and stretched out her bare legs. 'Things like that always happen when it's hot.'

Geenie fished out another letter. After scanning the first few sentences, she began to read aloud. 'Here's a good bit. *How can I apologise enough for the other night, my darling bird? Sometimes Rachel's talk does make me light-headed – as you said – but she doesn't have the hold on me you imagine, my darling, please believe that*—'

'Who's Rachel?'

'She was Jimmy's fiancée before my mother came along. Jimmy married her, but he always loved my mother.'

'Why did he marry Rachel, then?'

'It was a formality.' This was the word Ellen had used when Geenie asked if it was true that Jimmy had married Rachel.

'What else does it say?'

Geenie skipped the next few lines, then resumed. '*When the operation is over and done, we'll make a new start – Paris, Geneva, Rome – wherever you want…*' She stopped.

Diana was looking out of the window again. 'Actually,'

she said, 'I don't think they are in love, you know.'

Geenie sat at the desk and rested her cheek on the typewriter keys. The metal was cool against her skin. She closed her eyes and remembered it: how she'd come home from school and Dora had said, *Don't go up there*, and there were voices in the drawing-room, and she'd heard her mother's low wail. She'd started to shake, and had the sudden urge to go to the lavatory. Then, sitting on the icy seat, shivering, she'd waited for the sound of her mother's voice; and when it didn't come, she'd knelt outside the closed drawing-room door, and the doctor had appeared, saying, 'Little girls who listen at doors will hear things they don't like.' She'd never understood why *he* was the one who'd looked angry. For days after, Ellen had said that Jimmy was still in the hospital but was too ill for visitors, but Geenie knew he was dead; her mother's hands trembled and she hadn't changed from her blue knitted suit since that afternoon. Then Geenie caught pneumonia and everything was hot and still for a while, and there was only her headache, which seemed to thud in every part of her body, and Dora bringing up bowls of tapioca each evening. When she was better her mother said, 'We've got to be brave and get right away from here, it will be better that way, now Jimmy's gone.'

'Are you all right?'

Geenie lifted her head from the keys.

'Shall we look at some more letters?' Diana moved from the window and flicked through the pile. 'They were just starting to get interesting.'

Brushing the other girl's hand to one side, Geenie stuffed the papers back into the cardboard folder. 'No,' she said. 'I don't want to read any more.'

... Twenty-one ...

Ellen drove into Petersfield carefully. It was early morning, not past nine o'clock, and for most of the way she was stuck behind a cart spilling straw and mud over the road, for which she was glad. It gave her a chance to think, and she'd never enjoyed driving fast. James had thrown the Renault she'd bought him around like a chariot, thinking only of speed, of getting there in time for aperitifs, while she'd hung on to her seat, laughing nervously, her heartbeat shrill in her ears.

Crane had suggested the picnic, saying they should take Kitty and Arthur with them to the beach at Wittering. A summer treat for the whole family. He seemed to be referring to the staff more and more as *family* lately, but Ellen didn't much mind; at least it meant he was seeing her and Geenie as family, too, despite their not being married and there being no progress on the divorce from Lillian. But it was Ellen, of course, who had to oversee the whole outing, get Kitty going on the right foods (the girl had looked so crestfallen when Ellen had said no to Scotch eggs that she'd had to change her mind), and order suitable cold meat from Mr Gander; she'd even considered having some foie gras sent from Fortnum's, but had decided against it because of the expense.

Thinking about it now, this afternoon's outing would be the perfect time to make her announcement to the girls about her hopes for another child; if Kitty and Arthur heard it, all the better: everyone would know, then, of her seriousness about becoming domesticated. And it was absolutely right to have her hair styled before the event. No matter how it was set – pin curls, bias waves, brush curls – her hair always seemed to go its own way, but the new place in town looked surprisingly good – marble surfaces, a very clean front window, a list written in gold lettering which advertised MacDonald and Vapour Permanent Waving and promised *Life Experienced Operators Only*, whatever that meant. It was called Marie-Christine in the way of all such places in England; people seemed to think that some girl's name or other would stamp the place with a certain glamour.

She parked the Lanchester near the market place and walked along the High Street, passing a young man in chalk-stripe flannels and shiny shoes who smiled at her so widely that she almost stopped to ask his name. After he'd passed, she realised that she'd forgotten to wear a hat again. It was better just to put one on, although it was far too hot and she hated the sensation of the thing pressing down on her head, making her scalp sweat. Otherwise, the shop girls just didn't take you seriously, and you had no chance to convince them of your actual calibre after that first impression was gone.

The hairdressing salon was down a narrow cobbled lane next to a butcher's shop where whole rabbits and headless deer hung outside, giving the street a slightly ripe aroma which, in this rising heat, reminded her of Naples. She'd never quite become used to the particular scent of this town

– it was unlike any other she'd experienced in Europe. In the mornings, it smelled a bit like glue, but also, powerfully, of scorched clothes. Crane had told her it was the rubber factory. She found it vaguely unsettling: it was an intimate smell, a domestic sort of smell, that didn't seem right out of doors.

She pushed open the glass door of the salon. The floor was green tiles, the walls washed in pale pink, and it was already steamy inside. The girl sitting at the back of the shop was painting her nails; she nodded at Ellen and asked her to sit in a chair next to the window and wait for Robin, who would be out in a minute.

Ellen was surprised when a man of about twenty-five said good morning to her; she'd assumed Robin would be a young girl who would duck her head, laugh at all the wrong moments, and probably fix Ellen's hair into some tight and rather matronly shape which she'd have to comb out at home. The man was tall and wore a tunic that came high up his throat, like a dentist's. His own hair was slick and blond, and he wore it long at the front. His nose tapered to a blunt point, as if it had been chopped off at the end, and his cheeks were spattered with tiny scars which must have been caused by acne, but which now gave his face a weathered, worldly-wise look.

Touching the hand of the girl who was painting her nails, he twisted round to survey the appointment book. 'Mrs Steinberg?' he said, glancing across to where Ellen was sitting. The girl nodded.

'Get her washed, then. And don't take too long about it.'

The girl called Ellen to the back of the shop and the usual business of the water too cold and then too hot began.

Once she was in the chair and the curtains – which were

a hideous mustard yellow velveteen – were drawn around her cubicle, Robin pumped her into position. Then he stood behind her, examining her reflection.

'Can you make it shine?' she asked. 'And wave? I'd like it tidy, but not too tidy, if you see what I mean.'

He gathered bunches of her hair in his fists. 'Strong hair,' he said. 'Good condition. Never needs much.' His voice was hushed, important.

She'd never thought she had strong hair, but now he'd said it, it made perfect sense. 'That's probably why it'll never do a single thing it should,' she said.

'Is Madam from America, by any chance?'

'New York. But I haven't lived there for many years.'

'How glamorous! May I suggest a Hollywood wave? With some sculpture curls?'

What was his accent? He didn't sound like a local. More like one of those London actors who James had occasionally invited round for drinks. Slightly nasal, but with a lot of air in the voice.

'I don't want anything permanent.'

'Quite. A soft Hollywood wave will suit Madam very well. Such an elegant neck should be framed.'

She beamed at this, but he didn't return her smile. Instead, he reached for the glinting rack of scissors on the shelf below the mirror, and his hands began to fly with the blades, darting in and out, slicing through the air. Fronds of brown went this way and that as he cut Ellen into shape. As his fingers worked, her face seemed to come into focus. A head-on view of herself was always the most flattering: seen from this angle, her nose looked almost a normal size.

He'd nearly finished cutting by the time he spoke again. 'Going somewhere special today, Madam?'

His hands were so quick and light.

'Just a picnic. Myself and my – husband. And our daughters.'

'Really, Madam? You don't look old enough, if I may say so.'

She laughed at this, but he was silent, easing his fingertips around the top of her scalp to tilt her head to one side.

'Your husband must be very proud.'

She caught his eye in the mirror. 'I'll let you into a secret, Robin.'

He'd begun working on the waves, dousing her head in setting lotion and easing ridges of hair around steel curlers.

'What's that, Madam?'

'He isn't my husband.'

A smile grew on Robin's lips. 'Shall we curl it here, so it's soft on the cheek?'

'Oh yes,' she said. 'Let's.'

.....

After half an hour under the drier, Robin reappeared, whisked Ellen's chair round, and held a hand mirror to her face so she could inspect the back of her head. 'Better,' he said.

Her hair was indeed a sculpture of waves and light. Robin turned her this way and that, taking her in from all angles. As he swung the chair around, she noticed that his groin was level with her shoulder. When she looked in the mirror, her cheeks were flushed and her eyes were bright, and he was smiling at her, his tough cheeks wrinkling.

'Delicious,' she said. 'Absolutely delicious.'

'Would Madam like anything else?' He fingered the hair around her ears, allowing his thumb to touch her lobe for a second. 'We offer all sorts of services to help a lady relax.

Facials, mud wraps, personal massage. It's very cool,' he added, 'in the back room.'

She could, of course, pretend not to know what he was suggesting; or she could pretend to be shocked, storm out of the place without paying and then collapse with laughter outside. But what would be the point, apart from saving herself a few shillings? She and James had gone to a brothel together in Paris once, and she'd watched as a tiny blonde rode him with an expression of utter boredom on her sour face. For James's sake, she'd allowed another girl, much larger, with dimpled cheeks and the shiniest teeth, to suck her own breasts while she looked on. Throughout, she'd had the sense of being somewhere else entirely, and had wanted to brush the plump girl from her chest, like an irritating child from her lap.

But there had been no men on offer there. No young men with tough cheeks, airy vowels, and smiles like satisfied iguanas.

'Maybe some other time,' she said, liking the way her voice suddenly sounded very New York.

'As Madam wishes.'

There was a pause.

'And might I suggest a longer visit – perhaps even a permanent wave – next time?'

'What a good idea,' she said, admiring her own head of perfect curls in the mirror.

.....

Something was happening in the town when she drove back along the High Street. People were standing in shop doorways and along the edge of the pavement, looking towards the market square. Up ahead, a truck was swinging across the road and there was an awful racket, like children screaming in a playground. Ellen stopped the car and got out. The truck was coming towards her, swerving, its engine crunching as the driver changed gears. The screaming noise became louder. Then she saw something beneath the vehicle, being dragged along the road. Whatever it was was bellowing and kicking. At first she thought it must be a horse: there was brown hair, and hooves; but as the lorry came nearer, she saw the fleshy open mouth, the flared nostrils and the wet, black eyes. It was a cow, caught somehow beneath the wheels of the truck and being hauled along the road, its spindly legs kicking frantically, its hide scraping the asphalt. It must have cut loose at the cattle market, she thought, only to meet the wheels of this truck. Everyone in the street was standing perfectly still, watching the scene with wide eyes, and the driver himself seemed intent only on getting away. She could see his red face behind the windscreen. His lips clenched as he scraped the gears again. There was a hot smell of cow and rubber in the street.

'Stop!' she yelled. 'You've got to stop!' Her arms were up and waving, and she was stepping towards the truck. 'For God's sake! Stop!'

But he didn't stop. A hot blast of air hit her face as he drove past, finally getting the engine into gear. By now, the beast had stopped moaning. As the truck reached the end of the High Street, it spat the dead cow out behind, and roared away.

She ran towards the crumpled body of the thing. 'Bastard!' she cried. 'He must have seen it!'

All around her, a crowd of people were gathering in silence, staring at the mangled cow. Its hide was ripped down one side and its guts had left a steaming trail along the road. Its legs were impossibly skewed, as if it had skidded and fallen on a frozen lake.

'Bastard!' she shouted again.

A man took off his cap, stepped forward and held her elbow. 'No need for language, love. Are you all right?' He spoke gently.

She looked around her. A woman in a hat like a flattened fruit basket was whispering to a young boy whose hand was jammed in a paper bag of sweets. A girl with a freckled face was picking her nose and studying Ellen's hairstyle. No one seemed to be looking at the dead cow. Instead, everyone was staring at her. The man holding her arm cleared his throat and dropped his eyes to her stocking-less legs. 'Can't be helped, eh?'

'Can't be helped?'

'It's only an old cow. Nothing to fret yourself over.' He smiled.

'Why did no one stop that driver?' She shook the man's hand from her arm and turned to face him. 'Couldn't you see what was happening?'

The man looked at the ground. She noticed that his hair was thinning and speckled with scurf.

'Why didn't someone stop him?' She realised she was shouting, but she didn't care. 'Someone should have stopped him!'

The woman with the fruit basket hat spoke up. 'Nothing to be done, now, is there, missus? Best to leave it.'

Ellen looked at the dead creature. Flies were already beginning to settle on its bloody head. It seemed to have sunk, somehow, into the road; its legs were limp, its neck lolled, its eye drooped. It was, she saw, utterly broken.

'Someone could have stopped it,' she said, but her voice was quiet now.

She was still trembling as she walked back to the Lanchester. Slumping into the car seat, she covered her face with her hands.

'Bloody Yanks,' she thought she heard someone say.

... Twenty-two ...

It didn't look nearly sturdy enough. 'Borrow it. You have just the figure for it, Kitty,' Mrs Steinberg had said yesterday. '*Petite*. Compact.' The top of the bathing suit was like a vest, but with thinner straps; the bottom had a tiny pleated skirt sewn onto a pair of shorts. It was pale blue cotton with white vertical stripes. Just the thing, her mistress had said, for a beach outing. Kitty stood in front of the small mirror propped up on her chest of drawers and held the garment to her body. Without even trying it, she could see it was far too big for her. When they'd gone to the beach at Bognor as girls, she and Lou had swum wearing just their bloomers and knitted vests, but Miss Weston, their Sunday School teacher, had never got past the paddling stage. Kitty found it hard to imagine a grown woman throwing herself into the sea, in full view of the beach, wearing just a bathing costume. It was all right in the films, where they wore make-up and didn't have to actually get wet, but the reality was a different matter. She reached for her sewing bag and stuffed the bathing suit in with her embroidery. It was really the least of her worries, as she still hadn't quite managed to tell Arthur that she couldn't go dancing tomorrow night.

'All in, all in,' called Mrs Steinberg, waving to Kitty from the driveway. Her hair was, for once, settled in neat, shining waves around her head. In her halter-neck top and wide linen trousers, her shoulders broad and tanned, she actually looked quite handsome. Kitty smoothed her lily-print dress and climbed into the back of the car.

Mr Crane, who was sitting in the driver's seat, turned to face her. 'Glad you could come, Kitty. Glorious sunshine, isn't it? Perfect day for an outing.'

Kitty hadn't thought she'd any choice about coming, but she nodded and smiled, trying not to look at the exposed base of Mr Crane's neck. He'd unbuttoned his collar and was not wearing a tie. Unlike her mistress, he still looked pale, although his nose, Kitty noticed, had caught the sun and was rather pink.

'Here comes trouble,' he said, turning back to face the windscreen.

Geenie and Diana clambered in beside her, forcing her up against the car door. Geenie had on the long white robe she'd worn on Kitty's first day, and had drawn black lines around her eyes. Diana was wearing red shorts and a cream blouse, and was holding a book, but she also had lines drawn around her eyes. Both girls looked up at Kitty and blinked.

'What's in your bag?' Geenie asked.

'Embroidery, Miss.'

'You mean sewing?'

'Yes, Miss. Except you sort of make pictures with it.'

'Are you good at it?'

Kitty gripped the sewing bag tighter. She was about to say 'not bad', but she saw Mr Crane incline his head slightly towards her, as if waiting to hear the answer, and she changed her mind. 'Yes, Miss. I'm quite good. But mostly at dresses and that.'

Geenie kicked her foot into the back of the driver's seat but Mr Crane did not turn around.

'Does that mean you could make *outfits*?'

'Yes, I suppose so, Miss.'

The girl grasped both her knees and sat up very straight. 'Could you make me and Diana Pierrot outfits?'

'I – suppose I might...'

'Ellen!' shouted Geenie. 'Kitty's going to make us Pierrot outfits so we can do a proper show!'

'Where's Arthur got to?' Mrs Steinberg was standing outside the car on tiptoe, looking around.

'It isn't quite eleven yet,' said Mr Crane. 'Give the fellow a chance.'

Mrs Steinberg got into the passenger seat and sighed.

'Can we ride donkeys?' asked Geenie.

'If there are donkeys, you can ride them,' said Mr Crane.

'There are always donkeys on English beaches, aren't there, Ellen? It's because the British don't know what to do with themselves by the sea.'

Mr Crane gave a short laugh.

'They're for poor people who can't afford horses,' corrected Diana. 'Aren't they, Daddy?'

Kitty remembered the donkeys at Bognor: stinking, insect-ridden animals that Miss Weston had warned all the children to stay well away from.

Mr Crane looked round then, frowning. 'They're for anyone who wants to ride them, darling.'

'There you are!' Mrs Steinberg trilled. 'Put the deckchairs in the boot, would you, Arthur?'

Arthur did as he was told, then sat beside Diana. The girls moved along the seat so Kitty was now crushed against the car door, and Geenie was almost in her lap. He was wearing a pair of twill shorts, boots, a soft shirt and tie, and a knitted tank-top. His knees were red and knobbled. When he glanced in her direction, Kitty looked out of her window.

'We're so glad you could come.'

'My pleasure, Mrs Steinberg.'

'Kitty's going to make us Pierrot outfits,' Geenie said to Arthur.

'Is she now?'

'You did promise, didn't you, Kitty?'

She could feel all three of them staring at her. Looking round, she smiled at the girl's hopeful face. 'I did, Miss,' she said.

'Blotto! Come on!' The dog jumped onto Mrs Steinberg's lap. 'Let's go, then, Crane! To the beach!'

.....

Mrs Steinberg strode ahead with Blotto; Mr Crane carried the picnic basket; the two girls dawdled behind him. At the back of the line, Arthur was puffing with two deckchairs and the rug, and Kitty followed, cradling her sewing bag.

A heat haze was distorting Wittering beach. A few families were sitting on the sand, legs bared, heads under newspapers or handkerchiefs, their bodies seeming to bend and buckle. A greasy shine had settled on the sea, which swelled lazily forward, then back. It wasn't at all like Bognor, where there was a narrow strip of gravelly sand, striped deckchairs for hire, Punch and Judy, fortune tellers and ice-cream parlours. Here it was all ridged sand and grassy dunes, no entertainment, and not a donkey in sight. And everything wobbling in the heat.

Arthur stopped to wipe his brow and Kitty had no choice but to catch up with him. They walked a little way together in silence, Kitty sneaking sideways glances at

Arthur, whose face was now brick red and sweating. His arms were covered in pale ginger freckles that seemed to get bigger the further up they went.

'All set for Friday?' he said, looking straight ahead. 'I hear it's going to be cracking. There's a new band coming.'

'I've been meaning to tell you. I can't get the time off.'

He stopped, resting the deckchairs in the sand. 'You can't?'

'She needs me Friday.'

'What for?'

'His sister's coming.'

Arthur looked at his hands. 'Well. That is a pity.'

'Yes,' she said, and began walking again.

He caught her up. 'You do want to come still, though?'

Ahead, Mr Crane had stopped and was looking back. His hand was raised to his eyes, but she could tell he was looking directly at them.

'We'd better catch up.'

'Kitty. Wait.' Arthur gripped her arm tightly and she almost gave a yelp. 'I want you to come with me. Say you'll come.'

She glanced at Mr Crane, who was now sitting on the picnic basket, watching her, his image trembling in the heat.

Arthur pulled her towards him. 'Kitty…' His hand was warm, and softer than she'd expected. 'Say you'll come. If not this Friday, then next.'

His eyes were searching hers, his mouth, with its set-back teeth, hung slightly open. 'Come with me,' he said.

Then he put his other hand on her behind, and let it rest there. 'We could dance together all night.'

A hot pressure shot up her back.

'What's the hold-up?' Mr Crane was standing now, shouting, his hands cupped around his mouth. 'Get a move on, Arthur. We'll need that rug.'

'I'll try,' Kitty said, tugging free of Arthur's grip and walking towards the rest of the group.

.....

Geenie pulled the white robe over her head, revealing an orange bathing costume with an anchor motif. With her smudged black eyes, gangly limbs and fuzz of blonde hair, the effect was pretty peculiar. A little like an overgrown doll, Kitty thought. Carrying Blotto in her arms, she ran down the sand. Diana followed, slowly, still wearing her shorts and blouse and holding her book, picking her way carefully through the seaweed and stones which edged the shore.

Mrs Steinberg was also undressing, bending over and using Mr Crane's shoulder as a balance as she stepped from her slacks.

Kitty stood for a moment, watching the woman's long legs appear.

Arthur removed his empty pipe from his mouth and cleared his throat. 'I'll go and fetch the rest of the chairs,' he announced, heading back for the car.

'Sit down, Kitty,' said Mr Crane, offering her a deckchair beside him.

She did as she was told, trying not to stare at Mrs Steinberg's naked thighs. The woman was wearing a very small black-and-white spotted bathing costume with a thin red belt around the waist. In it, her body looked as though it had been flattened: her chest and hips were wide rather than full. But her legs, every inch of them now revealed, were astonishingly long and thin. Kitty thought of the emu she'd seen in a picture book at school.

'Wonderful thing, isn't it, to be near the sea?' Mr Crane

stared out at the water. 'So refreshing.'

She wasn't sure if he was expecting an answer. Mrs Steinberg, who was now lying on the rug, having placed a large pair of sunglasses on her face, was certainly ignoring him.

Kitty shifted her feet. Her shoes were full of sand and her toes were cramped and hot, but she could not think of a way to remove them without drawing attention to herself.

After a while, he said, 'Have you been on any walks lately, Kitty?'

'Not lately, Mr Crane.'

'No. Well, you've been busy. Looking after us. That's real work.'

Mrs Steinberg lowered her sunglasses and shot him a look, but said nothing. Above them, gulls were screeching like knives on china. In the distance, Kitty could see Geenie throwing Blotto into the waves, and Diana sitting in the shallows, reading.

'There's a lovely one, you know, if you don't mind hills. Straight out of the cottage, through the farmer's gate on the left, cut across the wheat field. You know there's a little patch of woodland there?'

Kitty nodded, trying to picture it, but failing.

'Well, there's a path right through the trees and up to the top. First-rate views all round.'

She said nothing. She was watching his bare wrists move as he gesticulated.

'Kitty's more interested in dancing, George.' Mrs Steinberg's glasses flashed. 'She's got real *swing*.'

Kitty brushed some imaginary sand from her lap.

Mr Crane turned to her. 'I didn't know you were a dancer, Kitty.'

Not in the way you think, she thought. Not like your ballerina wife.

'She has what you might call natural rhythm.' Mrs Steinberg kicked a leg in the air, scattering sand over the rug. 'Quite the showgirl,' she said, pointing her toes and wiggling her lower leg back and forth.

'Is that so?' He was smiling now, his left eye almost winking at her.

'Oh no, I—'

'Don't be modest, Kitty! Isn't it infuriating, Crane, the modesty of the working classes?' Mrs Steinberg's leg waved frantically. 'Why must they always bow their heads and mutter? Why do they never *admit* to anything? Take responsibility for themselves? In America, a working man's just proud to be alive, and to hell with the rest of them.'

Mr Crane ran a hand across his mouth. Kitty sat very still, staring at her mistress's slim leg as it swung back and forth.

'I don't think it's quite as simple as that, Ellen.'

'What's complicated about it? You either hold your head up, look the world in the eye, or you don't.'

Mr Crane shook his head and gave a short laugh. 'You can't compare the two in any level way. In America,' he said, his voice becoming louder, 'there isn't a long history of oppression. There isn't the same – ah – insidious class system, ingrained into the minds of the masses from birth …' He rubbed vigorously at his eye. 'It's not the same at all!'

'But nothing will ever change, will it, if the workers can't hold their heads up. They've got to do that, at least. They've got to say, *I've got swing, and to hell with the rest of them!*'

She hitched herself up on her elbows and grinned widely, but Mr Crane was scowling. 'You're being ridiculous.'

Mrs Steinberg looked at Kitty. 'Why don't we ask Kitty what she thinks? I'm sure she has an opinion.'

Kitty had taken her embroidery out of her sewing bag, and now she sat, clutching the frame, staring at her stitches, thinking of the way her mother went to the pub every night and left her and Lou to put themselves to bed. To hell with the rest of them had certainly been her motto. And, thought Kitty, it was Lou's too.

'Kitty? Am I being ridiculous?' Mrs Steinberg had taken off her sunglasses and was pointing them in Kitty's direction.

'Ellen…' Mr Crane pulled on his collar, as if it were suddenly too tight. 'Perhaps we should drop this—'

'I think,' said Kitty, surprised by the force of her own voice, 'it's not just about what class you are.'

They waited for her to continue.

She kept her eyes focused on the waves as she spoke. 'What I mean is, it's personality as well, isn't it? What a person's like.'

Mr Crane nodded. Slowly at first, but then more vigorously. 'Yes,' he said. 'Yes. That's – ah – one opinion. A good opinion.'

Mrs Steinberg laughed. 'I agree with you, Kitty. In the end, it's all about *personality*. What else is there?' She stood and stretched her arms above her head. 'Anyway. We're wasting bathing time. I'm going in.' She adjusted the straps of her costume. 'Aren't you two even going to take your shoes off? It must be a hundred degrees out here.'

'I'd say that's a *slight* exaggeration, wouldn't you, Kitty?' Mr Crane flicked a smile at Kitty, raising his eyebrows as though in apology. Then he started to remove his scuffed brogues, impatiently tugging at the laces. Kitty bent down and began to do the same, tipping the sand from her upturned shoe.

Mrs Steinberg was watching her. 'You can take those

stockings off, you know. Mr Crane won't watch, will you, George?'

Kitty looked at her lap.

'Go on, Kitty. Show him you've got *personality*.'

Mr Crane had removed his socks and turned up the ends of his trouser legs. He stood up. 'Look. I'll go for a stroll. Disappear for a bit. All right?'

When he'd gone behind the dune, Kitty hitched up her dress. Her mistress was still watching, a little smile on her face, whilst Kitty unrolled her stockings. The breeze whipped about her legs.

'That's better,' said Mrs Steinberg. 'Much better. Maybe we'll even get to see you in that bathing costume one day.'

Kitty watched the woman run into the sea. Then she took up her embroidery and began to work.

.....

Ten minutes later, Arthur arrived with the windbreak and remaining chairs and began hammering in the posts. Kitty unpacked the hamper. That morning, she'd ironed and folded the checked tablecloth, washed out the flasks with bicarbonate of soda, and polished the silver cake forks. She'd boiled six eggs, wrapped the poppy-seed cake she'd baked yesterday, assembled the shrimp paste sandwiches and cut off the crusts, packed a whole gala pie, and rinsed and hulled the first strawberries from the garden, wrapping them in a clean tea cloth.

Now she spread the tablecloth across the rug whilst Arthur assembled the windbreak. They said nothing as they worked, Arthur bending over the canvas, his brow knitted as he slammed the posts into place. Then he began on the deckchairs. Whilst he worked, she laid out the plates, the napkins and the glasses, and unwrapped the food. She glanced over to him. She'd never seen anyone handle a deckchair so confidently. The legs slotted into the right grooves first time round.

When she'd finished, she sat back on her heels.

'Let's have one of them strawberries.' Arthur reached across and plucked a fruit from the cloth. 'Proper scarlet,' he said, popping it into his mouth. 'Have one.' He held one in his palm for her. She looked around. Mrs Steinberg and the girls were still in the sea, and there was no sign of Mr Crane. She took the strawberry and held it to her nose: that sugary perfume was almost better than the thing itself. Taking a bite, her mouth was filled with acid sweetness. Arthur watched her, his lips open.

'Ah. Lunch.' Mr Crane sat on a deckchair. Kitty scrambled to her feet.

'Take a chair, there's enough for everyone. The girls can sit on the rug, I'm sure they'd prefer it anyway.' He looked out to sea and began waving both arms above his head. 'They'll be as wrinkled as prunes, staying in so long.' He waved and waved, but no one saw his signal.

'I'll call them, shall I, Mr Crane?'

'No, no, Arthur. No need. We'll wait.'

There was a silence. Kitty picked up her embroidery again. She meant to start work on the crab in the foreground of the scene. Looking at it now, she thought how the embroidered beach was much more pleasing than the real thing. There was no sand to get in your shoes, the little girls paddled elegantly, still wearing their white dresses, and the sun shone softly in the sky. Whereas here, on the actual beach, the light was so bright she could barely see to get the orange thread through the eye of her needle.

'Have you thought any more, Arthur, about what I mentioned to you the other day?' Mr Crane's face had become still, his voice hushed. 'I think it would be a really wonderful thing, you know, if you'd join us.'

Arthur tapped his pipe on the wooden frame of the deckchair and looked across the dunes. 'I've certainly thought about it, Mr Crane.'

'And what did you conclude?'

'I still haven't made my mind up, to be truthful, Mr Crane.'

'The party needs honest workers like you, Arthur. You'd be a valuable addition. Most valuable.'

Arthur produced a pouch of tobacco from his shorts pocket and tucked a tiny amount into his pipe. 'It's not that I don't think your lot have a point...' he struck a match, lit the pipe and sucked deeply on it. 'It's just I'm not sure if it's my thing, exactly.'

Mr Crane and Arthur regularly had discussions on the step of the writing studio in the late afternoon. Kitty had watched them standing together, Arthur on the lower step, nodding and tugging at his moustache whilst Mr Crane looked up to the sky and seemed to search for the right word. She'd presumed they were discussing the garden, or plans for the renovation of the cottage. But this seemed to be an entirely different matter. This seemed like politics, something that Bob always said women should never meddle in. Lou often pointed out that was a bit rich, coming from someone whose heroine was Queen Elizabeth.

'How do you mean?'

'Well.' Arthur took his pipe from his mouth and looked at it. 'I hope you won't take this the wrong way, Mr Crane, but I think it's more a thing for your intellectual type.'

'Intellectual?'

'Educated men, such as yourself.'

The crab was an odd shape. One pincer was definitely larger than the other. Kitty wondered if she could correct it.

'Come the Revolution, Arthur, we'll all be educated men. And women. That's the point.'

Kitty felt the men's eyes shift towards her and she focused hard on the crab's pincer. Her fingers were sweating in the heat, and her needle kept slipping. She'd have to be careful she didn't prick herself and let blood on the cloth. Then it would be ruined.

'Why,' Mr Crane continued, 'even Kitty here could join the Communist Party if she wished. She's a worker, a comrade, like you – like me – isn't she?'

Arthur sucked on his pipe and said nothing.

'It's my firm belief,' continued Mr Crane, 'that Kitty, and all her sex, have some very valuable views which should be heard.'

Mrs Steinberg and the girls were coming out of the sea. If the men would just keep talking for a minute more, the women would be back and Kitty would not be asked, for the second time today, for an *opinion*, when all she wanted was to finish embroidering her crab, eat some shrimp paste sandwiches (which would be turning crisp in this heat), and then cool her feet in the sea.

'I'm sure of that, Mr Crane,' said Arthur.

Bugger. She'd pricked her finger. Luckily there was no blood, yet. She sucked her reddening skin. If she didn't look up from her work, they might not ask her anything. They'd just keep talking as if she weren't quite there.

'Thank God! Lunch. I'm absolutely ravenous.'

Mrs Steinberg, still dripping from the sea, fell gratefully on the food. 'No Scotch eggs, Kitty?' There was a glint in her eye, but Kitty ignored this. If the woman had given her more than a day's notice, she would have been able to make both the Scotch eggs and the poppy-seed cake.

'I didn't have time, in the end, Mrs Steinberg.'

'*What* a shame. Well, tuck in, everyone. Don't stand on ceremony.' Mrs Steinberg took three sandwiches and a piece of pie, sat in a deckchair and began to eat with wet hands.

The girls helped themselves to the food, water dripping from their hair over the tablecloth. Diana sat near her father's feet and got to work on the crust of a piece of gala pie. Geenie helped herself to a strawberry and sat beside her, examining the fruit. Both girls' make-up had run down their faces, making them look like soggy chimney sweeps.

Mr Crane offered a sandwich first to Kitty, then to Arthur, and finally took one for himself.

When she'd finished her pie, Mrs Steinberg wrapped herself in a towel and stood to uncork a bottle of wine. Collecting four glasses together, she filled each one with red liquid, spilling some of it on the sand. 'Kitty, Arthur, have a drink with us.' She thrust a glass at Kitty, then took two cups and half-filled them. 'You too, girls. I have an announcement to make, and I want you all to have a drink in your hand.'

Mr Crane gripped his knees.

Mrs Steinberg was swilling her wine around, poking her large nose so far into her glass that Kitty imagined her mistress might begin to suck the drink up through her nostrils.

'An important announcement.'

Geenie stood and helped herself to a piece of poppy-seed cake.

'It's not time for cake yet, darling.'

'I hate shrimp paste.'

'Put the cake back. Only barbarians eat sweet before savoury.'

Geenie threw the cake down, but Mrs Steinberg was still wearing a clenched smile. Glass in hand, she knelt by Mr Crane's deckchair, shrugged the towel from her bronzed shoulders and gave her wet hair a shake. 'In fact, it's our announcement. Isn't it, George?'

Diana moved closer to her father, dropping her slice of pie as she did so. Only the meat was left. The girl had eaten all the pastry, the jelly and the egg. There was just a blob of pink pork with a hole in it, looking up at Mrs Steinberg. But the woman kept smiling. 'Never mind, Diana. Sit down, Geenie.'

Geenie gave a heavy sigh before looking around and choosing to sit at Kitty's feet.

'Girls. I have some very exciting news for you.'

Mr Crane was staring down at the nibbled pork.

'Very exciting news.' Mrs Steinberg tossed her head back. Her wet cheeks were glowing.

'There'll soon be another person joining our family.'

Mr Crane passed a hand across his mouth.

Kitty would have liked to have taken up her embroidery again, to have something else to look at, but with the glass of wine in her hand, she didn't dare.

'Blotto! Blotto!' Geenie was suddenly on her knees, calling for the dog. Gathering her fists to her chest, as if in an effort to summon all her strength, she screeched again, this time at the top of her voice. 'Blotto!'

Everyone watched as the dog came running, its ears blowing behind. Geenie stretched out her arms to greet the animal, but Blotto ran straight past and through the picnic, his wet paws landing in the strawberries and knocking over the flask of tea. Then he doubled back, sat by Mrs Steinberg and plunged his head down to gobble the remains of Diana's gala pie.

There was a silence, but Mrs Steinberg was still smiling. She held her glass high. 'A toast, please. Raise your glasses. Kitty, Arthur. Join us.'

Kitty lifted her glass.

'To our new baby.' Mrs Steinberg tipped the wine to her mouth and swallowed, her throat contracting.

No one else drank. The girls were staring at each other, their streaked faces dark. Mr Crane stood his glass in the sand and got up. 'Excuse me,' he said. 'I think I need some – ah…' he hung his head for a moment, and when he raised it again, his eyes were squeezed shut. 'I think I'll get my toes wet.' He walked towards the sea. Diana scrambled to her feet and followed him.

Biting her lip, Mrs Steinberg reached for the bottle and refilled her glass. 'Isn't it wonderful news, Geenie darling?'

The girl ignored her mother and raised her face to Kitty. 'Will you still make me a Pierrot outfit?' she whispered.

Kitty nodded. 'I promised, didn't I?'

The girl gave Kitty a weak smile. Mrs Steinberg drained her glass and filled it again.

... Twenty-three ...

Holding hands, the girls walked behind George. It was the morning after the picnic, and he'd announced over breakfast that he was taking them to see the bee orchids on Harting Down. 'You never forget your first bee orchid,' he'd said, gulping down his tea and pushing back his chair. 'We'll go at once, before it gets too warm.'

But it was already too warm. Geenie and Diana trailed along in the sun, their fingers sticking together, their sandals slapping on the dry chalk bridleway. George was striding ahead, his shoulders high, a dark patch of perspiration forming on the back of his shirt.

Geenie's eyes felt as if they'd been scratched. She hadn't slept much last night, in Diana's bed. The two girls had stayed up for hours, whispering. It had been another sweaty, still night and the air under the covers was damp and heavy, but they'd huddled together beneath the canopy of the eiderdown, hair sticking to their foreheads, discussing the day's events, and what to do about them.

'We could say I'm very, very ill,' Diana had suggested. '*Gravely* ill. That might stop them.'

'How?'

'I could pretend to have an awful disease. TB or something. Then Daddy would have to take me home, and they could never get married, and your mother would have to—' she put her lips close to Geenie's ear, 'get rid of it.'

In the darkness, Geenie couldn't see her friend's face properly, but she felt her breath become quicker.

'I can make myself go awfully white when I want to. And if you go under the bedclothes and breathe really quickly for five minutes, you raise your temperature *and* your pulse. And I'm very good at coughing. Listen.' She flung her head back and hacked out something that sounded like Arthur's hoe scraping the garden path.

'It wouldn't work. You'd have to pretend for ages, and in the end they'd get a doctor and find out,' Geenie said, feeling pleased with herself for being so sensible.

'Couldn't you tell your mother you hate my father and you'll just have to kill yourself if they get married and have this baby?'

Diana, Geenie decided, had read far too many novels. 'She wouldn't believe me. And I don't hate your father. He's nice.'

Geenie listened to Diana chewing on a length of her own hair.

'I suppose,' said Geenie after a while, 'I suppose they might not get married.'

Diana shook her head. 'If there's a baby, my father will marry your mother, and I'll never get home to London. We'll both be stuck here in the middle of bloody nowhere forever.'

Geenie didn't really mind being stuck in the middle of nowhere. She'd become used to the cottage, the garden and the stream. She liked the way the willow trees whispered in the night. She liked the way the house was small enough for her to know the whereabouts of her mother, when Ellen was at home, at any time of the day. She liked riding her bicycle down the lane. She was even beginning to like Kitty, especially since the cook had agreed to make the Pierrot outfits. But the thought of her mother having a new baby was too much to bear. She would definitely be sent away to school then, and she'd probably never get to sit on her mother's knee and hear her read from *The Last Days of Pompeii* again.

'I've got it!' Diana clutched Geenie's arm with clammy fingers and gave a little squeal. 'Kitty!'

'What about her?'

'We'll say Kitty's having an affair with my father. Then your mother will throw him out, I'll go back to London, and your mother will have to, you know, not have the baby.'

'But – Kitty isn't having an affair with your father, is she?'

'I know that! Really, Geenie, you're most awfully literal sometimes. We'll have to pretend. Like in a play.'

'How?'

'It'll be easy. It's a perfect, perfect plan. It's like I said. Cooks and housemaids are flighty. Everyone knows that. Your mother will believe us, not her.'

'Can we wait until she's made the Pierrot outfits?'

Diana let out a huff. 'I suppose so.'

.....

'Keep in step!' Diana said, and Geenie put her right foot forward in time with her friend's. Left, right, left, right. They bobbed along the bridleway, shoulders occasionally bumping together. Geenie had never seen Diana look so happy. She smiled as she walked, swinging Geenie's hand in hers. No more details of the plan had been discussed, but just the knowledge of a plot was enough to make them giggle whenever they looked at each other.

'You two are very gleeful today,' said George, holding a gate open for them. Beyond him, the wheat swayed in the sunshine.

'We're happy, Daddy, about the new baby.'

George frowned.

'Won't it be wonderful, Geenie, to have a little brother or sister?' Diana reached for her father's hand and gave him a brilliant smile.

'Well.' George looked into his daughter's face. 'It's lovely to see you looking more cheerful, darling, but don't get too – ah – excited, will you?' Dropping her hand, he closed the gate and walked ahead.

The hill was very steep, and Geenie's fingers kept slipping from Diana's as the other girl marched on, breathing heavily. They were walking through long grass now, and all around the grasshoppers were scratching, scratching, scratching. Geenie could feel the weight of the sun's heat on her hair. As she walked, the grass whirled round her bare legs. 'Can we stop?' she asked.

Diana didn't seem to hear. She'd let go of Geenie's hand and was following her father to the top, her black hair swinging.

If Jimmy were here, he would stop. Jimmy had been keen on walking, and had taken Geenie with him sometimes. One night, at Heathstead Hall, they'd climbed the hill at the back of the house to look for badgers. Jimmy always wore walking britches and long woolly socks, whatever the weather, and carried a special stick which he said had seen him across the desert in the war. Ellen told Geenie never to ask Jimmy about the war because he'd killed a German and he hated himself for it. He'd held Geenie's hand and pulled her along after him, so she hardly had to move her own legs through the damp grass. Occasionally she thought her arm would come loose in its socket, but she'd said nothing. When they reached the top, they stood and looked back at the house, its lights winking in the darkness. Geenie could imagine her mother down there, her face at the window, waiting for them to return.

'You're not frightened, are you?' Jimmy had said.

Geenie shook her head. 'Only if I look this way.' She turned towards the black mass of trees on top of the hill. 'As long as I can see the lights, it's all right.'

Jimmy had held her hand, tightly, all the way back down to the house.

.....

'Right.' George stopped and wiped his brow. They'd reached the top, and were standing on the edge of a clump of gorse. A warm wind blew around them, and they all stood for a moment, watching patches of cloud shadow inching across the fields below. 'They're up here, somewhere. Careful where you stand, girls.' Bending towards the grass, George began to study the area. 'They're delicate specimens.'

Geenie could see the whole village, the green spire of the church pricking the air, the sweep of the main street, their own cottage standing slightly apart, surrounded by trees. She wondered which one Diana had climbed, and thought of Kitty taking off her shoes and stockings, her face serious and pink.

'Daddy?' Diana sat on the grass and hugged her knees to her chest.

'Yes, darling?' He didn't stop studying the ground.

The girl shot a look towards Geenie and winked. 'You know Ellen said she was going to have a baby...'

George straightened up.

'How does that happen, exactly?'

He blinked. 'How does it happen?'

Diana put her head to one side and widened her black eyes. 'How is a baby made? We were wondering, weren't we, Geenie?'

Geenie knew how babies were made. Ellen had related the facts years ago, demonstrating with a pair of Red Indian dolls. She'd said she didn't want her daughter to suffer the same 'agonies of ignorance' she had as a young girl, and asked Geenie to repeat all the information back to her when she'd finished. Geenie had always presumed Diana knew, too. They'd never discussed the afternoon noises, but Diana had read enough novels, even grown-up ones like *Tess of the D'Urbervilles* and, she'd boasted, things by D. H. Lawrence.

George ran a hand over his mouth and looked to the sky. 'Hasn't your mother told you?'

'How could she?' said Diana, looking straight at him. 'Mummy's in London.'

'Well. Ah. Yes.' He'd begun to pace up and down.

Diana sat on her hands and waited. Geenie stood beside her, watching.

'Well. Yes. No point in being kept in the dark about these things. Much better to be in full possession of the facts.'

There was a long silence, broken only by the busy song of the larks.

'Well. If we observe nature, for example...' he stopped pacing and looked around him. 'It's a question of an egg being – ah – germinated. Just like those buttercups there. Well, not exactly like them. The lady has an egg, you see, and that egg must be germinated by the man's seed.'

'What egg?' asked Diana. 'Where does the lady keep the egg?'

'It's in the tummy, darling. Deep inside. That's where the baby grows.'

Diana placed a hand on her own stomach and swallowed. 'How does the seed get there?'

The larks were still singing. Jimmy had told Geenie that the males went as high as they could, singing all the time, before plunging to the earth, to impress the females. 'Like men talking clever, clever, cleverer,' Ellen had said, 'until they can talk no more.'

George wasn't talking now. He was sitting on the grass next to his daughter, looking out at the village, a deep frown on his face.

'Daddy? How does the seed get there?'

If Diana really did know, then she was very good at pretending she didn't, thought Geenie. She wondered if her friend was practising, for when she'd have to pretend that Kitty was having a love affair with George.

'Well. It's quite complicated. And yet simple,' his face brightened a little. 'Wonderfully simple, really. And – yes – beautiful.'

Diana waited.

'You see, what happens is. Ah. A man and a woman are in love, and probably married—'

'But you and Ellen aren't married.'

He looked at Geenie and sighed. 'No. No, we're not. It's not necessary to be married, you see, but most people are, because that's what society demands, marriage, and family. It's a way of sort of keeping people in order. The Soviet peoples have a different view of it, of course; there it's *community* that counts, not family, not some archaic, superstitious idea of religion—'

'But you have to be in love?' Diana asked.

'Yes. Yes, it helps to be in love. Personally speaking, I'd say that helps. Is necessary, in fact. Although not everyone agrees.'

The girls looked at one another. Diana arched her eyebrows. 'So how does the seed get there? Is it through *kissing*?' She giggled.

'Well, yes, that's a part of it. There will be kissing, yes, and touching, touching each other, holding one another. And then – and then—'

'The man puts his thing up you,' interrupted Geenie. 'The man puts his penis in the lady's vagina and he produces semen which makes her pregnant. If she's started menstruating, that is.'

George stared at her. His bad eye twitched. 'Yes. That's it,' he said, finally. 'Exactly.'

'Urgh,' said Diana. She jumped to her feet and gave a shudder.

'We ought to get back,' said George. 'It must be almost lunchtime.' He walked ahead. The patch of sweat now covered his back.

'What about the bee orchid?' called Geenie.

But he didn't reply. He just waved a hand in the air and carried on down the hill.

When he was so far in front that they kept losing sight of him, Geenie turned to Diana and said, 'Didn't you know that?'

'Of course I did.' Diana trailed one hand through the long grass. 'Aunt Laura told me, ages ago.'

'Why did you ask, then?'

'Because I wanted to see what he'd say.' As she squinted against the sun, her dark eyes looked small but bright. 'Now I know we're going back to London, I don't have to be nice to him all the time, do I?'

Geenie tightened her grip on her friend's hand and tried to keep in step.

··· Twenty-four ···

Dearest Bird, Ellen typed.

If I were another man, I would write of what a tonic the country air affords, of how I am getting better, *whatever that means, out here on the bleak hills, being blown into goodness by the unforgiving wind; but all I can think of is how long it will be before I am home again in London with you and Flossy.*

Mother, of course, occasionally tries to bring up the subject of Rachel (whom she now knows is, in name at least, my wife – it seems Rachel has written to tell her), but those tweed skirts and double strings of pearls seem to keep her from speaking too plainly, and she won't allow herself to become emotional with her only son, who, she can see, needs rest and quiet, to recover from his nerves.

She stopped. James had sent this one whilst visiting his parents' home in Northumberland. It was one in a series of letters she kept separate from the others, in a folder marked 'personal'. She'd never thought of publishing these. But, today, something had compelled her to begin work on them. They were, she realised, the key to the collection. Without them, the book would be incomplete.

I will stop drinking, darling; I know I've promised before, but now I am away from London, all that madness, all that pressure to perform, *I do feel I can do it.*

The library window was open but the air refused to move. She was sitting in her nightgown at three o'clock in the afternoon, and she could smell her own skin in the heat. Burying her nose into the fleshiness of her upper arm, she reflected that Crane hadn't really touched her since their al fresco encounter. Last night, after the picnic, he'd come to bed late after spending all evening in his studio, and she'd pretended to be asleep. This morning, she'd heard him rise early, but she'd stayed in bed as long as she could, counting the boatmen on her curtains. How could he have abandoned her in that damned dramatic fashion on the beach? She'd had to sit there with Arthur's silence and Kitty's infernal fiddling with needle and thread. In the end she'd plunged into the sea again and swum until her eyes were stinging. She didn't notice the ache in her arms and legs until she was sitting beside him on the silent drive home, watching his long fingers grasp and wrench the gear knob into place.

Pushing her hair back, she began typing again.

It's partly for the physical pain (I won't go into the mental pain; it's too tiresome even to consider), you know that, don't you, darling? Whisky seems to be the only thing that stops my blasted ankle hurting, but when I return, and have had the operation and it's all re-set, I know I will feel one hundred per cent better.

There was something about hitting the keys that soothed her. It wasn't about re-living the past. It was about typing it up and putting it away. Getting it all onto clean white sheets. Seeing it as it was, in black ink, for one last time.

She ripped the page from the typewriter and placed it on the pile with the rest. Then she riffled through the folder. It was a while before she found what she was looking for: the letter she'd received from Crane after James's death.

She knew this one couldn't possibly go into the book, but, scrolling paper into the machine, she began again.

My adored Ellen,

I do not know how to begin this letter. It is so sad and strange. I am so sorry for your loss. I cannot imagine what you are feeling now. I can hardly imagine what I myself am feeling. It's a terrible shock for all of us. You most of all.

Everything has happened so suddenly – all of it – that it's hard to know how to act, what to do.

I did not mean to write this letter.

Please forgive me for still wanting you. This is hardly the time to write about such things, but our afternoon in Laura's flat was quite the best thing to have happened to me.

If you choose not to come again, I will respect your wishes. You will not hear from me any more.

But if, when the time is right, you decide to live again, to love again, please live with me.

I can be patient.

He hadn't had to be, of course. Two weeks later, she'd been here, in this library, holding his arm and telling him she was going to buy the place, despite its cramped, dim little rooms. He'd kept calling her his Cleopatra. On the train back to London to pick up Geenie, her thighs aching from three days of sex with Crane in the White Hart Hotel, she'd found she couldn't stop weeping. A woman in a bright yellow hat with a greasy Yorkshire terrier on her lap had moved carriages in disgust. Ellen had lain on the seat, beaten her fist against the antimacassar, and wailed. She'd thought she would never be able to catch enough breath to cry even harder, but somehow she'd managed it, the snot running into her mouth, her throat clenching. When she'd reached Waterloo, the tears had stopped, and she hadn't cried again. She'd told herself it was for her daughter's sake. It was necessary to begin anew, wipe the slate clean, for Geenie.

She'd long suspected that her daughter knew. Geenie must know, surely, that James's death was Ellen's fault. Her daughter would have heard, of course, the terrible row the night before the operation. James had been drunk again, and it was just after she'd first slept with Crane, but it was all over some silly thing – James saying they should try to persuade Dora to keep working after she was married, at least until she had children of her own, Ellen insisting she could bring up her own daughter perfectly well. It was when James had faced her and said, 'You have no idea who that girl is,' that she'd snapped and thrown her tumbler of whisky at him; he'd ducked, and the glass had smashed on the wall and dripped down one of his maps, soaking the countries and the seas, staining everything brown. James had brought back his hand and slapped her like a child. What she'd felt, she remembered now, was relief that finally he'd done it, just as she'd always known he would, just as Charles had hit her almost every week for the last year of their marriage. She'd sunk to her knees and started to pick up the pieces of glass from the leopard-skin rug, the short hairs bristling beneath her fingers. James stood above her, watching in silence. When she was finished she'd gone to bed, knowing he would sit in his study all night. She'd never thought, not for a moment, that there would still be enough alcohol in him to react so badly with the anaesthetic. It simply hadn't occurred to her to mention it to the anaesthetist the next morning, when he'd arrived with his leather bag, warm hands and onion breath. James was going to stop, after all; he'd promised her he'd stop, just as soon as the operation was over and all the pain was gone. And, she remembered, her own head had felt as though a knife were stuck in her scalp, her tongue was coated and her stomach tight, and all she'd wanted was to close the door of the sitting room and lie down in the dark.

Still. It was, she felt even now, sitting at her desk in this strange little house in the wilderness, looking out onto a garden blighted by fierce heat, entirely her fault.

She left the sheet of paper in the typewriter and went upstairs to bed. The only thing to do on an afternoon like this was to close her eyes and hope sleep would take her somewhere else.

.....

At half past seven, she managed to comb her hair into some sort of shape (there was nothing left, now, of that sculpture of waves and light created so carefully by Robin), dust her nose with powder without looking too closely at the evil thing in the mirror, and put on her cream silk dress, all without crying. Laura was already downstairs. Ellen could hear the click of her heels on the wooden floor, the slow, confident timbre of her voice. She'd have to go down and face them all: the girls, Crane, his pregnant sister and her drip of a husband. And the dinner, of course, instructions for which she'd left scribbled on the back of an envelope last night: *KITTY: Tomorrow's dinner menu. Pea and lettuce soup. Chilled poached salmon and new potatoes. Strawberries and cream.* Then she'd added: *I won't be available to help so have kept it simple. E.S.*

They were all seated when she arrived downstairs. Kitty had extended the mahogany table to its full length. Ellen had brought it with her from the London house, and even with the two rooms knocked into one, it was a squeeze to fit it in comfortably. Crane seemed very far away, sitting on the other side of the room, studying his napkin. The feeble central light hung too low over the table, giving the room a rather shadowy feel. For once, she was glad of it: her reddened eyes wouldn't be so obvious in the gloom.

'There you are,' said Laura. She was wearing a jade shot-silk tunic with metallic blue feathers for earrings. Everything about her looked fuller: her curved lips and eyes, her black bobbed hair.

'Here I am,' agreed Ellen, trying a smile.

Next to Laura was a girl of about twenty, wearing a man's paisley waistcoat and no blouse. She stood up and bowed her head towards Ellen.

'This is my new friend, Tab,' said Laura, stretching a hand towards the young woman's elbow. 'She's a singer. Awfully talented.'

Ellen looked Tab up and down. Her bare arms were sleek and muscled; her small breasts seemed to be holding themselves up without any support, apart from the waistcoat, and her hair – dyed red to the point of being almost purple – was short and set in neat waves.

'Where's Humphrey?'

'Where indeed?' replied Laura.

Ellen glanced at Crane, but he was still studying his napkin. She pulled out a chair at the opposite end of the table and sat down. 'Welcome to Willow Cottage, Tab. Do sit.'

The wall seemed to be very close behind Ellen's back, hemming her into place. 'A singer. How interesting. What sort of thing?'

Tab cleared her throat. When she spoke, her voice was high and reedy. 'Anything, really,' she said, gazing at Laura. 'I mean, I love the French songs…'

'She does a marvellous "Mômes de la cloche", interjected Laura. 'Extraordinary.'

'I'm working on widening my repertoire.' Tab's accent was hard to place. It was a bit like the barmaid's in the Wheatsheaf, but not quite that coarse.

'She's been a great success at the Café Royal, haven't you, Tab darling?'

Ellen smoothed her napkin over her lap. 'I rather thought it had all blown over for the dear old Café now.'

'When was the last time you were there?' asked Crane, looking up.

Ellen laughed. 'Oh, I don't know. I've been stuck here in the wilderness with you for an age.'

'It's lovely here,' said Tab. 'A right breath of fresh air.'

'Tab's a Brighton girl,' said Laura, sliding her eyes sidelong. 'Isn't it a blast? A fisherman's daughter singing in the Café Royal.'

The colour rose in Tab's face.

'She used to help her father haul the nets up the beach,' said Laura.

'How interesting,' said Crane, putting down his napkin and leaning towards Tab. 'Wasn't it wonderful work, though, Tab, out there? There's something so – ah – rewarding about physical work out of doors, isn't there?'

Tab shrugged her shoulders. 'I prefer the Café Royal.'

'Shall we eat?' said Ellen, ladling herself some soup from the tureen and passing it to Tab. She could tell the stuff wasn't nearly hot enough as soon as she lifted the lid: there was hardly any steam. Taking a breath, she decided to let it go. She would have to ignore these little things in order to get through this evening. It was strange; despite being so upset this afternoon by re-reading the letters, she found what her mind kept returning to was the image of that cow being dragged along Petersfield High Street. She saw again the huge open wound of its stomach, the way it had seemed to sink helplessly into the road.

Picking up her spoon, she looked around the table and forced herself to focus. Geenie's normally pale face was, she noticed, now quite tanned, which made her appear somehow more defined; her chin wasn't pressed so far into her chest, and her hair had been bleached almost white by the sun. Instead of eating her soup, she was studying the prongs of her fork, holding the silver close to her nose. Next to Crane, whose eyes were fixed on his soup, was Diana. She, too, was tanned. Dark as an Italian, thought Ellen, and eating like one, too: nothing could stop Diana once she'd started on her food.

'Tell me,' Ellen began. 'Did you girls have an interesting day?'

Crane swallowed. 'I was just telling Laura. We went up Harting Down, looking for bee orchids.'

'But we didn't find any, did we, Daddy?' said Diana, between mouthfuls. 'So we had a very interesting discussion instead.'

Geenie gave a giggle.

George ducked his head.

'Fascinating,' said Laura. 'You're so lucky, living here in the country all year round. I long for it whenever I'm in London.'

Ellen was silent. In the half-light, she was trying to make

out how much Laura's stomach had grown since she last saw her. Beneath her silk tunic, there was a sizeable bump.

'Have you been in town lately, then?'

'Heaps. I have to occupy myself. Can't seem to get my mind off this damn pregnancy. Tabs has been an absolute tonic.' Laura pushed her bowl away. 'Sorry, darling, I can't eat anything this green at the moment.'

'You must be very excited,' said George.

'Must I?'

Crane reached across the table for more bread.

'Can't you ask for that to be passed?' flashed Ellen.

There was a pause before Laura gave a little laugh and said, 'Don't mind me. I'm not the slightest bit bothered by manners. I've been teaching Tab: just because everyone else does these silly things – ladies first, endless apologising and all that – doesn't mean we should. She was *terribly* polite when I first found her.'

Tab grinned.

Ellen filled her own glass with wine. 'Your brother is usually such a stickler for manners, Laura. He's really surprisingly bourgeois, for a Bolshevik.'

There was a long silence, throughout which Diana continued to slurp her soup.

'Has everyone finished?' Crane stood and began to collect the bowls.

'What on earth are you doing?' demanded Ellen.

'Clearing the table. Kitty's had a lot to organise this evening, and we always said we didn't want her waiting on us.'

'How is the little thing coming on?' asked Laura.

'She's coming on very well,' said Crane, carrying the stack of bowls out of the door. 'Very well indeed.'

Ellen bit her lip. The lukewarm soup had left her

stomach feeling bloated and oddly empty.

'We must have some light,' she said, suddenly pushing back her chair and squeezing herself free from the table. 'It's too damned dark in here.'

She left the room and went into the library. Ignoring the bespectacled gaze of the stuffed fox (why had she allowed Crane to keep that thing?), she rummaged in her desk drawer for some matches. When she'd found them, she flung open the window, sat on the ledge and looked out into the evening. The sky was a deep pink, and the house martins were circling. There was no air, even here: just the smell of the baked earth after another boiling day. She told herself to concentrate on that. To breathe in the earth. To not think about the hot stink of cow. She glanced over at her typewriter and the folder of letters. She should get back, she knew, but first she had to re-read one part of Crane's letter.

But if, when the time is right, you decide to live again, to love again, please live with me.

I can be patient. Who knows how two people should act, at a time like this? All we can know are our feelings for one another.

She'd known her feelings, hadn't she? It had seemed to be the right thing to do at the time. There must be some way to make it the right thing to have done.

She placed the letter back in the folder, rubbed her scalp, and returned to the dining table, clutching the box of matches.

Crane had brought the potatoes through, and provided everyone with a dinner plate. Ellen struck a match and leaned across to light the long candles in the centre of the table. Her fingers were trembling a little and she had some trouble getting the last one going.

'Are you all right?' asked Geenie, looking up at her mother.

'I'm perfectly fine.'

'You do look a little odd, darling,' said Laura.

'It must be the heat.'

'You were always complaining that it was cold before,' said Crane.

'But this heat – it's too close, isn't it? It gets under your skin.'

'You ought to try carrying a damned baby around in your stomach,' said Laura, lighting a cigarette. 'That really warms things up.'

Kitty came in with the salmon. She was still wearing her apron, and her face was round and pink about the cheeks. Ellen watched her as she placed the fish down. The girl really wasn't bad looking: a tidy little figure and a neat waist. A shine on her lip. She seemed to be standing straighter, too, and her hands no longer shook when she put something on the dining table.

Kitty made a small bob, then backed out of the room.

'How many times must we tell that girl not to do that?' asked Ellen, standing to dish up the salmon. It looked passable: its eye still firm, its skin lightly crisped, garnished with parsley and lemon. Using a fork and spoon, she peeled back a strip of silver to reveal the rose-coloured flesh beneath, thanking God it wasn't beef.

'Pass plates, please.'

'Have you told Aunt Laura the good news, Daddy?' Diana was looking at her father with a bright face.

Crane's eyes met Ellen's. He looked very tired. She thought again of the wounded animal being dragged along the street.

'We'll tell Aunt Laura later, Diana dear,' she said, firmly.

'Tell me what?' Laura had her elbows on the table and was leaning towards Diana, cupping a hand around her ear. 'Whisper it to me. I love secrets.'

Crane put a hand on his daughter's shoulder. 'Yes, it is good news, actually. I've been offered some work. With the Party. Lecturing.'

As soon as Ellen plunged the knife in, she knew the fish was overdone. There was no give to the flesh, no room. It was dry, and when she lifted a slice and dropped it on Crane's plate, it stood absolutely still.

'Didn't I tell you?' Laura said, blowing out a stream of smoke. 'I'm a vegetarian now.'

'Lecturing?' said Ellen, slicing another piece of fish.

'Don't vegetarians eat fish?' asked Geenie.

'I don't eat anything that's drawn breath.'

Tab held out her plate. 'I'd love some. Salmon's my favourite.'

'She's such a carnivore.' Laura traced a line along Tab's jaw with one finger. 'Or should that be a pescivore? I've never met a girl with such a taste for the sea.'

'Lecturing? Where?'

'I want to be a vegetarian,' said Geenie loudly, folding her arms across her plate.

Ellen stuck a fork into the fish and let it stand there, stiffly upright. 'Where will you be lecturing, Crane?'

He was helping himself to potatoes. 'All around the country.'

'You'll be travelling?'

'Quite a bit, yes.'

'And when were you going to mention it?'

'I thought now might be a good time, seeing as Diana brought up the subject of good news. I'll be speaking to the people about the importance of politics in great literature.'

'Can I have some fish?' asked Diana.

Ellen ignored her. 'The importance of politics in great literature.'

'That's right.'

'And what's happened to the great literature you're supposed to be writing?'

'Haven't you finished that blasted novel yet, Georgie?' Laura laughed. 'What's he been doing all this time in that studio of his, Ellen?'

Crane began to dissect his fish. 'The novel is not as important.' His voice was low and steady. 'This is real work. Work that can change people's minds. Work that can change the way things are.'

Ellen snatched Crane's plate from the table. 'Don't eat that.' She began clearing everyone's plates and cutlery. 'In fact, don't eat any of it.'

'Ellen—'

'It's awful. Ruined. I'm going to have to do something about that girl. She can't cook anything. She never could.'

Crashing the plates down on the table, she shouted, 'Kitty!'

Crane put his hand over his eyes.

'Kitty! Come here please!'

'Ellen, don't—'

'Kitty!'

There was the sound of a door slamming and footsteps along the corridor. Kitty appeared in the doorway, her face flushed.

'What have you done to that poor fish?'

Kitty's mouth moved but no sound came out. The sight of her downcast eyes made Ellen even more furious. 'It's ruined!' She couldn't help yelling. 'Absolutely ruined! What did you think you were doing? Incinerating it? The point is to cook it, not kill it.'

There was a loud bang as Crane smashed his fist on the table. 'Ellen! Not here. Not now.'

'Why not? It's my house. I want to know what this stupid girl thinks she was doing. I want this explained.' She stepped closer to Kitty. 'Do you think I didn't know you weren't a cook when you first came here? Do you think I couldn't see right through you? I gave you a chance, and this is what I get in return. Fucking incinerated fish.'

Kitty was staring at the floor.

Crane went to her. 'Kitty,' he said, softly, 'you can go now. We'll talk about this in the morning.'

Ellen's hands were shaking. She brought them to her scalp and rubbed at her hair to try and still them.

'Leave the washing-up,' added Crane. 'We'll do it.'

Ellen looked at Laura. 'Give me a cigarette.'

Laura took one from her silver case, lit it against her own, and handed it to her.

'I did it like it said in the book.'

They all looked up. Kitty was staring at Ellen, her chin trembling but her eyes fierce. 'Mrs Steinberg. Madam. I did it how it said.'

Crane put his hand on her elbow. 'You can go now, Kitty. Take the rest of the evening off.'

But the girl was still staring directly at Ellen. Then there was a sudden crackle, and the room went dark.

'Blasted generator,' muttered Crane. 'I'll see if Arthur's still about.' He stepped from the room and held the door open for Kitty to follow him, but she remained where she was, staring at Ellen.

'Nothing works in this damned house,' said Ellen, sinking into a chair.

'Just like it said in the book,' Kitty said again before

turning to go.

The girl's footsteps echoed down the corridor. Ellen's cigarette smoke evaporated into the air.

... Twenty-five ...

Kitty had been sitting on her bed for the last hour, staring at her embroidery. It was no use, she knew, trying to tackle the girl's face now. Without the electric light, she couldn't see enough, and her fingers felt too large and hot for the work. It was partly that the blood was still thick in her head; she could feel it pumping down her neck, along her shoulders and through her arms. Anger made her body want to move, to lash out at something, but still she sat with the embroidery on her lap, her work-box open at her feet, and tried to concentrate on the stitches.

The embroidery was heavier in her hands now. She brought it close to the paraffin lamp she'd placed by the bed. The sky and the sea, the crabs, starfish, pebbles and rocks were done. She'd unpicked and corrected the wonky claw, and the crabs looked almost solid, she'd been so careful to keep her satin stitches absolutely even and close together. Each one was snug up against the next. Kitty was particularly pleased with the contrast of the burnt orange thread she'd used for the shells with the black French knots of the creature's eyes. She was now halfway through the girl stooping with her net in the foreground. The outline of the girl's face, which Kitty had begun in stem stitch, was tricky:

she knew that if she got it wrong, the whole thing would be skewed. With hair a few extra stitches were all right, but you had to be careful with faces. One stitch too many and a face could turn into a shapeless blot.

She put the embroidery down on the counterpane beside her, stood up and went to the wardrobe. Opening it, she smelled cinnamon and decided she must scrub the whole thing clean. There was something wrong with having another woman's perfume in your wardrobe. The emerald frock was still hanging there, unworn, above the single green shoe given to her by Mrs Steinberg on her first day. What had the woman been thinking? No one could do anything with one shoe. She should have refused it straight away.

It was no good. She was thinking again of them all sitting round their dinner table, watching her. Of Diana with her little smile. Of Geenie with her worried eyes. Of that strange woman with the purple hair who looked like a lovely boy; she'd been the only one who hadn't stared. Of Mrs Steinberg's face, like Lou's was when Kitty had told her just before Mother died that she should've come sooner. Like a child who'd been smacked. Knowing they're in the wrong, but willing you to be the one to blame.

After Mrs Steinberg had shouted, Kitty went into the kitchen and, still feeling the touch of Mr Crane's fingers on her arm, removed her apron and hung it on the door. The generator hadn't yet got going again, so she'd lit a paraffin lamp she'd found in the larder and washed the soup bowls he'd brought through for her earlier, thinking *he carried these for me*, not thinking of Mrs Steinberg's face, of her voice, of *fucking incinerated fish*. It was almost funny, wasn't it? Getting that annoyed over a bit of salmon. Mrs Steinberg had told her she wasn't to spend more than two shillings a week on the MacFisheries order – so what did she expect? She wasn't a miracle worker. Lou would have pointed that out to her employer, quick as you like. *Well, what do you want? Bloody miracles?* And Arthur would have laughed. Shrugged his shoulders. *Whatever you say, Mrs S.* Walked away. Neither of them would have stood there trembling, only managing to squeak something about doing it like the book said.

When she'd finished washing the bowls, she'd fetched her sharp scissors from her work-box. Back in the kitchen, she'd sliced straight through the Chinese lantern's tassel and thrown it in the bucket she kept by the door for the compost peelings.

Now she glanced at the clock on her chest of drawers. Only nine. He might be out there, in his shed, even now.

She peeled off her old work frock and changed into the blue lily print. Looking in the glass, she noticed that her hair had lightened in the sun, and her cheeks were still flushed from the incident. That wasn't a bad thing. She bit down, hard, on her bottom lip, to bring the colour up, dipped her finger into her pot of Vaseline and ran it round her mouth. It was a trick Lou had shown her, years ago: not quite lipstick, but almost as good. Should Arthur ask her again, she decided, she would miss tea at her sister's on Sunday afternoon in favour of the dance she knew they held at the Crown and Thistle Hotel in Petersfield. It was mostly girls dancing with one another, of course, and only tea to drink, but maybe that would be for the best.

Then there was a knock at the door.

Kitty stood very still. If the woman was coming to start on again about the bloody fish—

Another knock. Quite a light knock. A bit of hesitation in it.

She held her breath, wondering how long it would take for Mrs Steinberg to retreat.

Then there was a voice – 'Kitty. It's Mr Crane. May I come in, please?'

She looked around. Her room wasn't untidy – it never was – but the embroidery was on the crumpled counterpane and her work-box was open on the floor. Hurriedly, she stuck her old frock on a hanger and closed the wardrobe.

'Kitty? Are you in there?'

Taking a breath, she pulled the door open. He was holding a candle. As soon as she saw his face – lined and a bit startled looking in the wavering light, as if he hadn't expected her to actually open up – she turned away and sat on the bed, trying to hide the work-box under her feet.

'Sorry to disturb – may I come in?'

She nodded.

'Thanks.' He stood for a moment, looking around. 'I thought you might need this,' he said, pointing at the candle. 'But I see you've sorted yourself out.'

'Yes. Thank you.'

He put the candle on her chest of drawers. 'Look here,' he began. 'I – ah – sorry it's a bit late – but I thought...' he trailed off.

She waited.

'Are those your parents?' he gestured towards the framed photograph.

'Yes.'

'May I?' Picking up the photograph, he held it at arm's length, inclining his head first this way, then that, as if studying some exquisite object he might be about to buy.

'Your father has a very fine look about him.'

Kitty glanced up. 'Does he?'

'He appears – full of humour. Doesn't he?'

Kitty thought about her father going up the passage to fart. *Don't tell, Kitty-Cat.*

'And what a smart jacket.'

'Oh, that's not his.'

Mr Crane raised his eyebrows.

'He didn't have a suit. I expect he hired it, from the photographer.'

'Quite. Yes, I see.'

He put the photograph down and dug his hands into his pockets. 'I'm so awfully sorry, about earlier.'

She focused on the place where his grey flannel trousers were going thin at the knees. There would be a hole in the left one soon. What would it take to make him a new pair? She'd never made a pair of men's trousers before, but she estimated three yards of a light gabardine – perhaps navy blue, it would go with his dark hair – and a high waist, with a slimmer fit. She could run them up for him on Lou's machine in no time.

'You see, Ellen – Mrs Steinberg – is a bit out of sorts at the moment. Not that that's any excuse. But I'm sure you'll – ah – understand.'

Had she sent him here, to apologise on her behalf? Kitty knew she should say *it's all right*, but couldn't bring the words into her mouth.

He sat down heavily then, right next to her on the bed. 'I want you to know that I'm very pleased with your work, Kitty. Very pleased indeed.'

It didn't seem to get cooler any more, even at this time in the evening. She could smell the sweetness of his sweat. There was still that pulse of blood in her neck and shoulders, making her body warm, making her want to move, to lash out. She swallowed it down.

'Is this your work?' He was looking at the embroidery she'd left on the counterpane.

She nodded.

He picked it up and held it close to the candle to examine it, just as he'd examined the photograph. 'It's the most accomplished craftsmanship, Kitty. It really is.'

'It's just a bit of sewing, Mr Crane. Something to pass the time.'

'It's much more than that, surely! Look at the detail in it!' His voice had become hushed, urgent. 'It's, well, it's remarkable.'

She fixed her eyes on his hands as they held the cloth, but she knew he was looking at her face now.

'Kitty…' His fingers were stroking the Cretan stitches she'd made for the clouds. Then he ran the flat of his hand over the surface of the rocks and the sand. He brushed the French knots of the crab's eyes, the gentle zigzag chain she'd sewn for the surf of the sea. 'You really care about your work, don't you?'

'About the house and the cooking, Mr Crane?'

'No, I don't mean that. I mean this. Your craft.'

She looked into his face. His eyes were so bright that she had to look away. 'Yes,' she said. 'I suppose I do.'

'That's a gift, Kitty. You know that, don't you?'

His voice was soft, and she was sure he would touch her now. He would touch her arm again, that would be how it would start. She moved her elbow closer to his hand. All along her forearm, her skin seemed to prickle, despite the heat. She steadied her breathing. If she could just wait a moment longer – if her skin could just move a little closer to his – surely he would respond to that pulse in her – surely they would move together—

He stood up, making the bed springs creak.

'Are you going?' As soon as she'd said it, she put her hand to her mouth.

'I'd better get back, see what the others are up to.' He smiled faintly from above. 'I'm glad we had this talk, Kitty.'

Once more, she fixed her eyes on the worn place at his knees.

'Keep up the good work, won't you?'

He left the room. Kitty listened to his footsteps over the kitchen flags, followed by the sound of voices in the sitting room. He'd gone back to them, then. Telling Mrs Steinberg, no doubt, that it was all sorted out. Probably the others had forgotten about it by now, anyway. She continued to sit, staring at her open work-box. There was the slap of bare feet on the flags, and the clink of bottles. Mrs Steinberg fetching more wine. Eventually, the electric light came back on, laughter started, and there was a woman's voice wailing a song. The girl who looked like a lovely boy must be singing. Kitty listened to the song for a few minutes – it wasn't one she recognised, and the girl's voice was too cracked to be really beautiful – then she stood, opened her door, walked through the kitchen and, without even a glance at the washing-up piled in the sink and sprawled over the table, went outside into the night.

It was cooler in the garden, and she was suddenly aware that she should have washed. She'd been cooking most of the afternoon, and she could smell the tang of salmon grease as well as her own sweat. But at least now she was moving, the blood in her head thinning, her limbs growing lighter as she walked towards the shed.

A line of light leaked onto the grass from the open door. She decided not to knock. Instead, she stood in the doorway and said his name.

Arthur looked up from where he was sitting, a book on

his knee. He didn't appear to have been sleeping this time.

'Do you sit here every night?' she asked.

He spread his hands on his lap and yawned. 'What makes you think that?'

'Your lamp's often burning.'

'Have you been watching, then?'

'Don't you want to go home?'

'Not especially.'

There was a pause.

'What's for me at home?' he asked. 'Empty chair on the other side of the table. Tin of Skipper's. Nothing on the wireless.'

'But you have to go home, eventually.'

'Eventually,' he agreed. 'But here there's folk about. And they needed me tonight, didn't they? The beast needed a kick.'

She shifted from foot to foot. 'Arthur—'

'Are you coming in or not?' He dragged a camp stool out from behind his deckchair and patted the top to show her where she should sit.

'Why have you got that shoe?' She pointed at the green high-heeled shoe, which was still beneath Arthur's deckchair.

He narrowed his eyes. Then he took his pipe from his top pocket and began tapping it on the frame of the deckchair and brushing away the debris.

When he'd re-loaded his pipe with fresh tobacco, placed it in the side of his mouth and got it lit, he reached beneath the chair and brought the shoe out. 'I was keeping it for you,' he said. 'I thought I might find the other, one day, but it hasn't turned up.' He knocked the heel on the floor and mud flaked from its sides. 'Don't suppose one shoe's much good to you, is it?'

'Let's go to the tea-dance Sunday,' she said.

He gave a short laugh. 'This Sunday afternoon?'

'Yes.'

'You're sure you want to?'

She let out a sigh. 'I said, didn't I?'

He replaced the shoe beneath the deckchair and patted the stool again. 'Come and sit, then. Sit with me for a bit.'

'Sunday,' Kitty repeated, ignoring his offer. 'Three o'clock. The Crown and Thistle. I'll see you there.'

She turned and walked back to her room, knowing his eyes were following her.

··· Twenty-six ···

Ellen's face was closed. Geenie knew the signs: chin tucked tight to her chest, eyes unblinking.

'I've got a hairdresser's appointment and you're coming with me.'

'Kitty could look after me.'

'I'm not leaving you with that girl.' Ellen pressed her lips together. She was wearing orange lipstick, which made her look as though she'd been sucking on a lolly, a green shiny dress, and a string of orange glass beads. Geenie could see where the powder had settled in the pores of her mother's large nose. Something important was going to happen in town. Her mother's orange handbag and matching shoes with heels and straps – rather than laces – confirmed it.

Alone with Ellen. All summer Geenie had wished she and her mother could be alone together, but now it was just the two of them, she wanted Diana and George back. This morning they'd caught the train to London; George had stated over breakfast that he'd some urgent work to attend to and was taking Diana to stay at her mother's for a few days. Ellen, still wearing her dressing gown, had stood at the window, looking out and saying nothing. Geenie had groped for Diana's hand, but her friend had jumped from the table, knocking her toast to the floor. Then she'd run straight upstairs to pack, leaving Geenie gazing at her mother's back.

'Go and put something decent on.' Ellen stared down at her daughter. 'And wash your knees.'

'It's too hot for something decent.'

'Just hurry up.' Ellen snapped her handbag closed. 'Please, darling. We don't want people to think we're completely hopeless.'

.....

Geenie lay on the back seat of the car and let herself roll around as her mother drove. Instead of looking out of the window – she knew the sky was white with heat and the fields would be crisped and dusty – she stared at the stitching on the inside of the roof. If she counted each stitch, they might get there quicker, and whatever was going to happen would be over, and Diana would be back.

Ellen held her by the upper arm as they slogged through the market place. Smells of old cabbage and rabbit cages rose up from the Saturday stalls. No one was buying much in this heat. Outside the pub on the square, men were sitting on the steps in their shirtsleeves, fanning themselves with their hats, sipping from pint jugs. They watched Geenie and her mother as the two of them walked by. Geenie stared back, and one of the men, wearing thick glasses and no tie, nodded to her.

Ellen quickened her pace. 'Don't stare.'

'Why not? It's interesting.'

'English people don't like it.'

'Can we stop for a lemonade?'

'Later.'

They walked down the cobbled lane to the hairdressers'. Next door, flies were buzzing around the butcher's chain-link curtain and there was a solid, meaty smell. Geenie tried to peer through the gaps as her mother dragged her past. There was always blood and sawdust in butcher's shops, which was all right to look at, as long as you didn't have to touch it. It was like the Italian paintings Jimmy had taken her to see in the National Gallery. All flesh and blood. It looked strange and sort of lovely, but you wouldn't want it on your hands.

The front door of the shop was open and an electric fan was groaning in the corner. The air, heavy with a chemical smell, seemed thicker, coarser, inside the shop.

A man in a white coat came to greet them, holding out a strong-looking hand.

'Hello, Robin,' said Ellen, smiling and touching his fingertips. 'I'm afraid I've had to bring my daughter with me.'

The man glanced down at Geenie. The skin on his face looked like cheese.

'That's quite all right, Madam.' He narrowed his eyes but did not smile. Instead, he knelt on the green tiles beside Geenie and whispered, 'How would you like to look like Garbo?'

His breath reeked of milky tea. Geenie kept a tight hold on her mother's hand.

'She'd love it,' said Ellen. 'What girl wouldn't?'

'Then I shall arrange it,' said the man, still kneeling, still breathing tea. 'Hilda will take off all the excess weight…' here he plunged a hand into Geenie's hair and lifted it away from her face – 'and then set it for you. How about that?'

Geenie snatched a long strand of her hair away from Robin's fingers, placed it in her mouth, and began to chew.

Between chews, she said, 'Cut it off, do you mean?'

'I mean, lick it into shape.' He winked. 'Hilda will make you look very sophisticated. It's her speciality.' Straightening up and facing Ellen, he added, 'It will take about an hour. Enough time for a special treatment for yourself, Madam.'

Ellen pulled her hand free of Geenie's and gave her a little shove forwards. 'You'll look beautiful, darling,' she said, her eyes still on Robin. 'Think how jealous Diana will be when she comes home.'

.....

Hilda held out a pink paisley gown. 'Slip this on love, and we'll get you washed.'

Pushing her arms into the scratchy material, Geenie asked, 'Are you going to make me look like Garbo?'

Hilda gave a short laugh. 'You and all the others.'

The basin was cold against her neck. Hilda's fingers sprung about Geenie's scalp as she rubbed in the shampoo. She wore very red lipstick and had a splodge of freckles on her nose. Her hair was shiny yellow and her curls bounced as she rinsed the soap away. 'What a lot of hair,' she said.

'Some people call me Flossy, because it looks like candy-floss.'

'Do they now? Come over to the mirror, then, and we'll see what we can do about that.'

It had been a while since Geenie had studied her own reflection. Sitting in the curtained cubicle, she looked in the large round mirror before her. Her hair now reached her waist and her face looked darker than before.

Hilda pulled a metal comb through the ends of Geenie's hair, making her yelp.

'This is a right old tangle. Doesn't your mother brush it for you?'

Geenie shook her head.

Hilda frowned as she tugged the comb through. 'We might have to cut some of these out I'm afraid, love.'

The metal teeth sang as Hilda tackled another knot.

'Cut it all off.' Geenie stared at her own mouth as she formed the phrase.

Hilda stopped combing. 'All of it?'

'Really short.'

Hilda ran her fingers through the thick mass. 'It would be a shame to lose *all* of it…'

'I don't want it any more. Get rid of it.'

'Are you sure, Miss? What'll your mother say?'

'She won't say anything.'

Hilda hesitated. She put one hand on her hip and held the comb in the air. 'How old are you, if you don't mind me asking, Miss?'

'Thirteen,' Geenie lied.

Hilda sighed. 'And you're sure you want it short?'

'Yes. Quite sure.'

'Right.' Hilda reached for the scissors. 'Put your head forward.'

And she began to cut.

The hair sprayed down to the floor. Once cut, it twisted helplessly to the ground. It was like when Kitty lifted the pie dish to trim the edge of the pastry. The stuff fell cleanly from the knife, as if relieved to be set free.

Hilda's bosom pressed against Geenie's shoulder as she angled the girl's head. Geenie closed her eyes, breathed in Hilda's currant-bun scent, and stayed absolutely still in the chair, waiting to be transformed. It would be like the dancing princesses being set free by Jack. Everything would be different, after this; once the yellow curtain was drawn back and she stepped out into the shop, everything would change. When Jimmy was alive, she'd been Flossy. But Jimmy wasn't coming back.

'Short enough?'

Geenie opened her eyes. Her hair brushed the tops of her shoulders.

'Shorter,' she said, closing her eyes again.

Throughout the cutting, Geenie heard only one noise from the back room: it was a familiar, long 'yes'.

.....

After an hour, it was done. Hilda had cut a bob so short that the lobes of Geenie's ears were partly exposed. She felt her hair prickling the skin there. Turning her head to the side, she saw how white her neck was, and reached up to touch it.

Hilda laughed. 'Nothing there any more, is there?'

Geenie looked in the mirror again. She wasn't sure who was staring back at her. The reflection didn't seem to be one she quite recognised. Instead of a mass of hair, there was her face: her pale blue eyes, her receding chin, her small mouth, all looking strangely prominent.

Hilda swept the blonde strands into an enormous pile. 'Do you want to take it home?' She swished the curtains back so Geenie was exposed. Geenie looked around, expecting to hear her mother's shocked response to her new look. But there was no sign of Ellen.

'Miss? I can put it in a bag for you, if you like.'

Geenie looked at the mound of dead hair. 'My mother might want it,' she said.

.....

When Ellen eventually emerged from the back room, she was no longer wearing orange lipstick, and her hair looked exactly the same as before, but the green shiny dress was creased across her thighs and bottom.

Geenie sat in the chair by the reception desk with a paper bag full of hair on her lap, and waited for her mother to notice.

'Robin said my daughter's hair would be included in the price.' Ellen leaned across the desk and spoke to the top of Hilda's head.

Hilda glanced at Geenie, and Ellen's eyes followed.

There was a tiny silence, during which Geenie listened to the groaning of the electric fan. Her head felt light and cool. Gripping the bag tightly, she knew she was ready for whatever happened.

'What have you done?' There was a tremble in Ellen's voice which Geenie hadn't heard for a very long time.

'What,' Ellen repeated, staring at her daughter's head, 'have you done?'

Holding out the open bag, Geenie shook it in her mother's direction. Then she watched as Ellen closed her eyes very slowly, put a hand to her mouth and shook her head. 'Your beautiful hair!' she whispered.

Geenie placed the bag back on her lap, expecting Ellen to take a swipe at it, but instead Ellen came and knelt on the floor before her. It was a moment before she spoke, and, when she did, her voice was so quiet Geenie had to lean forward to make out what she was saying. 'Jimmy loved your hair! You were his Flossy.'

Geenie studied her mother's eyes. They were smaller, greyer, than her own. They looked, she thought, washed out.

'Don't you remember, Geenie?'

Slowly, Geenie put the bag of dead hair on the floor. 'Of course I remember,' she said. 'I remember everything about Jimmy.' Her voice sounded loud in the empty shop.

Ellen reached out and touched the new, blunt ends of her daughter's hair. She took a strand between her finger and thumb and rubbed at it, as though it were a fine fabric.

Then Geenie said, 'But he's gone, hasn't he?'

Ellen pulled Geenie into her arms and held her. Geenie pressed her cheek into her mother's shoulder and felt her shuddering breath on the back of her own naked neck. They both held on tight.

When Ellen let go, she scooped up the bag of hair, carefully folded the top over, and tucked it under her arm. 'I'll keep this safe,' she said.

··· Twenty-seven ···

Arthur said they should have tea before dancing, and Kitty was relieved to have an excuse to put off the moment when he'd touch her, remembering the way he'd placed his hand on her backside at the beach. He led her through the quiet hotel and out into the tea garden. The Crown and Thistle wasn't nearly as upmarket as the White Hart: there was no revolving door, the girl on the desk didn't have a uniform, and it was a smaller place altogether, in the centre of town rather than out by the lake; but it was, Kitty thought, quite posh enough, and much better than the Drill Hall for dancing, even in the afternoon. Most people seemed to be sitting outside in the small garden, under the shade of the hotel's blue umbrellas, and she'd been right: the place was full of young women – some of them probably worked at the Macklows'. She didn't look too closely at individual faces in case there was one she recognised. Over the tinkle of 'Tiptoe Through the Tulips' there was the clatter of teaspoons on porcelain. As they crossed the lawn, there was a limp round of applause between numbers.

She was wearing her lily-print dress and a neat white tricorne hat, to the front of which she'd appliquéd a violet. It was her only hat besides the beret, and she was fond of it, even though Lou always said it looked like a boat washed up on her head. She'd pinned the hat so tightly to her hair that she could feel it pull every time she nodded to Arthur as they tried to find a table.

Arthur got out his hankie and wiped the lattice-work chair before Kitty sat. There was a blob of jam on the cloth and no parasol. Kitty removed her hat and wondered if she should have worn gloves to hide the fact that the tips of her fingers were damp.

'Well,' said Arthur, squinting at her. 'This is nice.'

He straightened his jacket sleeves. He was wearing the same suit she'd seen him in at the pictures, and she saw, now, that the fabric was shiny with wear on the elbows. His face was ruddy and he'd put something on his hair to keep it down. What with this, his flushed cheeks, and his damp brow, his whole head looked as though it had been covered in a film of grease.

Taking out his pipe, he twisted round, searching for the waiter. 'I'm parched,' he announced.

'Have you been here before?'

'Couple of times. In the evenings.'

Kitty was surprised but tried to hide it by looking down at the tablecloth.

'It's what you do, isn't it? With women, I mean.'

She'd never heard him say that word, *women*, before. It sounded slightly obscene.

'No doubt you've been here plenty, Kitty. Dancer like you.'

Kitty thought of the times she'd been to the Sunday tea-dance with Lou when she was younger: the two of them had clutched at each other's dresses, and Lou always hissed that Kitty should lead in case any boys were watching them.

She lifted her head. 'What do you mean, with *women*?'

Arthur tucked some tobacco into his pipe and smiled. 'You know. Girls and that. *Ladies*. A twirl around the floor in some hotel. It's what they expect, isn't it?'

Kitty wiped her palms on her skirt and raised her chin. 'What do *you* expect, then?'

Arthur lit his pipe. 'Oh,' he said, 'I don't know. Bit of company, I suppose.' He paused before looking straight at her. 'Someone to share things with. Doesn't really matter what they are, does it? As long as you do them together.'

Kitty looked across the lawn. The sun blazed down, bleaching everything in sight.

Arthur put his hand up for the waiter, but the boy didn't seem to see them.

'Do you want to stay in service, Kitty?'

The question caught her off guard. It wasn't something she'd thought much about. She'd just been glad not to have to live with Lou and Bob any more, and it didn't seem like there was any choice other than to stay in service – at least until she was married. Not that getting married seemed very likely to Kitty. She didn't allow herself to picture that scenario very often, and when she did, she always thought of the wedding photograph, with herself in a tidy marocain silk frock, perhaps, and a feather in her hat, which would bear no resemblance to a boat. But she couldn't imagine the man at her side at all.

'It's not a bad life, is it?' she answered.

'Well,' said Arthur. '*I'm* all right. Come and go as I please really: do a bit of gardening, see to the beast. They don't seem to mind, as long as I show my face and things keep going. It's better than slogging it down at the rubber factory, at any rate.' He sucked on his pipe. 'But I don't know about you. Seems to me you're wasted, with them lot.'

The waiter was near them again, and Kitty raised her

hand a fraction of an inch. But he swept straight past.

'You could be cooking in some proper house,' Arthur continued. 'For proper gentry. Have some girl do the skivvying for you. Those cakes of yours are smashing. Especially the – what is it? French sponge.'

'French buns.'

'That's it. Smashing.'

She smiled. For a while now, she'd had an idea that perhaps she'd be able to move and get a position as a real cook somewhere else, somewhere there'd be a kitchen maid to help her. But after the salmon incident, she knew she wouldn't get anything like a decent reference from Mrs Steinberg.

'Or, of course...' he licked his bottom lip. 'Of course, you could decide to go off and get married to some lucky Joe.'

'Didn't we ought to dance?' she said, standing up so she wouldn't have to look at his shining eyes. 'It's getting on. The band only plays until four.'

'What about your tea?'

But she was already heading for the open patio doors.

.....

As they walked to the floor, Arthur let his hand rest on Kitty's hip. In between the mopping of brows, the band was playing a drowsy 'Continental'. Kitty noticed that the lead trumpeter's shirt was wet through; you could see the outline of his vest. A few girl-couples limped through the dance, gazing over each other's shoulders, but there were no men in sight, apart from an old gentleman still wearing his jacket, who was guiding his wife slowly around the floor, his eyes half shut.

She let Arthur pull her quite close before they began to move to the music. His hand was warm and dry as it clasped her fingers. He'd left his jacket on the chair outside, and his chest was against hers; she could feel its rise and fall. She thought again of the movement of Mr Crane's shoulders as he put on his shirt. The leap of his muscle.

Forwards, backwards, turn. Arthur wasn't a bad dancer at all. His waist was stiff, but his feet knew where to go. The trumpets let out a long blast in an attempt to get some life into the tune. No one here would dance on the tables, Kitty thought. She tried to concentrate on following Arthur and not think of how she'd danced in the kitchen with Mrs Steinberg, how she'd let her hips lead the way. Here she must sway, rather than swing. She mustn't force him with any sudden movement. His breath was on her forehead. He smelled slightly of his shed: warm mud and fraying string.

'That girl's very fond of you, you know.'

Kitty looked up.

'She told me what happened the other night, with Mrs S. Damned liberty, if you ask me.'

Kitty stopped moving, but Arthur swung her round.

'You should be careful, though. It's never good to let them get too close.' He was looking over her head. 'Better to stick with your own.'

'How do you mean?'

He swung her round again. 'I mean, they're all right and that, but in the end they'll always be them, and we'll always be us.'

The only reply Kitty could think of was, 'Geenie's just a girl.'

Arthur ignored this. 'Take Crane. He's on at me to join the Bolshies, but I know it's not for me, it's for them. I listen to what he has to say, and I even agree with some of it, but

I keep my distance.'

The music stopped for a moment. He released her and wiped the back of his neck with his handkerchief.

'It's not as if I'm really close to – to any of them—'

'Didn't say you were. But the girl was gabbing about you making her some costume or other. Rang alarm bells, that's all.'

The music started again. He took her hand and smiled. 'Just looking out for you, Kitty. Seeing you're all right.'

She said nothing.

'Told you I could dance,' he said, dropping his hand lower on her back and pulling her in closer.

'I think it's good,' said Kitty, keeping her fingers taut in his, 'the way Mr Crane stands up for the working classes.'

Arthur gave a loud laugh over her head. 'He's just playing at it. Underneath all that talk, the *Daily Worker* and all that claptrap, he's like the rest. He's one of them.'

'At least he cares.'

Arthur pushed his hip into her body and moved his mouth close to her ear. 'Crane doesn't know anything about the working classes, Kitty. Have you ever seen him do any actual *work*?'

She tried to move her face away from his breath. 'He did that room, didn't he? Knocked it through?'

'I did that, with a mate who's a brickie. Crane just handed us some tools now and then.'

'He's writing a book.'

'That's not work, is it? Sitting at a desk making up stories.'

Kitty didn't reply. She didn't mention Arthur's love of Westerns. Instead she closed her eyes and remembered the feel of Mr Crane's fingers on her elbow, and was glad Arthur hadn't touched her there.

'Ladies and gentlemen, I'm sorry to announce this will be the last dance of the afternoon. I thank you.' The trumpeter made a salute and let out a loud blast, and the band began a new tune with more vim. Yelping girls suddenly squeezed through the patio doors and piled onto the dance floor. They began spinning each other around and laughing. Arthur kept his back straight and squeezed Kitty's hand.

But Kitty had decided to let her hips lead the way. Her thighs took the strain as she dipped, then straightened, taking Arthur with her. She hardened her jaw and looked to the right, then the left, aware of Arthur watching her with a slight frown, his feet stumbling in an attempt to keep up with hers. The floor itself seemed to be moving with the rhythm. Everything was much too hot and fast, but the only thing to do was keep dancing. It was the last number and you had to keep dancing. The girls bounced around them, giggling, overheated, swinging.

Arthur hooked his knee between her legs and swiped it to the side, almost causing her to topple. 'You're leading,' he hissed.

Regaining her balance, Kitty continued to dance, gripping his fingers in hers and twirling him around. Their feet tangled but she carried on.

'Kitty!' As he tugged his hand free of hers, she span out of his path; Arthur lunged forward, arms flailing, and she watched him and thought, *he's going to fall*, but she made no move to save him. He batted his arms in the air, as he'd done when trying to fend off that wasp in the garden, and somehow, through this frantic windmilling action, managed to stop himself going down.

The music stopped and a great wave of chatter and applause broke over their heads. Immediately, waitresses appeared and began to move through the crowd, pushing their way out into the tea garden with trays.

They stood apart in the bustle, staring at each other.

'You were leading.'

She put a hand to her hair. 'Was I?' she said, panting slightly from the heat and the exercise. 'I didn't realise.'

He seemed to be waiting for some sort of explanation, but she couldn't think of anything to offer him.

'We'd better go,' he said eventually, starting for the doors.

Standing in the middle of the dance floor, she watched him leave. She was sure he would turn around when he reached the doors and call for her to follow; he'd extend an arm, his trimmed moustache would twitch, and he'd say, 'You coming?' She waited, her eyes fixed on his short back. But he stepped right through the doors without so much as a glance over his shoulder.

The room had emptied around her. Kitty looked up at the stage. The band was packing up, but the trumpeter was still sitting back in his chair, his shirt soaked. Raising his hand to his brow, he saluted her.

··· Twenty-eight ···

It was incredible how close the girl could be. As Ellen walked down the garden path in the Sunday afternoon sunshine, she was sure she could hear Geenie breathing. It was almost as if the girl were trying to stick herself to Ellen's own skin. When they reached the stream, Ellen stopped abruptly, and Geenie crashed into her back, her face crushing against her mother's spine. Blotto nosed Ellen's ankles.

'Is it possible,' asked Ellen, 'that you could walk *beside* me, like a normal human being?'

Dog and daughter looked up with big eyes. She sighed. 'Right. All off.' She began unbuttoning Geenie's blouse, but the girl pulled away.

'I can do it.'

'Suit yourself.'

Ellen was wearing a knitted sleeveless top with nothing beneath, so was naked to the waist with one peeling motion. She unbuttoned her linen slacks, stepped out of her knickers and kicked them aside. They landed under the willow tree.

'Ready?'

Geenie had undressed, and was standing with both hands clenched around her backside.

'What are you doing that for?'

'In case anyone sees my bottom.'

Ellen laughed. 'It's the front you want to worry about,' she said, looking her daughter up and down. Over the summer, Geenie had filled out a little: there was now a definite curve to her hip, a fullness to her nipples; even a few pubic hairs were beginning to show.

Ellen stretched her arms above her head, swivelling her hips around and bending at the knees before balancing on the edge of the bank. It was what James had always done before bathing. After weeks of sunshine, the earth was powdery between her toes. She looked over her shoulder and held out a hand. 'Come on, Flossy. Nothing matters when you're naked.'

Geenie stepped to her side, and together they launched themselves into the water.

It only came up to Ellen's thighs, but it was cold enough to make them both yelp, which set Blotto off. The dog ran back and forth along the bank, yapping hysterically, ears bobbing and throat jerking with effort.

'Watch this!' Geenie cried, and there was a great splash as she threw herself backwards into the water, her limbs splaying, her newly shorn head going under. She held herself there, her face warped and silvery beneath the surface, and Ellen watched her daughter, wondering how long she would hold her breath this time. Ellen counted thirty seconds, concentrating on the sticklebacks pulsing around the girl's waist. Blotto's yaps turned into howls. Sixty seconds. Geenie's cheeks ballooned and her eyes were squeezed tight. A minute and a half. Longer than she'd ever done before. The dog's howls reached a higher pitch, and, in the shade of the willows, Ellen felt the top half of her body begin to cool and prickle.

'Geenie,' she said, trying to keep her voice steady. 'Come up now.'

Two minutes.

'Come up.'

Two and a half minutes.

'Come up.' Ellen plunged her hands into the water and grasped her daughter by the shoulders. 'For God's sake—'

But Geenie twisted away, burst out of the water, sucked in a huge breath, and, using her hands as paddles, began to scoop the stream in her mother's direction, almost knocking her down.

It took Ellen a moment before she steadied herself and fought back. She ran the length of both arms across the surface of the stream, pushing water over her daughter's head. The stream was a white fury of crashing foam as the two of them shrieked and splashed, and Blotto rushed around the base of the willow tree, barking.

.....

Ellen spread a towel on the lawn and they lay down to dry themselves in the sun. Next to Geenie, Blotto flopped on his side, panting hoarsely. Overhead, the sky throbbed blue. Ellen closed her eyes and let the sun warm her from head to toe. She'd always loved to sunbathe, and believed the sun's energy penetrated her very core. She smiled to herself, remembering the heat in the back room of the hairdressers'. When Robin unhooked her bra he'd made a sort of dive straight for her nipples, which had been tiresome, but she'd soon guided him back to her face and slowed him down. Then he'd carried her to the divan, which was something she hadn't expected. No one had carried her anywhere since she was a child.

'When are George and Diana coming back?' Geenie had buttoned up her blouse and pulled on her skirt, and was kneeling on the towel, looking down at her mother.

'Soon.' Crane hadn't said anything specific about his return when he and Diana left yesterday morning. He'd just mumbled something about being away 'a few days', and, at the time, Ellen hadn't the will to tackle him about it. He'd hardly taken a thing with him, though, so he'd have to come back, if only to pick up some clean underclothes.

'How soon?'

Ellen shielded her eyes from the sun and peered at her daughter. 'What would you say,' she asked, 'if I told you that it might be just you and me, for a while?'

'Aren't they coming back?'

'I didn't say that.'

Geenie tucked her chin into her chest and looked towards the house.

'But if they didn't come back for a while, it would be all right, wouldn't it?' Ellen continued. 'We'd get on all right, wouldn't we? The two of us.' She sat up and put a hand on her daughter's arm.

'Why did we come here?'

'You know why, darling.'

'I don't.'

Ellen's head began to feel tight with heat. She drew the towel around her shoulders so she wouldn't have to answer her daughter's question while fully naked. Then she looked at her hands and tried to think how she should begin.

Geenie sat very still. Blotto had begun to snore.

'When Jimmy died,' Ellen said, 'when he died, I didn't know what to do. I know it's hard to understand, but I needed to get away…'

'Will we go back?'

'To London?'

Geenie nodded.

Ellen pulled the towel tighter. 'I don't know, darling, maybe—'

'Because I don't want to go back. I want us all to stay here.'

Ellen caught Geenie's chin and twisted her daughter's face towards her own. 'So I did the right thing, didn't I?'

There was no response.

'Geenie? Don't you think I did the right thing?'

There was a pause, during which the dog's snores grew louder.

Geenie closed her eyes and replied in a flat tone, 'Yes, Mama.'

Ellen's head was aching now; she could feel her pulse behind her eyes. She'd have to go and sit inside, in the dark. The sun's energy was too much for her today. A gin and it would help. She removed the towel and reached for her clothes.

'How did he die?' Geenie's voice was quieter, but she still spoke in the same flat tone.

Ellen dropped her clothes on the grass. The dog woke with a piercing yap and tore down the garden towards some unknown crisis.

'How did who die, darling?'

'Jimmy.'

Ellen took a breath. Blotto was rushing around the willow tree again, barking with abandon.

'You know how he died, darling. I told you. He died during the operation on his ankle.'

'Why?'

'Operations are very dangerous—'

'People don't usually die of a broken ankle.'

'Well, Jimmy did. The operation went wrong. Sometimes it happens.' Ellen stood up and shook the towel out. She must get inside before the dog started howling again. 'Jimmy was unlucky. We all were.' She dressed quickly, being careful not to look directly at Geenie, who was staring at the house, her blank face steady and unblinking.

Leaving her daughter on the lawn, Ellen walked to the writing studio. The door wasn't locked, and she went straight inside and managed to close it before the tears came. The afternoon sun had made the studio like a glass house, and she leant back on the door and wept and sweated silently, one hand across her mouth, the other clenched tight across her belly.

When she'd managed to stop, she sat in Crane's armchair and steadied her breathing by telling herself, over and over: *he will be back*. She could smell the muddiness of the stream on her hands. Her nails were full of it. *He will come back*. He'd sit here again and look at her while she scolded him for not getting on with his novel. He would have to come back, and when he did, she would make it all right. After all, hadn't she been thinking of him, of their first time together, even when Robin had been inside her yesterday? It was amazing how one man could seem like another during the sexual act, how you could almost forget who the man was entirely, and become lost in the act itself. Robin had been a sure-touched and attentive lover, but hadn't she been thinking of Crane's trembling hands? It was outside the bedroom that men were so very different.

Perhaps if she waited long enough, Crane would arrive and find her in the chair, and she could say she'd been sitting there, waiting, all the time he'd been gone. Then he'd call her his Cleopatra, and they'd make love on his desk. Perhaps there was still some hope for a pregnancy.

Wiping her wet cheeks with the heel of her hand, she stood and, telling herself that she didn't mean to, opened his top desk drawer. She didn't think about what she was doing, or of what she was about to do; she just clasped the brass handle and pulled. Inside were several photographs of Diana as an infant (one in a knitted bonnet on her mother's slim lap); a couple of pens with broken nibs; a letter from the publishing house saying they would always welcome him back; and a dirty handkerchief. Ellen pulled the second drawer open. Apart from a clutch of rubber bands and a few pencil shavings, it was empty. The final drawer was the deepest, and felt heavy as she pulled. She knew this was it: the manuscript. And sure enough, there was a pile of paper, the top leaf of which read:

LOVE ON THE DOWNS
a novel
by G. M. Crane

What did that M stand for? He'd never used a middle name before. She stepped back from the paper and swallowed, becoming aware of how very quiet it was in the studio. Briefly she remembered Geenie, still sitting outside, staring blankly at the house, and thought that she should push the drawer back into place and go into the house to fetch them both some barley lemonade. Or maybe a gin and it. But instead she reached in, dragged the pile of paper from the drawer and placed it on top of the mess of papers on his desk. Then she stood a moment, looking at the top sheet, the rush of her blood making her feel light-headed. She gave a small laugh – how bad could it be? It was only the story of their love affair. It wasn't like she didn't know what had happened. What was happening.

She turned over the title page. The second page was

blank, apart from an inscription typed halfway down the sheet: *For my dear Diana*. Ellen stared at the words for a full minute, not quite believing it wasn't her own name there, before turning two more blank pages and coming to the heading: *CHAPTER ONE: The Arrival*. Turning another page, she finally found a whole typed paragraph, which she held before her and read.

It was going to be an endless summer. Georgina Chance had arrived at the Sussex cottage with her family two days ago. As soon as she set foot in the place, she'd left the crashing of teacups and the clatter of servants carrying goodness knows what up and down the stairs behind, and had climbed to the top of the green hill which rose up from the end of their long garden. For she was a young woman with scant respect for the oppressive gentility of her generation. Born into the aristocracy, she longed for one thing: escape from manners and money, and all that went with it.

So it *was* about her, albeit in a roundabout way. Realising that her fingers were sweating, making the thin paper wilt, Ellen sat in the armchair, placed the page flat on her lap, and read on.

No one could have been more relieved than she to be out of London. The Downs were there, wetly beckoning from every window.

She'd have to challenge him on that. 'Wetly beckoning' wasn't right at all.

What bliss it had been to walk barefoot through the grass, with no care for convention, and no one to see her shapely white ankles!

Yes, that was right. Although Ellen herself had yet to

walk the full height of the hill.

She'd allowed her thoughts to wander to her great love: poetry. Her father was against poetry, caring only for money and commerce, and her mother said it was 'all right until you get married'. But for Georgina, poetry was the life force itself, and out there, on the green hills, she could feel its power in her very bones…

Ellen rose and went to the desk to find the rest. But the next page was blank. She placed the typed page on top of the ones she'd already read and lifted another page. That was blank, too. And the one after that. And the one after that. She picked up the whole pile of paper and flicked through its corners with her thumb. But there was nothing. Not one more word. Just page after page of white, blank paper.

Perhaps this was a false start. The rest of it would be somewhere else, hidden. She bent down and looked beneath the desk, lifting the edge of Blotto's hair-matted old blanket. A ripe whiff like stewed meat came up, and she moved away, holding her nose. She looked around the room. Of course. The filing cabinet.

On her knees, she wrenched up the wooden shutter. The top drawer was stuck; as she tugged it open it made a squealing sound which reminded her of the lorry she'd seen dragging that poor cow down Petersfield High Street. But she blinked that thought away. When she'd finally got the thing fully open and delved her hand to the back, it was empty. The next drawer opened easily, but there was nothing in there apart from a copy of *The Socialist Sixth of the World*. Ellen threw it on the floor in disgust. The other drawers yielded only dog-eared envelopes and stray photo-corners. Then she looked beneath the low table with the wireless on top; all she found was the wastepaper basket, so she rummaged in there, too, fingering a drying apple core and a screwed-up piece of paper. She was about to move on when she noticed that the paper had something typed on it, so she smoothed it flat and read the words: *Sunlight. Shadow. The girl brings him cakes on a tray. His blood is heavy with wanting.*

She almost screwed it back up and threw it away – she was thinking about looking behind the filing cabinet now – but something made her read it again. *Sunlight. Shadow. The girl brings him cakes on a tray. His blood is heavy with wanting.*

Ellen stood, holding the page in her damp fingers. She smoothed it out once more, trying to get rid of all the creases this time, to make it completely flat, thinking that perhaps she'd missed something. She read it again. *The girl brings him cakes on a tray.*

There was no mistake, no hidden word, nothing missing in the creases of the paper. *Sunlight. Shadow.* Who else could it be? Who else could it be, this girl with cakes who made his blood heavy? Her stomach squeezed tight, and she felt a hot liquid at the back of her throat. She leant on the desk to steady herself until the nausea had passed. *The girl brings him cakes on a tray.* How had she not seen it before? His novel was nothing, the story over before it had begun, the heroine ridiculous, and nothing like her – apart from those ankles; it was clear to Ellen now that Crane had been sitting in this place for months doing absolutely damn all; but *who was this*? She heard herself saying it aloud. 'Who is this?' Her voice was small, strangled. 'Who is this?' she repeated, knowing the answer full well.

... Twenty-nine ...

They came back in the middle of the night. Geenie was twisted in her bed, waiting for sleep, when she heard the front door open, the low sound of George's voice, and Diana's quick footsteps up the stairs. She sat up and listened. The clack-click of Diana's door closing was louder than usual, and was followed by several bangs and crashes. Then there was George's even tread along the landing. A rumble – that would be him putting his case down. A couple of thumps – taking his shoes off. The squeak of her mother's bedsprings. And then – silence.

She threw back the covers and climbed out of bed. Tiptoeing to the door, she listened. Not a sound. Keeping close to the wall, she edged along the landing to Diana's room. Once inside, she could make out Diana's suitcase, still buckled, sitting by the window. There was also a large lump beneath the bedclothes. A large lump which didn't move when Geenie hissed, 'Diana!' So she sat on the edge of the bed, flicked on the lamp, and poked the lump. It twitched. 'You're back!' she whispered.

'Go away,' said a muffled voice, and the lump shifted.

Geenie sat a while longer, looking at the lump, wondering whether to leave it alone. Then she thought of the saggy centre of her own bed, and how lonely it was there, and she said, 'Something exciting happened, while you were away.' She stretched out a hand and tried to find the edge of the sheet so she could peel it back. Grabbing a piece of smooth cotton, she pulled, but a hand appeared and gripped the sheet hard, preventing it from moving.

'Please come out.'

'No.'

'What's the matter?' Again, Geenie tugged at the bedclothes. This time she caught Diana off guard, and the sheet came away suddenly, revealing Diana's back. The girl was curled in a cramped ball, and was still wearing her blouse and skirt. Her hair was pulled into a tight plait so intricate in design, and so securely knotted, that it must hurt to wear it. 'What happened to your hair?' Geenie whispered.

'My mother did it.'

Geenie tapped Diana's tense shoulder. 'Look at mine! Look at my hair, Diana!' She crawled around the bed, trying to see her friend's eyes. But Diana remained scrunched tight, her face pressed to the mattress.

'Please look.'

Diana covered the back of her head with both hands, as if ducking a blow, and curled into an even smaller ball.

Geenie sat on her heels and sighed. Deciding she may as well wait, she stretched out along what was available of the bed, and tried to stay as still as possible. Her friend couldn't remain in that position forever, she reasoned, and, in the end, her curiosity about the exciting thing that had happened would surely get the better of her.

Eventually, Diana stirred. Very slowly, she removed her hands from her head and caught hold of Geenie's wrist. Geenie waited a moment before whispering, 'I'm glad you came back.'

'Daddy said we had to. I could've stayed with Mummy.'

'Why didn't you?'

Diana lifted her head. 'It just wasn't the right time. Mummy's got a very important show on and it wasn't the right time for her. Any other time, I could've stayed.'

Geenie put her other hand on top of Diana's. 'I'm glad you came back,' she repeated.

After a while, Diana uncurled herself and knelt next to Geenie on the bed. 'What happened to your—'

'I cut it,' said Geenie, sitting up.

Diana clamped her fingers around the top of Geenie's scalp and twisted her head this way and that so she could examine the bob fully. Finally, she nodded her approval. 'Was it awful here without me?'

'Yes,' said Geenie, without thinking. 'Quite awful. Apart from the haircut. And Ellen and I bathed in the stream and I soaked her.'

'Well,' said Diana, yawning, 'I don't mean to stay long.'

'What does your father say?'

'You know Daddy. He hardly says anything. Unless it's about the workers.' She looked Geenie in the face. 'We have to carry out the plan, so I can get home.'

Geenie had almost forgotten about the plan.

'We have to start as soon as possible,' continued Diana, lying flat on the bed, stretching her arms and closing her eyes. 'We'll begin first thing in the morning.'

Geenie remained sitting upright, watching over her friend until Diana's plump bottom lip fell away from her teeth and she began to snore, softly.

.....

'Keep still, Miss.'

Kitty looked peculiar with all those pins in her mouth. Her face was set, her voice louder than usual.

'Now turn around, please.' She pressed the cool steel tip of the inch tape into the nape of Geenie's neck and ran the length of it down her spine. 'Two pompoms, was it?'

'Yes. And they must be black,' interjected Diana, who was sitting on a kitchen chair, watching, having already been measured for her costume.

'You said, Miss.'

'How long will it take?' asked Geenie.

'That depends.' The tape was now around Geenie's waist. Kitty held the ends together for a moment, then let it go and began spinning it around her hand, winding it back into a ball.

'On what?' asked Diana, swinging her legs and scuffing the tiles.

'That's you done, Miss,' Kitty said to Geenie. When she'd finished winding the tape, and had written some numbers down on a little pad, she turned to Diana. 'It depends on how busy I am, Miss.'

'Can you hurry?' Geenie pressed her palms together and gazed up at Kitty from under her brows. 'Please, Kitty? Can you?'

Kitty laughed. 'Well. I suppose it shouldn't take me so very long...'

Geenie hopped on the spot.

'Especially if I borrow my sister's machine.'

Diana stood and, with her hands behind her back, aimed a dazzling smile directly at Kitty. 'That would be really super of you.'

Kitty took a step back. 'Yes, well. I'll see what I can do.' She turned to the table and picked up one of the long white cotton nightdresses Geenie had dumped in her lap that morning. 'Are you sure it's all right for me to use these, Miss?' She held one up to the light from the window. 'They're very nice stuff.'

'They're old,' said Geenie, standing at her side and gazing at the fine cotton.

'But your mother said we could use them?'

Geenie nodded. 'She hasn't worn them in years.' One was from Geenie's dressing-up pile, the other she'd pinched from her mother's drawer this morning. But she hadn't told even Diana about that.

Kitty looked from Geenie to Diana and back again. 'Well, if you're sure—'

'When can you do them?' asked Diana.

Kitty gathered up the fabric, her notebook and her workbox. 'We'll see.'

Diana shot a look at Geenie. 'When?' asked Geenie, standing in front of Diana and grasping Kitty's hand. It was smaller than her mother's, and much rougher to touch, but she squeezed it as tenderly as she could. 'When do you think you might?'

Kitty looked down at her fingers, and Geenie gave another squeeze.

'I'm going to my sister's tomorrow, so I might be able to make a start then—'

'Oh, please do!' said Diana.

'But I can't promise anything, Miss. Now, I really must get on.'

Geenie could tell by the little flush rising in Kitty's cheeks that they would have the costumes soon enough.

.....

They began rehearsals right away in Geenie's bedroom, wearing just their knickers and vests (because no other costume would have been right), and with their faces painted white. Diana had appointed herself writer/director, and Geenie was in charge of costumes and set.

'First of all,' said Diana, standing on the bed with her hands on her hips, 'we'll both do a song.'

Geenie was sitting cross-legged on the paint-stained rug. 'I can't sing.'

'You can do a dance, then.'

But Geenie didn't think she could do a dance, either. 'Can I do Cleopatra?'

'You want to do *Shakespeare*?'

'No – just Cleopatra.'

'What will you do?'

Geenie thought. 'I'll die on stage. I'll collapse in a swoon, and I'll die. I'll wear my white robe.'

'But we'll be in Pierrot costumes. That's the point.'

Geenie was silent. From here, Diana looked rather frightening: her hair, now released from its complicated plait, had gone kinky and wild.

'I'll do a dance,' said Diana, kicking up one leg and managing to keep her balance perfectly whilst the earrings wound around Geenie's headboard rattled in a mad dance. 'You don't have to do anything. Anyway. That's just the *prelude*.'

'What's a prelude?'

'It's like an introduction. Something to whet the audience's appetite.' Diana strutted from one side of the bed to the other then launched herself to the floor, landing before Geenie with a quiet thud, her hair shuddering around her bare shoulders. 'What's important is the Main Act.' She licked her lips. 'Now. It's a one-act play called *What the*

Gardener Saw. You'll be the housemaid, Ruby, and I'll be the great poet, John Cross.'

'Can't I be the great poet?'

'No. My father's a poet and I know much more about it.'

Geenie lay on the floor and looked at the ceiling. 'Can't we do another play?'

Diana slowly walked around her friend before leaning over and looking into her face. 'You get to kiss me.'

Geenie sat up and the two girls' noses almost touched. 'What happens?'

'I'll show you.' Diana giggled and pulled the other girl to her feet. 'It's *hopelessly* romantic. We open with me.' She jumped into position, sitting at the end of the bed. 'I'm at my desk, composing, like this.' She crossed her legs and, resting an elbow on one knee, put a fist to her forehead. 'Then you come in with your duster—'

'Duster?'

'It could be a feather one, I suppose, or a tea cloth—'

'I'll have a feather one.'

'So you come in, and you say, *Oh, sorry to disturb you, Sir—*'

'How do I say it?'

'How?'

'You're the director.'

'Well. Sort of – quiet, you know, and hesitant. Look at the floor a lot. Just think of Kitty and copy what she does. Like this.' Diana stood, hunched her shoulders, and shuffled towards the door. '*Oh*,' she said, her voice barely a whisper, '*I'm so sorry—*'

'Kitty isn't like that.'

'But that's more or less it, isn't it? Anyway, you're not Kitty, you're Ruby. It's a general impression of a housemaid sort that we're after.'

'Kitty's not a housemaid. She's a cook.'

Diana sighed. 'Do you want to know what happens next, or not?'

Geenie nodded.

'Now we come to the good part.' Diana sat back on the bed. 'I'm struck by the thunderbolt, you see—'

'What thunderbolt?'

'The thunderbolt of love. I'm struck with love, and I just sit and stare at you, like this.' Placing her hand flat on her heart, she opened her eyes as wide as they would go, then closed them slowly and let her neck go limp before saying, in a deep voice, 'I am inspired as never before – inspired by love.'

'Oh,' said Geenie, 'that's good.'

Diana smiled. 'Isn't it?'

'Do you kiss me then?'

'Not yet. In the next scene, you're kneeling on the floor, scrubbing, like this.' Diana got down on all fours and rubbed furiously at the rug with her knuckles, pausing to wipe her forehead in a long sweeping gesture.

'We'll need some props for that,' said Geenie.

'Of course – that's your department. So you're scrubbing, working really hard, and I – the great poet John Cross – come up behind you and start reading my love poem.'

'How does it go?'

Here Diana looked suddenly shy. She sat back on her heels and tucked her frizzy hair behind one ear. 'I haven't finished it yet.'

'Never mind. What then?'

'Then I kiss you, passionately.'

'Show me,' said Geenie.

'All right.' Diana stood, readjusted her knickers and vest, and took a step towards her. Geenie closed her eyes and waited.

'Don't close your eyes yet.'

'Why not?'

'We have to build up to the *moment.*' Diana stretched out a hand and let it rest on Geenie's shoulder. She moistened her cushiony top lip with her tongue and opened her mouth very slightly. Geenie began to giggle.

'You can't laugh when we perform it for real, you know.'

Geenie covered her mouth with one hand and took a deep breath.

'In fact,' Diana said, 'when I touch you, I think you should swoon.'

'I can do that.'

'Go on then.'

Geenie closed her eyes, put her forearm to her brow and let her body buckle. As she went down, Diana caught her, spreading one hand flat in the centre of Geenie's back, cupping the other beneath her naked neck, and pulling her close. 'Pretend you love me,' she said, moving in for the kiss.

When it came, the kiss was dry and hard, and both girls stayed completely still as their lips locked. Geenie squeezed her eyes tighter and wondered if she really would faint: her knees were weak, her neck twisted, her heartbeat loud in her ears; she could taste the sweat on Diana's top lip. At first, she held onto her friend with a fierce grip to keep from falling, but as the kiss went on, Geenie let her lips go soft, and she found herself relaxing into Diana's arms.

Finally, Diana came up for air. 'Very good,' she said, a little breathlessly. 'I'll tell Daddy that we have a play to show them on Friday morning.' She reached past Geenie, grabbed her skirt from the bed and began to dress. Geenie did the same, her fingers slipping on the mother-of-pearl buttons on her blouse, her heart still jumping inside her vest.

… Thirty …

When Kitty arrived at Woodbury Avenue on Wednesday afternoon, Lou was waiting for her in the doorway, wearing a lilac crepe frock with matching hat, and cradling a lilac bag beneath her arm as if it were a small, fashionable dog. She peered through the net which half-covered her eyes with lilac crosses. 'We're going to the White Hart for tea.'

'Now?'

'It's your birthday, isn't it?'

Kitty hadn't expected her sister to remember. 'Tomorrow. Tomorrow's my birthday.'

Lou shifted her bag to the other arm and stroked it. 'It's nearly your birthday then, isn't it? I've booked a taxicab and everything.'

'Where's Bob?'

Lou didn't answer this. Instead, she looked her sister up and down and said, 'I'd have thought you'd make more of an effort, on your birthday.'

'It's not my birthday,' Kitty replied, running a hand over the skirt of her lily-print frock. 'Anyway, Lou, I really need to borrow your sewing machine this afternoon. Can't we go another day?'

Lou tutted. 'Don't be an idiot. Come inside. We'd better get you kitted out, quick.'

.....

In the back of the cab, Lou stared out of the window at the sun-stunned streets. Her face was flattened by white powder, and her hands wouldn't stay still. It was unlike Lou, Kitty thought, to keep fidgeting with her hat, her gloves, her handbag; but all the way to the hotel, Lou's fingers were busy with some clasp, seam, or pin. Kitty held on instinctively to the straw hat attached to her hair. It was pink, to match the pink frock with the white bib front Lou had donated to Kitty for the afternoon. The frock was too small for Lou ('that's what marriage does for you,' she'd said), but wasn't too bad a fit for Kitty. The crispness of the organdie on her skin made up for the slight sagginess around her bosom. Lou had also persuaded her to experiment with her Tangine lipstick, and Kitty could taste the stale-sweetness of it on her mouth.

'Perhaps I could run up the costumes when we get back,' Kitty thought aloud.

'You'd better not.' Lou patted her handbag. 'I'll have to get on – Bob's dinner...'

'I won't get in the way.'

'Why are you so set on these bloody costumes?'

Kitty said nothing.

'It's not like they do much for you.'

'It means a lot to Miss Geenie.' Kitty looked at her sister. 'I don't give a fig for the other one, but, well, you have to feel a bit sorry for Geenie.'

Lou huffed. 'Poor little miss millionaire. It must be awful, having all that money, and never having to lift a finger.'

'She's lonely, though,' said Kitty.

'Aren't we all,' Lou stated.

.....

It was cool and silent in the hotel reception. Yellow chintz armchairs were plumped and ready, but no one was sitting in them. A gleaming coffee table displayed a fan of expensive magazines, untouched. Kitty stepped across the deep pile towards the woman at the desk, whose head was bowed over a snowy white register.

'It's through here,' said Lou, taking her sister's arm and leading her through a pair of glass doors.

They came into a large, light room which smelled strongly of beeswax. Pictures of ships on stormy seas covered the walls, and in the middle of the room was a grand piano. All the tables, each one displaying a tight white rose arrangement at its centre, were empty. An electric fan at the back of the room puffed over a parlour palm, but apart from that, the air was absolutely still.

Lou took the table next to the open windows, sticking her face in front of the fan for a moment and blowing out her cheeks before sitting down. 'This place is like the morgue. The morgue in a heatwave. Not very good for the dead, this kind of temperature. We'll have a cocktail, liven things up. Where's the boy?'

'Tea for me, please,' said Kitty, noticing the softness of the cushioned chair, the yellow and scarlet monogrammed antimacassar: WHH, the two Hs entwined in fish-bone stitch. 'And cake. Victoria sponge, if they have it.'

'No you won't. You'll have a White Lady with me. It's your birthday.'

'Not until tomorrow.'

'Where did you get your damned uptightness from? It's certainly not from Mother.'

A waiter crossed the carpet noiselessly and stood over them, one hand behind his back. He was young, with a spray of spots up one side of his neck, but his cuffs were crisp, and his face did not move.

'Two White Ladies, a pot of tea and some cakes, please,' said Lou, the dots of rouge on her cheeks crinkling.

'Would Madam like the afternoon selection? Or a particular cake?'

Lou hesitated. She looked down at the tablecloth, then enquired in a quieter voice, 'How much is the afternoon selection?'

The waiter's top lip twitched very slightly. 'The afternoon selection is three shillings, Madam. It consists of a selection of our best sandwiches, cakes and dainties.'

'All right,' said Lou, looking up at him with a wide smile. 'That's what we'll have.'

'Very good.' The waiter moved away as silently as he'd arrived.

Kitty leant across the table and touched her sister's fingers. 'Can you afford it, Lou?' she whispered.

'Of course I can,' snapped Lou, taking a packet of Player's from her handbag and lighting one. 'It's always good to check the price in these places beforehand, that's all. Then they don't swindle you when it comes to the bill.' She drummed her painted fingernails along the tablecloth and blew smoke towards the windows. 'So. What's new in Bohemia?'

Kitty had been dying to tell someone – anyone – about the row over the salmon for days. But she couldn't think of a way to explain it that wouldn't make her sister angry, so instead she offered, '*He* left for a few days, all of a sudden.

It was quite peculiar.'

Lou took a long drag on her cigarette.

Kitty couldn't help adding, 'I think it might have had something to do with me.'

Lou gave a short laugh. 'What could it have had to do with you?'

'Maybe it didn't. But she shouted at me – and he didn't agree with it – and then, next day, he left.'

Their cocktails arrived in long-stemmed glasses. Lou thanked the waiter, who looked over their heads and gave a quick, stiff bow before retreating.

Kitty took a sip of her drink. The gin scalded her throat. 'It was all over nothing, really…'

'Don't give me that. What happened?'

Kitty swallowed another mouthful of White Lady. Her insides were suddenly cooled by the alcohol. It was lovely, like a cold, soft tongue flicking through you.

'Something about the fish being overdone. She got very upset over it.'

'What did she say?'

Having first checked over each shoulder to see if anyone else had come in, Kitty leaned across the table towards her sister and whispered, 'Fucking incinerated fish.'

Lou almost spat out her drink. 'No! She said that?'

Kitty giggled. 'They had this dinner party, and she went off her head, saying I'd overcooked the salmon – she called me in and said that it was—'

'Fucking incinerated?' asked Lou, wide-eyed. Kitty nodded. Both sisters took another drink, and then exploded with laughter.

Kitty was laughing so hard that she didn't notice the waiter had taken up position behind her chair. 'Oh!' she said, and giggled again as he placed the three-tiered silver tray and a silver teapot on the table.

'Will you require anything else, Madam?' he asked the air.

Lou shook her head.

When he'd gone, Kitty hissed, 'Did he hear us?'

'Don't think so,' said Lou, bypassing the sandwiches and helping herself to a cream slice. 'Happy twentieth birthday.' She held up her glass in a toast, and they clinked and drank. A happy flush of gin spread from Kitty's stomach to her thighs.

'So he didn't like it, then, when she shouted?'

Kitty's hand hovered over the sandwiches. Egg and cress, tomato paste, ham and mustard. Each one as flat as an envelope.

'I don't think he did, no,' she said, choosing a glistening éclair instead. 'He apologised to me.'

'He *apologised*?'

'Yes.' Kitty took a bite of éclair and licked a dollop of cream from her lip.

'He apologised to *you*?'

'Yes.' Two bites and the éclair was gone. She moved on to the pineapple meringue.

Lou sighed. 'He sounds *gallant.* I wish Bob was more like that. I don't think he's ever said sorry to me. Not once.' She pushed her plate away and lit another Player's.

'He is – polite,' said Kitty, through a mouthful of sugary crumbs. 'Very polite.' Then she dared to add, 'And thoughtful. He's the sensitive type, you know.'

Lou was staring at the tablecloth. 'Bob's never apologised. Not even now. After everything.'

'What do you mean?'

'Nothing.' Lou drained her cocktail.

Kitty swallowed the last of the meringue and eyed the

thin slice of strawberry gateau still on the silver tray. Before she could get it onto her plate, though, Lou sighed again, loudly.

'What's the matter?' asked Kitty, abandoning the gateau.

'Sorry.' Lou put a hand to her mouth and shook her head. 'I suppose I might as well tell you.'

'Tell me what?'

'I didn't mean to mention it, not now.'

'Tell me what, Lou?'

Lou opened and closed the clasp of her handbag. 'Bob and me have been having a spot of trouble.'

'What kind of trouble?'

'The marriage kind.' She smiled weakly. 'We might – separate. For a bit.'

Kitty stared at her sister.

'He's going to live – somewhere else.' Lou looked out of the window. 'With someone else.' She ground out her cigarette. 'I'll be glad to get shot of the old bastard, won't I?' Then she added, 'Sorry to spoil your birthday.'

Picking up the silver teapot, Kitty poured tea into Lou's cup, added milk and two knobs of sugar, and pushed it over to her sister. 'It's not my birthday.'

'Fucking incinerated fish,' said Lou, with a dry laugh.

.....

They travelled back to Woodbury Avenue in silence until, passing by the cemetery, Lou put a hand on the back of the driver's seat. 'You can drop us here, please.'

They hadn't been here together since their mother's funeral. Kitty stood on the path, watching a heatwave shimmer over the rows of gravestones fanning out in neat lines on either side of them. It was a new cemetery, and the trees had yet to grow large enough to offer any shade. The smell of the rubber factory, which was just behind the cemetery wall, was at its worst in this spot, and the sickly, burning aroma rose around them.

Lou pulled the net of her hat down lower. 'I hate cemeteries,' she said. 'Especially ones that stink.'

Kitty scanned the rows of crosses and slabs. She knew exactly where the grave was, but she wondered if her sister would. As they walked, Lou's heel caught in the crack of a paving stone. 'Bugger it.' She twisted round and yanked the shoe from her foot. 'It's come right off,' she said, showing the damage to Kitty.

'You could stick it back on.'

'It'll just come off again.' Clenching the heel in one hand, Lou limped on, and Kitty followed. To her surprise, Lou went straight to the right plot, over in the left-hand corner, by the wall nearest the factory. There was a small stone which read: *Douglas Allen, 1875–1921; Mary Allen, 1881–1934; At Peace with God.* The sisters stood before it in silence. It didn't matter how many times you read it, Kitty thought, it never became any more familiar, or comforting. She considered uttering her usual quick prayer – something about hoping they were both in heaven, and asking God to look over them – but she didn't want to kneel, not in front of Lou, and not in the organdie frock.

'It's been two years, almost,' said Lou.

'I know.'

'She would've been disappointed with me, wouldn't she? Her eldest daughter – the divorcee.'

Kitty remembered the way their mother had always referred to Bob as *The School Teacher*. It was a kind of reverence, but also a kind of scorn. 'She'd have wanted you to be happy.'

'No she wouldn't. She would've wanted what looked best on her.' Lou turned to Kitty. 'Not that she had to put up with Dad, did she? He went and died before she could get really fed up with him.'

Kitty said nothing.

'Listen,' said Lou, suddenly grabbing Kitty's elbow. 'Bob's going to let me stop on at the house, and pay me a bit. It's all agreed. I've just got to take the blame in the divorce. He gets to keep his reputation, but I get to keep the house. It's the least he can do, considering he's the one who's gone off with that old trout... do you know what he said to me? That he'd found paradise!' The net on Lou's hat quivered with anger. 'As if he'd know paradise if it came up and bit him on the arse.' She jabbed her broken heel in the air. 'But what I thought – just last night – what I thought was, why be on my own? Why be on my own when Kitty could come back?'

'Come back?'

'To live at the house. With me.'

Kitty took a step away from her sister. 'But – my job – the cottage—'

'You don't have to live in, do you? Anyway, you could get another, now you've the experience. The Macklows'—'

'I hated it at the Macklows'.'

'At least it was work. It got you out of the house, didn't it?'

Kitty gave a laugh. 'I still had to go home every day and get Mother's tea, while you were—' She stopped. The sisters faced each other. Lou's cheeks were puffy with heat and her lipstick had a tiny crumb of cake stuck to it.

'While I was what?'

Kitty concentrated on the crumb and kept her voice even. 'Married. In your own house. With your own things.

Away from us.'

They were silent for a while. Then Lou said, 'She had an all right life, when you look at it.' She gestured towards their mother's name on the gravestone with her handbag. 'Did what she liked, didn't she?'

'Not in the end, she didn't,' said Kitty. Then she added, feeling the heat and the gin in her limbs, 'I know I should have fetched the doctor, but you should have come sooner. We were waiting for you.'

Lou turned her face away. It was a minute before Kitty realised her sister was quietly crying.

There was a long pause before Kitty managed to say, 'I'm sorry about Bob,' and hand Lou her hankie.

Lou sniffed and nodded. 'Come back to the house with me?'

'What about Bob's dinner?'

'He's already gone. I just didn't know how to tell you, earlier.' Lou blew her nose loudly, three times. Kitty recognised the sound from their childhood: Lou's three blows in the morning, and three before bed.

'That was loud enough to wake the dead,' Kitty said.

Lou smiled briefly. 'You'll think over what I said? About coming to live at the house?'

'Maybe.'

The sun was getting lower and the yellow evening light was sneaking into their eyes. Kitty took Lou's arm, and the two of them walked back to Woodbury Avenue together, Lou hobbling, still carrying her broken heel in her hand.

.....

It was late when Kitty got back to the cottage. With the Pierrot outfits she'd run up on Lou's Singer bundled under one arm, she let herself in the back door. There was no light on in the kitchen, and she almost tripped over Blotto, who was snoozing on the mat. The dog groaned and stretched before tucking his head back into his chest and letting out a long, creaky sigh. Kitty turned on the kitchen light and looked up the hallway: no sign of any life there, either, so she fetched herself a glass of water and sat at the kitchen table to drink it down in large, grateful gulps. As she drank, she stared at the lantern's trimmed tassel. No one else seemed to have noticed that it was much shorter than before. She wondered, now, if she could remove the whole thing without anyone saying anything. The kitchen would be much brighter in the evenings if she did.

She wiped her mouth, took off her shoes, rolled down her stockings, laid her bare feet on the cool flags and closed her eyes. It had been a long evening, and she'd been glad of work to do while listening to Lou's story of Bob's affair with the older woman. Apparently she was a widow who lived in one of the big houses by the lake; they'd met at the local historical society and shared a passion for Queen Elizabeth. Lou said he was welcome to her, that she was glad to be rid of him, but as she spoke, she'd kept plucking at her collar and cuffs, and smoked a chain of cigarettes. Kitty had tried to listen while focusing on getting the seams of the outfits straight. They'd been quite simple – a bit like baggy pyjama-suits, with wide circular collars attached. All she had to do now was make the pompoms. She was sure she had some black wool somewhere in her work-box. She could even, she thought, get Miss Geenie on to making the pompoms herself. The girl might enjoy that.

After rinsing her glass in the sink, she turned off the light and opened the door to her room. Although it was quite dark, she knew immediately that someone was in there.

'Kitty – forgive me.'

On hearing his voice, she dropped the Pierrot costumes to the floor.

'It's the most unforgivable intrusion – please forgive me.'

She took a couple of deep breaths. She could see the outline of him now, sitting on her bed in his shirtsleeves. And here she was, standing before him, with no stockings on and a pile of silly costumes round her bare feet.

She snapped on the light and he flinched. His sleeves were rolled up to the elbow, and his hands – those beautiful long fingers – touched his hair, hiding his face.

'Forgive me,' he said again.

'What do you want, Mr Crane?'

He nodded. 'Quite. What do I want? What do I want?' He hung his head, his hands still in his hair.

'Have you been – drinking?' She knew he hadn't, but she couldn't think of anything else to say. A man was in her room without her permission, and she should be outraged.

He lifted his head. 'Kitty,' he said, and his voice was suddenly loud and deep, as if he were addressing an audience, 'Kitty, when I came here the other evening, I wasn't entirely straight with you.'

She should scream, shouldn't she? Scream and throw him out.

'I didn't say what I meant to say.' He nodded his head again. 'Yes, that's it. I didn't express what I wanted – needed – to express.'

Kitty didn't move. She was watching those fingers. They were on his knees now, each one evenly spread over the thinning fabric as he sat up very straight and nodded again. 'What I want, what I'd like very much, is for you to sit here beside me for a minute.'

He looked at her for a long moment, his eyes steady, his

face pale and thin in the electric light, and Kitty knew she'd have to do as he asked. She was shaking as she sat on the edge of the bed, her stomach pulling inwards as if a thread were being stroked and gathered inside her.

'Let me see your ears,' he said.

She looked at him.

'I've never seen them – the whole of them.' His fingers reached out and touched her ordinary hair, and he moved his face close to her neck. His breath was on her exposed skin, and she thought of how even she had never really looked there, behind her ear, in that hidden place. They were both very still, and the thread in her stomach pulled tighter. What was he seeing as he looked there, at that secret spot of white skin, which must be knobbled and strange? What shape were her ears? She tried to picture them, their folds and bumps, but could not. She felt a sudden urge to laugh as he moved closer, but then his face was in her hair, his lips on her earlobe, and the thread in her stomach snapped and everything came loose.

'They're lovely.'

'Mr Crane—'

'Please call me George.'

His lips touched her again, this time just below her ear, and her hand went up, first to her own throat, then to his. She wrapped her fingers around the back of his neck, and she held his head there while he kissed her.

··· Thirty-one ···

The letters were finished. It was Thursday morning, and Ellen sat back in her chair, flexed her aching fingers, and gazed out of the library window. On the lawn, the girls were laughing together. A minute ago Geenie had looked like she was scrubbing the grass clean: she'd been on her hands and knees, knuckles working the dusty ground, while Diana stood over her, proclaiming something with one arm stretched elegantly into the air. Some game or other, Ellen thought: it was good to see her daughter so engaged with another girl; it certainly made a change from hanging around rooms, waiting for her mother to do or say something. Not that Geenie had been hanging around much since they'd had the conversation about James's death. Ellen wished she'd been able to say more to her daughter on that subject, but somehow there were no words for it. And there was also the sense, she reflected now, taking another swig of her gin and it – a pre-lunch drink wasn't so out of the ordinary, was it? – that James wasn't much to do with Geenie. He wasn't her father, after all. He was Ellen's lover. His death was her business.

Pulling the final page from the typewriter, she set it on the pile. Then she finished her drink, pushed back her chair, and carried the manuscript from the room.

She was so surprised to find Crane's studio empty that she marched directly to where the girls were playing on the lawn. They saw her coming and Geenie pressed her lips together.

'Where's your father?' Ellen asked Diana.

For an answer she received a shrug and a smile. She looked from girl to girl, and Geenie slid behind Diana and began to laugh.

'What's the matter with you?'

'She's just excited,' said Diana, 'about the play.'

'What play?'

'The play I've written. We're performing it tomorrow morning. Eleven o'clock sharp. On the lawn.'

'Everyone's invited,' said Geenie, peeping over her friend's shoulder.

Ellen gazed at Diana, and the girl gazed back, her dark eyes amused, her face composed. Eventually Ellen turned and walked back to the studio, leaving the girls whispering behind her like lovers.

.....

Inside, she sat in Crane's armchair with the manuscript on her lap and wished she'd thought to fetch another gin. She had a notion that she would wait here until Crane returned, and she might need another drink. Ellen hadn't given much thought to what she would do when he did arrive; she only knew that she wanted him to see the letters, now they were finished. They'd managed to avoid each other almost completely since he'd got back from London on Monday night. By the time he'd climbed into their bed in the dark, she'd had time to think, and her urge to scream and slap him very hard had waned. Anyway, what would she have said, exactly? *I was snooping in your wastepaper basket and I found this*? Or, *I was looking for the novel you obviously haven't written and I came across these – words*? She couldn't admit she'd been prying, and even if she did, he would have said it was just a poem, something he'd made up. So she'd clenched her body into a tight bundle on the edge of the bed and pretended to sleep.

Crane had hidden in his studio for most of the next day, and she'd locked herself in the library, brooding over the letters, drinking too much gin, and then falling asleep in her chair, waking to find herself covered in sweat and ravenously hungry. At dinner she'd concentrated on filling her gasping stomach with Kitty's admittedly rather tasty chicken pie while Crane's eye twitched like some trapped insect. But by Wednesday morning Ellen was thinking of going to Robin again. After lunch, during which Crane revealed his busy schedule of talks for the Party, telling her they were to begin next week in Rochdale (where was that? she hadn't even bothered to ask), she'd taken the Lanchester into Petersfield and parked by the market square. Walking down the lane to the hairdressers' shop, smelling the mixture of carbolic and blood from the butcher's open door, she told herself that perhaps she would just book another appointment after all, then go straight back and face Crane and tell him it was over. Or perhaps she could cry a little, and relations would thaw. But when she walked through the door and saw Robin sitting at the back of the empty shop, a penny paper spread across his solid knees, she'd known exactly what would happen. If Crane's blood was *heavy with wanting* for the cook, why shouldn't she spend a little time with Robin? In the back room, he'd kept the wireless on, and his knowledgeable hands had slowly stroked her breasts to the rhythms of the *Afternoon Band Hour*. Just as he was sliding his fingers beneath her French knickers, she stopped him and said, 'I want you for the whole night.'

It had been expensive, of course. There was the room at the Royal Oak in Midhurst, where – after she'd telephoned Crane and told him she was too drunk to drive home and was spending the night at Laura's – they'd signed in as Mr and Mrs Crane; and Robin had still charged by the hour. But it had been worth it, she decided, as she rose from the chair to place the manuscript on Crane's desk, over his latest copy of the *Daily Worker*. It had been worth it, because since she'd got back to the cottage at ten o'clock this morning (and Crane hadn't been anywhere to be seen, even then), her head had been marvellously clear. Clear enough to finish work on the manuscript, and to add a note between the title page and the first letter:

To the memory of James Holt, my greatest love.
With this book, I ask for forgiveness.

– Ellen Steinberg

James's memory was the most important thing, after all. It was the thing she had to keep safe from now on. Crane had distracted her from it. At least, that was how it had seemed when she'd typed the dedication. She could always, she thought, change things later.

Leaving the pile of paper on the desk, she walked out of the studio and into the sunshine. She wouldn't wait for Crane, she decided. Let him find the letters there, just as she'd found his scrap of a poem. She wouldn't even wait for lunch. She'd drive into Petersfield straight away, buy flowers for the cottage from Gander's, perhaps stop at the White Hart for a drink, and then, if she still felt like it, drop by the hairdressers' once more.

... Thirty-two ...

Kitty woke early on Thursday, the morning of her birthday, still wearing Lou's pink organdie frock. The skirt was pressed against her thighs, as if something were pulling it back. She reached behind and smiled to herself as she felt Mr Crane's knee there, pinning her frock to the bed. It wasn't much past dawn: the birds were raucous outside her window, their songs clambering into the air. And he was still here. He was still here. She tried to stay unmoving on the edge of the bed so as not to disturb him. He was still here. She closed her eyes again. All night the feeling of his kiss was there, even when she'd turned from him and eventually reached something like sleep. They'd kissed until her lips were dry and her neck tired. Sometimes the kisses had been long and light; at other times he'd kissed her so hard she'd felt his teeth on hers. His hands were in her hair, on her throat, then his arms were crushing her to him and she thought, this is what they mean when they say *breathless*. He'd kept murmuring 'lovely', and she wasn't sure if he meant her or the kisses. Eventually he'd lain back on the counterpane and said 'come to bed now', and she'd frozen, thinking that he must want her to undress and not knowing how she could possibly start. But instead he pulled her to his side and cradled her head on his chest, and then he'd slept. Kitty stayed awake for hours, listening to his breath, inhaling the scent of him and staring at his chin, at all the little ticks of stubble there, so close to her face. And here he still was. She still had him. In her small room, on her small bed.

She opened her eyes again. It was already light and warm in the room. The Pierrot costumes were on the floor, where she'd dropped them last night. She wished the picture of her parents wasn't so visible from the bed. Her mother's face stared directly down at her, and she shifted her eyes away. The clock on the chest of drawers said six. She closed her eyes again and inched a little closer to him. No one would be up before nine. There were hours to go. Hours of just lying here, knowing he was next to her. If she could move slowly enough, she might even be able to turn over and watch his face while he slept.

Then the thought hit her hard and she sprang upright: Mrs Steinberg. *Fucking incinerated fish* would be nothing compared to this. She stole a look over her shoulder at the sleeping man on her sheets, taking in the length of his legs, the way one hand was thrown over his head, the muscle of his upper arm filling his shirt sleeve, the shapely wrist resting on her pillow. Just one more kiss, she thought, and then I'll tell him he has to go. She bent close and studied his face: the long nose, the black lashes, the slightly sunken cheeks. She was just about to touch his forehead with her lips when his eyes flicked open.

'Good morning,' he said.

Kitty drew back.

He gave a huge yawn and stretched his arms. 'I slept so well. I haven't slept so well in ages.'

Sitting on the edge of the mattress, Kitty fixed her eyes

on the door and waited for him to move from her bed. It would all be over soon: he'd get up, stretch again, say something about what a night of madness it had been, he didn't know what he'd been thinking, it was an unforgivable intrusion and could she forgive him, could she? Then he'd walk out without waiting for her answer, and she'd have to pretend nothing had happened, put his tea down without glancing at him, watch Mrs Steinberg casually touch his thigh beneath the table, listen to them laughing together in the sitting room, picture her dancing for him while that man's sweet, rasping voice unravelled from the gramophone. She didn't think she could do it. There was nothing else for it: she'd have to go back to Lou's.

'Kitty? Did you – ah – sleep well?'

'I think you should go.'

'What time is it?'

'After six. I think you should go.' It wouldn't be so bad at Woodbury Avenue, without Bob there to rattle the newspaper in her direction.

Mr Crane sat up.

'You should go,' she said again, keeping her voice low.

He rubbed his eyes. 'What's wrong?'

'You should go. You should go, otherwise – she'll know.'

He came to the edge of the bed, placed his hands on her shoulders and turned her towards him. One collar was dented, striking him in the chin, and his shirt was badly creased. His eye gave a twitch. 'Listen to me. It doesn't matter. None of that matters, not really.'

She twisted away from him. 'Not to you, maybe—'

He reached for her again. 'Kitty. Ellen – Mrs Steinberg – didn't come home last night.'

'How do you know?'

'She telephoned me. She stayed at my sister's house last

night. And she'll have the most dreadful hangover this morning, so I'd be surprised if she came back before lunchtime.'

'Oh.' Kitty stared at the floor. 'You should still go though, shouldn't you?'

He smiled. 'Let's go for a bicycle ride.'

'Now?'

'Now.'

'I don't have a bicycle.'

'You can borrow Geenie's. She's almost as tall as you. I'll adjust the saddle.'

Kitty let out a laugh. 'At six in the morning?'

'Why not? You told me, didn't you, that time I met you on the road. Don't you remember? You said you liked riding bicycles.'

'What about the girls? The breakfast…'

'We'll be back before then,' he said, springing from the bed and and holding out his hands to her. 'I promise.'

.....

It was exactly as she remembered: the breeze on your cheeks as you pedalled, the way the saddle made you sit upright and almost proud, the wheels throwing the road carelessly behind. Even now, the hedgerows were drying out in the early morning sun and heat was beginning to rise from the asphalt. Yellow wheat danced in the fields on either side of them, but the hills in front were a flat, grey green, yet to be touched by the sun. Mr Crane, still in his creased shirt and with his slick of dark hair splayed on the crown of his head, cycled on while Kitty kept a short way behind, in case anyone should see them. Not that she could think of any reason she should be cycling at this time in the morning at all, let alone so close behind Mr Crane, who was, to outsiders' eyes at least, her master. What was he in her eyes, then? Was he – she dared hardly think the word – her lover? Her lover, who was also a poet, although he didn't look like one. She smiled to herself at that.

When they came into the village, she saw it was deserted, the High Street stretching emptily ahead and the windows of the houses utterly blind, and she pushed down hard on the pedals to overtake him, calling quietly over her shoulder, 'Follow me.'

As she opened the gate to the churchyard, it seemed smaller than she remembered. She didn't look at him as they abandoned their bicycles by the wall and walked through the damp grass, past the Fetherstonhaughs' private enclosure, towards the back of the church. It was very cool here, just as Kitty remembered it had been on her picnics with Lou years ago. She gave a shiver, partly because of the cold dampness of the place, and partly because she knew what would happen if she kept walking deeper amongst the graves, away from the road and the church, to the stones in the back corner, by the flint wall. He was close behind her, and she knew he was watching her body move in the crumpled organdie frock, and he'd seen that place behind her ear which no one else – not even she – had seen; but she was going to follow through.

She stopped when she found what she was looking for, a long headstone beneath a large yew tree. Mary Belcher, who had died young and been alone underground all this time. There it was, the grave where she and Lou used to sit, still lying flat in the grass, splattered with lichen.

'This place,' she began, 'I used to think it was haunted.'

He was approaching her, a smile on his lips.

'I used to think,' she said, 'that the devil might hide here.'

'And does he?'

'Perhaps.'

He looked behind him in mock fear. 'Well. It's – ah – just you and me at the moment.'

She moved closer to the grave. The ivy and moss were thicker now, but the place had that same stillness, that same smell of mould.

'Today's my birthday,' she said, quietly.

Mr Crane stopped smiling, and for a moment she wondered if she'd said the wrong thing, but then he stepped forward, took hold of her waist and kissed her, pulling her in so close she could feel all the buttons on his shirt pressing through the bib front of her frock. Inching her hands down his straight spine, she felt for that dimple of flesh she'd seen when she'd spied on him getting dressed, and, feeling the indent, she tugged his shirt from his trousers, reached behind his braces and found his soft place. He gave a little moan as her fingers touched his naked skin. Thinking of Lou stretching out with her knees showing, waiting for someone to come along, Kitty broke away from him. 'Wait,' she said.

Mr Crane watched as she lay down on Mary Belcher's grave. The cold stone sent a shocking jolt through her skin, but she hitched up the hem of her frock and extended a hand to him. 'Here,' she said. 'Here.'

... Thirty-three ...

It was past seven o'clock when Ellen returned with half a dozen bunches of canna lilies on the back seat of the car, a gnawing hunger in her stomach, having skipped lunch, and a buzz in her thighs from her hour with Robin. Getting out of the car, she groaned to herself as she noticed Crane waiting in the front porch. She gathered up the lilies so he wouldn't be able to see her face and pushed past him without a word.

He followed her into the sitting room and closed the door behind them. 'I need to speak with you.'

Ellen stood in the middle of the room, her arms still full of flowers. '*I* need to put these in water.'

She made for the door, but he blocked the way and clutched her arm. 'Ellen. Please.' His voice was low, his face grey.

She laughed. 'You haven't needed to speak to me for the last few days, Crane; I don't see why you should start now.'

'It has to be now. But not here.'

'You're hurting my elbow.'

'Come for a walk.'

'Don't you think these will look sublime in here, darling?' She pushed the lilies into his face. The over-rich scent rose between them.

'Come for a walk, Ellen.'

'You know I loathe walks.'

He looked at her through the petals. 'Do you? You never said.'

She sighed. 'Does it have to be now?'

He pulled the lilies from her arms, dumped them on the dining table and held the door open.

.....

They crossed the field. Broken ears of wheat poked at Ellen's feet through her peep-toe shoes – there'd been no time to change. Crane walked ahead, saying nothing. His shirt was very creased, and was sticking to his back in streaks.

'Is that a grass stain on your shoulder?'

His hand leapt to the place. 'I was – lying on the lawn, earlier.'

A smear of swallows flew over them, circling and screeching across the field. Ahead, Harting Down was still brightly lit. Its chalk paths, gnarled bushes and scrubby grass glowed in the evening sun.

'When are we going to talk?' she asked. 'I thought it was urgent.'

'When we get to the top.'

She stopped walking then, put her hands on her hips, and was about to refuse, loudly, to climb to the top of that hill. But he ignored her actions and kept walking ahead, and she had a feeling that if she didn't follow him he would simply continue on his own. Then this thing, whatever it was, would never be said. So she trudged behind him, watching the sweat grow on his back, her feet swelling, her head beginning to pound heavily. Picking another sharp stone from her shoe, she wished she'd had time to wash the smell of Robin from her hands.

When they'd passed the little patch of woodland and gone through the gate, they reached the narrow chalk track. But instead of following it, taking the gentler route up the hill, Crane broke from the path and began climbing straight up the grassy slope, using his hands to help him.

'Crane!' shouted Ellen. 'This is ridiculous!' But he continued his ascent, almost leaping up the hill with irritating sprightliness.

Puffing with the effort, she followed. Her fingers clutched at dry grass, her feet slipped on stones. Once she fell, scraped both knees on the dirt and cried out for him. But he did not look back. Her head began to feel heavy and light at the same time: the blood still pulsed in her temples, but there was also a pressure in her nose which made her vision swim a little. Her throat was dry (she'd had nothing since those gin and its earlier on), her stomach empty, and the buzz in her thighs had become a dull ache. 'Crane!' she croaked, but still he pressed ahead.

When the hill had levelled out a little, she stopped to rest, sitting on the grass and gazing down at the village. She'd never seen the cottage from this high up before; from here it looked compact and insignificant: no more than a brown lump in the landscape. Inside, she thought, Kitty would be in the kitchen, fretting over potatoes; Arthur would be dozing in his shed (she knew he spent a lot of time doing this, but she'd never objected, since she only paid him for a few hours a day anyway); and Geenie – where would Geenie be? She realised that she had no idea. Her daughter might be anywhere at all.

'Crane!' Ellen shouted up to his disappearing legs. 'No

further! Do you hear me? No further!'

She waited. She wouldn't allow herself to fully imagine what he might be about to say, when he'd worked himself up sufficiently; but she told herself that if it looked as though he were about to break it off, she would do so first by pointing out that she knew all about him lusting after the cook, and she, Ellen Steinberg, was not a woman to tolerate such betrayal.

She heard him stepping carefully down the slope towards her, and knew he would be avoiding treading on any flowers.

'It's really unforgivably dramatic of you to drag me all the way up here,' she said.

He sat down next to her, breathing hard.

To her surprise, he didn't pause long to catch his breath. Instead, he began to speak almost immediately. 'I'm glad you've typed James's letters,' he said, taking little gulps of air between words, staring all the time at the village below. 'Thank you for letting me see them. They're exceptionally interesting and I'm sure they'll be published.'

'Yes—'

'And I think the dedication you've added is wholly apt, and absolutely right.'

'Yes – I wanted to talk to *you* about that—'

'There's no baby, Ellen, is there?'

The possibility of lying to him flashed into her mind. But how much time would that buy her?

'No,' she said. 'There's no baby.'

'Then I think we should part.'

She tried to speak but he continued in the same quiet tone, his eyes still fixed on the village below. 'It's been over a year now, hasn't it, since James died, and I've given it a lot of thought and I think now is a good time to end it. We both need to move on. I'm going to leave as soon as I can.' Then he added, in a warmer tone, 'I'm sorry, Ellen.'

He was so decisive, so calm, and he'd stolen her thunder so completely, that she almost laughed. She'd never heard him sound so resolute. It was as if he were reading out a letter he'd carefully composed weeks before.

Ellen gripped a handful of grass, pulled it from its roots and tossed it into the air. 'What have you been doing all summer?'

His head drooped a little. 'What do you mean?'

'Well. You certainly haven't been writing a novel.'

'No,' he said. 'I haven't...'

'Any poetry?'

'Not really.'

'Well,' she said. 'That's that, then.'

'That's what?'

'It's all been a waste of time, hasn't it? Being here, I mean. It's been a colossal waste of time for you.'

'Of course it hasn't.' He was looking at her now, but she refused to meet his gaze. 'I've been with you—'

She snorted.

'And I've been – ah – reading. Getting ready. Preparing myself for more important work. For the Party...'

She pounced. 'So *that's* where my money's been going. The development of the damned Bolsheviks. And there was me thinking I was a patron of the arts.'

'Ellen—' he reached for her hand, but she snatched it away.

There was a pause before she said, 'I meant what I wrote, you know, in the dedication.'

'I know you did. I know James was the love of your life—'

'Not that. I meant what I wrote about forgiveness. About asking for forgiveness.'

He sighed. 'Ellen, you shouldn't waste time with guilt. After all, we didn't do much, did we, until after his death – no one could blame you for getting on with life.'

She turned to him. 'I knew he was still drunk,' she said. 'I knew it, and I let them operate.'

Crane stared at her.

'Do you understand? It was my fault, George.' Her voice had become high and shaky. 'James's death was my fault, and Geenie knows it.'

He shook his head and put his hand over hers, gripping her fingers tightly. 'Geenie loves you,' he said. 'She loves you, Ellen.'

Suddenly there was an immense pealing of church bells. Thursday practice had begun. The chimes rose and fell, scattering sound over the village and echoing around the valley. Ellen had always hated the clanging racket of those bells, which went on for hours, drowning out her records and prohibiting any decent conversation.

'Damn those bells to hell,' she said.

He squeezed her hand. 'I'm so sorry.'

'You already apologised.'

They sat together, listening to the chimes racing up and down the scales, never quite making a tune.

After a few minutes, she said, 'I'd better get back. It's dinnertime. The girls will be waiting for me.'

He lay on the grass and squinted at the sky. 'I think I'll stay here a bit.'

Running a finger along his cheek, she looked at him, this slim and elegant man who was leaving her. Then she left him there and stumbled down the hill, sprinting in places, slipping on the grass but righting herself before she fell, her face blasted by the last rays of the sun, her stomach groaning for the food that was waiting for her.

... Thirty-four ...

That night, Kitty waited for Mr Crane to come again. She told herself that this was not what she was doing. What she was doing was finishing her embroidery, just as she would have done if nothing had happened. She was sitting on her bed – where he'd held her head to his chest, where he'd kissed her earlobe, and then her neck – with the embroidery in her lap, and she would finish it tonight. Looking towards the window, she saw there was a light in his studio. Her ears strained for the sounds of his door opening, his footsteps along the gravel path. It was half past eleven, and he hadn't had any dinner. Surely he'd come in soon. She threaded her needle with red silk. He hadn't said he would come. He hadn't said anything much as they'd lain in each other's arms on the grave, looking up at the patches of blue flickering between the yew's needles. He'd stroked her hair and said *Kitty. Kitty* he'd said, as if it were a beautiful sound.

She would fill the stripes on the girl's gown with fern stitch. Gripping the needle, she forced it through. The picture was almost complete, and the cloth had stiffened. How could he come? He'd left her as soon as they'd got back to the cottage, saying nothing about when he would see her again. He hadn't been at the dinner table when she'd left the cutlets and retreated without looking anyone in the face, not even Geenie, who'd kept thanking her for the Pierrot costumes. The thread creaked as she made the last stitches on the girl's sash. But how could he not come again? How could he not come, when he'd touched her between her thighs, running his forefinger along that secret nub of skin, building a fierce heat low down in her, a pressure that had to be released. It had been painful when he'd pushed himself into her, and she'd kept her eyes on his face and gripped the sides of the grave as her lower back pressed against the uneven stone. But she wanted it to happen again, now that she knew the pressure was possible, now that she suspected he would be able to release it.

She secured the stitch with another at the back of the calico, removed the frame, shook out the fabric and examined her work. Everything was correct – she'd managed to pick out the faces and the rocks well; the French knots were all even; the loop stitches of the fishing nets were almost perfect; the fern stitching was so close you could hardly see it was stitched at all – but the work seemed flat and bland to Kitty now. What was it *for*? There was no life to it, and no purpose in it: she realised that she'd sewn the whole thing without knowing what its use would be. She flung it down on the bed beside her, scooped her silks back into her workbox and slapped the lid shut.

The pink organdie frock was hanging on the door of her wardrobe. There was a long grass stain down the back of the skirt; a few stitches at the waist were broken, and a button on the bib front had been lost, leaving a trailing thread. She thought of that stray white button, buried somewhere in the grass and the fallen yew needles of the churchyard. Then she drew handfuls of the material to her face, covering her nose and mouth with it, inhaling the dampness of the grave, the salt of his skin, the musk of her own body.

Still holding the frock, she went to the open window and fixed her eyes on the light in the studio. If she concentrated hard enough, he might come. That's what lovers did, wasn't it? Called each other up out of the night. She waited, but there was no sign. There was just the gurgling sigh of the stream, and the willows, huge and quiet in the darkness. She would have to send a signal. Gathering up the frock, she hooked a button hole over the window catch, and threw it out into the night like a flag. For the next hour Kitty stood at her open window, touching the organdie and watching for him. But the light in the studio remained constant.

... Thirty-five ...

On Friday morning, Geenie jumped from her bed to put her costume on again. She'd found both the outfits hanging on the back of her door yesterday afternoon, with a note from Kitty: *Dear Miss Geenie and Miss Diana. Here are your costumes. I could not do the pompoms as I had no wool. Kitty Allen*. She'd called Diana, who'd suggested they 'run through a dress rehearsal' immediately, so they'd clambered into the pyjama-like trousers and white tunics and, after a moment spent congratulating each other on the effect, Diana stood on the bed, declaiming the poem she'd now finished, which was very good and all about the *turmoil of love*. It was full of words like *tranquil* and *tremulous*, and also featured a unicorn. The odd thing was, now that Geenie was standing before the mirror in her costume, she couldn't remember one word of the play; all she could picture was Diana closing her eyes as she moved in for the kiss.

.....

They were to perform in front of the rose bed, which was now in full bloom. They'd placed four kitchen chairs in a row on the cracked lawn, adding cushions as an afterthought; Geenie had fetched a bucket, feather duster and scrubbing brush from Kitty's cupboard beneath the stairs, and now they were in Arthur's shed, which they'd claimed as their dressing room, waiting for the audience to arrive. Geenie had been wearing her costume since she'd got out of bed, and by ten o'clock they'd both been fully made up, their faces sticky with white pan-stick, and two tears pencilled on each cheek. Geenie had drawn Diana's for her with a shaking hand.

'Where is everyone?' asked Diana, peeping round the shed door. 'I hope they're all coming, now we've gone to all this bloody trouble.'

All morning, a large, round pebble had been growing heavier in Geenie's stomach. Now it expanded a little and she gave a whine, like Blotto did when teased with food. When she put a hand on her friend's arm and tried to see past her huge white sleeve, she noticed that her own fingers wouldn't quite keep still. 'We could just do it for Kitty and Arthur,' she suggested, hopefully.

'What would be the point of that?'

'They might like it.'

Diana squealed. 'They're here!' Slamming the door shut, she turned to Geenie. 'Right. This is it. Plan into action.'

Geenie stared at Diana. With great clarity she suddenly saw that the costumes were all wrong. They should have pompoms. The black circles Kitty had sewn on instead were not the same. And Pierrot clowns were supposed to wear black skull caps, weren't they? All they'd done was scrape their hair back and tried to keep it in place with soapy water. Their tears were smudged. And their ruffs were really just wide, flat collars, not the stiffened pleats that real Pierrots wore. 'It's not right,' she said, clutching Diana's arm. 'I don't think we can do it. It's not right—'

'I'm on,' said Diana, pulling away and opening the door.

In the earthy gloom of the shed, Geenie looked at Arthur's neat rows of tools. Perhaps no one would notice if she just stayed in here. It was airless and hot, but she could stand it. It would be better than facing the four adult faces out there in the bright sunshine. She sat on Arthur's deckchair, twisted her hands together and sweated. Outside, Diana was singing *those charming, alarming, blonde women!* in her best Dietrich voice. Geenie closed her eyes and tried to remember what she had to do. Was she supposed to scrub the floor first, or pretend to be dusting?

As Diana was nearing the end of the song, Geenie gathered enough courage to crack open the shed door and take a peek. Her friend was bobbing around on the lawn, kicking her legs in the air. She'd pulled her black hair into a bun and her head looked small and determined on top of her baggy white costume. Ellen, George, Kitty and Arthur were sitting in a row. Her mother looked rather bored, which cheered Geenie a little. George had his hands behind his head and a smile on his face, but his eye was twitching. Kitty's cheeks were very pink, and she was looking at her knees, which was where Arthur's eyes were also fixed.

Diana gave a twirl and a bow, and everyone clapped.

'And now for our main attraction, which is a play written by me, Diana Crane. Ladies and gentlemen, *What the Gardener Saw*.' Diana bowed again and extended an arm towards the shed, her white sleeve gaping in Geenie's direction.

It was too late, now, to escape, and impossible to hide. Geenie's blood fluttered in her veins as she pulled open the door. She knew she *was* walking – she could see her feet stepping across the lawn – but she felt as though she were swimming. Was it the lawn, or the sky, that was wobbling? She stopped beside Diana and anchored her eyes on Kitty, who gave her a small smile.

'Oh!' said her mother. 'You both look so theatrical!'

'*What the Gardener Saw*,' said Diana again in a more urgent tone, gesturing to Geenie. This was a cue, but for what? Everything wobbled again. There was another small round of clapping, and Arthur began to chuckle.

The sun glared. Geenie stood and blinked. If she could just keep standing, things might stop moving around and glowing a ghastly pink.

Diana gave a short sigh before announcing in a loud voice: 'This is Ruby, the housemaid. And I am the great poet, John Cross.'

Arthur chuckled some more. Geenie stood very still, staring at Kitty's flushed face and searching her mind for some sort of command, some memory of the play, of the plan. What had it all been for? She could hardly recall.

Kitty nodded and smiled again, and Geenie let out a breath: she could see what she had to do now. Falling to her knees, she began to scrub the grass, not caring that her props were still in the shed.

'That's not the start,' Diana hissed from above. But Geenie continued rubbing her knuckles in the dirt.

'You've missed out the whole of the first act!'

'Just carry on, darlings,' laughed Ellen. 'The show must go on and all that.'

Geenie could hear Diana puffing out a series of snorts, but she continued to work at the grass with her invisible scrubbing brush.

There was a long pause before Diana stepped behind Geenie, threw an arm over her own face and began to speak. 'Who is this wondrous creature? What beauty there is to be found in a lowly housemaid! I am inspired as never before – inspired by love!'

Geenie heard her mother's high-pitched laugh again, but it was quieter this time.

'You beautiful creature! I must have a kiss!' Grabbing Geenie's arms, Diana hauled her to her feet, pinching her flesh so hard that Geenie winced. The pain seemed to reduce the size and weight of the pebble in her stomach, and stop everything from wobbling quite so violently.

'Kiss me now, and then I will declare my poem in your honour!' Diana's hot breath was on Geenie's face as she lunged forward for the kiss. 'Do not resist me, maid! I am struck by the thunderbolt!'

Planting both feet firmly on the ground, Geenie pushed her hands into her friend's chest. 'No,' she said.

Diana tried to hold her tighter, moving her hands to Geenie's waist and pulling her in, but Geenie struggled and pushed harder. The two of them almost toppled. 'My beautiful darling, my muse!' gasped Diana, closing her eyes and puckering her lips. 'One kiss is all I ask!'

Summoning all her strength, Geenie shoved Diana away. Just as the girl was regaining her balance and coming for her again, Geenie dodged sideways. 'Leave me alone!' she shouted.

Diana stood, staring at Geenie, who was faintly aware of her words echoing round the garden. Before the other girl could speak, Geenie turned to their audience. 'The end,' she panted, bobbing slightly.

There was no applause. George had his hand over his eyes. Kitty's mouth was hanging open. Arthur was looking at the ground, chewing his lip.

Ellen got to her feet and put an arm around her daughter's shoulder. 'Well done, girls. I'm not quite sure what that was all about, but I'm sure we all appreciated it.' She began to clap, but no one else joined in.

'I haven't done my poem,' said Diana in a small voice.

George stood and cleared his throat. 'Well done, girls. Most – ah – inventive.' He took Diana by the arm. 'Come and tell your poem to me,' he whispered, leading her across the lawn to his studio.

Geenie glanced up at her mother. 'That wasn't how it was supposed to be,' she said.

'Wasn't it, darling? I'd never have guessed.'

'It was better this way, though.'

'You improvised, darling, which is very clever. And I like your costume.'

'Kitty made it.' She turned to the chair where Kitty had been sitting, but it was empty. Looking towards the house, Geenie caught a glimpse of the cook running through the back door, one hand pressed across her mouth, the other frantically cutting the air.

... Thirty-six ...

Kitty sat at the kitchen table, struggling to control her breathing. She'd been so preoccupied with the sensation of being next to Mr Crane on the lawn – once his knee had touched hers and the thudding in her chest had become so strong that she thought she would have to go inside – and with not looking at him, despite the burning in her face and the irritation in her fingers, that she hadn't concentrated on what the girls were doing at all. It was only when Diana had declared *What beauty there is to be found in a lowly housemaid!* in that strange, hollow voice she'd adopted that Kitty had begun to pay attention to the play. And from that moment on, she'd prayed for the thing to be over.

Taking a deep breath, she laid her hands flat on the table, trying to steady her trembling fingers. The girls couldn't know, she thought, what had really happened. They couldn't. If they did, Geenie would never have pushed Diana away. But still. They must know something.

'Tea?'

She swung round to see Arthur filling the kettle. He hadn't come in for his late morning tea since they'd danced together that Sunday afternoon at the Crown and Thistle. As he measured out the leaves, tapping the spoon three times on the edge of the caddy, he whistled 'The Continental' under his breath. Setting the pot and two cups on the table, he pulled up a chair next to Kitty and sat down with a loud sigh.

'Weather's going to break soon,' he predicted, taking the lid from the pot and stirring the tea with considerable force.

She tried to say something suitable, but her mind couldn't settle on any one word. Arthur poured tea, then milk, into a cup and pushed it in her direction. 'That was a proper spectacle, wasn't it?'

She brought the cup to her face and blinked.

'Those girls.' He gave a laugh, leaning back in his seat and rubbing his eyes. 'When Miss Geenie gave the other one a shove! It was all I could do not to laugh. I thought they were both going over. Splayed out on the lawn like a couple of wrestlers.' He took a long slurp of his tea and ducked his head to catch Kitty's eye. 'You all right?'

She looked at her lap.

Then he said, in a low voice, 'What the gardener didn't see would've been more like it, eh?'

Kitty put her cup down. The china clattered and some liquid spilled into the saucer. She looked at Arthur, at his ridged brow, his neatly trimmed moustache. His eyes searched hers, and she knew he was waiting for her to deny it. But she could not.

A small smile passed over his lips. 'Well, it's like I said. It's never good to get too close to them.' He finished his drink and stood up. 'Better get back to it. I'm a busy man.'

'Arthur—'

He stopped, tea still glistening on his moustache.

Kitty swallowed. 'Will she sack me, do you think?'

Arthur gave a loud laugh. 'Well, I wouldn't wait around to find out, if I were you. If I were you, I'd get it over, before she does.' He laughed again, shaking his head. 'Bloody women!' he muttered, striding through the door.

.....

The weather did not break that day. Kitty spent most of it in the kitchen, her mind veering from one thought to the other. At first she'd vowed to find Mrs Steinberg right away and tell her she was leaving. Then she'd heard the crackle of tyres on the gravel, and looked out to see both cars disappearing down the drive. Going back to the kitchen, she decided she would wait just one more day – it was only a day, after all, since he'd kissed her, and she needed to see him again before making any firm decision. Standing in the larder, wondering why she'd gone in there in the first place, she decided she should disappear herself: just up and leave without a word. She imagined Mr Crane appearing at Lou's gate, looking for her, his thin face drawn. Washing lettuce leaves for the girls' lunch, she decided she'd pretend nothing had happened. If Mrs Steinberg tackled her about it, she'd deny everything.

In fact, the only decision she really managed to make was to bake a quiche, as she'd now learned to call it, after lunch. The bringing together of the pastry, having first run her fingers beneath the cold water tap, soothed her, and she found it was possible to concentrate on each small task. Then her heart would leap only when she heard what sounded like a car coming close to the cottage, rather than with every other breath. Leaving the pastry to rest in the larder, she scrubbed out the sink with Jeyes and wiped down all the shelves. She rolled out the pastry and put it in the oven to bake blind. Still only half past four, and no car in the drive. So she set to work on the kitchen and larder windows, rubbing them to a shine with a little vinegar. Whilst doing this, she noticed for the first time that the girls had been silent all day. Remembering Geenie's face as she'd stood before her on the lawn, her features stiffened with fear, Kitty considered going upstairs to check on the girl when she'd finished her chores. But after she'd swept out all the downstairs rooms with the soft broom, it was time to scrape the potatoes and shell the peas. And her heart was still flipping in her chest with every noise from the road.

The girls came down at half past seven to feed themselves, and Kitty left them to it, sitting alone at the kitchen table to try to eat the slice she'd put aside for herself. Although the bacon was crisp, the pastry softly crumbling, and the cream and egg filling shivered on her fork, she didn't swallow more than three bites. Going into the sitting room, she found the girls had left the table. She cleared the things away and washed up, running the water so hot that the geyser knocked against the wall and her fingers turned the colour of crabs in the sink.

It was past ten o'clock when she heard a car return, and by that time she'd decided what she would do. She even smiled to herself as she sat on her bed and listened to Mr Crane's deliberate footsteps along the path to his studio. The lamp's glow grew in his window. There was no time to waste. Unbuttoning her apron and taking off her dress, she changed into a clean pair of knickers, the ones with the lace trim that she'd sewn around the legs herself. Then she removed the emerald green Macclesfield silk dress that Lou had given her from its hanger. It was slippery and cool on her forearms as she lifted it and slipped it over her head. The heavy fabric rested on her hips and breasts and followed the curve of her thighs. It was a little long, but that didn't matter now. She combed her hair, tucking it behind her ears, pinched her cheeks and smeared Vaseline over her lips. Then she realised she'd no shoes. The green shoe – if it had had a partner, and if it had fitted – would have matched, but one shoe was worse than no shoes, and she couldn't very well ask Arthur for the other now. She'd have to cross the lawn barefoot. In a last-minute rush of daring, she left her stockings off, too.

She tiptoed through the kitchen and out into the night. The roses smelled their best at this time, but she didn't think about that. The damp grass licked her toes as she headed straight across the lawn towards the studio, her dress swishing behind her.

Pausing before the door, she gulped several mouthfuls of cool air and pressed the dress down around her hips. Her heart was rushing, her palms moist, her throat dry, but she couldn't stand here, exposed in her emerald silk dress and no shoes. She kept her eyes closed as she pushed on his door, and it was only when it was almost fully open that she thought: what if he's not alone in there? But it was too late. She was standing on the threshold looking in, and he was sitting in his armchair, looking back at her.

'Good grief,' he said. They were both frozen for a moment, Kitty grinning at the sight of him – he was real, breathing, here – Mr Crane's mouth gaping. Then he jumped to his feet, pulled her inside, and slammed the door closed. She came easily, stepping very close to him. He held her wrist and their hips pressed together, the dress crumpling between them as she looked into his face. Her hand reached for the back of his neck, but before she could kiss him, he said, 'Wait.'

She hadn't planned words. She'd planned only the dress, and the taking off of the dress, and their bodies moving together again.

He let go of her wrist and took a step back. 'Kitty, I – ah – I've been meaning to talk with you.' Then he looked her up and down and added, a smile growing, 'I'm glad you came. And in such a dress.'

'It's the first time I've worn it,' she said, wishing her voice didn't sound so small.

'It's lovely.' He touched her elbow.

'I wanted to wear it for you.'

'Did you?' His eyes were following the curves of the dress, of her body in the dress.

She smiled, and had to stop herself from twirling in front of him. Instead, she moved towards him again and looked up.

He cleared his throat, then said, very quickly, 'Look here. It's the most awful timing, but I have to go away tomorrow.' He held on to her elbow, as he had on that first day when she'd stood in his studio and almost curtsied. His fingers were very white against the green silk.

'It's a lecture tour, you see, with the Communist Party. Up and down the whole country. Very important work. Damned awful timing. But I have to take this opportunity.'

She blinked, and swallowed hard, before managing to ask, 'When will you be back?'

There was a silence. He dropped his hand to his side and looked away. 'I'm not altogether sure. But when I am, I hope we'll – ah – see one another again. Don't you?'

She fixed her eyes on the pile of old blankets beneath his desk. Blotto's bed. Picturing the dog curled up at his feet, warm and snoozing, she began to shake.

'It's important work,' he said again. 'And it's really very exciting. This country is going to change. Everyone says so. The working classes are going to rise up—'

'You should wash those,' she said, staring at the blankets. 'They smell.'

He drew a hand across his mouth. 'Kitty. I'm so sorry.'

Clasping her fingers behind her back to stop them trembling, she glanced around the room. His desk was empty. The typewriter was in its carrying case, by the door. A pile of books was stacked on top of the filing cabinet, and there were no pictures anywhere. 'How long have you known?'

He sat in the chair and patted the leather patch on its arm. 'Sit with me.'

'How long have you known?'

'Some weeks.'

The shaking became stronger, forcing its way from her knees to her stomach, then up her spine and out of her mouth in a short, audible gasp of air. She covered her face with her hands.

'Kitty. Dear Kitty. Sit with me. Please.'

She didn't move.

'Kitty. Please.' His hands were on her waist, pulling her towards the chair. 'Lovely Kitty,' he said, slowly drawing her hands from her eyes, 'It was lovely, wasn't it?' He slipped his fingers up her naked forearm. 'And this dress is – quite beautiful. You're quite beautiful in it.' He planted a kiss on her wrist, but she was looking over his head at her own reflection in the darkened window. The shaking had almost stopped now. The emerald dress flashed in the lamplight, her eyes were large and empty-looking, her mouth shining. She let him go on kissing the soft skin of her arm, all the way up to the elbow. He nudged the green silk sleeve higher. 'Kitty,' he said. 'Kitty.' He tried to rise from the chair, but she pushed him down again, grasping his hair and holding his head to her stomach so his cheek pressed against the heavy fabric. She gazed at her own reflection in the window, absorbing the image of herself with a man's face buried in her waist, and she kept him there until she was ready to leave.

... Thirty-seven ...

Geenie did not go to Diana's room that night. Instead she slept in the soft centre of her own bed, and dreamed of the maps on Jimmy's wall. In her dream, she drew all the countries and the seas on the floor of Jimmy's study, and when he came into the room, he was carrying his walking stick, and he was ready to take her anywhere.

In the morning, she rose early. Sitting at the dining table, rubbing sleep from her eyes, she watched Diana bring in a plate of toast, a pot of tea and two cups.

'Where's Kitty?' Geenie yawned.

Diana spread the toast with butter, being careful to get it in all the corners. 'There's no baby, you know,' she said, taking a bite.

Geenie had almost forgotten about her mother's announcement. The day on the beach seemed long ago, now. 'Isn't there?'

'Daddy told me yesterday.'

Geenie nodded. Then she asked again, 'Where's Kitty?'

'Haven't seen her. Daddy made me toast, and I made the tea.' Diana sipped her drink.

'You can make tea?'

'It's far better, actually. Not so strong. Want a cup?'

Geenie shook her head and watched in silence as Diana ate two more slices of toast, thickly smeared with raspberry jam.

The door opened. 'Five minutes, darling. We've got to catch the eight-forty.' Spotting Geenie, George stepped into the room. 'Don't look so worried,' he said, giving her a pat on the head. 'You two will see each other again. You'll have to visit Diana at her mother's. Won't she, Diana?'

Pushing past George, Geenie ran from the room and took the stairs two at a time. Dragging all her dressing-up things from the bottom of the wardrobe, she plunged her arms into the pile and threw stockings, hats, shoes, dresses and waistcoats over her shoulder until her fingers touched the cool sleekness of fur.

Diana was standing in the hallway with her suitcase by her feet when Geenie made it back downstairs. Geenie thrust the coat towards her friend. 'If you're going,' she panted, 'you'd better have this.' It weighed down her arms and draped on the floor about the two of them, like a king's cloak.

Diana hooked her hair behind one ear. 'But it's yours.'

'Take it.'

From the driveway, George was calling his daughter.

'It's Jimmy's,' said Diana. 'You have to keep it.' She stroked the fur collar. 'It suits you best, anyway.'

When the front door had closed, Geenie wrapped herself tightly in the coat and went in search of her mother.

.....

As far as Ellen was concerned, they'd already said their goodbyes on Harting Down, and there was little point in getting up this early in the morning. She burrowed beneath the bedclothes and closed her eyes. What she really couldn't stand was the thought of another drama. She'd spent all yesterday avoiding it. After the play, Crane had gone to Laura's to meet with Lillian and make the necessary arrangements for Diana, who was going to stay with her mother while he went on his lecture tour, and Ellen had gone to the hairdressers'. She'd actually had an appointment this time, and Robin had spent hours dyeing her hair jet black and then styling it in the same Hollywood wave as before. While she was sitting in the chair, watching his steady fingers move around her face, she'd thought again of Crane's scrap of poetry. *His blood is heavy with wanting.* Ridiculous. It had to be make-believe, Ellen decided, just like that amusing little play the girls had put on. Geenie had shown a lot of nerve, barking back at Diana like that, and almost pushing her over. It was actually very promising.

Once she was polished and set, Ellen couldn't quite face going back to the cottage in case he'd returned, so she went for tea at the White Hart before meeting Robin again, this time in the back room. It had been, as always, vigorous and refreshing, but she meant to make it her last visit. Since she'd decided her daughter should go to the local school in September, she should make the most of the few remaining weeks of summer with Geenie. Perhaps she could teach her to dance. Besides, Robin was getting to be an awfully expensive habit.

Ellen shifted in the bed. Crane had come up late last night, but she hadn't pretended to sleep. Instead, she'd opened her eyes and said, 'In the morning, will you just go? I don't think I can stand it, otherwise.' He'd brushed her hand with his, and she'd caught it and held fast. But now, as she lay between the sheets, looking at the little boatmen on her curtains, she did think about going downstairs and blocking the doorway. Forbidding him to leave. Begging him to stay. She covered her head with the pillow, but still she could hear the muffled sound of his careful tread on the hallway boards, the click and shudder as he pulled open the front door. She put her hands to her ears and closed her eyes, as she'd done as a girl when her father was leaving the house to visit his mistress. It was surprisingly comforting, especially with the pillow draped over your head and shoulders and your body curled in on itself. Almost like someone was holding you.

When she unfurled her arms and legs, the cottage was quiet. She lifted the pillow from her head. The sun was warming the sheets, and her daughter was opening the door and throwing herself on the bed beside her, wearing a beautiful fur that Ellen hadn't seen or touched for a long time. With a laugh, she recognised it: Jimmy's sable coat. Accepting it from the girl's hands, Ellen draped it across the bed, and she and Geenie lay down together and slept on top of the coat until lunchtime.

.....

Kitty was too exhausted to cry any more, but she wasn't refusing to get out of bed. It was just that she didn't see why she should. George (she thought of him as George for the first time, and it was less painful: *George* was not the man who'd kissed her goodbye last night) had said Mrs Steinberg knew nothing of their love affair (was that what it had been?), but Kitty couldn't believe him. The woman was sure to throw her out. She may as well try to sleep for another hour, and then, when she was stronger, she could face it.

But it was no good. Although her body was heavy, her mind was still alert. She peeped over the sheets. The green silk frock was sprawled on the floor, where she'd kicked it off last night. The best thing to do would be to give it back to Lou and tell her it could be altered after all. With enough determination, you could make anything fit.

Rolling over, Kitty covered her eyes against the sun, which was glaring through a gap in the curtains, and gave a little groan. Sounds were coming from the kitchen, quiet ones at first: shoes on the flags, the larder door creaking. Then louder: drawers opening, cutlery chiming. Pots being clashed together. Kitty turned over again, trying to ignore the row. Let the woman get on with it, she thought. She wouldn't know butter from margarine, or a skillet from a saucepan. Let her pull the kitchen apart, if that's what she wants. See how she fares.

Then she noticed something poking between the wall and the mattress. She reached for the corner of the material and tugged. Her embroidery. Sitting up, she spread it across her lap, flattening out the creases with her hands and remembering the day at the beach, how she'd felt the embroidered scene was so much better than the real one. Running a finger along its surface, she felt the thickness of the rocks, the pinched knobbles of the crab's eyes, the fine filigree of the girls' fishing nets. She'd had a thought that she might give it to George – Mr Crane – as a gift. But now she was glad she hadn't. Perhaps it was good enough to put on the wall. She could use it to replace the awful painting of the woman at the waterfall.

Then she remembered that by the end of the day she'd be back at Lou's, among her sister's things, where anything homemade was not tolerated.

There was a knock at the door. Kitty gathered the embroidery to her chest and turned her face to the wall.

'Kitty.' It was Geenie's voice. 'Kitty?'

She waited for the girl to go away.

'Ellen says, will you have lunch with us?'

So that was it. Even now, they couldn't make themselves a meal. Kitty threw off the bedclothes and, still in her nightgown, pulled open the door. 'Can't you get your own lunch, just for once?' She was almost shouting. Geenie stepped backwards, and Kitty looked beyond her into the kitchen. Mrs Steinberg was standing at the stove, stirring something. Her hair had changed colour: it was glossy and black, like oil, and it made her nose stand out even further. There was a smell of burnt toast, and a pot of tea was steaming on the table.

'It's only scrambled egg,' the woman said, frowning at the stove, ploughing her wooden spoon into the pan. 'Well, you can make up for it tomorrow, Kitty, I'm sure. But for now, we'll have to put up with my effort.'

'I helped,' added Geenie, hopping on one foot. 'I cracked the eggs.'

Kitty folded her arms across her chest. 'I'm not – dressed.'

'What does that matter?' Mrs Steinberg was dolloping mounds of egg onto plates. 'Sit down and eat.'

Kitty could tell by the way the egg fell with a heavy splat that it would be rubbery. The toast in the rack looked limp and cold. But her mouth filled with water.

Taking a chair, she sat at the table.

'Just a minute.' Mrs Steinberg disappeared from the room. Kitty looked at Geenie. 'The costumes were lovely,' the girl said. Then the cottage was filled with the thump and soar of music, and a man's sweet, rasping voice began to sing.

Mrs Steinberg returned. 'Much better,' she said. Pushing a plate of egg over to Kitty, she sat with Geenie at her side. Kitty took up her knife and fork. Together, the three of them began to eat.

··· Acknowledgements ···

This novel is based loosely on events in the lives of Peggy Guggenheim, her lover Douglas Garman, and their respective daughters Pegeen Vail and Deborah Garman, who lived together in Sussex from 1934 to 1937. The characters and setting have been fictionalised, but essential to me in researching this book was Peggy's own outrageous, tantalising, inconsistent account of her life, *Out of This Century: Confessions of an Art Addict*. Among many other useful books were Anton Gill's *Peggy Guggenheim: The Life of an Art Addict* and, for its wonderfully gutsy evocation of life in service, *Below Stairs*, by Margaret Powell.

I'd like to thank Cath Aldworth and Marge Phillips for sharing their fascinating recollections of the mid-1930s with me. Both ladies were wonderful company and extremely generous.

Thanks to Pete Ayrton, John Williams, Rebecca Gray and the team at Serpent's Tail, and to my agent, David Riding, for their commitment to this book. For their advice on drafts, I am grateful to Naomi Foyle, Claire Harries, Kai Merriott and Lorna Thorpe, and I remain deeply indebted to David Swann, who read the first half and convinced me it was going to be all right. Special thanks to my parents for their support, and to my brother Owen for his expertise on every subject. My greatest debt, as always, is to my husband Hugh Dunkerley, who is also my first and best reader.

Snooping in Other People's Houses

some thoughts on writing *The Good Plain Cook*

I was just eighteen when I first visited the Peggy Guggenheim Collection, housed in the Palazzo Venier dei Leoni, Venice. Eighteen, tired from inter-railing and longing for home, a good bath and a plate of my mum's chips. I bypassed most of the big boys of twentieth-century art and found myself in a small side room, filled with puzzlingly child-like paintings by Peggy Guggenheim's daughter, Pegeen Vail, who died aged forty-two. The room displayed a photograph of her, all huge eyes and no chin, beside which was a short elegy, written for her by her mother. For the Peggy Guggenheim Collection isn't only a museum; it's also where Peggy lived.

The wonderful thing about walking around the Palazzo is the illicit thrill you get from snooping in someone else's house. There's the white plastic sofas in the drawing room, where she would have sat, backed by a Pollock, gazing out at her private gondolier (I thought); there's the Calder silver bedhead, under which she took her pleasure with her fabled string of famous lovers... In short, I found the house, and the ghosts of those who'd lived in it, much more interesting than the art.

Fourteen years later, I was still interested enough to think that Peggy's story might give me something to write about, and I embarked on what writers call 'research', which is really more snooping about in other people's houses, keeping an eye out for anything that piques your interest or chimes with your own experience enough to get a story going. I knew that I wanted to write fiction, but thought that the facts of Peggy's life might open up some avenues in my imagination. I also thought, after setting my first novel in the industrial landscape of small-town Oxfordshire, this was the perfect excuse for some much-needed glamour. I saw a prolonged period of 'research' in Venice stretching out before me. Yes! I thought. This must be why so many people dream of becoming novelists.

But then I read that Peggy and her daughter had spent a few years living fairly near me, in West Sussex, and I was intrigued. I also read that she'd employed a local girl as a cook and, dissatisfied with the girl's performance, had decided to learn to cook herself. Everything changed. There they were: the seeds of my cast of characters, just down the road from me. Writers often talk about characters 'taking over' their work, and whilst I bristle a little at such a mystical idea, once I'd found my Good Plain Cook, the novel's direction became clear. I realised that Kitty's point of view – as that of the character so often written out of the bohemian dramas of the period – was a crucial one for me. Perhaps this is because my own family's stories are full of Kittys, whose work enabled the moneyed classes to indulge their passions for art, literature, partying (and politics) without having to worry about the washing up or incinerating the fish. I was fascinated by Peggy's life, by Peggy's house – the art, the lovers, the money – but realised that the story had to include something from my own house. *The Good Plain Cook* is my attempt to put the 'below-stairs' girl centre-stage, whilst also, of course, indulging in a little bohemian glamour.

the pools

Middle England, mid-1980s. The kind of place where nothing ever happens. Except something has happened. A fifteen year old boy called Robert has died, down by the pools. And half a dozen lives will come unravelled.

There's Kathryn and Howard, Rob's parents. Kath has been making the best of her second marriage after the love of her life died young. Howard has been clinging onto a family life he hardly expected to have. There's Joanna, the teen queen of nowheresville. She's been looking for a way out, escape from her parents' broken marriage. She thought Rob might take her away from all this, but lately she's started to think Rob might have other plans. And then there's Shane, with the big hands and the fixation on Joanna.

Bethan Roberts' strikingly assured debut novel subtly reveals the tensions and terrors that underpin apparently ordinary lives, and can lead them to spiral suddenly out of control.

writing the pools

The process of writing *The Pools* began while I was studying for an MA in Creative Writing at the University of Chichester. When I started writing it, I didn't know it was going to be a novel. I thought these characters, this situation, might be best explored in a poem, or – what was I thinking? – a radio play in verse. (A dark secret of mine: sometimes I attempt to write poetry, and I've always had a weakness for *Under Milk Wood*). I suspect this is because I could hear the voices of the book – especially Howard's – quite clearly in my head from the start. In fact, I did write *The Pools* as a rather hysterical radio play, but it didn't quite work, and it didn't feel like the end of my relationship with the material. I wanted the thing to be quieter, gentler, more expansive. I wanted to go deeper into the characters' minds. I wasn't quite ready to let them go. So, slowly – very, very slowly – it became a novel.

I had a lot of help: first from the MA – from both my tutors and fellow students – and then from the novelist Andrew Cowan, whom I'd 'won' as a mentor for six months as part of a Jerwood award for young writers. When I was writing, I didn't think to myself: this is my first novel. I just thought about the next sentence. And the next. And the next. I didn't have a grand plot structure in mind at first. I just wrote and wrote, getting to know the characters as I went along. And then I cut most of what I wrote, and re-wrote. And, eventually, I thought about the plot, and somehow I managed to reach the end. I don't know if this is the best way to write a novel. But it seemed to work for me.

Whilst I was writing, I tried not to think about getting published. But I can't deny that I have imagined what it would be like for a very long time. I've had day-dreams about book-signings. Seen covers and blurbs in my sleep. In the day-dreams I'm entirely happy and successful and everything is very shiny. But the reality is much more every-day. Of course, when my agent called to tell me that we'd found a publisher I didn't stop smiling for weeks (except to eat, which I'm very keen on doing regularly). It's utterly thrilling – and very surreal – to see your words in print, between covers, and on the shelf of a bookshop... You even start to think: maybe I am actually a writer. Could that be true? Could it? But then you get back to your desk. And there's the blank page again. Staring at you without pity. And you take a deep breath, and dare to put down one sentence... and then the next, and then the next.

And next: read the first two chapters of The Pools

Howard

Christmas, 1985

Since the night he disappeared, she's kept her hands to herself. No fingers stray towards me as we lie together, not sleeping. At seven o'clock I shake her shoulder. The brushed cotton of her nightie is soft against the rough skin of my fingertips. I know it's rough because she used to tell me, in bed. If I stroked her back she would say, 'Howard. Skin's catching.'

I shake her shoulder and she ignores me. So I speak. 'Time to get up, Kathryn. Come on now, time to get up.'

Her arm twitches, but there's no sound. So I try again, a bit sterner. 'Come on, now. You have to get up. This morning you have to get up.'

Neither of us has slept, of course. For the last hour I've been watching the blue-grey light push through the curtains, listening to her breathe. From her shallow, quiet breaths, I knew she was awake, too; probably her mind was stuck, like mine, on that moment when we saw the policewoman opening the front gate, carefully closing it again, and taking off her hat as she walked down our path. Then we knew they'd found his body.

I rise and leave her, knowing it'll be ten minutes before she'll move. But when I come back from the bathroom she's standing there in her winter nightie. Her hair is still in waves, but they're all in the wrong place, as if she's wearing a wig and it's slipped. There's a big patch of mottled red on her chest where the cotton has made its imprint.

On our wedding night she wore a very different nightie. It was all layers of stuff, a bit see-through, short, well above her knees. But it hung there as if it wasn't on her body at all, as if she'd just stepped into a tepee made of nylon. 'What's that you're wearing,' I said, smiling, wishing I could see more of her lovely curves. At the power station Christmas parties I knew the other men were watching her, their eyes following her movements; some of them even looked slightly scared if she spoke to them, I noticed that. They would lean towards her to catch her voice. They patted other women on the hips, shouted things out as they passed, but with Kathryn it wasn't like that. Even her hair seemed curvy to me, and her eyelashes, the way they swept up off her cheeks just as women's eyelashes are supposed to. I never saw any other girl with eyelashes like Kathryn's, except at the pictures. On our wedding night she touched a layer of nylon and gave me a twirl. 'It's a powder blue negligee,' she said. 'Can't you tell?' And she lifted up the hem and laughed.

I reach out and hold her elbow for a moment, but she doesn't make a sound; she just stands there, waiting for me to let go. I release her and she walks past me, out of the door. Then I hear water running in the bathroom.

When she comes back her face looks a little pinker so I ask her, 'What'll you wear?'

She looks up at me with clouded eyes. I lean forward and press my forehead to hers. The tip of her nose is cold against my cheek.

'What'll you wear, Kathryn?'

'Anything. Anything.' She lets her weight fall against me.

I sit her down on the bed. 'Right then, let's have a look.' I go through her whole rail, my fingers trailing over dresses, skirts, blouses, and there's nothing black. I pull out every drawer and pick through the folded corners of her knitwear, and there's nothing black. Plenty of brown, and quite a bit of blue, but no black. I think it best not to say anything. Instead I select a dark brown pleated skirt and a navy blue jumper.

'This is nice,' I say, laying it all out on the bed beside her. She stares at the skirt but doesn't move.

'Come on, Kathryn. Let's get that nightie off.'

I wait a few moments, in case she stirs.

She lets me hook the hem of the nightie round my fingers and lift it up to her thighs, and when I say, 'Lift your bottom up for me,' she does so. She sits there naked on the bed, her arms clutched round her waist. The skin on her forearms hangs. In the half-light of the bedroom I can see the curves are still there; a little wilted, but still there.

'Here's your knickers,' I say. 'Are you going to stand up for me?' I hold the knickers out so she can step into them. 'No? All right then.'

I lift her left foot, guiding it into the elastic hole. And as I lift her right foot I smell her there above me, all sleepy brushed cotton and something faintly vinegary, and I find myself stopping and dropping her foot back down again, so she's sitting there with her knickers round one ankle, and I'm resting my cheek against her shin and mouthing *Robert* without making a sound and knowing our son is dead.

She must feel my breathing go heavy, because she puts her hand on my head and we sit like that for a few minutes, my knees digging into our thin purple carpet, my cheek feeling the dry tissue of her shin and the knobbles of bone in there, all rounded, like a row of marbles.

'I should have bought a black dress,' she says.

I lift her right foot again. 'No, no. It's all right. People don't wear all black at funerals these days.'

I guide the knickers beyond her knees. 'Lift your bottom up for me.'

I keep thinking of the time I took Robert to the Tank Museum. Kathryn refused to come in, waited in a café down the road, wearing her red raincoat (she used to wear a lot of red), sipping a milky coffee, reading a novel. At least, that's how I imagined her as I walked around that place, yards of camouflage and unspeakable weapons everywhere.

In that museum there were lots of fathers and sons. All the fathers seemed to have big hands with which to guide their sons around the *Whippet*, the *Sherman Crab* and the *Somua* tanks. They would stoop and point, ruffle hair, share interesting facts. I didn't know anything about those grey and brown hunks of metal. I knew about turbine halls, not armoured vehicles.

I walked behind Robert as he ran ahead. I'd never seen him so excited. I let him weave between the tanks with his anorak wrapped around his waist in the way he liked. I smiled as he sat in the cockpit of the armoured Rolls-Royce, his hair sticking up on the crown of his head, his straight teeth shining.

When we got back to the café she embraced him as if he'd been gone for weeks, and he told her all about the tanks in one long breath, and her eyes lit up at the very mention of the word *missile*, even though she'd refused to set foot in that place. 'Did you enjoy it, Howard?' she asked me. I hesitated. Robert said, 'Dad *hated* it.' And they laughed.

The iciness of the kitchen floor seeps through the thin soles of my slippers. I warm my hands in the steam of the kettle. The blind with the fruit and veg print is moving slowly in the draught from the window. Sucked in, blown out. I drop the cold tea bag from the pot into the bin. I can't cook like Kathryn so the bin is full of empty tins. She used to feed Robert plenty of meat; chops grilled with a little salt, boiled potatoes and tinned peas on the side. I never understood it. She doesn't like meat much, but for her son she let the fat ooze over the bars of the grill and fill the kitchen with a sweet stink.

For the last fortnight she's said nothing as I've handed her beans on toast, spaghetti on toast, cheese on toast, night after night. She says nothing, chews on a corner, leaves the rest. Since the night he went, we've eaten our tea on our laps, in front of the television. And we do not watch the news.

I almost pour the tea into the mug he bought for her, years ago – the one with 'World's Best Mum' on the side. When I say he bought it, I mean of course that I got it, and said it was a gift from him on Mother's Day. He must have been about six. She looked pleased, but she never used it. Kathryn doesn't go in for that sort of thing, slogans.

I jerk the spout away so quickly the tea burns my hand. Then she's there, standing beside me in the kitchen, wearing the brown skirt and the blue jumper. She's put some earrings in.

'You've got earrings in,' I say, pushing the mug behind the teapot.

'I'll take them out,' she says, quickly, before I can tell her that I like them. 'It was a mistake. What was I thinking? Earrings.'

'Right,' I say. 'Tea.'

Eleven o'clock. The car arrives in plenty of time for the service. We stand in the hallway. I am wearing my only black suit; it's a bit tight round the waist. It's all right, though, because I've put a belt round and left the top button undone. I hold out Kathryn's wool coat. She slips her arms into it, and I heave it onto her shoulders. I button it right to the top; the collar is so high it's like I'm tucking her neck into it. I comb her hair, which sticks out above her right ear. The ends of it look frazzled, as if they've been burnt.

'Have you got any spray?' I ask.

She looks at me. 'Spray?'

'For your hair.'

'No,' she says.

'A hat then.'

'I've never had a hat.'

'Oh. Right then.' I smooth the shoulders of her coat. 'You'll do,' I say.

She reaches past me and opens the door. Outside, a blast of wind brings water to my eyes as I hurry to keep up with her, to keep hold of her herringboned elbow.

Joanna

Christmas, 1985

I know Shane's not coming. I sit on the seat of the twitchers. I know he's not coming. But I wait. I grip the seat until my fingers go dead, and I wait for him.

Pink hoop earrings, pink pencil skirt. I'm ready, should he stride past, Walkman blasting. I'm ready, but I know he won't come. No one's seen him since that night. Not even me.

Rooks scream in the spiky trees. Everything's frozen, even the air. It bursts in my lungs when I inhale.

The only thing moving is the steam in the sky. It coughs out of the power station cooling towers. It never stops.

I stretch my fingers out and let the blood flow back. Then I grip the seat again.

They found Rob's body down here a week ago. I saw it on the news, like everyone else. There were nets and dogs and more police than you've ever seen in Calcot. They came to my house and asked me, when was the last time I saw Robert Hall? How did I know him? Who were his other friends? How did he seem when I left him? I didn't leave him, I said. I went to look for him. But he'd gone. They'd both gone. The policewoman had lines scored around her mouth, and shimmery purple eyeshadow. I kept looking at it because she'd done one eye darker than the other, and it made her lopsided. I know it's hard, she said, but try to remember. She put her hand on my shoulder. Robert's friend Luke said there was someone else there. Was there anyone else with you? Was there anyone else there that night? No one, I said. No one else was there.

It's all quiet now, though. The police have gone. They found Rob's body, and they stopped looking for Shane.

Rob came into the shop where I work weekends not long ago and bought some Dairy Box for his mum, for Christmas. I told him that she'd want Ferrero Rocher, pointing to the gold pyramid I'd just stacked. We laughed. His flawless cheeks glowed.

They'll be grey now, though. Bloated from the water.

No one's found Shane. But he's probably looking for me. If I sit here long enough, he might come. I might hear his beat. He might put his hands on my head.

If he does, I'm not sure what I'll do. I might scream. I might run off. But I'll let him touch me, just once.

Shane's hand would have covered Rob's whole head.

Instead, Simon comes.

I know it's him before he sits down next to me. I recognise his sigh, the expensive-sounding crunch of his leather boots on the frozen mud.

We sit for a long time, looking at the pool. There's still police tape round the other side, where they found the body.

Mum didn't come to the funeral, but Simon did. He didn't come with me, he just appeared at the last minute, sat behind me and breathed his damp air on the back of my neck. I didn't ask him to do that. After the service, I slipped out before he could clutch my elbow and say my name.

He must have followed me down the lane to the pools, telling Mum he was going to do some birdwatching. Promising he'd bring her something back. Kissing her pout before he left.

He inches along the bench, closer. I let him sit there, in silence. I know he doesn't know what to say to me. He steals the odd sideways glance at my face. I keep looking at the pool, though. I don't want to see his eyes.

Then he reaches into his coat pocket. Brings out a bar of Bourneville. Slides a finger beneath the red paper wrapper. Pops it open. Rips back a piece of foil. Offers it to me.

I snap off a block and put it in my mouth. Let it melt.

THE ZORK CHRONICLES

Delve into the challenge and adventure
of the world of

ZORK

with the fantastic imagination of

GEORGE ALEC EFFINGER

"We (science fiction writers) stand
in awe of a writer so young, so strong,
so good. . . ."
Harlan Ellison

"Wry, inventive, nearly hallucinatory . . ."
Publishers Weekly

"Great entertainment . . ."
Fantasy Review

Other Avon Books in the
INFOCOM™ Series

ENCHANTER® *by Robin W. Bailey*
PLANETFALL® *by Arthur Byron Cover*
WISHBRINGER® *by Craig Shaw Gardner*
STATIONFALL™ *by Arthur Byron Cover*

George Alec Effinger

THE ZORK® CHRONICLES

A Byron Preiss Book

AN INFOCOM™ BOOK

AVON BOOKS NEW YORK

ZORK: THE NOVEL is an original publication of Avon Books. This work has never before appeared in book form. This work is a novel. Any similarity to actual persons or events is purely coincidental.

Special thanks to Marc Blank, Dave Lebling, Richard Curtis, Rob Sears, John Douglas, David Keller, and Alice Alfonsi.

AVON BOOKS
A division of
The Hearst Corporation
105 Madison Avenue
New York, New York 10016

Published by arrangement with Byron Preiss Visual Publications, Inc.

Library of Congress Catalog Card Number: 89-92497
ISBN: 0-380-75388-X

Cover and book design by Alex Jay/Studio J.
Cover painting by Walter Velez
Edited by David M. Harris

First Avon Books Printing: July 1990

Printed in the U.S.A.

RA 10 9 8 7 6 5 4 3 2 1

To Rob Sears of Infocom, and Brett Sperry,
Mike Legg, and the rest of the gang at
Westwood Associates, who have made my own
Infocom game, *Circuit's Edge*, a reality.

And to David M. Harris, the editor whom
I tormented with this manuscript.

ACKNOWLEDGMENTS

I'D LIKE TO MENTION THAT I used two reference books extensively in creating the characters as well as devising the progression of their adventures. The first of these books is *The Hero*, by Lord Raglan, published by New American Library in March, 1979. This is a classic study of the common elements and themes that occur in the "biographies" of heroic characters from myth and fiction.

The second book is *The Hero with a Thousand Faces*, by Joseph Campbell, published by Princeton University Press in 1968, which attempts to find a single, coherent pattern among the many heroic quest myths from around the world.

I've always found such literary analysis and synthesis fascinating, and I've always wanted to use these two references as the basis of a fantasy of my own. I'll be the first to admit that *Zork* is not on the same level as, say, the Arthurian cycle; but if anyone becomes interested in writing a long, critical study of this work, I can often wax eloquent upon the subject over a free lunch.

CONTENTS

Prologue: *Die Göttercocktailpartei* 1
Chapter One: We Can't All Be Heroes 12
Chapter Two: The Importance of Being Brave 33
Chapter Three: A Traveling Companion 47
Chapter Four: The Myth of Wickedness 64
Chapter Five: Hell's Twice the Labor 80
Chapter Six: A Dead Man's Embers 100
Chapter Seven: Waiting for Santa 120
Chapter Eight: Glarbo Speaks! 135
Chapter Nine: Not Doing Nothing 153
Chapter Ten: A Better Class of Enemy 172
Chapter Eleven: The Formula for Success 191
Chapter Twelve: A Proof of Genius 212
Chapter Thirteen: Inspiration, Inc. 229
Chapter Fourteen: Good Grounds and Bad 243
Chapter Fifteen: Fathers and Sons 259
Epilogue: *Die Göttercocktailpartei II* 282

The composite hero of the monomyth is a personage of exceptional gifts. Frequently he is honored by his society, frequently he is unrecognized or disdained. He and/or the world in which he finds himself suffers from a symbolical deficiency. In fairy tales this may be as slight as the lack of a certain golden ring, whereas in apocalyptic vision the physical and spiritual life of the whole earth can be represented as fallen, or on the point of falling, into ruin.

—Joseph Campbell
The Hero with a Thousand Faces

>Kill troll with sword.
>You can't see any sword here!

—Message in *Zork I*

PROLOGUE

Die Göttercocktailpartei

THERE WERE SUPPOSED to be some eager acolytes meeting Glorian and taking him right to the hotel; but of course the acolytes never showed up, and Glorian had to find his way on his own through one of the hugest stations in the supernatural world. He trundled his two heavy suitcases and felt ever more as if he should have just skipped the entire weekend. He could have stayed home and dabbled at the human pursuits he found so rewarding. He could have worked some more on his book, for instance: *A Guardian Spirit Speaks to Troubled Teens.*

The fact that the awards banquet was in the Valhalla Hilton didn't improve his mood. He hated having to come to Valhalla for these stupid banquets. He preferred the alternating years when they were held in the Elysian Fields. At least the food was a lot better. Valhalla was cold and gray and blustery no matter what time of year you came, but for some reason the Campbell Awards banquet committee always picked the grimmest weekend of the year. It was even grimmer if, like Glorian, you were one of the anxious award nominees.

Finally, Glorian got his luggage up to the Registration Desk of the Valhalla Hilton. The desk clerk looked down at him as if Glorian had stumbled into the posh establishment expecting to find a soup kitchen. "Yes?" said the desk clerk. There was a world of "No" packed into that single syllable.

"Glorian, party of one. I confirmed my reservationa three months ago."

The desk clerk riffled briefly through a plastic box of index cards, then punched a couple of keys on a computer keyboard. He looked up at Glorian with a broad smile of absolute satisfaction. "Sorry, sir," he said, beaming, "nothing here at all under that name."

"Having some trouble, young man?" came a deep, booming voice from behind Glorian's left shoulder. He turned around and was shocked to see one of the supernatural world's greatest and most influential members, Shiva the Destroyer.

"Well, actually," said Glorian, a little abashed in the great being's presence, "they seem to have lost all record of my reservation."

Shiva gave a loud *hmmph* that wobbled the stone columns of the Valhalla Hilton. "Happens to me all the time, too. I think they get some kind of perverse pleasure out of it. These desk clerk types have no idea of the kind of afterlife that could be waiting for them." He glowered at the frightened desk clerk for several meaningful seconds.

"Mr. Destroyer," said the desk clerk in a small, strangled voice, "I seem to have cleared up the problem just this very moment." He produced a card, had Glorian sign it, and punched a button that caused a computer printer to spit out a page of information no guest ever read.

"Thank you, sir," said Glorian to Shiva.

The destroyer laughed, causing another frightening rumble in the huge lobby. "I was a young supernatural being myself once. I remember what it was like. You're Glorian, aren't you? One of this year's Campbell Award nominees?"

Glorian's eyes opened even wider. He was amazed that such a personage as Shiva the Destroyer would recognize him. "Yes, sir," he said.

"Well, good luck in the voting, son. But remember what they always say: It's an honor just to be nominated."

"You bet," said Glorian.

Glorian had picked up his key and luggage and was heading off toward a bank of elevators, when Shiva's gruff voice stopped him. "You know, quite a number of influential people have their eyes on you. This weekend could be the beginning of something very important for you, whether or not you win the Campbell."

Glorian carried his bags up to his room, wondering what Shiva had meant by that. He assumed it would all be made clear eventually, because that was the way things tended to work out with The Powers That Be.

The room itself was okay, in a minimal way, although certainly not worth what Glorian was paying for it. The entire wall opposite the king-size bed was a window, but when Glorian pulled back the drapes, there was only a kind of opaque, moiling murk beyond the glass, and a few tiny words in the bottom right-hand corner: *This space intentionally left blank.* Glorian shuddered and closed the drapes again.

Except for the bed, there was only a bureau, a chair, a television, and a closet. On the door to the closet was a framed sign that told him what to do in an emergency. "In case of fire," the occupant was reassured, "do not panic. After all, you may be invulnerable. If after several minutes you discover that you are in fact beginning to burn, you may exercise any of several options. First, this may be only Magic Fire, in which case you will only fall asleep for centuries and centuries and be awakened with a kiss. The management of this hotel makes no guarantee that the fire you encounter will be of this variety. Second, the fire may actually be Zeus or Marduk or one of the truly major personages who frequently accept the amenities of this hotel, and they may be merely attempting to seduce you in their typically obscure way. In such a situation, your response is best left up to your own moral posture. However—and this point cannot be stressed too highly—it may indeed be that the fire is just regular old fire and that you are in serious danger of dying in a horrible conflagration. Our advice to you in this third scenario is: Don't. Escape will seem like the most profitable course of action, even to the dullest-witted." Below that, in tiny letters, were the words Powers That Be Printing Office. Publication No. 0154-G.

There wasn't much else to see in the room. When Glorian turned on the television, there were only two channels operating. One played a rerun of a once-popular sitcom called "All-Father Knows Best," which pretended to portray what daily life among the Powers That Be might conceivably be like. Today's episode featured Ed Asner in the role of Oceanus, who was a lazy Titan who just lay around in his sea-bed all day until his wife Tethys, played by Carol Kane, came in and announced that she was going to get a job singing with a Cuban dance band. Glorian had seen the episode at least three times before, so he changed the channel. The other one that worked gave information about events at the Valhalla Hilton. It said that the cocktail party preceding the Campbell Awards ceremony would begin shortly, and that all award nominees were entitled to two free drinks.

Two free drinks sounded good. He didn't even bother to unpack his bags, but just tossed them into the narrow closet. Whatever secrets were hidden in the bureau would have to wait until later that evening.

Glorian stopped briefly in the bathroom and glanced at his reflection in the mirror. As a middle-level supernatural being, he had the ability to change his appearance at will, and this talent had come in very useful on some of the difficult and dangerous quests he'd been assigned in the past. Now, though, he thought it best if he assumed the guise of a modest, friendly, generally charming young man. If he needed to change sex or size or particular attributes later, that could be accomplished easily enough. As he pocketed his room key and stepped out into the hall, he looked like any bright young man who wanted to talk to you seriously about buying into a time-share apartment.

Glorian was pleasantly surprised to meet an old friend while he waited for the elevator to take him back down to the lobby. Her name was Amitia, and she was a supernatural helper of heroes of about the same rank as he. She was lovely, with her long blonde hair done up with strings of pearls, and she wore a shimmering gown of silver. "Glorian!" she cried when she saw him.

"It's been a long time, Amitia," he said.

"When was the last time our paths crossed? It was on Earth, wasn't it? In the future? When you were leading that old woman on some senseless quest, and I was traveling with that bright young man and his lecherous uncle."

"The three of you were dragging a Vanguard missile behind you!" said Glorian, laughing.

"Nobody ever said these missions had to make sense. Not to us, anyway. They're always life-and-death matters to the poor, misguided heroes, though."

Glorian jabbed again at the elevator button. "Just think how much easier our life would be without the heroes."

"Really? How? What would we do?"

He stared at the beautiful non-real woman for a moment and then shrugged. "I don't know. But I'm sure the Powers That Be would think of something."

The elevator arrived just then, and they entered. Amitia pressed the button for the lobby. "Nervous, Glorian?" she asked.

"About what? The Campbell Award? Hey, I've been nominated nine times before, and I've never won. The first couple of times, I went along with everybody who kept telling me 'It's an honor just to be nominated.' Now I just want to win one of those suckers."

"Some of us have never been nominated, not even once," said Amitia glumly.

"It's politics," said Glorian quickly. "It's who you know."

The elevator reached the lobby before they could discuss the matter any further. There was a comfortable bar in one corner of the hotel's lobby that was filled with other non-existent, mythical characters, and Glorian and Amitia took a table near the entrance. A waitress dressed as a medieval woodland sprite came over and took their orders. "Gin and tonic," said Glorian.

"White wine," said Amitia.

"Typical," said the woodland sprite in a sarcastic tone. She turned her attention to another party of customers.

"She could at least have left us a bowl of peanuts or pretzels," said Glorian.

"What's the matter?" asked Amitia. "You *are* getting nervous, aren't you? Admit it! This whole Campbell Award thing has you climbing the walls!"

"What are you talking about?" asked Glorian. "The Campbell Award? I don't care that much for the Campbell Award," he said, snapping his fingers. "And besides, there are plenty of other qualified people nominated this year. It wouldn't be any disgrace to lose to Polylapidus or the Hanged Frog or Isvahaken."

"What about the Princess Dawn des Malalondes?" asked Amitia with a smug leer.

Glorian's path had crossed the princess's before, when he learned that her real name was Narlinia von Glech, and that she was about the phoniest, sleaziest, slimiest sylphidine in Creation. "Well," he said, sipping at the gin and tonic the supernatural waitress had just left at his elbow, "there's very little chance of that, is there? Everyone knows Narlinia. I think my real competition is Polylapidus. The Hanged Frog is maybe just a little too melodramatic, if you know what I mean, and Isvahaken shows real talent, but just hasn't had enough exposure yet. Maybe next year."

"So you do care?" said Amitia, sliding her glass of white wine nearer.

"Of course, I care," said Glorian. "Winning the Joseph Campbell Award for Best Semi-Actual Persona is what we all aspire to. It could make my career. It could lift me out of the dull range of supernatural sidekicks and into the category of demigod or even better! Sure, I want to win, but I've been here often enough in the past to know that, well, if I don't win, the world won't come to an end."

"Sometimes it does," said Amitia, swallowing a little of her wine. "There was that time that Chilean thunder-god, Pillan or something, lost and got so disappointed and angry that he just clapped the universe out of existence. Then the committee had to get together and start everything from scratch again, and they put in those new by-laws—"

"You know I'd never do anything like that. These awards just don't mean so much to me. They're—"

"Hush, Glorian!" murmured Amitia. "They're going to start!"

There was a podium set up at the front of the bar, and the current president of the Supernatural and Fantastic Wayfarers Association tested the microphone. It was Savitri, the Indian golden god of the sun. He tapped the microphone and murmured into it. "Everybody hear me all right out there?"

"Yes, yes," muttered Glorian in an ill humor. "Just get on with it."

"Well," said Savitri, "we had a guest speaker lined up for tonight, but before she could come up here to address our group, she apparently ate a few pomegranate seeds and was carried off to the underworld. We're still trying to sort that all out. In any event, in the meantime, I think I'll just get right to the matter at hand, this year's Joseph Campbell Award."

There was a smattering of applause, and Glorian realized that he was feeling very lightheaded. He decided that the cure for that was a couple of sudden gulps of gin. The next thing he knew, Savitri was tearing open an envelope and announcing—

"And the winner is . . . Narlinia von Glech, the Princess Dawn des Malalondes!"

There were a few boos, some smatterings of applause, and quite a loud ripple of murmured comment. Narlinia von Glech stood up, looking like a reincarnation of a 1940s Hollywood beauty queen in her long, dark hair and tight red, sequined gown. She made her way as quickly as she could to the microphone, where she spoke briefly about how proud she was to win the Campbell Award, and how she hoped to live up to its standards, and how much she wished her father had lived to see this day, and how very much she loved everybody. Her voice sounded exactly like Edie Adams doing Marilyn Monroe.

"I don't believe it," said Glorian. "I just don't believe it. It must have been some kind of strange voting conspiracy. People casting their ballots on the basis of breast size rather than genuine craft and dedication. I just wonder how many actual missions Narlinia completed last year." He'd turned aside, not even watching Narlinia's performance at the podium. Savitri handed her the Campbell Award, the bronze mask of a god, and Narlinia gushed some more, then wiggled her way back to her own table.

"Can we go now?" asked Glorian.

Amitia laughed. "Come on, Glorian, at least be gracious. You've got to congratulate her."

"Why? Do you see the Hanged Frog being gracious?"

"Glorian," said Amitia with a frown, "if you don't congratulate her everyone will notice, and you'll just get a big reputation for being a sore loser."

"I *am* a sore loser," he said grumpily. "This is the tenth time I've lost." Nevertheless, he made himself get up and ease his way to Narlinia's table. "Congratulations, Narlinia," he said, his eyes pointed down at the tiled floor. "You know that I wanted to win that Campbell Award myself, but if I didn't get it, then I'm glad you did."

"Ooh, that's just so sweet, Glorian!" Narlinia cooed. She leaned forward, putting dangerous stresses on the upper buttresses of her sequined gown, and gave him a quick peck on the cheek.

"Now can we go?" muttered Glorian.

"Now we can go," murmured Amitia.

All the way from the bar to the elevator, people stopped Glorian again and again, telling him that it was a shame he hadn't won the Campbell Award, but that it was an honor just to be nominated. "You bet," he said each time. He'd really begun to hate hearing about it. He told Amitia that he had a terrible headache and that he just wanted to go upstairs alone and get some rest. They made plans to have breakfast the next morning.

Upstairs in his room, Glorian unpacked his bags in the bureau drawers, turned on the television, and then stretched out in his mythic underwear to watch an episode of "My Mother the Slug," with the voice of Bea Arthur as Ka'apiti the World Slug of Ghidan. He had started to doze off to sleep when the telephone rang. "Hello?" he said, yawning.

"Glorian, there is an envelope for you in the upper left drawer of the bureau."

"Who is this? I just unpacked my things, and there wasn't an envelope in that drawer."

"There is now," said the mysterious voice. There was a jagged sound, and then Glorian was listening to the dull burr of the dial tone. He shrugged, got up, and went to the bureau. He opened the top left drawer, and there, on top of his socks and underwear, was a white envelope. He tore it open and read the sheet of paper inside:

> Glorian, here are instructions for your most important mission. You must meet a hero by the name of Mirakles by the usual old white house. You must help him regain the vital Switch that has been dipped in gold. The fate of this and every other reality depends on your courage and devotion.
>
> Good luck to you,
> and may God bless.

He'd received many other directives in his career, most of them in mysterious white envelopes just like this, but in every case, those orders had come from The Powers That Be.

This one bore the mark of the signet ring of the Autoexec himself. Glorian tossed the paper on the bureau, lay back down on the bed, and watched the end of "My Mother the Slug." The fate of universal reality could wait until morning.

CHAPTER ONE

We can't all be heroes because somebody
has to sit on the curb and clap as they go by.
—Will Rogers

NOW, GLORIAN ISN'T THE hero of this tale, not in the sense of the guy who carries the broadsword and takes all the risks. In fact, the authentic hero, Mirakles of the Elastic Tendon (at least, that's the best way of rendering his epithet into English) was having a little trouble finding his way through a deep, dark, mysterious forest. Gloomy, threatening woods were nothing new to Mirakles, of course, so he wasn't yet getting the least bit uneasy. He was just getting bored, which was one of the occupational hazards of the broadsword-toting caste when there was nothing nearby to hack and hew. Mirakles had been through all this before; he was certain that sooner or later a giant bat or something would cross his path.

How would a great poet like Homer or Byron describe Mirakles? It's impossible to say, naturally, but we could make a modest beginning by mentioning that in the physique department it would have taken at least two of the Greek or Trojan warriors to be his equal. Say, Achilles and Ajax together, and you could have a little change back. That's how huge and strong Mirakles' arms were, that's how barrel-chested he was, how broad and great his back, how powerful his legs. And he was of fine features, too, for a wandering swordsman—after all, was he not the son of Desiphae, queen of the Sunless Grotto?

And we haven't even mentioned his sword yet. Let's talk about that for a moment. When Mirakles was but a stripling, his father, King Hyperenor, passed on to the boy a mighty weapon that had been in their family for centuries. "Take this blade and guard it well," said the king, "because it will always stand you in good stead. It is the fabled sword Redthirst. Its edge is keen and fashioned with a magic that has nothing to do with hammer and anvil. The steel is guarded by sorcerous incantations, and you will never be defeated in battle so long as you remember three things."

"What three things are they, Father?" asked young Mirakles, stricken with awe by the terrible beauty of Redthirst.

"Your mother knows. Before you slay your first dragon or band of brigands, talk to her. Now go away. I am an old king, and soon you'll have to take my place, ruling our people wisely, showing up for strawberry festivals, all that kind of lunacy. This afternoon I think I will put on my ceremonial feather headdress and go boar hunting all alone without my courtiers and no weapon but a pointed stick."

Mirakles was shocked and for a moment forgot his place. "Father, that's stupid! Why would you even think about doing such a thing?"

King Hyperenor just gave his young son a sad look. "Another thing you'll learn as you get older is that this is the way old kings move things along so history can happen."

They looked at each other for a moment, and then Mirakles understood. He gave his father a strong, manly embrace, took the magic sword Redthirst, and went to find his elusive mother, Queen Desiphae. Mirakles never saw his father alive again, and on that very day he changed from a headstrong, impulsive boy into the shrewd, courageous, taciturn hero it had always been his destiny to become.

His mother had been very mysterious when Mirakles questioned her about Redthirst. "The first secret," she'd told him on that sad, long-ago day, "is that this blade will provide you greater protection against supernatural and demonic enemies than against mere human villains. Whenever you're in the presence of a supernatural enemy, the sword will begin to grow warm in your hand and there will be an aroma as of bread baking."

"Bread baking, Mother?" asked Mirakles, puzzled.

Queen Desiphae waved her hand in dismissal. "All right, it's not very warlike, I admit. I suppose you wished the sword would shriek aloud or sing to you or something. I'm sorry. You've got to learn to take what you're given."

Mirakles was duly chastened. "Yes, of course, Mother," he said. "And the other two secrets?"

"You'll learn them when you need to know them."

Mirakles stood and regarded the Queen of the Sunless Grotto with a calculating expression. "Then this is the end of my education?"

"Yes, my darling son."

"And there will be no further magical gifts or ointments or spells or purses of gold or anything else?"

The queen shook her head sadly. "The great sword Redthirst is our family's one great treasure."

"Ah," said Mirakles. He bent to kiss his mother's brow. "I'll be off, then. I'll leave you as regent of this great underworld realm until my return. I hope soon to have won my own fair kingdom."

"Yes, of course, my son. Good fortune attend thee. Take a sweater."

Mirakles slung Redthirst in its great scabbard across

his back. "Well, so long," he said, and he left his mother sitting on a rock in the middle of her unplumbed pool.

Now, years later, he was thrashing noisily through a dimly lit forest. He was using Redthirst to hack his way through the underbrush, when suddenly he felt the sword's hilt turning hot in his strong right hand. Mirakles' eyes narrowed, and he turned around slowly, searching for some leather-winged, fanged fiend to attack. He saw nothing but the trees. "By Thrag!" he shouted in his strong, deep voice, "I know you're waiting for me in cowardly ambush. Come out and face the wrath of Mirakles, son of Hyperenor!"

There were some gentle rustling sounds from overhead. "Hey!" cried an old man's voice. "Is that you? Baking bread down there?"

"By Thrag, show yourself and you'll soon learn the difference between a baker and a master swordsman!"

Mirakles heard more branches swish above his head, and then he saw a small, round-shouldered old man dressed in a brown leather jacket and brown leather trousers. The old man was climbing painfully down from the very top of the tree. In one hand he carefully protected a few small objects. "I don't know," said the old man in a hoarse voice, "it's just not clear to me why a person couldn't be both a baker *and* a swordsman."

Mirakles looked the little man up and down, then sheathed Redthirst. "Because both callings require a lifetime of dedication," he said.

The old man laughed. "Only if you want to be great at one thing or the other. Me, well, I wouldn't mind being just an okay baker and just an okay swordsman. The rest of my time I could spend however I chose."

"Like climbing trees in lonely forests?" asked Mirakles suspiciously.

"Possibly. You're not the only man on a mission around here, you know."

"What makes you think I'm on some kind of mission? I'm not, you know. Anyway, my sword tells me that you're not a human being. What were you doing up in that tree?"

The old man held out his hand. "Malted milk balls," he said. "There's a bird's nest up in that tree that's empty now. I was putting some malted milk balls in it."

Mirakles was feeling more exasperated with every question and answer. "Why, in the name of Thrag?" he thundered.

"Somebody has to do it," said the old man, shrugging. "Let me introduce myself. My name is Glorian. Glorian of the Knowledge, actually. And you were quite correct, I am a supernatural being, a kind of mythical helper to adventurers on heroic quests. I've been assigned to give you a hand."

Mirakles was so astonished that his mouth dropped open. "I'm not on any kind of heroic quest," he said. "I already told you that. I'm just out on my own, living day to day. You know, looking for fame, fortune, a kingdom to conquer, the hand of a beautiful princess. Nothing more. You must have the wrong man."

Glorian shook his head. "Trust me on this. Very soon now, you'll receive what we in the trade refer to as The Call to Adventure. From then on, you'll be glad to have me around. I have lots of useful magical talents."

Mirakles laughed, a deep, booming sound. "Magical talents? A little, wizened-up old man like you?"

Glorian joined in the laughter without anger. "I don't *have* to look like this, you know," he said. "I chose this appearance because I thought it was appropriate for our relationship at this point. I can easily change it if you don't like it, though. I can be young or old, male or female, human or some scungy, roiling, fetid cloud of interdimensional horror."

Mirakles thought that one over. "Why don't you just stick with the kindly old gnome look for a while?"

"Fine. My knees complain when I put myself through this, but you can't have everything."

Mirakles took a deep breath and looked around at the forest again. "So here we are. How do you plan to help me? I mean, if I was actually on a heroic quest—which I'm not, remember—but if I was, what would you do first?"

Glorian reached into his jacket and pulled out a pamphlet. "Here," he said, giving the literature to Mirakles, "this is standard. Look it over later when you have a few minutes."

The pamphlet's cover was a light gray color. The words on it were printed in blue. Mirakles had some trouble sounding them out. *"Heroic Behavior,"* he read haltingly. *"Some Do's And Don'ts.* Powers That Be Printing Office. Publication No. 6014-B."

"I'm sure you know most of that stuff already," said Glorian. "And next, I suppose I should get us out of this forest. The house should be right over there." He turned and pointed south, then started marching along a narrow path. He didn't even wait to see if Mirakles was following him.

"Hey," cried the hero, "who do you think you are, handing me this stupid pamphlet? As if I need helpful hints on heroing or something! I was rescuing maidens almost before I knew what a maiden was. Hey! Wait a minute!"

The path widened until it entered a clearing. There was a white house in the clearing. It had no door on the north side, but workmen were busily tearing down the boards that covered the windows.

"Renovation!" said Glorian. "And about time, too."

There was a billboard on the property that advertised *3 Rms Barrow View, Spacious Downstairs Excellent for Playroom, Etc.* A number of prices covered the billboard, each lower than the previous one, all of them crossed out. Now a poster slashed slantwise from lower left to upper right and proclaimed *Coming Soon! Casa Blanca Condos! Only 6 Left!* Below that was the address of the Frobozz Magic Realty Company, a wholly-owned subsidiary of Frobozzco International.

"As I recall, this used to be a pretty marketable parcel of real estate," said Glorian, leading Mirakles around behind the house to the east. "There was serious talk of constructing an entire community to go with it, with a school, a shopping mall, a massive Cosmoplex for car shows and auctions of sofa-sized art, and all that sort of modern convenience. Today, though, there's still only the house, but at least Frobozzco seems to be taking an interest in the property."

"What's Frobozzco?" asked Mirakles.

"Well," said Glorian, frowning, "Frobozzco is the parent corporation of a million little specialized companies, whose board of directors seem to be made up of interlocking combinations of the Implementors, who function just beneath the Powers That Be, who are supervised by the Autoexec."

"Ah," said the brawny hero. "So if I want to make my mark quickly in this world, I should just skip all those intermediaries and face down this Autoexec in person."

Glorian and Mirakles walked around the third side of the house, where there was another path back into the foreboding forest. "I'm not entirely positive that the Autoexec is at the very top of the corporate ladder, if you understand my meaning. I just know that I get occasional memos from him, and I've learned not to ignore them. Furthermore, the intermediaries, as you called them, generally won't let themselves be skipped."

"By Thrag!" shouted the wrathful Mirakles. "What am I supposed to do now?"

"Let's just finish walking around the house. There's a mailbox there that I want to check."

"Fine," said Mirakles sulkily. "And then I want to kill something. I want to rip something to pieces and then char it over a fire and eat it all bloody and raw in the middle."

Glorian looked off into the distance, where the tall trees were bending in the stiffening breeze. "I could have gone into some other line of work, you know. I thought once about moving to Taiwan and beginning a career painting the little paper umbrellas that go in those phony Polynesian drinks. Or I could spend the rest of eternity filling foil packets with peanuts for no-frills airlines. Anything but this."

"Having a grave moment of philosophical doubt, O clever and resourceful occult guide of mine?"

Glorian grinned. Because he was still in his old, liver-spotted, massively misshapen and choleric persona, it wasn't an attractive grin. He really only had one useful tooth, a huge, perfectly white formation that hung down like a stalactite and made him look somewhat like Ollie the Dragon. "No, master," he said in an unctuous, crafty voice, "no doubts or second thoughts at all! My will is entirely submissive to yours! Tell me what you wish, and I will work tirelessly to bring it all to pass."

"Does that include winning for me the hand of certain mortal women of surpassing beauty?" asked Mirakles.

"You bet," said Glorian. He knew that in the early stages of these hero-helper relationships absolute and utter falsehoods played a frequent and indispensable role.

"How about Kim Basinger?" said Mirakles.

"Uh huh," said Glorian, "I'll make a note. Now, as to the mailbox, it should be just around here. Yes, here it is! Look, master! Just as I said! You can rely on me, master!" Glorian was already getting fed up with pretending to be subservient to Mirakles, who was probably much like Glorian's other hero-clients, most of whom had been born ignorant and had continued to lose ground. They'd all taken too many sword-whacks to the head, as well as wizardrous whipsaws that dazzled their senses—usually forever, and they frequently had had their pitiful pea brains parched too long in the heat of dragons' breath.

"Well," said Mirakles, "what about the mailbox?"

"There's always something important inside, master! Let me open it up and see!" Glorian moved around to the west side of the house and threw open the small mailbox that had been set up on a wooden stake. Inside, there was an envelope. It was addressed to Glorian. "Ah, I was correct, master! Come see!"

"What is it?"

Glorian tore open the envelope, wholly expecting to find the usual brochure that one always found in this particular mailbox outside this particular house. Instead, there was a cryptic message from the Powers That Be:

> Glorian:
> You may already notice that the obligatory brochure has somehow been mislaid. On top of all your other duties regarding Mirakles and his heroic quest, it is incumbent upon you to find the appropriate brochure and restore it not only to its proper place but to its proper time. You will find the means of accomplishing this within the house. All of us in the upper echelons have nothing but the highest confidence in your ability.
>
> Good luck to you,
> and may God bless.

"Great," muttered Glorian. He was beginning to feel as if he were trapped in someone else's nightmare.

"Some problem?" asked Mirakles, trying to read the page over Glorian's shoulder.

Glorian hurriedly tucked the message inside his leather jacket. "Oh, no, master! Everything's just fine and dandy! Everything's just moving along without a hitch! We ought to be finished with your quest, oh, maybe by tomorrow night, unless the weather turns bad! In the meantime, let's go inside the house and see if there's anything to eat."

Mirakles' handsome face clouded with anger. "I've told you again and again that I'm not on any heroic mission, not any kind of mission at all. The next time you mention it, I'll have to chastise you from one end to the other. Is that understood?"

"Yes, master, of course, master," said Glorian unhappily. Things were not beginning auspiciously, but then again, they never did.

"There might well be food inside the house," said Mirakles. "The first strategy that presents itself is a frontal assault. In such a situation, my experience tells me that it would be best for me to make the primary incursion toward the objective, holding you in reserve."

"Oh, right, master," said Glorian. "So in case you get slashed to ribbons, I can come up from the rear without a weapon of any kind and reinforce you."

Mirakles shook his head. "I'm merely thinking out loud now. Obviously, there are some flaws in that scheme. For one thing, we don't have any idea how many people may be inside the house guarding the food. We don't know if those workmen doing the construction on the house are closely allied with the hypothetical defenders within the objective, or merely neutral noncombatants."

"Then what do you propose, O glorious leader?"

Mirakles frowned and spat in the dust. "Surveillance," he said. "We must gather intelligence, so that we can formulate a battle plan that has a reasonable chance of success."

Glorian shrugged. He reluctantly admitted to himself that Mirakles knew what he was talking about. His estimate of the hero's mental ability went up a few points. For many years, Glorian had been used to dealing with brawny, room-temperature-IQ types; it surprised him now to learn that Mirakles was perhaps the smartest hero he'd ever met in his long, mystical, unreal, transcendental life. Of course, it wasn't Glorian's place to judge his client, but he did so anyway. In this business, you had to take what small pleasures came your way.

"We could try peeking in the small window on the east side of the house," said Glorian. "I noticed that it was slightly ajar. I'm sure that wouldn't be interpreted as a pre-emptive strike, and so it would be unlikely that we'd draw hostile fire. If there's food in there, we could eat it. If there's not, then we're no worse off than before."

Mirakles thought about that for a long time. "You know," he said at last, "there's a certain wisdom in what you say. You may yet prove to be a worthy companion."

"Thank you, master," said Glorian. He'd never yet quit in the middle of a mission; but already his stomach was starting to hurt, and he was having trouble remaining civil to his client. He didn't know how much more of Mirakles he could stand.

They stealthily approached the open window from behind the house. There were several construction gangs performing various maintenance projects around the building, but none of the workers noticed Mirakles and Glorian. Some of the workmen were covering the old white weathered clapboards with new vinyl siding; others were replacing worn soffits, fasciae, gutters, and downspouts; still more were touching up the landscaping, covering rocks with white paint and setting them alongside the paths that led around the house.

"They're doing a good job, master," said Glorian, as he and Mirakles reached the slightly open window.

"I suppose," said the hero. "Houses are fine for people who can no longer feel true contact with their Mother Earth, people whose innate oneness with the world has been worn away by luxury and ease. My own mother, the Queen of the Sunless Grotto, lives on a rock in the middle of a big pool. You never hear any complaints out of her."

"And your father, master?" asked Glorian.

Mirakles was silent for a moment. "My father is no longer alive," he said in a grim voice. "He tripped over a wild boar and stuck a pointed stick through his eye."

"I'm sorry to hear that, master, but now you've brought up a matter we must discuss. You see, I know for a fact that King Hyperenor was not your true father."

Mirakles' face contorted in rage, and Redthirst sang as the mighty warrior ripped it from its scabbard. "By Thrag!" he shouted. "No man may cast aspersions on my parentage and live! Prepare for a pitiful and piecemeal death, coward!"

Glorian backed off a few steps, raising his hands in front of him as if they might ward off a sudden roundhouse slash from Redthirst. "No, it's true! All of us in the Supernatural and Fabulous Wayfarers Association have heard the story. Your beautiful mother, Queen Desiphae, was visited once by Thrag the Dogface God in the guise of a year's supply of microwave popcorn. Nine months later, she gave birth to you, master, as well as to a hideous monster—Smorma, the great ravenous anemone that guards the vast treasure at the bottom of the Sunless Grotto. King Hyperenor did his best to kill Smorma at the instant of its birth, but it slipped from his hands and fell into the Grotto. The king was understandably distressed and confused by this entire ordeal, and he picked you up and threw you into the water after the anemone. Your mother cried out in anguish and alarm, certain that you would drown instantly, but a miracle occurred. A magic creature, Akubasimé the Loon of Truth, swam up with you clutching its long neck. Akubasimé flew away with you, master, and for many years you were raised by laughing, happy, joyous gypsies in a land far away."

Mirakles took a few seconds to assimilate all this new information. "So King Hyperenor wasn't my true father?"

"No, he wasn't. He never learned the truth about your parentage, though, and he loved you deeply and fiercely in his own somewhat eccentric way."

"And my true father is Thrag, the God of Smiting?"

"Yep. That explains your own superior warlike attributes."

"And I've got a twin monster guarding a vast treasure at the bottom of my mother's realm?"

Glorian was pleased that Mirakles had grasped the essentials of the story so quickly. "Uh huh," he said. "I suppose it's your destiny to return there someday and destroy Smorma and claim the treasure."

"No hurry," said Mirakles. "Now, one last question: What about the popcorn?"

Glorian was completely confused. "The popcorn?" he asked.

Mirakles nodded. "Did the popcorn endow me with any particular powers or abilities?"

Glorian shook his head slowly. "The popcorn just

sort of disappears right out of the whole story. I don't think it's important at all."

"Okay, fine," said the hero, "so where does all that leave us now?"

"Well," said Glorian thoughtfully, "one of us should inch the window open a little more and then ease on into the house. If everything looks safe, he can signal the other guy. Then we'll be in possession of our main objective. What do you think?"

"Listen," said the darkly-tanned hero, "you said Thrag appeared to my mother as a year's supply of microwave popcorn. I was born nine months later. Whatever happened to the other three months' worth of popcorn?"

"Here," said Glorian, raising the window with a great effort. It made a loud, shrieking sound. He looked around, but none of the workmen were paying them the slightest attention.

"By Thrag!" cried Mirakles. "I've been an assassin, a mercenary, a bodyguard, and a kidnapper, but this is the first time I've ever been reduced to breaking and entering."

"It's all part of the mythos," said Glorian. "Trust me. Someday, they'll sing songs about this. These crummy little events will be glorified beyond all recognition."

"Hey!" said Mirakles. "I'm forcing my way into this house to find food, right? Because we're hungry, right? You got any more of those malted milk balls?"

Glorian shrugged. "Nope, master, sorry. I left them all in the bird's nest. In the future, that will be in the song, too."

With a long, grim recitation of muttered curses, Mirakles squeezed through the narrow opening of the window and into the house. Glorian waited patiently. He knew from experience that there was nothing to fear—yet. He and the hero from the Sunless Grotto would first be lulled into false security before the first true, horrible monster showed up. You just didn't expect a Gastropod from Hell in the kitchen of an old house undergoing renovation. There would have been signs outside. Someone would have posted a warning, something like Keep Out! Mean Gastropod on Guard! But the whole day was just as peaceful and serene as—

"Are you coming, by Thrag?" roared Mirakles from inside the house. "You're the most useless, pigeonhearted, giddybrained excuse for a boon companion I've ever met!"

"Oh, sorry, master," said Glorian quickly. "I was scrupulously guarding our rear." He was actually quite happy that Mirakles had called him a boon companion. It showed that the hero had actually begun to accept their relationship. The next step would be to get the Prince of the Elastic Tendon to admit that he was on a quest, as well.

"Forget our rear and get in here, by Thrag!"

"You bet, master." Glorian gave the window a dubious glance, wondering whether to go in headfirst and risk sprawling on his belly on the kitchen floor, or kind of back in with first one leg and then the other in an even more inelegant style. He wished he'd paid more attention to how Mirakles had gone about it. He didn't wonder longer, because the hero just grabbed Glorian by the arm and pulled him through the opening, cracking his figmental friend's head on the edge of the window in the process.

"Well," said Glorian, taking a deep breath, "here we are. Inside the house. Adventure awaits."

Mirakles just looked at him and shook his head. Still, he pulled Redthirst from its scabbard and stood all bent over, as if he expected to be attacked at any second by hordes of ghastly-faced, stone-skinned, insatiable mountain ogres.

To be honest, the kitchen seemed like a very nice place. The workmen had pretty much finished with the room. There was a huge linoleum-topped work table in the center, with copper-bottom pots and pans hanging from a rack overhead. There were two walk-in refrigerators against one long wall, the kind of coolers you usually find only in a sizable restaurant; a modern eight-burner stove stood against the northern wall, giving further proof to the theory that someone planned to do a lot of cooking in this kitchen; a capacious double stainless-steel sink stood against a third wall; and there was a small table and a comfortable chair by the fourth wall. On the table was a stack of buttered toast, a pitcher of milk, and a recent issue of *The New Zorker* magazine propped up on a rack.

Mirakles' face brightened considerably. He went to the small table and began wolfing down the buttered toast. Glorian winced as he listened to the hero grunt as he ate. He winced again as Mirakles lifted the pitcher and gulped down the milk, letting it spill down his face and onto the floor.

"You barbarians are all the same," said Glorian, reaching inside his jacket and bringing out a green footed tumbler in a pattern known as Tearoom.

"Don't need that," said Mirakles. He belched loudly. "Had enough milk. Where did that glass come from, anyway?"

"Oh, master, you'll see that I can come up with many essential items as our travels continue! Anything I had in my bags I can make appear here. I unpacked my bags last night in the Valhalla Hilton. I always pay extra to get a room that has a bureau with Drawer Forwarding. I find the service can literally be a life-saver."

Mirakles' brow narrowed, and he took a menacing step toward Glorian. "Are you mocking me, little man? What are you talking about?"

Glorian sighed. He couldn't expect a mere hero to comprehend even a little bit of the Knowledge. He put the Tearoom tumbler away again. There was no more milk to drink anyway.

A loud voice came from the outer room. "Do I have visitors?" it called. It did not sound pleased.

"Who's that?" asked Mirakles, grasping Redthirst in both hands.

"I don't know, master," said Glorian, "but I suspect it is the rightful owner of that toast and milk. Now I wonder if there's going to be a fight to the death over breakfast."

There was only a warning growl from Mirakles, but laughter sounded from the living room. "Come, both of you," called the man's voice. "Join me, and I'll explain our little problem."

Mirakles and Glorian looked at each other, then went from the kitchen west into the living room. The son of Thrag did not sheathe his weapon. The room was large, with a high ceiling. Against one wall stood a tall, glass-fronted trophy case. It appeared that some of the items that had once been housed in the case were now missing. Shelves of books lined the other walls, and on the floor was a beautiful and costly Oriental rug, mostly yellow, a Keraghan or a Shirvan; Glorian wasn't sophisticated enough to tell. The room was filled with many other curious and fascinating objects, but their attention was seized immediately by a large man sitting in a huge chair with tapestry arms. Beside the man stood a heavy dictionary on a stand, and the man was idly paging through it. The only other feature in the room was a gigantic golden machine of some mysterious purpose, which was completely out of place in that studious chamber. The heavy man in the chair pretended it did not even exist. He turned his attention to his visitors.

"Welcome to my house," he said in a gruff voice.

"I could hear from this room that you took the opportunity to refresh yourselves. I smell the delicious aroma of baking bread, so my surmise is that you are now thoroughly familiar with my kitchen. Now that you've accepted my hospitality, I wonder if you'd indulge me by accepting a small task in the way of repayment."

"We're not baking bread, you obscene toad!" cried Mirakles. "Your nose is but warning you of my magic sword, Redthirst."

"No matter," said the heavy man. He languidly lifted one hand and indicated the golden machine. "This device, gentlemen, is a time machine. You can use it to travel backward or forward in time, as you will. Or, at least, you used to be able to do that. This machine rested for many, many years in the Technology Museum, the greatest historical collection in the Great Underground Empire. It has cost me dearly in time, money, and labor to have this machine brought up from that distant, ruined Royal Hall, but at last I've succeeded. Or *nearly* succeeded.

"You see, I plan to use this time machine to restore the Great Underground Empire to its former splendor. There is so much I could accomplish, if I could only get the time machine to operate once more. The single button that sent it backward or forward is still there, and it seems to be in fine condition. I've had experts examine the machine from top to bottom, and they all agree on one thing: An important component is missing."

"You want us to find that component, is that it?" asked Glorian.

"Yes," said the fat man, raising his shoulders half an inch and letting them fall again. "Within the actual mechanism of the time machine, there were three special switches. One switch had been dipped in copper, one had been dipped in silver, and one had been dipped in gold. Now, the golden switch is missing. You must find this dipped switch and return it to me."

Glorian leaned closer to Mirakles. "What did I tell you, master? The Call to Adventure! Here it is!"

Mirakles took a step toward the large man in the chair. "By Thrag, no one issues commands to Mirakles, son of Desiphae, Queen of the Sunless Grotto!"

"I knew you'd say that, young man," said the languid-eyed owner of the house. "I have a scroll for you. You must understand that this scroll is from your father, and its message controls your destiny. Beyond that, I can say no more, because the scroll is written on a steel harder than any I've ever encountered. The scroll has been wound tightly and fastened with a Frobozz Magic Scroll Lock."

"Then how can I read it and learn my destiny?" cried Mirakles.

The heavy man nodded slowly. "For every Frobozz Magic Lock, there is also a Frobozz Magic Hot Key. You must seek out that key, unlock the scroll, read the words of your father, and then act on them. But I can tell you this: You will find the Hot Key in the very same place as the Dipped Switch."

Mirakles took a deep breath and let it out. He sheathed Redthirst in the scabbard on his brawny back. Then he approached the man in the chair and accepted the magic steel scroll.

"Excellent, O master!" cried Glorian. "You've accepted the challenge, and our dire, daring, perhaps deadly undertaking begins with this moment!"

"I want you to know something," said Mirakles, glaring at Glorian. "I'm holding you personally responsible for everything that happens to us. If I so much as nick myself shaving on this idiot's adventure, I'll make you pay for it tenfold! Do you understand?"

"Yes, master, but you needn't worry! I've accompanied heroes of all sizes and shapes and ages and conditions, and I've never been as impressed by a warrior as I am by you! We'll win our way to our goal, master! Between the two of us, I'm sure we'll overcome every difficulty along the way."

"Right," said the massively-thewed hero. "How do we start?"

"There," said the large man, lifting his hand again and pointing at the Oriental rug. "Push it aside."

Mirakles did as he was directed, and was surprised to find a wooden trap door built into the floor. "I'm not happy about this," he said, looking squarely at Glorian. Still, he pulled open the trap door. The quiet study was filled with the awful screech of protesting timber, but when the trap door was finally thrown open all the way, it revealed a rickety staircase descending down into darkness.

"For the glory of Thrag, and the honor of my mother, the queen!" cried Mirakles, as he proceeded down the shaking stairs.

"Yes, good!" said the fat man. "Now you must follow him. It's time for me to go upstairs to my attic. The workmen have finished putting in the glass skylights, and I can begin working today."

"Well," said Glorian, "we'll be back as soon as we find your switch."

"If I'm not here," said the heavy man, "I'll be upstairs with the plants."

Glorian followed Mirakles down the rickety staircase. He hadn't gone three steps when he heard the sound of the trap door crashing shut and someone barring it. "Oops," said Glorian. He hoped Mirakles hadn't heard the same noises.

It was also pitch dark. "Oops, again," said Glorian.

"What do you mean by that?" said Mirakles nearby.

"I mean, master, you're usually supposed to take the brass lantern from the trophy case. In this darkness, we're likely to be attacked and eaten by hordes of grues."

"By Thrag, my patience is wearing thin, you rattlebrained gnome! What is a grue?"

"I suppose I should've warned you about them. They live in the darkness and they're deadly dangerous—" And the rest of the description was lost as the first grue attacked.

CHAPTER TWO

The important thing when you are going to do something brave is to have someone on hand to witness it.
—Michael Howard

SOMETHING HUGE, FURious, and foul-smelling hurled itself against Mirakles, throwing the hero back against a damp, moss-covered wall. Heavy footsteps pattered all around, so it was obvious that the first attacker was not alone. "By Thrag!" shrieked Mirakles. "I can't even see what I'm fighting!"

"Just keep whacking at 'em, master," said Glorian. "There are probably so many, you could hardly miss."

"Aarrgghhh!" cried Mirakles. "I've taken a minor wound to the heart area."

"Don't worry, I'm working on getting us out of this mess even as we speak."

"Don't *speak*, for Thrag's sake, fight! Help me drive off these grues!"

Man and beasts struggled in the narrow confines at the foot of the rickety staircase, and Mirakles' weary panting mixed with the vicious snarls of the ravenous creatures. The monsters roared their hatred, but Redthirst was scoring often enough to fill the air with the horrible screams of animal pain and terror. "How are we doing, *yaa Sidi?*" asked Glorian. His voice was now considerably lower in pitch.

"Some of us are starting to get a little worried, you brainless fool!" There was a loud echoing *whang!* as Mirakles swung his magic sword against a stone wall in the darkness.

One of the grues gave a piercing bellow that contained an ominous note of victory, and then there was the crash of two heavy bodies falling over each other to the floor. Just then, a bright light blazed forth. The grues, terrified by the sudden illumination, fled as quickly as they had come, through passages to the north and south. All that remained at the foot of the staircase was Mirakles, savagely wounded but still alive, and a tall, heavily muscled man with coffee-brown skin. The grues must have eaten their dead and wounded pack members, or dragged their bodies away, because there was no sign of them now at all except for spatters and pools of vile-smelling blood.

The giant brown man wore a pair of baggy blue satin harem pants, but he was naked from the waist up, and his massive chest was nearly the equal of Mirakles himself. He wore a huge golden earring in one ear, and his skull was shaved completely smooth, except for a single thick lock of black hair that dangled from the very back of his head.

"Glorian?" gasped Mirakles weakly. He lay where he had fallen. Bright arterial blood pumped furiously from his chest.

"Yes, *yaa Sidi,*" said the brown giant, aiming the light on his companion. "It took me a few moments to find this electric lantern. Drawer Forwarding again."

"But you also took the time to transform yourself?"

"Yes, as you see. I was frankly getting a little tired of hobbling around after you, calling you master all the time and acting like Dr. Frankenstein's schlemiel of a lab assistant."

"You may notice, Glorian," said Mirakles in as clear a voice as he could manage, "that while you take a few more seconds to fill me in on exactly what you were up to while I was fighting for my life against a throng of monsters I never actually saw, my own heart's blood is spurting out of me at what is, to me at least, an alarming rate. I'm wondering if there might be something you could do about that, unless you had other plans for the immediate future."

Glorian's huge black eyes opened wider. "Oh, forgive me, *yaa Sidi!*" he cried. "I've been inexcusably self-involved, while you lie there with your life ebbing from you with every tick of the clock! The Powers That Be will surely hear of this, and I'll be duly censured, you can be sure!"

"Glorian . . ."

The professional accompanier turned modestly away, because he no longer had a jacket he could reach into to pull out Drawer Forwarded objects. When Glorian faced Mirakles again, he knelt beside the grievously wounded hero and opened a flat, round metal can.

"Some enchanted herbal substance? A gift from the theological improbabilities with whom you frequently share nectar and ambrosia?"

"No, not actually," said Glorian. "This is Byelbog's Balm. I used to sell it when I was a kid. They had advertisements for it on the backs of cenotaphs and palimpsests, and if you sold enough balm, you could earn all kinds of neat things. I tried to save up enough points to get a rubber glaive once, but I never did."

"Do you think," murmured Mirakles faintly, "do you think you could actually apply some?"

"Very definitely, *yaa Sidi.*" Glorian smeared the strong-smelling yellow stuff all over Mirakles' arms and legs and especially his chest. "Now I'll apply direct pressure," he said.

"How long will it take?"

Glorian looked puzzled. "How long will *what* take, *yaa Sidi?*"

"For this slimy magic unguent to heal me?"

Glorian shrugged. "It's not magic, O Prince. It's not magic at all. It just smells bad."

"Then, by Thrag, I'll rip you limb from limb!" shouted Mirakles, getting painfully to his feet.

"You're making a remarkable recovery," said Glorian judiciously. "Take a moment to reflect on that. You're healing at, shall I say, a superhuman rate."

Mirakles stopped and looked down at his mighty body. Glorian was correct: All the minor wounds had stopped bleeding, and the hero couldn't even feel the slightest sting from them anymore. The major wound, the rip in his chest, was also closing nicely. "This is not the work of your cursed balm," said Mirakles evenly. "This is due to the holy blood of Thrag, which flows through my veins."

Glorian wiped along the rough flagstones with one slipper-shod foot. "Well, *some* of Thrag's blood still flows through you. There's actually a good deal of it on the floor here. I'm glad we're under no responsibility to the man upstairs to keep things nice and tidy on our travels."

Mirakles gave Glorian a contemptuous frown as he cleaned Redthirst and slid the bewitched blade back into its scabbard. "There are questions you must answer, Weasel Spirit."

"Yes, of course, *yaa Sidi.*"

Mirakles looked about the cellar room, then headed back up the wooden stairs. "First, what is this '*yaa Sidi*' thing you keep calling me?"

"It means the same as *monsieur* or *sahib* or any other similar term of respect. As you see me now, I am in the form of an ancient Persian man at arms, ready to fight at your side. The lock of hair at the base of my skull is what Allah will use to pull me instantly into Paradise at the moment of my death."

"Unless some wiseguy clips you bald first and then slits your throat," said Mirakles. He grunted as he threw his shoulder against the closed trap door at the top of the stairs.

"There is no way back, *yaa Sidi,*" said Glorian sadly. "There never is. The trap door will not open. We must go on. We must go down. We must follow the trail of the Golden Dipped Switch through the vast expanse of the Great Underground Empire."

Mirakles pounded furiously on the underside of the trap door, but as Glorian had foretold, it remained firmly, silently, solidly locked. "I will kill that fat, self-important peasant when I see him again!" cried the Prince of the Elastic Tendon. "Who in the name of Thrag's bloody sheep does he think he is?"

"Come, *yaa Sidi.* Let us go back to the cellar. The large man in the house upstairs is, perhaps, a trifle mad. You see, he doesn't actually plan to use the time machine to go back and fix up all the nice palaces and markets and statues and paintings and things. He actually wants to change history."

Mirakles shoved angrily by Glorian, which was somewhat more difficult now that Glorian was a seven-foot Persian warrior instead of a little old gnome in a leather jacket. Nevertheless, the prince stomped down the wooden steps and stood in the center of the cellar, looking north and south, wondering which way to go.

"As I was saying," Glorian murmured in Mirakles' ear, "the dour-faced man upstairs has taken for himself the title of File Restorer. He cares nothing for the faceless ranks of average people, but he has horrible plans for one certain file, a clan that once governed all the wondrous subterranean geography through which we must pass."

"Look, it may seem heartless to you," said Mirakles,

"but I care nothing for the faceless ranks of average people, either. The only purpose they have in life is to run behind me across a battlefield. If it weren't for them, when I got to the other side, I'd be all by myself except for the enemy. And what good is running single-handed into a waiting army of the enemy? Glorian, sometimes your lack of good sense is astonishing."

"He intends to use the time machine to prevent the bungling and mismanaging of that file of men I mentioned, the Flathead Dynasty, which brought the Great Underground Empire to an end in 883. His scheme is to replace Dimwit Flathead on the throne, unite the Eastlands, the Westlands, and the island of Antharia under his rule, and plunder the entire country of Quendor of its vast wealth. Then, using the time machine again, he'll transfer that unimaginable mountain of loot to the present, where he'll set himself up as the richest and most powerful man in the world."

"North," said Mirakles decisively, following a path through a low-ceilinged tunnel. "You know, Redthirst doesn't smell like fresh bread any longer. I think it's finally gotten attuned to you."

Glorian grabbed Mirakles by the arm. The two men stared each other coldly in the eye. Finally, Glorian let his hand fall. He muttered an apology.

"Next time," said Mirakles in a low, dangerous voice, "next time, I will cut that offending hand loose from its wrist."

"Haven't you been listening to what I've been saying?" cried Glorian in frustration. "Don't you care?"

Mirakles looked at him in surprise. "Why should I care? What is it to me if this File Restorer amasses more money than anyone since the dawn of Creation? I have my own worries."

"Exactly! With his almost infinite wealth and power, the File Restorer will extend his influence across the entire world, down even to the Sunless Grotto itself! Think of your beautiful mother, helpless in the hands of—"

There was a sudden, sharp sound in the cold tunnel as Mirakles reached up and slapped Glorian across his broad, brown face.

"Forgive me, *yaa Sidi,*" said the magical comrade, "forgive me if what I say offends you. Yet you must understand the threat that's involved. You must see that the File Restorer must be stopped!"

Mirakles seemed to stagger, and he leaned for a moment against one of the rough-hewn stone walls of the underground cavern. "I should have guessed it was him," he said quietly. "I should have recognized him. He is Morgrom, the Essence of Evil whose name is spelled the same backward and forward. He must have bewitched me so that I knew him not, and did not fear him. He is Thrag's Bane, who from the morning of the first fresh rainfall that fed into the Sunless Grotto has dared to boast that he will be Queen Desiphae's ultimate husband."

"*Yaa Sidi,* he means to do more than despoil the lands of the great Underground Empire, the ancient kingdom of Quendor," said Glorian.

"By Thrag's steely beard, he means to despoil the holy queen herself!" said Mirakles. "How else would he have known about King Hyperenor's scroll? I was such a fool!"

Glorian pointed the flashlight down the tunnel ahead of them. There was a small room with a passage to the east and a forbidding hole leading west. The walls of the chamber were marred by bloodstains and deep scratches. "Tell me, *yaa Sidi,* what do you wish to do?"

Mirakles' expression became grim and determined. "We go east, my friend. We hope King Hyperenor has hidden for us the means to defeat the File Restorer, as you call him. Morgrom, Thrag's Bane—it is our mission to wreck his schemes and bring him low! I swear that I will never again seek out the pleasures of the sunlight world above until I deliver Morgrom in chains to the temple of Thrag, my holy father!"

They walked in silence along the stone passage for a few seconds. "That was some oath, *yaa Sidi,*" said Glorian.

"I meant every word of it," growled Mirakles. "In our family, we go in for mighty vows, and we rarely fail to fulfill them."

"Unless things just get too tough," said Glorian. "I can imagine sometimes an oath is just too impossible to do anything about."

"That goes without saying," said the brawny hero. "But this time, I mean it. I really do. Which way, straight ahead or to the left?"

They turned north and followed the passage farther as it angled northeast, coming at last to the edge of a deep chasm that ran off into the distance far beyond the beam of Glorian's flashlight. Near the edge of the chasm, in a pool of cold, limpid water, was a huge shelled reptile, sunning itself as it were in the gloom of the cavern.

"Look," called Mirakles in astonishment, "that must be the biggest turtle I've ever seen! I swear by Thrag's lidless eyes, not even in the Sunless Grotto is there a creature like it!"

"You are only partly correct," replied the beast. "I am technically a tortle, a fifty-fifty mix of tortoise and turtle. That's why you see me resting this way, half in the water and half out. The turtle part of me prefers to remain submerged, while the tortoise part is more comfortable on the dry, stony shore."

"And it speaks!" cried Mirakles.

"Have you known this guy long?" the tortle asked Glorian. "Is he always so slow on the uptake?"

Glorian shrugged his broad shoulders. "You have to make allowances for him," he said. "He fought a desperate battle not long ago, and we've been wandering in hunger and thirst ever since."

The tortle moved restlessly on the loose rocks at the edge of the chasm. "I think I can help you out there," it said. "You see, the greatest problem involved with my intrinsic nature is that I am incapable of feeding myself. The tortoise half abhors diving under the water in search of fish, and the turtle half doesn't feel up to scrambling on shore for whatever I might find there."

"Then how do you stay alive?" asked Glorian.

"I've always depended on the kindness of strangers," said the tortle. "Not much farther up the chasm, you'll find several coin-operated vending machines. I'd deeply appreciate it if you'd do me the favor of fetching me something to eat. And you'll be able to refresh yourselves at the same time. By the way, I strongly suggest you buy your beverages from the machines. The water here is not entirely pure. I mean, would you want to drink from a pool that had a big, talking animal in it?"

"Hold on a minute," said Mirakles slowly. "This is just too suspicious. I mean, why should we do what you ask? By Thrag, this sounds just like one of those weird, senseless tasks that always trap innocent people in fairy tales. We could end up turned into donkeys or something."

"Like I said," whispered Glorian to the tortle, "he's very tired."

"All right," said the beast, "I'll make it worth your while. If you look closely, you'll see that I'm wearing a glowing amulet around my neck."

Mirakles knelt down beside the edge of the pool. "Thrag's beard, you speak the truth. Tell me more about this amulet."

"If you bring me something to eat, I'll trade you the amulet. You can see for yourself that its light is brighter than your friend's flashlight. It's obvious that his batteries are starting to run out."

"I'm afraid he's not exaggerating, O Prince," said Glorian, shaking the flashlight up and down. "I don't know how much longer this thing will hold out."

"How much will this meal cost us?" asked Mirakles. "I've heard fables of this kind where a burger and some fries were worth a king's ransom."

"Well," said the tortle pleasantly, "the lighted amulet alone would be worth far more than the few zorkmids you'll spend to feed the three of us, but wait! There's more! I call this my Swiss Army Amulet, because it also has a built-in pencil sharpener, compass, secret compartment, decoder, and a special whistle that only grues can hear."

Mirakles frowned in thought. "Why would I ever want to call a pack of grues?" he asked.

The tortle shrugged, a gesture Glorian had never before seen such a reptile make. "Listen,' said the beast, "you may never need to use it, but it's there, along with all the other great items. All you have to do is trot up the chasm about a hundred yards, drop a few zorkmids into the machines, and bring me back a nice little supper, low on the carbs, please."

Mirakles stood and glanced at Glorian. "What do you think?"

"I think it may be our only chance to get something to eat tonight, *yaa Sidi.*"

"Well, all right,' said the hero dubiously, "but what's a zorkmid?"

"The local coin," said the tortle. "They're left over from the last of the Flathead kings."

"Well, Thrag knows we don't have any zorkmids. I have a pouch filled with gold and silver from many kingdoms and states, but not one single zorkmid."

"There's a zorkmid changer right next to the vending machines," said the tortle.

"Too convenient," said Mirakles of the Elastic Tendon. "Just too convenient. There's something about all this that I don't trust."

"Then forget about it," said the tortle, shrugging again. "I have a lifespan measured in eons. It won't bother me to wait until the next couple of bumbling adventurers comes my way. Maybe they'll be smart enough to recognize a terrific deal when they hear one."

"Speaking as your supernatural guide," said Glorian, "I strongly advise that we make this trade. Your etheric projections are getting weaker, and down here in these endless passages, you never know when you'll need to be at full strength. The next talking animal we run into might not be so friendly."

"By Thrag, I hate this!" cried Mirakles. "But I must eat and drink and rest. Fine, I'll do it. First, give me the amulet."

"Feed me first and *then* I'll give you the amulet."

"I'll have the amulet first, or tonight I'll dine on roast tortle!"

The beast didn't react with anger. "How about if I call that pack of grues now?" it said calmly.

Glorian just started walking in the direction of the vending machines, taking the flashlight with him. After a few seconds, Mirakles joined him. He was furious. "As the royal son of Thrag the Well-Hated, I can't stand haggling with . . . creatures!"

"Calm yourself, *yaa Sidi*. I think I see the vending machines."

The machines were just as the tortle had described them. They all bore small plaques that said they belonged to the Frobozz Magic Vending Machine Company. There were two that served various kinds of hot food, one beverage machine, and a Frobozz Magic

Zorkmid Changer. Mirakles dropped in a few silver coins and received a handful of zorkmids. "What a cheat," growled the prince. "Who set the exchange rate around here, Morgrom the Malignant?"

"Actually, that's probably true. These vending machines weren't here the last time I passed by. I think they're part of the File Restorer's renovation project." They made their selections and carried the food back to where the tortle waited at the edge of its pool. Together, the three dined on boiled furtwänglers with red cabbage, kubelik with horseradish cream sauce, a fresh fruit ansermet, and an aromatic tea made from the leaves of the knappertsbusch.

When they had all eaten and drunk their fill, they relaxed comfortably. "I must admit," said the son of Thrag, "that was the best food I've ever had from vending machines."

"I quite enjoyed it, too," said the tortle. "And I thank you for your kindness."

"You're very welcome," said Mirakles, "but now it is time for you to give me the amulet."

"Certainly," said the beast. "Come closer, and take it from around my neck."

Mirakles stepped right to the edge of the water, his eyes narrowed as he watched for the first hint of treachery. But the tortle was as good as its word, and allowed the hero to bend and lift the amulet free. Mirakles held it aloft, then slipped it around his own neck. For a few moments, the odd greenish glow of the amulet caused fearsome, strange shadows to dance madly on the rough-hewn walls of the cavern. Then, suddenly, the light went out. The chamber was plunged into nearly total darkness, relieved only by Glorian's weakening flashlight.

"What is this?" shouted Mirakles. "Some evil trick?"

"I never promised that the amulet would remain

alight for anyone but myself," said the tortle. "Anyway, you still have a useful compass and pencil sharpener."

Redthirst shrieked as Mirakles whipped it from its scabbard. "By Thrag's crimson chariot, there will be one less tortle in the world before I draw another breath!"

"My tortoise half is going to hate this in the morning," said the beast, sliding out of sight into the dark depths of the water-filled chasm.

Mirakles took a few steps into the water, but then dropped off a ledge and disappeared beneath the surface. He rose again almost immediately, thrashing and kicking and gasping for breath. He made his way to the stony shore and sat down beside Glorian, dripping and shaking with fury.

"Useless!" cried the prince in a murderous tone, grasping the dark amulet around his neck. "Cheated by a reptile with a brain the size of a peach pit. And it's all your fault."

"My fault?" said Glorian. "I just gave you the benefit of my experience and judgment, as I understood the situation at the time. You still could have refused the bargain."

Mirakles glared at him. "Not long ago, I called you Weasel Spirit. How perceptive I was then, and how much I loathe your attempt to deny responsibility now! I warn you, supernatural being or not: My sword is still unsheathed."

"Then sheathe it, son of Thrag," said Glorian wearily, "and count this the first lesson in the ways of the Great Underground Empire. After all, *yaa Sidi,* we have eaten well, and now we may rest."

Mirakles thought about Glorian's words for a few seconds; then, still grumbling, he returned Redthirst to its scabbard. "Yes," he said, "it is time for sleep. But let us move away from this accursed pool."

"Whatever you say, Prince," said Glorian. He aimed his flashlight around the cavern until it picked out a low-ceilinged corridor to the south. The two companions stood and followed the faint beam of light into a circular stone room with passages leading off in many directions. Morgrom's renovation hadn't progressed very far here, because some of the tunnels were still blocked by cave-ins.

"Here," said Mirakles, dropping to the dusty floor. "We sleep here. When we awaken, I will take complete command of our journey. I do not wish to hear any advice from you in the future, unless I specifically ask for it. Do you understand?"

"Yes, O mighty Prince," said Glorian. "Would you like me to get some new batteries for the flashlight?"

Mirakles sighed. "How, in Thrag's name? Did we pass a battery vending machine that I failed to notice?"

Glorian turned his back to the brawny hero. "Drawer Forwarding again, *yaa Sidi*. I can take the batteries out of my clock radio and put them in the flashlight. That will protect us from grues as we sleep."

Mirakles did not reply. He was already dreaming of bright, sunlit meadows and semi-naked princesses.

CHAPTER THREE

It is easier to find a traveling companion
than to get rid of one.
—Art Buchwald

"GOOD MORNING, MIRakles of the Elastic Tendon! Good morning, son of Thrag the Cordially Despised! *Yaa Sidi*, it's time to be up and about our work. We have desperate dangers to vanquish, legendary exploits to perform, and a mission to fulfill laid upon you by the Powers That Be themselves!"

Mirakles rolled over on the stone floor and opened one eye. "By the black, swollen tongue of Thrag, are you always so cheerful in the morning?" he asked.

"Yes," said Glorian with a broad smile. "I suppose it's just part of my nature, something that marks me as just the sort of ghostly guide a hero would want to have along on a perilous journey."

Mirakles sat up and stretched his cramped muscles. He had not enjoyed a good night's rest. "Well, let me tell you one thing, friend of phantoms," said the prince in a gravelly voice. "I personally have such utter contempt and disdain for early-morning jubilators that there are very few left alive in the realm of my stepfather, King Hyperenor. *Very* few. Do you understand me?"

Glorian gave a hearty laugh. "You're young, *yaa Sidi*, and you have your health. You think of yourself as a night owl. I understand perfectly that you resent waking so early and moving around; but I assure you, the cutthroats and monsters waiting for us along our path were up and about their dastardly deeds long before now, plotting their evil day's work and laying their abominable traps."

"I'll worry about the cutthroats when the time comes," said the hero. "In Thrag's name, what o'clock is it, anyway?"

Glorian shrugged. "I had to take the batteries out of my clock radio to power the flashlight, remember, *yaa Sidi?* Still, I have the supernatural aide's fine attunement to the movement of the celestial spheres. That will help me make a fairly accurate guess."

"The movement of the celestial spheres? Even though we're down here in these vast caverns, buried under tons of rock and stone, completely out of sight of the sun and stars and planets?"

Glorian shrugged; he also permitted himself to look the least bit superior. "Whether or not we see them, *yaa Sidi,* the sky-spheres turn. My finely gauged preternatural mind tells me that it's about half past six in the morning."

"Half past six!" roared Mirakles. "By Thrag and all his minced minions! At half past six, I'm usually dismissing the last of the night's handmaidens, the one who rubs my entire body with jasmine flowers when she's finished her other duties. I know what half past six looks like only because I stay up all night and recognize it before I fall asleep! And you want me to rise at this ungodly hour and begin the day? When I haven't been touched by even a single jasmine flower?"

Glorian stood and worked the kinks out of his back and shoulders. "I'll tell you what, *yaa Sidi:* I'll take the flashlight and explore the environs a little. You stay here and go back to sleep if you like. After all, you're the hero and it's up to you to set the day's agenda. I'll be perfectly happy to go along with whatever you decide."

"Great," said Mirakles, yawning a mighty yawn, "you just do that." He had settled himself back on the rocky floor when a stray thought flickered like feeble lightning through his mind. "Glorian, wait!" he cried. "If you take the flashlight, I'll be helpless against the grues!"

"Why, yes," said Glorian in a dry, sarcastic tone, "how clever of you to make that connection."

"All right, I'll get up," said the prince, thoroughly dismayed but courageous enough to begin the day at half past six. "Remember, though, that according to you I am a quasi-demigod. We potential immortals have long memories. I assure you, eventually you'll pay for all this disrespect. You may laugh behind my back now, but sooner or later, after I recover my stepfather's scroll and rescue my dear mother from the filthy clutches of Morgrom the Palindromic, I'll deal with you as you deserve. You may end up spending the rest of eternity mediating the never-ending arguments of Ometeotl, the Aztec creator of the universe who is both male and female in one body. Or, in the next day or two, I may think up an even more suitably horrible fate for you."

"Whatever you say, *yaa Sidi,*" said Glorian, smiling emptily like an employee in an expansive and costly theme park. "Shall we go on together?"

"What choice do I have?" said Mirakles in a surly tone. "You have the accursed flashlight. Of course, Thrag knows it wouldn't be much of a contest if I decided to wrest that item from your possession. I could do it, too. You must have noticed by now that I can pretty much make you do whatever I wish. In addition to my matchless strength and boundless courage, I have a certain force of personality that comes from being born to command. Average people like you are almost helpless in my presence."

"Yes, *yaa Sidi,* once again your wisdom has displayed itself in all its stunning depth. However, with apologies, may I point out just the smallest flaw in your virtually perfect chain of reasoning?"

"Flaw?" cried the hero. "What flaw?"

Glorian sighed, as if he really hated bringing up the subject. "There is the matter of the batteries, *yaa Sidi.* Now, the ones in the flashlight are fairly fresh, but they were being used all last night while we slept. They're not magic batteries, and they won't last forever. If you claim the flashlight—as is your right, I admit—and leave me alone in this dark and noisome cave, then sooner or later your batteries will fail. How will you replace them?"

The burly Prince of the Sunset Grotto frowned. "I suppose the idea of permanently borrowing the flashlight is not without its logical difficulties. But by Thrag's double navel, I am no thief! I was only thinking out loud, examining alternate paths toward my destination. We have forged a bond of friendship and blood spilled in battle. My blood, anyway. Such a union is stronger than any immediate profit that might be taken as circumstances arise."

"You are wise beyond your years, *yaa Sidi.*"

"I am also growing increasingly impatient. We must leave this Round Room and seek my stepfather's scroll and the Dipped Switch. But first, let me ask you a question. When the batteries in the flashlight burn out at last, do you have others?"

Glorian the Imaginary gave the hero a generous smile, the kind that Prometheus wore, after that Titan gave fire to mankind, and before he began having serious concern over the regular discomfort in his liver. "Oh yes, *yaa Sidi,* I had battery-operated conveniences almost beyond number in my bags. Cordless toothbrushes, electric shavers, cassette players, you name it. The quantity of batteries available to us is certainly vast enough to see us through to the end of our quest."

"I'm overwhelmed with joy," said Mirakles. "Now, by the sacred spear of Thrag, which way do you suggest we travel this morning?"

"You arrived from the west," came a strange, high-pitched, nasal voice, "then turned northeast toward the chasm. You could continue east from here, or you could go on to the southeast. There are any number of fascinating chambers in either direction."

Before the voice had spoken five words, Mirakles had drawn forth Redthirst. "Hold!" he cried. "Who dares interrupt the planning of a prince's most urgent campaign?"

"It is I, The Protector," said the high-pitched voice. Mirakles and Glorian turned to face the intruder, who rose from behind a high, tumbled pile of rocks. The Protector didn't look very fierce or very clever, and Glorian had serious doubts about the person's chosen epithet. After all, down here in the abandoned Great Underground Empire, one could call oneself virtually anything.

The Protector was surely no more than four feet tall, lanky-limbed, and thin as six stalks of wheat. Its sex was difficult to determine, but neither Glorian nor his heroic patron were in any particular hurry to solve that enigma. The Protector's ears were conspicuously pointed, and they stuck up out of long, unruly blond hair. Glorian noticed the young person's eyes were long and almond-shaped, and colored the palest shade of gray that he'd ever seen. The rest of the intruder's body was hairless and naked, except for a torn and ragged shift of tiger-striped nylon worn for the sake of modesty. The only other remarkable feature about The Protector was that the small being's entire body glowed. It gleamed a luminous golden yellow, so bright that Glorian could have read his pamphlets in the light.

"Let me get this straight, by Thrag," said Mirakles, incredulous. "You know where we came from and where we've been. How long have you been hiding behind those rocks, listening to us?"

The Protector shrunk back a little at Mirakles's wrathful tone. "To be absolutely frank," said The Protector, "I was in the Round Room even before you arrived. I hid myself behind the rocks, and spent the night keeping watch over you."

"Keeping watch over us?" said Glorian with a slight sneer of contempt. "You don't look capable of wrestling your own weight in damp towels."

The Protector's expression turned fierce. "There's no need to make personal remarks now. Besides, although I admit that my physique is neither imposing nor threatening, I have other, more occult means of providing protection."

"What other means?" asked Mirakles.

"I choose not to reveal them at this time. Suffice it to say that they were great enough to win me entrance into the select circle of the Supernatural and Fantastic Wayfarers Association only last month."

"The Supernatural and Fantastic Wayfarers Association," said the hero thoughtfully. "That's your outfit, isn't it, Glorian?"

The Protector's eyes widened. "You're Glorian? Glorian of the Knowledge? Why, I've been a big fan of yours since I could glow only as bright as half a firefly. It's a great honor to meet you, sir!" And The Protector stuck out a long-fingered elfin hand.

Glorian accepted it with distaste. "Neophyte probationaries, we call 'em in the organization," he murmured to Mirakles. "Neopros. They all think it's just a matter of time before they're creator gods with worlds of their own to run. They're all just itching to make reputations for themselves, but most of them have never even seen any real danger. None of them have been allowed to guide so much as an unenchanted frog. They're all in a hurry to establish their credentials, so they can get into the secret parties they think we have. I don't know what these kids think we do in the organization, but by Quetzalcoatl's quincunx, it's certainly not worth risking your hide against even a single grue or dragon or ill-mannered troll."

"Then why do you belong, Spirit Guide?" asked Mirakles mockingly.

"For the publications, *yaa Sidi,*" said Glorian, raising his eyebrows as if the answer should have been obvious. "Look at this one: *The Tortle, Fact or Actuality?* Powers That Be Printing Office. Publication No. 127-DJH. Before I fell asleep last night, I spent some time looking through the first few chapters. It turns out that the tortle wasn't nearly so smart as he thought he was. Did you know that all tortoises belong to the turtle family anyway? That beast was just fooling himself, or indulging himself in a bizarre neurotic joke at our expense. As it turns out, he could quite easily have found his own food in the water, choosing from a rich and varied array of aquatic plants and animals. There are over two hundred and thirty species of turtles, and their bodily architecture is spectacularly fascinating. There is no other animal in the world whose protective armor is so structurally laudable."

"Except for the kimono dragon, of course," said The Protector.

Glorian laughed a tight, humorless laugh. "You mean the Komodo dragon, and compared to the tortle we saw last evening, the Komodo dragon is a much greaer threat. I slashes its victims with huge jaws then hangs on for dear life. Sometimes it actually waits for its prey to die of massive infection before finishing its meal. I'm truly grateful to the Powers That Be that our journey won't take us anywhere near even the smallest Komodo dragon. Nevertheless, I believe it's safe to say that neither Mirakles of the Elastic Tendon nor myself—with my centuries of practical knowledge and woodcraft—would be so foolish as to fall victim to a Komodo dragon's primitive survival strategy."

"Well," said The Protector, "but yestereve, did not the vaunted Mirakles put himself at risk by lifting an amulet from around a strange beast's neck?"

The prince's face began to flush a deep, angry red, but before he could reply, Glorian raised a hand and cut him off. "Listen, little one," he said, peering down at The Protector from his superior height, "do not criticize what you obviously don't understand. The great prince was slaying beasts of field and fantasy long before you were a pale yellow, flickering glimmer in your father's eye. It's time for you to learn to respect your elders, or you'll find a cold reception in the Supernatural and Fantastic Wayfarers Association. Our organization judges each member on his actual accomplishments, and not on empty bravado and unfulfilled wild schemes for the future."

The Protector looked unperturbed by Glorian's harsh words. "I was not speaking of the Komodo dragon. I am quite willing to admit that it may be a fearsome beast, if you're the innocent type of tourist who chooses to stretch a leg across the serrated, backwardly-curved fangs of a hungry monitor lizard, just to pose for a cute holiday snapshot for the folks at home. Yet as cruel and voracious as those monsters are, they are as nothing compared to the kimono dragon, one of which has recently taken up residence in the Great Underground Empire. It resides now in the same Dragon's Lair where once dwelt a more traditional type of dragon, which you may remember was killed by the adventurer who plundered these caverns of their wealth. Your path takes you very near to that Dragon's Lair, and I warn you that it seems unlikely that you'll manage to sneak by without some sort of bloody confrontation."

Mirakles laughed. "The kimono dragon has its fierceness and guile, while I have the intelligence of a semi-godlet—and Redthirst as well, by the scarlet skin of Thrag!"

"Sure, fine, terrific, wonderful," said The Protector caustically. "Yet know this, son of Desiphae: Naught will avail you unless you heed well the advice of The Protector. I'll lead you past all the dangers to come, and I'll whisper in your ear the vital ploy that alone holds the hope of defeating the full fury of the kimono dragon."

"Now wait just a damn minute here!" cried Glorian. "Who are you going to listen to: me, who's already proved my worth to you many times over in the short period of our acquaintance, or this short, sneaky refugee from a bioluminescence lab?"

"You, The Protector," said Mirakles dubiously, "what proof—"

The slender glowing person broke in on the hero's words. "We're companions now, one might even say we're bound together in battle. You don't have to call me The Protector. That's just the official *nom de guerre* I chose for myself when I joined the Supernatural and Fantastic Wayfarers Association. Just between us, though, I'm Spike. That's what all my friends back home call me."

"Spike, The Protector," said Glorian, with an expression as sour as if he'd bitten into something rotten. "I believe that my lord, Prince Mirakles of the Sunless Grotto, was about to ask you for some sort of proof. Proof of your abilities, proof of your background, proof of your knowledge of these underground passages, and proof that you can be trusted to lead us in good faith and not sell us out to the first villain who comes along. Like Morgrom, the Essence of Evil. How do we know you're not in the employ of Morgrom at this very moment, and plotting our destruction behind your smiling face?"

"Morgrom?" asked Spike innocently. "Who's that?"

"By Thrag's neck," shouted Mirakles, "we're making no progress here! I'm getting no nearer the completion of my great task, I haven't moved the first step in the direction of the lost scroll of my stepfather, and my poor, trusting mother is still unprotected on her rock in the middle of the Sunless Grotto, unaware of the demonic intrigue that Morgrom has set in motion to violate her virtue!"

"Calm yourself, *yaa Sidi,*" said Glorian. "I gave this all a great deal of thought while we were forced to listen to Spike's rambling and somewhat incoherent explanation. I believe there is a collection of rooms to the southeast that will be both educational as well as possibly providing important clues as to the whereabouts of King Hyperenor's scroll."

"You lead this great man astray, Glorian," said Spike. "His path leads to the north, across the drained reservoir."

"What sort of clues?" asked the brawny hero.

"Engravings," said Glorian. "Engravings of ancient and mystical import. It is very possible that they relate in some half-forgotten way to the eternal battle between your mystic parent, Thrag the Generally Abhorred, and Morgrom of the Reversible Name."

Mirakles stood a moment in thought. "There is nothing in this chamber but tumbled-down rock. I think it best at this point that we go on to view the engravings. But I warn you, Glorian: I have no need of *two* supernatural guides. At your first failure, you will meet Redthirst most intimately, and then you will swiftly hasten to join your ancestors."

Glorian suppressed a shudder in his seven-foot, thinly-clad frame. "There will be no failure, *yaa Sidi,*" he said with more confidence than he felt. "I am no neopro such as Spike, but a seasoned veteran of scores of dangerous assignments. Follow me with confidence, and we'll shortly have this entire matter brought to a happy conclusion."

"I hope you didn't misunderstand me, Glorian," said Spike. "We're not in some sort of competition. That would be against the holiest bylaws of our association. I have nothing but the highest esteem for you personally, and total regard and respect for your illustrious achievements in the past. I also thought it was a crime that you didn't get the Campbell Award. You had *my* vote."

Spike was glowing so effulgently that the subterranean chamber was as bright as late afternoon above ground, so Glorian switched off the flashlight to save the batteries. "Thanks for voting for me," said Glorian gruffly. "You know, it's an honor just to be nominated."

"Uh huh," said Spike. "We all believe that."

"Southeast," said Mirakles, his face clouded with uncertainty. "Which way is southeast?"

Glorian and Spike looked at each other. There was silence in the Round Room for some time, until it occurred to Mirakles that he was the one wearing the amulet with the built-in compass. "That way," he pointed, and he marched off before either of his non-existent escorts could give him an argument.

The two members of the Supernatural and Fantastic Wayfarers Association hurried along, not wanting to be left behind. "Not so fast, sir," cried Spike, The Protector. "I've got the light, you know. You don't appreciate how many types of evil adversaries, human and otherwise, you may suddenly run up against down here."

"Oh, right, Spike," said Glorian, "and I suppose you've made a thorough survey."

Spike turned to look up at him. "You've earned your sterling reputation, and so you're known as Glorian of the Knowledge. You have the knowledge of the workings of things. You were fully capable of telling Prince Mirakles everything he ever wanted to know about turtles and tortoises, and much more besides. I make no special claim to such all-encompassing knowledge. I don't possess the benefits of your years of travel and experience. I do have *one* area of expertise, however."

Glorian took a deep breath and let it out. "And what is that?"

"The Great Underground Empire. There is not one vault, one passage, one chamber, not even one broken gray boulder that I do not know intimately. I've lived in this subterranean maze for most of my life, studying it in the finest detail. I knew that someday, a need would arise for an expert on these things. It's common knowledge that after the fall of the Flathead Dynasty, a nameless adventurer entered the great Underground Empire and emptied the caverns of every treasure, defeated every threat that crossed his path, and then passed on to a higher plane of existence. Still, I knew that this vast territory could not remain empty forever. And behold! I was correct! Already, new monsters and new heroes populate this portion of ancient Quendor—and who is there to say that we won't also discover dazzling treasures, as we traverse the dark miles of these dungeons? Perhaps the old adventurer failed to claim each and every one, or perhaps someone else has since begun planting treasure for some inscrutable purpose. It's an exciting time to be alive, Glorian, and it's especially thrilling to be part of this mythic quest. Don't you feel it? Aren't you proud in your very bones to be a member of this expedition?"

"Spike," said Glorian slowly, keeping his eyes on the heavily-muscled back and shoulders of the determined Mirakles, who paced along not far ahead of them, "I wonder if you would object to a simple though personal question."

"You are Glorian of the Knowledge!" cried The Protector. "You are one of my oldest heroes! Ask me anything, I'll be proud to answer!"

"Well—and I'll try to put this as delicately as possible—what actual sex are you?"

Spike laughed. "That is one of the darkest secrets of the Great Underground Empire. There is no simple answer, my friend, or else I would give it to you. I have no desire to dissemble or create an air of mystery where none exists. The circumstances of my . . . my *coming into being* are quite unusual. Perhaps, as we amble along after Mr. Elastic Tendon, I can shed some light on all that."

"Light-shedding seems to be your best and only talent, as far as I can see," said Glorian.

"Well," said Spike, shrugging, "you've not yet had the opportunity to see me in action. I'm quite good at what I do, and that includes finding my way through these hopelessly tangled mazes, solving new traps and puzzles put in place by the evil forces at work here, and providing protection for those who willingly put themselves in my care."

"I see," said Glorian. "You speak at great length, yet you convey no actual information."

Spike laughed. "As do you. As do all the best of us."

Glorian took offense at that remark. "Look, young one," he said in a tone that was more than half growl, "did you not listen to my recitation concerning the tortle and its excellently devised protective shell? Was there not whole volumes of information in there, for he who chose to hear it?"

"That's just it, Glorian," said Spike with a yawn. "You accuse me of talking too much and relating nothing at all. I accuse you of talking too much and relating immense quantities of material that does not and cannot serve any useful purpose under the circumstances."

"Hey," cried Mirakles over his shoulder, "I'll stand for no dissension in the ranks. How are the two of you getting along?"

"Just fine, *yaa Sidi,*" shouted Glorian.

"We're becoming the fastest of friends," called Spike.

The Prince of the Sunless Grotto came to a halt at the entrance to a low-ceilinged chamber. "What's this?" he asked.

"The Engravings Room," said Spike. "It's quite safe, as long as you don't spend any length of time here in absolute darkness."

Mirakles grunted. "You have no plans to stop glowing, do you? I mean, we don't have to worry about the glow disappearing in the middle of the night, leaving us vulnerable to hunting grues."

"What the son of Thrag means is," said Glorian, "the glowing is a natural thing, right? You just do it, like breathing. It's not something that you do for an hour, and then you have to rest up for another hour, and then you can glow again. Or is there something about it that you haven't told us?"

Spike attempted to reassure the hero and the senior spirit, although The Protector stopped just before patting Mirakles on the arm. "The glowing just goes on and on. There doesn't seem to be anything I can do about it."

Glorian walked slowly around the Engravings

Room. In addition to the passage they'd used to enter, there was another exit leading east. "I imagine that could be a pain in the neck," he said, turning to face Spike. "Not to mention downright dangerous. I mean, surely there are times when you don't want your presence known, and there you are, glowing all over the landscape. Talk about having to hide your light under a bushel!"

Spike laughed, but there was no humor in it. "I've never encountered such a situation before," said the neopro.

"You, Spike," called the son of Desiphae, "you claim to know these caverns well. By Thrag's bloody lips, can you decipher these engravings?"

"Some of them," said The Protector, "although they're recorded in an archaic form of the language of the Great Underground Empire. Some are pictographs showing the daily life of the people who once populated this part of ancient Quendor. Others give more details about their primitive yet pious religious beliefs. You can see here and here—in many places, as a matter of fact—where later hands belonging to reformists or visionaries or fanatics have attempted to deface or even remove the records of the earlier people."

"Behold, *yaa Sidi,*" said Glorian in a low, urgent tone.

Mirakles, heir to the throne of the Sunless Grotto, stepped nearer to where Glorian was shining his flashlight. There was a carving on the wall that appeared to have been incised there more recently than the others. It showed a tall man wearing a high, feathered headdress, and the figure seemed to be holding out a large sealed scroll in one hand. "The headdress, the depiction of the locked scroll!" cried the prince. "By Thrag's thirst, it *must* be a likeness of my stepfather! But what is it doing here, and who could have carved it?"

Not far away to the east, from another chamber, came the chilling sound of low, ominous laughter.

Spike stood in the center of the Engravings Room and sniffed the damp air. "Am I crazy, or does anyone else smell fresh bread baking?" asked The Protector.

Glorian and Mirakles exchanged anxious looks. "Speaking as your supernatural guide, *yaa Sidi,* I strongly advise that rushing forward hastily may only aggravate our problems unnecessarily."

"You're right, my phantom friend. This could very well be a trap of some kind."

"Hey," called Spike, "what did we come down here out of the sunlight for? To stand around getting older and grayer in these empty, crumbling caves? No, we came down here to help Mirakles guard the safety of his realm and fulfill his destiny. We're not going to do that by rocking on our heels here and admiring the stick figures on the wall. Besides, what's there to be afraid of?"

Glorian started to say something, then closed his mouth.

Mirakles completed the thought. "Just a few minutes ago, you yourself were about to run through a catalog of all the malevolent entities we're likely to meet down here."

Spike shrugged. "I don't deny that there are some dreadful beings in these dungeons. I'm just saying that we really shouldn't paralyze ourselves with worry. Look, we've got Glorian's vast supernatural experience. We've got the mighty hero, Mirakles, and his magic sword, Redthirst. And last but not least, we have me: The Protector! So are we moving out now or what?"

The three companions exchanged tight, nervous smiles. "Which way did that laughter come from?" asked Mirakles at last. "From the east, right?"

"East it was, *yaa Sidi,*" said Glorian. He let Thrag's

son lead the way, then Spike went second to provide light, and Glorian brought up the rear. For some reason, all he could think about was how nice it would be right about now to have another gin and tonic with Amitia in the lobby of the Valhalla Hilton. Instead, he followed close on the heels of his comrades, marching east toward deadly danger.

CHAPTER FOUR

Wickedness is a myth invented by good people
to account for the curious attractiveness of others.
—Oscar Wilde

THE VARIOUS PASSAGES between the significant rooms of the Great Underground Empire had begun to take on a wearying sameness, just as do the carpeted corridors repeating the customary muted earth tones, the floor coverings one finds in one luxury hotel after another, if one is cursed with having to do much business traveling. Glorian, a sagacious veteran, had reached the point where he'd come to abhor the large hotel chains, and preferred to stay in small, intimate, renovated old hotels. Unfortunately, his missions often took him to places where there was simply no choice of accommodations. Such a place was the Great Underground Empire.

The stone tunnels were generally of the same height, except for a) the occasional novelty passage that was vastly tall and which might very well conceal all sorts of evil and deadly creatures in the impenetrable gloom of its upper reaches; and b) the amusing how-low-can-you-go passages, through which even the aristocratic Mirakles was forced to crawl on his belly, cursing and demanding that Glorian and Spike find an easier, more comfortable route. Yet both of these types of corridor were rare, and the majority of galleries appeared to have been hand-hewn according to a single serviceable design, all in ages past.

Mirakles, the Prince of the Sunless Grotto, pushed on fearlessly, even though Spike, The Protector, and Glorian both warned him that there were surely more fearsome dangers up ahead than anything they'd faced thus far. "And besides," Glorian added, "Redthirst is giving off a definite aroma of freshly baked bread. Something supernatural awaits us in the next chamber."

"The Dome Room," said Spike. "Actually, the Dome Room itself houses little of interest. There's a big stone dome overhead, of course, and a narrow walkway encircling a deep dropoff guarded by a wooden railing. Where the danger lurks, no doubt, is far below, in the Torch Room. Or perhaps farther south, in the Temple."

"Ah," said Glorian. "Maybe you and I should wait here, out of danger. The noble son of Thrag will no doubt prefer to reconnoiter for himself."

"Yet you are his supernatural specter of guidance, and I am his source of protective light," said Spike.

Glorian thought that over for a few seconds. "Look, you've just said that at the end of this passage, there's a Dome Room where nothing horrible is likely to happen. And as for light, I can lend him the flashlight. What purpose would it serve for all three of us to fall simultaneously into some evil trap?"

Spike laughed scornfully. "Be thankful that Mirakles is far enough in advance that he could not hear you! Now listen: I always wanted to join the Supernatural and Fantastic Wayfarers Association because I carefully followed the careers of the hemi-demi-semigods who were my heroes. All of them! I could recite statistic after statistic, like a walking encyclopedia of the wraith wonders who'd made the grade. I was a callow fan, I admit it, but I knew all of your exploits and triumphs, Glorian, and even your dismal failures when you were overwhelmed by the forces of evil. Now that I've earned the ultimate honor of being accepted as a member myself, I'll have no part in your faint-heartedness. Our patron deserves better from us, and we have a debt of honor to our organization."

Glorian's expression changed abruptly and he put a hand on Spike's bright yellow arm. "What you call faint-heartedness," he said in an instructive tone, "I call caution. I've been on hundreds of missions, little one. This is only your first. I would appreciate it if you'd give me some credit for knowing what I'm doing."

Spike shrugged away from Glorian's grasp. "Okay, sir," said The Protector, "if you say so."

"I do say so," said Glorian. "Have you never heard the proverb, 'Discretion is the better part of valor'? We shall follow closely enough behind Mirakles; if he discovers trouble, we can be beside him in an instant, ready to provide whatever supernatural aid is in our power."

Spike chewed a thin lip. "All right," said the neopro, "I'll grant that you have much more worldly wisdom than I do." They trudged a few steps farther before Spike spoke again, this time in a suspiciously friendly tone. "As I followed behind you and Mirakles earlier, I heard the story of his early life. Would it be too much to ask you of your origins?"

Glorian's brows narrowed as he wondered at Spike's sudden change of subject. What could The Protector's true motives be?

"Impertinence," said Glorian, "is the first word that comes to my mind. Maybe today our society has degenerated to a point where well-known people can be asked any and all absurd questions. Why must celebrities be expected to reveal hidden secrets about their past to absolute strangers? Current morality seems to condone such lapses of common decency. Maybe I belong to the old school, Spike, but I resent unsolicited intrusions into my own private history. That part of my life is also none of anyone else's business.

"But I'll go this far, Spike: Because you are a new member of our supernatural college, I'll let you ask certain questions about my personal history that would be forbidden to mere mortals, and I hope my answers will help you in dealing with similar situations when they arise for you in the future, as they certainly will."

Spike blushed, becoming a kind of delicate, emotional shade of orange that derived as a composite of Spike's natural saffron glow and an embarrassed pink blush. "First, Glorian, great sub-godling of the Knowledge, what is the story of your own origins? I've heard many contradictory stories, and some of them actually deny you the Knowledge and power you've naturally earned for yourself with your exploits, wisdom, and cleverness. Unfortunately, many of your most valiant achievements have not been recorded in our organization's official Bulletin. Because of that, many of your enemies are agitating for your removal from the Supernatural and Fantastic Wayfarers Association, on the grounds that you haven't truly performed the essential requisite wonders and miracles for your mortal charges over the years."

Glorian was so astonished that he could barely speak. "Here I was, just nominated for the Campbell Award! And just because my sense of modesty has kept me from writing up each victory in the form of an article for the Bulletin, this vicious group that's always disliked me is now trying to remove me entirely from our magical conclave?"

Spike frowned sadly. "Yes, sir," said The Protector, "and there are quite a number of influential inhuman geniuses in that group."

"So," said Glorian, "you say I must account for myself now, after all these years, just to maintain my status in our society?"

"It seems to be that way," said Spike.

All three of the adventurers were still making their way through the long, dark, and narrow passage between the Engravings Room and the Dome Room. "All right," said Glorian glumly, "but I've never before gone into the details of my early life. They're not very interesting, for the most part. As the supernatural guide to scores, if not hundreds, of heroic figures—some mythic heroes even more magnificent and memorable than the mighty Mirakles—I've learned that my own humble beginnings are not interesting.

"There are certain resemblances, of course, between the outrageous origins of those eternal heroes and my own foolish, unlucky situation—the difference, of course, is that a chance meeting with the Enchanted Ur-Flamingo may have world-shaping implications for a hero; but for simple symbolic support personnel such an event is never even recorded anywhere in the official mythology."

Spike ran a long-fingered hand through unruly blond hair. "So what you're saying is that you've had plenty of opportunities to pal around with these cosmic Ur-Flamingos and whatnot, and it hasn't affected the world the least little bit."

"That's exactly right, Spike," said Glorian morosely.

Spike's expression displayed intense disappointment. "And that I myself have nothing better to look forward to, as far as my own career as a member of the Supernatural and Fantastic Wayfarers Association is concerned."

"Well," said Glorian, "there you're wrong. I'm trying to make you see that you're missing the point. Being the companion, being the helper—hey, that has its *own* wonderful benefits. Sure, you don't get your name in the headlines in the Bulletin or Forum, but if you do your job well, everyone in the organization will hear about it. The word gets around. Even though some lean-witted, broad-shouldered, unimaginative sword-wielder gets all the column inches in the reviews and write-ups, you can feel proud of a job well done. Just be confident that the right people will always know who was really responsible for the triumph of a vital mission—and those influential people understand full well that it's not usually the guy with the great latissimus dorsi."

Spike took a few steps without saying anything. "What happens on an assignment like this?" asked The Protector after a while. "I mean, where there are two supernatural guides, instead of one? Who's going to get the credit?"

"To be honest," said Glorian, "I have no idea. This is an entirely new situation for me. Right now, I'm just concerned that Mirakles fulfills his destiny and protects the virtue of his mother, Queen Desiphae of the Sunless Grotto. I'm sure that beyond that, there will be enough glory to share between you and me."

There was a brief pause before Spike replied. "Yes," said the neopro, "yes, I'm sure you're right about that. I just hope no one else joins our group along the way." Then they all hurried along the final few yards to the entrance to the Dome Room.

Just before the party passed through the opening into the Dome Room, there was a sudden, loud, frightening sound. It rumbled and echoed in the underground stillness for several long seconds.

"What was that?" cried Spike.

"You'd think someone who called himself The Protector would be less inclined to panic," said Glorian.

"It must have been one of these ancient blocks of stone," said the son of Thrag, "let loose at last from its accustomed position on the wall, and tumbling noisily to the ground, thanks to the force of gravity."

"See?" said Glorian. "I keep telling you that he's smarter than the average hero."

"Okay," said Spike in a quavering voice, "I'm reassured now."

Glorian shook his head and smiled at Spike's trepidations. "If it will make you feel any better," he said, "I'll take a quick look around."

'Don't take too long," said Spike, "because I have an absolutely riveting lecture on the Dome Room and the Torch Room below."

"Wouldn't want to miss that," said Glorian, walking back the way they'd come. His flashlight picked out grotesque rock formations, many seeming like the distorted and horror-filled faces of human beings, others definitely those of demons and evil spirits summoned from some nethermost hell. Fortunately, over the years, Glorian had seen gargoyles like these, and many that were much worse. He didn't suffer a moment's nervousness until the dimming beam of his flashlight illuminated what was obviously a brick with a note tied around it.

"Here," he thought, "I'll bet this was the source of that sudden racket." He bent over and examined the brick, which was red and heavy and rough-textured, very similar in many superficial ways to other bricks Glorian had encountered in his long and theopneustic life. Next, Glorian carefully untied the note from the brick and read it:

To: Glorian
From: The Autoexec
Re: Your possible demise through treachery

The Powers That Be have been keeping me well informed of your progress, and I must admit that so far I think you're doing quite an admirable job, considering how witless your companions are. Also, you haven't faced a truly menacing threat as yet (in the Great Underground Empire, a grue is as common as a sinus infection, although the grue tends to inflict more grievous and less localized harm in the long run).

Now here is some valuable information that should make your journey just a trifle less life-threatening. First, the being you know as Spike, The Protector, is a young male. This bit of intelligence provides you now with whole lists of appropriate pronouns. Even more important, Spike is a human being, and has no supernatural qualities at all. He is not, repeat not, a member of the Supernatural and Fantastic Wayfarers Association. You may treat this bit of classified data as you see fit. We do not yet know what Spike's ultimate ambition is: He may be a perfectly dependable young aide-de-camp, or he may be planning maniacal, devious intrigues of his own. I can only advise that you keep your eyes open from now until your mission has been brought satisfactorily to a close. Spike's trick of glowing is temporary, the result of using a great quantity of luminia. These are short, scrubby, flowering plants thought to be extinct here in the Eastlands; they can be made to give off light only when exposed to the light of the full moon, or if some other source of light (such as a pocket flashlight, cresset torch, or any number of sorcerous devices) can be artfully used to simulate the correct amount of brightness available from the full moon as seen from above ground. Spike must indeed be skillful in deceiving the luminia in his possession, and it's very unlikely that you'd be able to match him at this task.

Once excited by the proper level of light, the glowing florets of the luminia can be rubbed on a person's body. I'm sure that Spike has sufficient access to this rare weed, but I cannot say how often he must repeat this process. It occurs to me that the importation of luminia from the Westlands and its cultivation in the Great Underground Empire would do much to protect the uninformed adventurer, the sort who perishes each day from voracious grues and other dangers.

Glorian of the Knowledge, I have one more bit of admittedly unconfirmed information for you: Spike seems to have dwelt in the Great Underground Empire for his entire life, or at least for a major portion of it, and his knowledge of the unmapped byways below ground is second to none. Further, our best sources believe he is an ally of one of our greatest enemies. So do be careful where Spike is concerned, but remember that we do not wish to do the lad a grave injustice.

Good luck to you,
and may God bless.

The note bore the mark of the Autoexec's signet ring, just as had the first message Glorian received in his room at the Valhalla Hilton. The non-human shepherd of heroes hastily dropped the fractured brick. After reading the message twice more, Glorian shuddered. His simple assignment of guiding this year's barbarian-warlord to his precious treasure had become something much more worrisome, something unfamiliar and chilling. Recalling all the threatening things the message had implied, Glorian's stomach began to ache. He knew full well that he was neither immortal nor eternal—not yet anyway—and that he had his own set of weaknesses and Achilles' heels that Spike could attack at any moment.

Glorian carefully folded the message from the Autoexec, and Drawer Forwarded it back to his bureau in the Valhalla Hilton. Then, as he slowly followed after his companions, two alarming thoughts chased themselves through his anxious mind: What did Spike know, and when did he know it?

The others were standing on the vertiginous walkway that circled a precipitous shaftway. Glorian peered over the edge and immediately regretted it; he saw a stone-sided pit that dropped like a mighty troll excavation to the Torch Room, a great, gloomy distance below. "This chamber that we presently occupy," expounded Spike, "the Dome Room, was once constructed of the same mineral-flecked gray stone as most of the rest of the Great Underground Empire."

Mirakles of the Elastic Tendon leaned toward Glorian and whispered a few words into his ear.

"The Prince of the Sunless Grotto," said Glorian, "has made it clear to me that he cannot stand heights, and the sooner we depart this decrepit walkway, the better. Also, he wishes to understand what you meant when you said the Dome Room was 'once constructed of the same gray stone as the rest of the Great Underground Empire.' "

Spike gave them both an indulgent smile and continued in a tone learned from too many visits to various museums and other local attractions, and derived from too many bored and remorseless tour guides. "First let me point out," said The Protector in his high, nasal voice, "that instead of the self-glorifying tributes to the questionable achievements of the Flathead kings which we normally encounter throughout this vast network of tunnels, you no doubt witnessed in the previous passage and here in the Dome Room, hideous, gibbering travesties of human likenesses, as well as what could only be described as diseased, disfigured, malevolent creatures from some outer darkness."

"How can you tell if a carven stone image is gibbering?" asked Glorian.

"Let's move along now to the next panel of the Dome Room," said Spike. "Notice the discoloration of the rock itself. If we had a blade—and I'm surely not going to ask the noble Mirakles to lend us his enchanted Redthirst—we might be able to scrape away the greenish tarnish from the mountain's bones, as well as the fetid, obnoxious slime that now covers the vertical surfaces here."

"What in the name of Thrag's fierce favor does that all mean?" asked Mirakles.

"Only this," said Spike, and his voice turned grim and ominous. "Some gruesome, leprous, depraved contamination has claimed residence here, and will certainly do its baleful best to keep us from traveling onward."

Mirakles laughed. "Gruesome contamination, indeed!" he cried. "I'd like to see any horrible mucous from beyond time and space withstand my own partially divine prowess, as well as the ensorcelled excellence of Redthirst!"

"You'll have your contest, surely enough," said Spike, shuddering. "And sooner than you think! There is ghastly evil here!"

Glorian didn't like the sound of any of this. "You know," he said, "we could always go back to the Round Room and take the east tunnel. No sense challenging these engraved monstrosities, which I recognize as the Gods of the Nameless Night. Besides, my belly is feeling a little hollow right about now. Isn't anyone else hungry? We skipped breakfast, and the Powers That Be insist it's the most important meal of the day. Why don't we—"

"Too late," said Spike in a mournful voice, "oh, too late! Behold!"

Glorian and Mirakles looked where Spike pointed across the circular walkway. Suddenly, out of thin air, two figures had appeared. One was a very old man, tall and straight, with bushy eyebrows and piercing eyes. He carried a stout hardwood staff and was dressed in a garment of shining cloth of magical workmanship, a long gray cloak, a tall pointed blue hat, a silver scarf covered by his long, gray beard, and on his feet a pair of admirable black boots.

The second figure was a young woman, lithe and tender in years, with hair the color of the palest early morning light. She wore a figure-hugging dress of copper-colored material, and the figure that it hugged was desirable in the extreme. She clutched the old man's arm with one delicate hand, and stood a step or two behind him, as if deferring to anything the staff-bearer might say or do.

"Don't I know you?" asked Glorian, straining his memory to recall where he'd met these two magical people before.

"No," said the old man, who was obviously a wizard, "I don't think so."

"Aren't you a member of the Supernatural and Fantastic Wayfarers Association?"

The wizard laughed scornfully. "What? And pay those inflated dues, just to get a couple of publications that tell me less than my own secret sources?"

"Gandalf, isn't it?" asked Spike. "One of the world's greatest sources of magical power. It's an honor to meet you, sir."

The old wizard bowed politely. "I'm afraid you have me mixed up with someone else," he said. "My name and Gandalf's are vaguely similar, and we're often mistaken. To be perfectly honest, I am simply Bardalf, the basis for a character who appears and reappears throughout Shakespeare's works, although he persisted in misspelling my name. I was merely one of Sir John Falstaff's companions, and I matched that late, lamented worthy drink for drink. My alcohol-ravaged nose is what gives me my particular sobriquet: Knight of the Burning Lamp. I have no actual magical powers of my own."

There was an embarrassed pause. After a moment, Bardalf laughed, then the beautiful young woman at his side, and finally, uncomfortably, Glorian and Spike.

Suddenly, Mirakles spoke up. "Thrag knows I'll not be fooled again!" he cried. "Does no one else smell the aroma of freshly baked bread? This is no creature of the beloved bard! This is Morgrom, Thrag's Bane, in yet another disguise!"

"And beneath that spun-gold wig," said Glorian fiercely, "I recognize Narlinia von Glech!"

"Oh," she said petulantly, "you're still upset over that Campbell Award thing. You should learn to let go of disappointments, Glorian."

"What foul work have you planned for this corrupted chamber?" demanded the Prince of the Sunless Grotto. "Are these horrible distortions of human faces carved now in the blackened stone your doing? Are you the source of the green slime that oozes down every rocky panel?"

Morgrom only shrugged. "These things you mention are nothing," he said. "Mere symptoms of a vastly greater evil. By the way, I was of course lying when I said I had no magical powers, while I was pretending to be the drink-besotted Bardalf. Look, if you dare, at what rises to meet you even now, from the depths of the room below!"

Spike peered over the wooden railing and gave a high-pitched shriek. Glorian was in no hurry to discover the truth, but at last he, too, looked and saw a vast monster rearing slowly up from the darkness. In all his centuries of experience, he'd never seen anything as loathsome or as dangerous.

"In Thrag's name, what is it?" asked Mirakles, as Redthirst sprang into his mighty hands.

"I have no name for it," said Glorian in a shaky voice. "All I know is that it must be one of the Gods of the Nameless Night."

"Yipe," said Spike.

"I will give you its name," said Morgrom with the laugh of a lunatic. "Behold Shugreth the Unenviable, and await your doom. You'll excuse us if Narlinia and I make a quick exit. We'll come back later to scavenge what meager items you leave behind." And with that, the two villains disappeared in a cold cloud of noxious vapor.

Higher rose a monster so hideous that it would have frozen the blood of less-experienced adventurers. Soon it had elevated itself to the level of the wooden railing. Its body was cloaked in a shapeless, roiling mass of oily vapors, so that none of the three humans could get a good view of it. It was immense in size, greater than the largest natural animal ever seen on Earth. Its dreadful head—it very definitely had a head, although the amorphous vapors formed and reformed, so that the slimy head was not always in the same place—varied from moment to moment in the number of restless eyes and sabered maws it possessed. Reaching out toward them were many rubbery, pulsating appendages. Shugreth uttered a vile, yammering yawl in no earthly language, and as the three humans watched, it seemed to them that the monster's rage increased to a stupendous pitch.

"Let me try something first," said Glorian. "I have a left-over furtwängler from dinner last night. I'll toss it to Shugreth, and see if it appeases its mad hunger."

"You're nuts, Glorian," said Spike, "but give it a try."

Glorian approached the frail wooden railing as closely as he dared, and threw the cold furtwängler into the nearest of the unearthly creature's maws. There was an enormous, disgusting, smacking sound from Shugreth, but then the monster immediately returned its attention to the overmatched trio of adventurers.

"Well, by Thrag's square shoulders, now it's my turn," said Mirakles the near-naked hero. "Here goes." He approached the railing and took one mighty swipe at the pustular head area of Shugreth the Unenviable. The fearsome blow had little effect on the God of the Nameless Night, which turned all of its pitiless eyes on Mirakles.

"Blow the whistle, O Prince!" cried Glorian.

The brawny hero turned to question his Supernatural Guide, but before he could speak, Shugreth seized Mirakles with its abhorrent tentacles.

"Quickly!" shouted Glorian.

Just before the odious being from beyond drew him to its nearest, nauseous maw, Mirakles blew a powerful blast upon the whistle built into the otherwise useless amulet, while at the same time hacking with Redthirst at the encircling tentacle with the last of his remaining strength.

"Now," said Glorian, shoving Spike westward toward the Engravings Room, leaving the Dome Room in total darkness, "let's hope my plan works."

"Plan?" said Spike in an astonished voice. "I didn't see any plan! All I saw was Mirakles in the grasp of Shugreth the Unenviable, about to be chewed up and spat out by any of a dozen enormous mouths!"

Yet a moment later came the unholy sound of many large, ravenous beasts. "Grues!" cried Glorian. "They answer the call of the whistle!"

The fiendish, fearful sound of battle came from the Dome Room, as the dreadless and starving grues attacked the misshapen but possibly edible creature that floated there in the blackness. At last, the malevolent noises of battle came to an end, leaving an even more disquieting silence. Glorian and Spike waited a reasonable amount of time; and then, using Spike's natural glowing ability as well as Glorian's flashlight, they re-entered the Dome Room.

There was very little to be seen. There were tiny shreds of blubbery, decomposing matter here and there on the walkway, evidently ripped from the glutinous mass of Shugreth the Unenviable. Of the grues, as before, there were no signs at all. The only other items on the walkway were the magic sword, Redthirst, and the still form of Mirakles, Thrag's son, Prince of the Sunless Grotto.

Glorian hurried to Mirakles' aid, but it was soon apparent that either Shugreth or the grues had made short work of him. He of the Elastic Tendon was dead, as dead as a valiant warrior had ever been. The passing of Mirakles not only left Glorian with an unfinished assignment, it filled his semi-magical eyes with very real drops of saline fluid.

"Well," said Spike, looking around the Dome Room and even peering over the railing, "let's grab up the enchanted sword and get the Hades out of here."

Glorian glanced up at his human companion, and he realized he'd never before felt such a loathing for anyone, flesh and blood or otherwise.

CHAPTER FIVE

Many might go to heaven
with half the labor they go to hell.
—Ben Jonson

HALFWAY AROUND THE parapet that marked the edge of the deep pit of the Dome Room, Glorian and Spike came upon an old, dusty, not altogether trustworthy rope tied to the wooden railing. "This rope was left here by the nameless adventurer, as he ventured below to plunder the astonishing chambers in the deeper part of the caverns."

"Wonderful," said Glorian, "but what's the point?"

"There are miraculous and semi-holy rooms below," said Spike, "and they may give us a chance to resurrect Mirakles. The path through the Torch Room and the Temple leads circuitously to the very gates of Hades."

Glorian stared at his companion and shook his head in disbelief. "That Hades is reachable from below I have no doubt," he said at last. "But may I remind you, that's exactly where Shugreth the Unenviable rose from to slay Mirakles in the first place? Perhaps Shugreth, that foul malevolence, was not killed by the Prince of the Sunless Grotto. Perhaps that inhuman creature still waits, and that if we clamber down this frail and perilous rope, we may find ourselves each dropping into a separate and loathsome maw."

Spike only shrugged. "No guts, no glory," he said.

"Fools rush in," Glorian countered.

Spike at last lost his temper. "Look," he cried, "what good in heaven's name are a Protector and a Supernatural Guide without a hero to work for? It's our sacred duty to do our utmost to recover Mirakles, if it's at all possible."

"*Some* Protector!" said Glorian in a voice dripping with venomous scorn.

"*Some* Supernatural Guide!" said Spike in the very same tone.

The two stared at each other for a long moment. Then Glorian realized that he had only two choices: a) He could return to the surface and the white house, and admit to the Autoexec and the Powers That Be that he'd simply let the hero assigned to his care get killed by a nightmarish monster out of someone's diseased imagination—thus blowing forever the possibility of winning the Joseph Campbell Award—and was there some other, possibly less terrifying mission that needed accomplishing? Or b) He could climb down the godforsaken rope that looked like it wouldn't bear the weight of a pair of furtwänglers, let alone Spike and himself, and go on to the very gates of Hades. He'd never been to the gates of Hades before, but he'd heard about them, and he wasn't all that profoundly interested in seeing them up close and personal.

"All right," he said at last, but not at all happily, "we'll climb down. But I'm taking Mirakles's magical sword, Redthirst, to warn us of supernatural enemies as we dangle helplessly on this ancient rope."

"Good try," said Spike, "but if you look closely, you'll observe that both the body of Mirakles and his sword have disappeared. We'll find them together—if we're supremely lucky—in Hades."

That made Glorian almost spitting mad. "When are things going to start going *right* for us?" he cried.

Spike gazed thoughtfully upward at the stone dome. "I suppose not until the very last adventure, which is usually the final confrontation with the enemy. In this case, that will be Morgrom, the Essence of Evil. If we do manage to resurrect Mirakles, either he'll defeat Thrag's Bane and the Great Underground Empire will be safe forever, or Mirakles will die again, this time in so utterly permanent a fashion that not even a quick jaunt back to Hades will help. There are worse places than Hades, you know, and Morgrom is familiar with them all."

Glorian, overcome for the moment with hopelessness, leaned forward against the railing, peering down into the darkness. "Then what's the point?" he asked. "Why bother going on? It's only going to be one horrendous encounter after another. I'm going to be exhausted of magical resources and completely fed up with monsters before this is all over, if I myself am not supernaturally killed first."

Spike smiled and slapped Glorian on the arm in a comradely fashion. "Catch a falling star, right, Glorian?" he cried. "You're not down yet! You've got to have heart! You've got to try, though your heart is breaking! Climb every mountain! You know the rest!"

"Please," said Glorian wearily, "spare me the show-tune philosophy. All right, from here on in, it's one step at a time, one chamber at a time, one abominable, ichorous, obscene monster at a time."

"Right, pal. Now, let's get going!"

Spike insisted on being the first over the railing, but before he began climbing down the frayed rope, Glorian stopped him. "You know," he told The Protector, "I know a lot about you. I know you're just a young man with no special powers at all. I know all about the luminia and the glowing."

Spike only shrugged. "Hey," he said, "I admit it, *you're* the one with the magical abilities. I'm just the guy with the encyclopedic knowledge of this vast underground network of tunnels. Together, we make a powerful team!"

"That remains to be seen," murmured Glorian, as he watched Spike climb slowly into the abyss below. Finally he, too, raised a leg over the edge of the railing. Feeling just a trifle foolish and more than a bit vulnerable—he imagined Shugreth the Unenviable waiting for them with whetted appetites—he followed Spike into the depths.

He was thankful for the young man's luminian glow, which relieved the utter darkness of the shaft. Glorian had half-expected the sides of the well to have been decorated with the heads of evil gods and monsters, or warnings to the foolish adventurer. Instead, halfway down, in tiny letters, was the legend *This space intentionally left blank*. All in all, Glorian considered that a good sign.

"Now, I got to warn you," called Spike from below, "this rope doesn't reach all the way to the ground. There'll be about a ten-foot drop at the end."

"Gotcha," said Glorian. "Just as long as there aren't any crocodile-headed demons waiting for us when we get there."

"To be perfectly honest," said The Protector, "I can't promise there *aren't* any monsters or demons. It's just not very likely. There's no chamber in the entire Great Underground Empire that's completely free of monsters at all times. We just have to hope for the—unnh!"

"Spike?" cried Glorian in a worried tone. "What happened? Did something—unnh!" He had, like the glowing young man, come to the end of his rope and dropped the last ten feet to the floor of the Torch Room.

Mirakles' two guides got up and brushed the antique dust from their clothing. Glorian was still wearing his blue satin harem pants, and Spike's tiger-striped nylon shift had suffered greatly during the recent events. "Just a second," said Glorian, sighing. "It's time for a change of costume." He turned his back, and when he faced Spike again, he had a complete set of more appropriate adventurer's clothes in each hand. He had also taken the opportunity to change shape. He no longer resembled a seven-foot Nubian slave. Now he resembled, in an off-hand way, Stewart Granger, down to the gray at the temples the actor wore in *The Prisoner of Zenda*.

"By the blood of the Zorkers!" cried Spike, taking one set of clothes. "You look so much more appropriate this way!"

Glorian gave The Protector a tight smile and began donning the tough, well-designed outfit he'd chosen for himself.

"Where'd you get this stuff?" asked Spike, putting on a pair of good, long, cotton socks, and a pair of thermal underwear.

"Drawer Forwarding. You heard all about that before."

"No," said Spike, "where did these great clothes come from originally?"

"Oh," said Glorian casually, "I order lots of stuff from the Kiwi Republic catalog. It always comes in handy."

"The Kiwi Republic? I thought it was another fruit entirely."

"Well, there may well be imitators," said Glorian deprecatingly, "but the Kiwi Republic catalog is, in fact, the major industry of the Kiwi Republic. They don't even bother with selling postage stamps to tourists."

"I never even heard of the Kiwi Republic," said Spike. "Maybe you mean Fiji instead of Kiwi."

Glorian gave him a long, disdainful look. "This from a young man—who, I might add, has not even the most minimal magic power and is a total fraud when it comes to claiming membership in the Supernatural and Fantastic Wayfarers Association—and who managed to lead his trusting charge directly into the plurifanged faces of the worst monster it's been my misfortune ever to see. But I suppose everyone is entitled to a blunder now and then. The Powers That Be are certainly aware that I've blundered on occasion. So we'll speak no more of that.

"Let us move on to more practical matters. Now, as you say, it's likely to be cold and damp where we're going. In that case, be sure to wear the cotton, long-sleeved aviator's shirt with the epaulets, and tuck it into the rugged, many-pocketed, khaki twill pants. There's also a dependable olive-drab belt with a brass buckle that should fit you. I advise throwing on the British black, woolen sweater over the shirt, and topping it all off with the foldable canvas hat with all the eyelets. Then, finally, lace up those sturdy, warm, waterproof boots. They'll see you through whatever landscape the Great Underground Empire throws our way."

"Well," said Spike after a long moment, "you've left me almost speechless. I don't know what to say except thank you. You've certainly been a better friend to me than I have to you."

"As I said before," said Glorian with the greatheartedness that came from many centuries of helping those less fortunate than himself, "we can leave all that sort of talk until another time." He turned his back, and when he faced Spike again, he had two large rucksacks, filled with extra clean socks and underwear. "This should hold us," he said, "and I have plenty more shirts and khaki trousers in my bureau in the Valhalla Hilton."

Spike accepted the rucksack with a look of awe on his face. "You know," he said in a low voice, "I wish from the bottom of my heart that I was who I presented myself to be, and that I could join your wonderful organization."

Glorian took a deep breath and let it out slowly. "I'll tell you this: If things end up as I hope they do, and everyone involved in this little undertaking achieves his proper reward or punishment, I may do all that I can toward sponsoring you for membership."

"You would? Even after I lied to you?"

Glorian raised a finger and shook his head. "We'll have to see how well you perform in the future. You know, you've told me nothing about your real heritage. There's just the slimmest chance that you'd be eligible to join the Supernatural and Fantastic Wayfarers Association on a technicality."

Spike was evidently very excited by this news, but Glorian turned away, not wishing to waste any more time discussing that matter. He began examining the Torch Room in great detail. It was a large room with a prominent doorway leading to a down staircase. In the center of the room was a white marble pedestal. There was nothing on the pedestal except a small brass plaque that said Frobozz Magic Pedestal Company.

"Torch Room, eh?" said Glorian in the tone of a schoolmaster whose students have just shown themselves not quite up to snuff. It may have been the influence of the British woolen sweater.

"Yes, this was the famous Torch Room," said Spike. "But the Torch was a great treasure. It was magical and never went out, unlike the batteries in the brass lantern the adventurer carried. I suppose the torch is upstairs, in the trophy case of Morgrom the Malignant."

"So then, what you're saying is that we can pass on through the Torch Room as quickly as ever we can, and forget all about it."

"I suppose so," said the pseudo-neopro, "although maybe we could get a few bucks for the marble pedestal if you Drawer Forwarded it back to your hotel room."

"That would be theft! Spike, you must learn that there is good theft and bad theft, and we have no immediate use or need for the pedestal, so—unnh!"

"What happened?" cried Spike.

"I seem to have tripped over a large rectangular mass," said Glorian, sitting up and repositioning his canvas hat on his head.

"Look!" cried Spike. "It's a case of beer! It's a new treasure!"

"A case of beer, a treasure?" said Glorian dubiously.

"Sure, don't you see? Morgrom plans to use the time machine to return the Great Underground Empire to its former glory, and he's already begun stocking it with new traps and new monsters and a few new, not very expensive treasures. This beer is ours! We're the adventurers, we found it!"

"I suppose you're right about all that. I'm rather disappointed, though. I'm not a big beer-drinker."

"So Drawer Forward most of it back to your hotel room for safekeeping, and we'll have a bottle or two each while you Drawer Forward some delectable food for dinner. Or lunch. Or whatever meal it is now. And it very definitely *is* mealtime. I'm sensitive enough to know that much."

"Yes," said Glorian, "that's quite a good plan.

You are becoming an increasingly worthwhile companion."

Spike opened the case and took out a dusty bottle. "Flathead Beer," he read from the label, "a product of the Frobozz Magic Brewery beside the clear, sky-blue waters of the Frigid River."

"Does beer age well?" asked Glorian.

Spike only shrugged, wrestled off the bottlecap, and tasted a healthy mouthful. "It ranks somewhere between not very refreshing and terrible."

"In my opinion, so do most beers. All right, let me set out a hearty meal. First, as an appetizer, we'll have *Huîtres en coquille à la Gentile*, which differ from Oysters Rockefeller by being not nearly so rich. They come baked beneath shredded lettuce mixed with a secret sauce you can buy in a bottle. It's good enough for us today, though."

"I'll say," said Spike. "Am I right in believing this food is coming from the Valhalla Hilton?"

"Yes, of course, in a way," said Glorian. "I have an account with Antoine's of the Mystic Plane, who always caters our Awards Banquets. Many of their dishes resemble those of Antoine's of New Orleans, although some differ for better or for worse. The oysters, for instance—Antoine's guards its recipe for the green sauce so jealously, not even our combined magical might could pry it loose from them. Now, soup?"

Spike hadn't even finished gulping down his dozen oysters, but he nodded his head.

Glorian produced two steaming bowls of *Potage alligator au Sherry*. "Now, you may never have tasted alligator before, but give it a try. It's a good, rich meat much like beef. I'm sure you'll like it."

Following the soup, they had a choice of entrees. Spike decided on the *Poulet sauce Boudreau*, while Glorian went with his all-time favorite, *Tournedos sauce Boyer*. Almost entirely filled, they both still had room for the *pièce de résistance: Crêpes Dubaldy*. Glorian explained that Dubaldy had once been the Huguenot spelling of the family name of Abner Doubleday. The dessert had been invented in celebration of that old Cooperstown resident's accession by acclamation to the higher plane. In honor of the great Father of Baseball, the crêpes came with an interesting filling of peanuts and popcorn, and were stitched together with red licorice strings. This remarkable treat was available only at Antoine's of the Mystic Plane, and nowhere on Earth.

"Wow," said Spike, leaning back and patting his stomach, "I've never had a meal quite like that before."

"Thank you," said Glorian, pleased, as he disposed of the dirty dishes through the rucksack, Drawer Forwarding them back to the Valhalla Hilton.

"May I ask you something? Why didn't you offer this alternative when the tortle cheated you and made you fetch food from the vending machines?"

Glorian shrugged. "I thought about telling Mirakles that I could supply dinner more simply, but I knew that he truly desired that blasted amulet. I'm very glad now that I can perform this little function, because I just realized that Mirakles took all the money with him, in that leather pouch of his. The vending machines would be useless to us."

They left the Torch Room by passing beneath the great stone doorway between huge marble pillars. "Well," said Spike when they arrived at the north end of the Temple, "at least we found a treasure."

"One monster, one treasure," said Glorian. "Except that twenty-four bottles of Flathead Beer don't quite make up for Shugreth the Unenviable. And that doesn't even address the question of our lost hero—"

"Hey," said Spike more cheerfully, "I told you

not to worry about that. We're going to Hades and we're going to spring him."

Glorian only nodded. On the east wall of the Temple were more inscriptions in the long-dead language of the original inhabitants. "If this is a Temple, that must be a prayer of some kind. Can you read it, Spike?"

"Well, like before, this is all obscure stuff. It's kind of a religious tract concerning certain practices. All I can make out is that it seeks protection from absentmindedness, from encountering small insects, and forgiveness for the picking up or dropping of small objects. Or else, depending on some of the ancient characters that seem worn away with time, it could be a deadly warning, meaning exactly the opposite. All I can state with sureness is that the final verse very clearly consigns the trespasser to the Land of the Dead."

"Some mighty religion they had, didn't they," said Glorian curiously.

"Aren't they all?"

"What's that about the trespasser? Do you think we have to worry about that?"

"Hey," said Spike with a grin, "we were invited down here! As they say in German, *'Sweatlos!'* We're not trespassing; and anyway, even if we were, the Land of the Dead is where we're heading in the first place."

"Maybe so. I just want our method of arrival to be our own choice. Did you notice the west wall? It's solid granite. It's the biggest undecorated wall I've seen in all the time I've been in the Great Underground Empire. What do you think it means?"

Spike shrugged. "Probably doesn't mean anything. The Flathead Dynasty probably came to an end before the Royal Engraver got around to chiseling all their portraits up there. Now let's hurry on south to the altar for a second. There's something interesting I want to show you."

At the south end of the Temple, down a beautifully constructed stone staircase, there was a small altar. There was also a hole in one corner, one that looked as if it had been broken through by a trespasser, and not designed nor intended by the builders. It was a small hole. Glorian could see nothing by peering into it, even with his flashlight.

"Watch out for that hole, O Supernatural Sage," said Spike. "You can travel down it with ease—indeed, we'll need to go that way to approach the entrance to Hades—but the path is too difficult for you to return that way to this altar."

"Then after we rescue Mirakles, how—?"

"I know plenty of other ways, Glorian. Relax, you worry too much. Now, I want to tell you this, but after I describe the magic, please don't try it. That will only waste an hour or so. If you kneel at this altar and pray, you'll find yourself back out in the forest near the house. It's a quick escape if someone—or something—is running hard on your heels."

"Kneel at the altar, pray, back out in the forest." Glorian frowned in concentration for a moment, then smiled. "All right, it's all filed away in my imaginary brain," he said. "What about that room we skipped?"

"The Egyptian Room? Oh, there used to be fabulous treasure there, but of course it's all gone now. Not a thing left by that blasted adventurer!"

"You don't want to go look?" asked Glorian in surprise.

"No, I don't even want to go look. We have to keep our priorities straight, Glorian. You, of all semipeople, should know that."

Glorian clapped his companion on the shoulder. "I was just testing you, Spike. We're doing fine."

Spike stopped and looked at Glorian. "Don't test

me," he said in a grim tone. "I don't like to be tested. Just take me as I am."

Glorian was surprised by his vehemence. "I know just how you feel, Spike. Let's go on, then. Down that rathole, I suppose?"

"Whoever said that the road to Hell was paved with good intentions probably never had to crawl there on his hands and knees. Yes, we go down that rathole. Let me crawl in first, for the light."

"No one ever really said that about the road to Hell," said Glorian, following Spike down into the steep, tight shaft. "St. Francis de Sales said something like 'Hell is full of good intentions or desires.' Other similar quotes are attributed to George Herbert, a proverb mentioned by Samuel Johnson, George Bernard Shaw—"

"Whatever they said, the floor of this burrow is neither smooth nor well-paved, so watch yourself. I don't want you slipping on a loose rock fragment and tumbling into me from behind."

"Less well known," continued Glorian, "are the words of C. S. Lewis, who said, 'The safest road to Hell is the gradual one—the gentle slope, soft underfoot, without sudden turnings, without mile-stones, without signposts.' "

"Listen," shouted Spike, "your constant bragging about every book you've ever read or heard about is starting to make me sick. Lewis was probably saying that a good man gradually turned evil over the decades through love of gold or unsuitable women was more surely damned than someone who only, say, threw a sackful of aunt into a river. But none of that makes the slightest bit of difference now. Mirakles is already dead and gone, and if he ended up in the darkest corner of Hades, it doesn't make any difference how he got there. We got to get him back out."

"You're right, of course," said Glorian. "I wasn't bragging, either. I was just talking to keep my spirits up. I'm sorry."

There was a short pause. "I'm sorry, too, then," said The Protector. There was another pause, of about the same length. "I thought you were, you know, well beyond all those usual human worries, and didn't have to do things like 'keep your spirits up' as you clambered down toward Hades."

"To be absolutely frank," said Glorian, who could see a lighter area beyond Spike's left shoulder, "I don't need to keep my spirits up. It's a regular service of the Supernatural and Fantastic Wayfarers Association. It's done for me; I don't even have to give it a thought. I was doing all the up-keeping of spirits for you. My thought was that you're much newer at this, and you might not be feeling very confident about soon facing some of the most fearsome supernatural entities ever created."

"One more time," said Spike in a low and dangerous voice. *"I can take care of myself!* Stop worrying about me. If I suddenly feel an attack of panic coming on, I'll give you fair warning. Until then, I'd be grateful if you'd just give me the credit I deserve, the same respect I've extended to you."

"Fine," said Glorian.

"Fine," said Spike. The two men just glared at each other for a few moments. It was clear that after their mutual goals had been achieved, they would spend very, very little time in each other's company. Even birthday cards were probably out.

"We seem to have fallen out of that rough-hewn chimney," said Glorian. "Does that mean that we're finally there? In Hades at last?"

Spike stood up and stretched his cramped muscles. "No," he said, walking about the small cave. "It just means that we've gotten on to the next destination. This is just one of your ordinary, nondescript, not too terribly remarkable caves. If it weren't surrounded by all the other nutty things down here, this cave would be perfect for, like, Injun Joe or hidin' stuff from Long John Silver."

"Did Jim Hawkins ever hide stuff from Long John Silver in a cave?" asked Glorian. "I ask purely as a matter of information."

Spike's smile faded. "You'll notice three exits from this bare cave. The one to the north and the one to the west both lead around to an interesting mirrored chamber we'll have to visit if we get out of Hades all right. Our main concern at this point is down there."

When Spike and Glorian made their way down the dark and forbidding staircase to the small, plain, almost peaceful forecourt to the terrible nether world, both characters kept absolutely still. It was as if they didn't want to attract attention, although their very purpose for coming here in the first place was to storm the Gate of Hades and recover, forcibly if necessary, one of the new infernal residents.

"Not bad so far," said Glorian.

"Trying to be hearty again?" demanded Spike. "Not bad so far, as the old maid said as she poured tea for the paroled convict."

Glorian only shrugged. "I only meant that I've been in the Great Underground Empire before, and I'm not usually surprised by what it has in store for me, but I've never actually set foot here at the Gate of Hades. To be absolutely honest with you, I was expecting worse. I was expecting—"

Just then, there came ghoulish voices raised in supplicating moans from beyond the gate.

"Well," said Glorian, "that, for one." He shuddered.

There was a large gateway that looked as if it had been made of wrought and cast iron pieces, but iron couldn't have survived a century in the atmosphere that seeped from within the abode of the damned. Clouds of noxious water vapor would surely have reduced the gate to rust, and the poisonous vents of sulfurous gases would've done worse, especially after the two vapors mixed, making sulfuric acid fog. So the fence that kept out the living and kept in the ghastly dead must have been constructed of some other substance. At another, later date, Glorian might have been interested in discovering the true nature of that workmanship. Now, however, his attention was fixed firmly on the motto inscribed in an antique style over the Gate itself, the motto about "abandon hope" and "enter here."

"How we doin'?" asked Spike in a trembling voice.

"Whatever else happens," murmured Glorian, "*do not* let that luminia glow of yours fade!"

Actually, the Gate itself was already open. Getting into Hades was apparently always easy enough to manage. It was getting back out alive that provided the intellectual and sometimes physical challenge.

Through the Gate, Glorian saw a boundless desolation, unlike anything he'd ever imagined, dwarfing the worst earthly battlefield or urban housing project. The battlefield metaphor was most apt, because on one side, near the fence, were heaps and piles of dead bodies, all in varying states of decomposition. Heavy on the fetid air he heard more of the terrible voices, each lamenting its own, no doubt well-deserved fate.

He glanced behind him, and Spike, The Protector, was there. Glorian had not been deserted, even here. Spike's expression was unnaturally pale, however, but Glorian understood immediately that it was from the horror of the situation, and not because the effect of the luminia weed was beginning to fade.

When Glorian tried to walk through the Gate, he was pushed back by the evil spirits. The purely metaphoric hero of this portion of the story thought at first that the evil spirits envied him, or hated him, or were jealous according to some incomprehensible plutonic reason. He tried again, pushing forward at the Gate against the legion of evil spirits, who began to jeer at his poor effort to gain entry.

"Now it's my turn," said Spike, stepping forward confidently. "Here's where I saw an adventurer perform the sacred rites that will let us get safely past these guardian spirits, and allow us to wander as long as we need within the infernal kingdom itself."

"How?" asked Glorian. "There's nothing in any of the Supernatural and Fantastic Wayfarers Association's handbooks covering this situation."

"That's 'cause the jealous dead don't want us living folks traipsing all over their fire and brimstone. Now look on the ground. See? There's some kind of ancient Zorker religious text, a bell, and two unlit candles. There's a certain combination of things we've got to do, and we've got to do them in the proper order, or we're in a lot of trouble."

"And you know all about the proper order, don't you, Spike?" said Glorian nervously. He may have changed his looks so that he appeared like Stewart Granger in jungle gear, but he still had his own doubts and fears.

"You bet. You'll see. A few minutes from now, you'll be shaking hands with dead people and thanking me for the experience. Now, let's see: Was it the book first, then the bell, then the candles? Or the bell, the book, and the candles? Or—"

"The familiar phrase is 'bell, book, and candle,' " suggested Glorian.

Spike glanced at his companion and his eyes narrowed shrewdly. "We'll try that one first, then, if you say so. If you insist. If you're so sure you know everything there is to know about Hades all of a sudden."

"Do what you wish," said Glorian wearily.

"Well, then," said The Protector grimly, "we'll do it the way I recall it. I'll ring the bell first." As Spike rang the handbell, it became red-hot and the young man dropped it to the ground.

"Was that supposed to happen?" asked Glorian in a loud whisper. "Was it supposed to get all hot like that? What if you have to ring it again?"

"Take a look," said Spike. The wraiths slowly stopped their gesticulating and catcalls, and they stood in place as if they'd suddenly become paralyzed. Not quite paralyzed—each one had turned to face Glorian and Spike with an expectant expression on its face.

"What's that mean?" asked Glorian, his hands shaking.

"I don't know, I don't know!" cried Spike.

On the ashen faces of the long- and newly-dead were expressions of a long-forgotten terror.

"What now?" shouted Glorian, starting at every motion, every noise.

"I think we're all right," said Spike.

"Should we get out of here, try again tomorrow?"

The Protector faced his older colleague and slapped him once, briefly, across the face. "I'm sorry, sir."

Glorian raised one hand to his cheek. "Do you remember what you said to me upon the occasion of my giving you a similar reproof?"

"Yes, O Supernatural Guide, but just now I felt you needed it."

"Perhaps you were right. Go on."

"Next the candles," said Spike. "Matches, please."

"Oh, I have no matches," said Glorian. "I'm quite sure of it."

"Well, I don't have any, I know that for a fact. You'll have to Drawer Forward some matches quickly if we're to survive this ritual. We've begun it, and we have to complete it, or else we're as good as dead."

Spike lifted one hand and swept it in an arc at the ghouls and other ghastly beings silently observing them.

Glorian wiped his forehead with one hand. "I can't even Drawer Forward matches. There are none in the rooms of the Valhalla Hilton."

"*No matches!*" shouted Spike. "*Every* hotel supplies books of matches in the guests' rooms! If there's nothing else, there's at least a book of matches!"

Glorian stubbornly shook his head. "The vast majority of guests at the Valhalla Hilton have no need of external means for creating fire. I, unfortunately, am one of the minority. I do not have the power to produce fire from my fingertips, and I cannot Drawer Forward matches from the hotel. A nice mint from the pillow, maybe."

Spike's expression was absolutely terrified. "We're *doomed* now, Glorian! And, once again, it's all *your* fault! You think you're such a great—"

Glorian held up a hand for silence. "I did not mean to suggest that I was completely helpless. It just appears that, once again, despite your youth and enthusiasm, we will have to proceed according to my ideas, my plans, my thinking, and my experience. Spike, as a glowing young man, you're superb. Otherwise—" Glorian just shrugged.

"Really?" said the murderously angry Spike, forgetting for the moment his desperate danger at the very Gate of Hades. "Just how do you propose to get inside and rescue Mirakles?"

Glorian stood up and leaned back against the fence, pretending not to be bothered about the nearness of the ghosts and other hellish creatures within reach from the other side. His expression was absolutely unconcerned. "Which would you prefer, depending on whether you've read Virgil or Homer?" he asked Spike. "A ram and ewe whose throats we'll have to cut, or a few gallon cans of blood. Either will work just fine.''

The Protector stared at him for a long moment. Then he said, ''You *can't* Drawer Forward me a pack of matches, but you *can* get me a live ram and ewe, or gallon cans of blood?''

''Exactly,'' said Glorian. ''Now choose fast. I think the natives are starting to get restless again!''

CHAPTER SIX

Few are wholly dead:
Blow on a dead man's embers
And a live flame will start.
—Robert Graves

THEY ARGUED THE MERITS the live animals as opposed to the esthetically neater cans of blood for quite some time. The big problem was that because of the various times of day—first here in Hades' hallway, then in the Great Underground Empire generally, and above-ground in what some folks are pleased to call "the real world," and finally at the Registration Desk of the Valhalla Hilton—Glorian's request would not be noticed for quite some time.

The reason was that back in Valhalla, it was the middle of the night. That meant that Glorian's note which he Drawer Forwarded back to his hotel room —a hotel room from which he was deriving very little pleasure at very expensive rates, he reminded himself gloomily—wouldn't be picked up until morning by the housekeeping maid.

"She's going to wonder why nobody's slept in that bed again," said Glorian to himself.

"This hotel," said Spike slowly, "you really think they've got rams and ewes and gallon jugs of blood stacked up in Room Service? And blood from obscure sources, too?"

"Of course, they do," said Glorian, in a tone that made it clear he thought The Protector was a blockhead. "Every day the Valhalla Hilton accommodates everyone from Shiva the Destroyer to, well, semi-super, lower-level types like me. They serve wizards, witches, elves, trolls, dwarves, demons, elementals, ghosts, sylphs, gnomes, ghouls, fairies, sprites, specters, djinn, brownies, pixies, gremlins, hobs, pookas, kobolds, banshees, leprechauns, nymphs and dryads of all persuasions, undines, nixies, naiads, kelpies, sirens, fauns, satyrs, centaurs, dybbuks, fiends, in- and succubi, afrits, lamias, zombies, imps, poltergeists, goblins, boogeymen, Furies, Fates, were-things, seraphim, cherubim, and angels of other ranks, phantoms and phantasms, wraiths, apparitions, *Doppelgängers*, pagans and heathens, heretics, the good, the bad, and the ones who could maybe do something with their hair."

"Yipe," said Spike.

"Then you have everybody from the Tooth Fairy to the Sandman to Reddi Kilowatt getting away from it all. And checking in you've got every god and goddess and godling from Aa Nefer, the sacred bull of ancient Egypt, to Zuttibur, the forest god of the Slavs, too. *With* their entourages."

"They do a big trade in gods?" asked Spike. He had the look of the genuine acolyte on his face, and Glorian felt that if Spike could stay out of too much trouble, he would definitely make it into the Supernatural and Fantastic Wayfarers Association. After all, there were worse types than The Protector in the group. Glorian had had a few memorable lunches with Loki at the table, for instance.

"And on top of everything else, remember that each one of these gods or supernatural beings assumes he'll be able to carry on his regular and often obscene rites either in his own room at the Valhalla Hilton, or in one of the function rooms. They also expect the hotel to supply whatever weird, unreal, or merely rare item might be needed at any moment. Blood's a cinch for them. They've got vampires calling down at all hours of the night for it."

"What about basilisks? You didn't mention—"

"Basilisks, too," said Glorian. "You didn't think I was giving you a complete list, did you? That was just off the top of my head. The Valhalla Hilton serves supernatural beings you wouldn't even be able to put a name to, I'd bet on it."

Spike was getting a sick look on his face. "Let's get out of here," he said in a quavery voice. "If we're not going to make the journey into Hades tonight, let's at least get out of the reach of its inmates."

"Good idea," said Glorian. "Back up the dark stairway to that small cave?"

"We have to kill the time someplace, and the cave is as good as any." Spike shuddered. "Have you put through your request yet?" he asked.

"No," said Glorian, yawning and starting the climb up the staircase to the tiny cave.

"Let's go with the cans, okay?" said The Protector in a plaintive tone. "I'm not real good when it comes to slashing the throats of things that aren't trying to hurt me."

Glorian turned and put his hand on Spike's shoulder. "Fine," he said. "I was planning to go ahead with four gallon cans, two of ram's blood, two of ewe's. Ought to be plenty for what we've got to do."

They sat on the floor of the small cave for a while. Glorian Drawer Forwarded his note. They talked a little more, and then they fell asleep. One of them should have stood watch, but they both fell asleep. You can only expect so much from these people, you know. Besides, Mirakles had been the hero; it wasn't

Glorian or Spike's job to think like a military genius. And they probably needed the rest, okay?

When Spike awoke, he found Glorian already stalking impatiently around the small cave. "You didn't do any exploring on your own, did you?" asked the young man.

"No, I stayed in the cave. I've only been up for fifteen minutes or so. Why?"

"Oh, nothing," said Spike. The two stared at each other wordlessly for a moment.

"Want coffee and a sweet roll?" asked Glorian at last. "They come with the room, whether you want 'em or not. I don't like to eat early in the day."

"Sure," said Spike gratefully, "I'll take them. Thanks."

"Don't mention. I've been reading."

The Protector had a mouthful of sweet roll, so he just looked up and wiggled his eyebrows.

Glorian held up a Powers That Be Printing Office pamphlet, this one entitled *Hades on Five Zorkmids a Day*. "Just checking on procedure," he said. "It's more complicated than I thought. The official policy seems to be to ignore Virgil and go with Homer, for the sake of seniority if for no other reason. Well, it turns out that I need a lot more than a few buckets of blood."

"I don't really want to hear this."

Glorian laughed. "None of it's so bad. There's just a long tradition to follow. Fortunately, I had plenty of time to put through another request and—" He looked surprised, turned his back on Spike, and produced two large, sturdy, burlap sacks, bulging with contents. "And here we go!" he announced with satisfaction.

"Burlap sacks," said Spike. "I've always admired how useful they can be. Now, what do you have in 'em?"

Glorian just set the sacks on the floor of the cave

and let Spike examine them. "There are two cans in each sack," said The Protector.

"About the size of a can of paint. They get heavy fast, so I had the hotel divide the load."

"A sword?"

"Non-magical. Apparently, I have to dig this trench, and at the last minute I realized that I needed a tool. I also read in the pamphlet that you need a sword to keep back all the billions of ghosts you don't want to talk to, just so you can make yourself understood by the ones you do."

Spike shuddered. "I didn't know we wanted to talk to *any* of them, except Mirakles," he said. "I hadn't pictured this adventure as being so social, if you know what I mean."

"Use the sword to pry off the lids of the blood buckets, too. The pamphlet advised me that we wouldn't be able to bring any non-magical items back out of Hades, so we'll have to leave the sword behind."

"Aw. Now, look, you got milk and honey and wine and a plastic jug of water. I figured on a kind of quick, quiet guerrilla raid into Hell to get your pal back, and you're turning it into some kind of picnic or something."

Glorian stopped his pacing and stared hard at Spike. He drew himself up to his full Stewart Granger height, which was considerable, and stared down at the glowing young man. "If you really object to any of this," he said in a cold voice, "you can stay here in the cave, or go off somewhere else in the Great Underground Empire. We never even have to see each other again. But this is something I *have* to do, and I have to do it according to the book and by the numbers. Understand?"

Spike did not reply. "What else we got in here?" He lifted out a paper bag and opened it. "Round rice."

"White barley."

"Jeez, and I'm full already."

"It's not for you and it's not for me," said Glorian.

Spike closed the burlap sack and threw it over his shoulder. "Is looking like one of Santa's helpers enough to get me into the Supernatural and Fantastic Wayfarers Association?" he asked, laughing.

Glorian didn't dignify the question with a reply. He hoisted the second sack and led the way back down the forbidding staircase. Spike followed.

When they got to the vestibule, it was just as it had been the previous evening. "This is going to be rough," said Spike. "Wish we had the matches. No good ringing the bell and reading the book without the candles."

"Don't worry. I've got an alternate solution to the problem of getting past all those ghastly guardians." Glorian walked right up to the open gate and tried to enter. Once more, the moaning, gesticulating shades of the dead pushed him back, trying to keep him out of Hades. Glorian opened his burlap sack and took out one of the heavy gallon cans. "Look!" he cried. "Blood! I bring blood!"

There was a bare instant of silence, and then all the ghosts began going "Ahhhhh!" as if they'd just witnessed the lighting of the Christmas tree at Rockefeller Plaza. The sound grew and grew, until it was a deafening roar. Glorian turned to look back at Spike, who didn't look happy but at least gave him a positive nod.

Glorian entered Hades, holding up *Hades on Five Zorkmids a Day* and reading aloud from it. "Stride boldly into the Kingdom of Decay," he quoted. "You will see on one hand the River of Terrible Fire, and on the other the River of Wailing, which is a branch of the Styx. You will see the two rivers unite around a bald and barren mount of rock, and the dreadful waters then hurl themselves with a great thunder into the Great River of Acheron. This is the spot you must go to. Here is where Charon arrives to ferry the recent dead into the Underworld proper, but you may have no need of his services, if all you want to do is speak with the Guardians at the Gate."

"I expected a dog," said Spike in a voice that trembled so much that Glorian barely understood him. "You know which one I mean. Three heads."

"Herakles took him away, but later he brought him back. I passed a note on to Hermes last night. Hermes is the Guide of the Dead, you know, and Cerberus is like a little puppy with him. I'm glad Hermes was at the awards banquet, because I begged a favor and had him take care of the Hound of Hell for us—but we're on a tight schedule."

"Great," said Spike. "I have to admit, I'm having trouble following you deeper into Hades."

"This will all redound to your credit, you can be sure."

"Terrific, if I live to see the world ever again," said The Protector.

They marched around for quite a while looking for the island rock, with the entire pack of horrible phantoms following them in the hope of snatching a few drops of the promised blood. "I think I see the pinnacle we're looking for, about half a mile through this miasma," said Glorian, pointing.

"You know something? Hades is paved with exactly the same kind of rock and chips of stone that you find in the tunnels of the Great Underground Empire. As if the G. U. E. was just an extension of this monstrous place, or a kind of intelligence test for adventurers, and the dumb ones have to stay here through eternity. Anyway, I've never experienced anything that smelled this bad, not even Shugreth the Unenviable. It's like the gods of the underworld contracted somebody to scoop up tons of rock from the passages above, soak them in some horrible solution until every stone reeked with a supernatural stink, and then they brought all that rock back here and paved the place with it. I'm chattering, aren't I? I'm just talking to hear the sound of my own voice."

"You have a scientific turn of mind, that's all."

Spike peered in the direction Glorian indicated, but all he could see were throngs of ghastly guardians everywhere, cutting off their retreat. "I *do* believe in spooks," he muttered. "I *do* believe in spooks, I do, I do, I do."

"Aha!" cried Glorian. "Here we are!" They stood on the bank of a mighty, black, fuming river.

"Scary place," said Spike, "but I'm glad we made it this far."

Both trespassers dropped their sacks, and Glorian opened them. He drew his sword and cleared a shallow trench one cubit square. Then he passed the sword to Spike. "Hold 'em back. *All* of 'em."

"You're kidding," said The Protector.

Glorian poured libations around the square trench, first milk mingled with honey, then the bottle of sweet wine, and last of all the plastic jug of water.

"You think these ghosts get anything out of all that stuff you're dumping into the ground?" asked Spike dubiously.

"It's traditional. I don't know how it works." Then over all he'd spilled, he sprinkled the white barley. "Got to pray now," he said, kneeling by the trench. The racket of the frustrated phantoms was growing louder and more threatening. Glorian ignored it, and addressed prayers to the ghosts themselves, and promised that he'd make a special offering to Tiresias when they returned to the upper world.

"Who's Tiresias?" asked Spike.

Glorian ignored him. He said, "Dread Hades and awful Persephone, Lords of the Underworld, I have no live animals to sacrifice to you now. I swear by all I hold dear, however, that when I return to my home on the Mystic Plane, I will make a generous contribution to your favorite charity."

"Huh?"

Glorian looked over his shoulder quickly. "You're supposed to cut the ram and ewe's throats and let the blood pour into the trench, then flay the dead animals and sacrifice them, burning the flesh to Hades and his wife, Persephone."

"But all we've got are gallon buckets."

"Right," said Glorian. "So I'll make a big cash donation to their favorite charity."

"They have a favorite charity? Hades and Persephone? *What* charity?"

"The Heart Association."

"The Heart Association? That's good, I guess."

Glorian shook his head. "You don't understand. On the Mystic Plane, there is a different Heart Association. Its goals are more in line with what you'd expect from the gods of this place. It has many professional and volunteer employees whose job it is to spread stress and other leading factors of heart disease on the Mundane Plane. That will cause even more humans to die, and swell the kingdom of Hades and Persephone."

Spike stared up at the hazy, bronze-colored sky. "I'm never going to be happy again, just knowing these things."

"Now the blood," said Glorian. He took back the sword and used its tip to pry loose the flat lids to the four gallon cans. Spike helped him pour the buckets into the trench. The ghosts almost went wild with desire, but Glorian turned and held them back with his sword.

"That didn't fill up the trench as much as I thought it would."

"Should've gotten more," agreed Glorian. "But it would've been a lot of trouble to carry it all."

"Not as much trouble as I see brewing in the faces of these terrible wraiths."

"I think we're all right," said Glorian with forced cheerfulness. "I think we have plenty. We only have to question Tiresias, and then we can get the hell out of here. To find Mirakles, I mean."

Meanwhile, from the fluttering ghosts swarming back and forth by the blood-filled trench there came an outcry frightening enough to chill anyone's bones. Spike looked around, and noticed each spirit as an individual for the first time, some with gaping wounds or other proofs of their violent deaths, some were just children, or lovely maidens. "Oh, please don't take too much more time," begged the glowing young man. "I don't know how much more of this I can stand."

After a few minutes, a tall, burly, curly-haired apparition pushed his way to the front of the crowd, as if that was his right and customary honor.

"It's him, I think," said Glorian, letting out a deep breath.

"Tiresias? Who was he anyway?"

"One of the greatest of the soothsayers of ancient Thebes. He was stricken sightless because, purely by accident, he happened upon Athena in her bath. Athena took away his physical sight, but tried to make things better for the innocent man by giving the gift of seeing the future."

"I've had days like that," said Spike sourly. At this point, he just wanted to get it all over with and get back to the relatively safe passages and chambers of the Great Underground Empire, but Glorian kept adding new chores and duties to their time in Hades.

"Need something, right?" said Tiresias, leaning on his staff. He spoke in a faint, whispery voice like the rustle of fallen leaves. "Let me drink, and then we'll get down to business. As if I don't have better things to do than give advice to every hero and quasi-hero who pushes his way in here."

"Do you?" asked Spike rudely. "Have anything better to do, I mean?"

Tiresias had bent over, but had not yet put his lips to the sheep's blood. "Well, actually," he said, "beyond drinking my share of this offering, no. I have nothing better to do. Remember where we are. It hasn't yet occurred to anyone here to organize us all into teams or anything."

Glorian put a hand on Spike's arm, preventing him from saying or doing anything further to delay Tiresias. At last, the blind soothsayer stood up straight, his lips stained with the dark blood. "The canned stuff, right? Nobody ever bothers going through the old true ritual anymore." Now his voice was deep and booming. "Ah well, young men, what can I do for you? Want to speak to your Mommy, find out where she hid the silverware?"

Glorian held his silence for a moment. "My name is—"

"Glorian of the Knowledge," said Tiresias. "Yes, I know."

"And my mission was to be the Supernatural Guide to a sort of warrior-hero—"

"Mirakles," said Tiresias. "You've come to talk with Mirakles. Well, if you sit here by this trench full of blood long enough, he'll show up. Every person who ever lived will show up, if you wait long enough. Even when you think the last molecule of blood is gone, they'll still crowd up to you. This is not a pleasant place. Now that I've given you the benefit of my wisdom, I'll just—"

"No, sir!" cried Glorian. "Please wait just a moment! We've come to take Mirakles back with us. You see, he wasn't a mortal hero. He's sort of a hemi-semi-demi-god, the son of Thrag the Undelighted. We need to find Mirakles, and then travel back through the gate. We must continue our quest."

Tiresias studied them for a moment. "That will be difficult," he said.

"Why?" asked Spike. "Because of Cerberus? Because of the interference of Hades or Persephone? Because—"

"Because Mirakles likes it here too much, that's why."

Glorian was astonished. "Where is he, then? Have you seen him?"

Tiresias just turned his white, sightless eyes on Glorian and waited for an apology.

"Sorry," Glorian murmured.

" 'S all right," said Tiresias. "You'll find Mirakles with the rest of the real ruffians, wranglers, and brawlers. On the Plain of Constant Conflict. That way." And he pointed across the Acheron. "You'll find it easily, by the unending clash and shrieking of warfare. Finding your friend will be simple. Getting him to quit and go back to the dull world above may prove more difficult. One last bit of advice: Charon, the ferryman, requires an obolus, an ancient silver coin of Greece, from everyone he transports. You don't have any, do you?"

Glorian shook his head sadly.

"Get some!" said Tiresias cheerfully. Then he disappeared into the massive crowd of wailing ghosts.

"Get some," muttered Glorian. "How does he expect—"

"Let me," said The Protector, stepping in smoothly. "Who wants a drink of fresh sheep's blood?" he cried. "Who has a silver obolus for a drink of fresh sheep's blood?"

The uproar of the ghastly guardians went up again

to an even more unbearable level. Most of the shades had a coin, because it had been the custom to bury the dead with an obolus to pay to Charon; but would they give up their ferry-fare for a drink of blood?

The spirit of a tall, lean, and hungry-looking man stepped forward first. "You'll need two oboli, so that both of you can cross the river," he said in a faint, ghostly voice. "I don't know if Charon charges the same fare to come back across, because no dead souls ever make that return trip. Just in case, however, you should get three more oboli, for the two of you and for your swordsman friend. I'll pay five oboli, then, for a good, long, healthy drink of the blood."

"Done!" cried Glorian, gratified that one of this adventure's complications had been so easily solved.

"This is the shade of my father," said Spike in a husky voice. He just stared at the ghost, his emotions nearly out of control.

Glorian looked at Spike and saw that what the young man said was true. He found himself deeply moved, and he gave the sword to The Protector. "Here, Spike," he said, "I'll let you talk in peace with your father. Use the sword to protect yourself from the crush of the throng. I'll meet you at Charon's ferry landing."

Spike looked from the shrouded spirit of his father to Glorian. "Thank you," he said softly.

Glorian moved away, pushing his way easily now through the crowd of thirsty shapes. Finding the ferry landing was no trouble, either. He stood there and waited, feeling great sadness, wishing that someone in Hades would pay so much just to speak with him. Once again, it struck him that being a supernatural being was not always the most pleasant or rewarding thing in the world. Supernatural beings were either successful in their assignments, or failures; they were rarely happy.

Apparently, Glorian's innate time-sense didn't function very well in Hades, because he had no idea how long he waited for Spike to return. In the meantime, an elderly woman ghost, more robust than the others, approached him. Glorian assumed that she had drunk from the trench of blood, and that accounted for her purposeful stride.

"Are you Glorian of the Knowledge?" she asked.

"Yes, ma'am." Glorian uttered a silent prayer to the current administrative board of the Supernatural and Fantastic Wayfarers Association that this old lady wasn't about to start some crazy, time-consuming subplot.

"Then this is for you." She handed him a white envelope with the signet ring mark of the Autoexec on it and hurried away.

"Wait!" he cried. "Where did you get—" But she was gone. Glorian opened the envelope and read the single sheet of paper within:

> Glorian, we all here in the upper echelons are perfectly elated with the job you're doing. I can promise you that when you've accomplished your goal of seeing Mirakles all the way to the end of his quest, you will have set new standards for all supernatural guides on your level to live and work by. I think I can also guarantee that you'll soon have to get used to living and working on a higher level, although I'd rather not get into that just yet. You've probably already recognized that your companion, Spike, is the son of the thief, the adventurer's constant competitor and antagonist. Now, certainly Spike has given you valuable help, but please remember that Morgrom the Multi-Faced is still at large, and that Spike may very well be in his pay. I know that currently you're working your way through a little hitch in your scheme involving Hades, so I won't

take up any more of your time. We here just wanted to be sure you didn't begin trusting anyone or anything.

Good luck to you,
and may God bless.

Glorian put the note back into the envelope, then crumpled them both up and stuffed the wad of paper into one of the many pockets of his safari jacket. He'd had suspicions about Spike before—he didn't need the Autoexec interfering and lending a helping hand as if Glorian had never been on an adventure alone before—and now he knew just who the young man's father was. The thief, who'd caused a great amount of trouble, up to and sometimes including death, for many adventurers who had tried to map out the Great Underground Empire before it had finally been conquered by *the* adventurer.

But standing at the boat dock, gazing out over the vista of Hades, Glorian just didn't care. He knew that he couldn't completely trust Spike, but the theoretically real agent of The Powers That Be had met very few people, supernatural beings, or even gods whom he had been able to trust completely.

"Very unnerving," said The Protector, joining Glorian at Charon's landing. The glowing young man had kept his burlap sack, which he'd tucked through his brass-buckled belt, as well as Glorian's sword. Glorian himself had abandoned all the rest of the items they'd brought into Hades. After all, they'd be able to take out only magical things. Spike would have to lose both his souvenirs at the gate. If they ever made it back there.

They didn't have to wait long. The number of dead souls arriving daily in Hades over the years had increased at a drastic rate. At an obolus a ride, Charon must have collected more silver than anyone in history, even Croesus or the Hunt brothers. Sometime, Glorian would like to find out what Charon did with all his wealth.

The two adventurers shuffled along in a large group of wraiths. When they got to the ferryboat itself, Charon gave them a surprised look. "You two are still alive! It's been centuries since anyone's tried a stunt like this! Oh well, the best of luck to you. I'll take your coins the same as I'll take the ghosts'."

Glorian and Spike paid and found seats near the front of the ferry. They sat down and tried to look inconspicuous, which, in that situation, was as frankly impossible as wrapping themselves in branches and leaves and trying to sneak around with a bevy of wood nymphs. The voyage across the river was an assault on every sense. The water was the foulest either had ever smelled, and it stung fiercely when it splashed up against them. It had a black, boiling surface—not muddy, but something more like the total absence of anything in the water that might sustain life for any creature that had ever lived. The Acheron boomed and roared as if it were falling from immense heights, although within their sight this was not true, and when a few drops landed on Glorian's hand and he automatically licked the burning fluid off, the taste made him vomit instantly. This was not the kind of boat ride you took on a moonlit night with your best girl. Already, Glorian was dreading the return voyage.

They disembarked on the opposite shore. "Plain of Constant Conflict?" asked Glorian.

"The other boy's got the sword, and you don't look the type," said Charon in a friendly manner. "But I guess you know what you're doing. Head that way for a little while, you'll pick up the din."

"Thanks," said Glorian. Charon only shrugged and began poling his boat back into the terrible waters of the Acheron.

"Let's hurry up and get out of here," said Spike. "You're supernatural, so maybe all this isn't getting to you as much as it is to me."

"I'm not dawdling, either, you'll notice," said Glorian. They walked as quickly as they could, until they came to a huge, flat, barren field that was filled with men hacking and hewing and stabbing and doing everything else they could think of to kill their thousands of companions.

"These are serious warriors," said Spike.

"There's a place for them in the world, and I guess there should be a place for them down here. Now, as to finding Mirakles." It took a considerable amount of time—hours, days, who could tell?—to walk around that battlefield and look into the faces of all the combatants. The contending wraiths eagerly turned to attack Glorian and Spike, but as soon as they discovered that the young men were still alive, they lost interest and looked elsewhere for an opponent.

"Look!" cried Glorian finally. "Mirakles!"

"Look!" cried Spike. "A treasure!" The glowing young man bent over and picked up an envelope. He tore it open, and inside there was a fifty-dollar gift certificate from the Kiwi Republic Catalog. "Terrific!" yelled Spike. "I can order some—"

Glorian looked at him impatiently. "This is another minor treasure, put here to distract us. And you know Morgrom, the Essence of Evil, has probably been watching us every step of the way. He knows you liked these clothes."

"I don't care," said Spike. "Now I have this dandy gift certificate."

"Which you won't be able to take out of Hades because it's not magical."

The Protector thought about that for a while, then let the piece of paper flutter to the ground.

"All right," said Spike angrily, "where's Mirakles?"

"Over there, fighting that bloody, hacked-up guy."

Spike's eyebrows went up. "He appears to be winning."

"I'll bet these bouts go on forever," said Glorian. "Defeat brings temporary death, then the victim jumps up good as new and attacks someone else."

They pondered the situation for a few seconds. "What's your plan?" asked Spike.

"*My* plan! I have to have a plan? Okay, we'll get his attention and persuade him to follow us back out through the gate."

"Are you watching what he's doing to all those poor soldiers?" said Spike. "He's cutting them to bits!"

"Of course, he is," said Glorian. "He's the son of Thrag, the God of Just This Kind of Thing. All right, let me make a try. Give me that stupid sword."

"You're braver than I am," called The Protector.

Glorian went up to Mirakles, who'd just vanquished his most recent opponent and was looking around hungrily for another. His eyes lighted on Glorian, but then, like the others, he immediately lost interest.

Glorian took the opportunity to make one sudden, fierce attack on Mirakles's swordhand with the flat of his own blade. Mirakles wasn't expecting such a thing from a mortal, and he dropped Redthirst, more in surprise than in pain. Glorian was too quick for him, however, and scooped up the magic blade—which was giving off the aroma of freshly baked bread as if it was prepared to air-condition all of Hades forever.

Mirakles stood and blinked, confused. He looked at his empty hand, and he looked at the two swords Glorian held. "Hey!" cried the Prince of the Sunless Grotto in a stupid voice.

Glorian cracked the hero across the jaw with the pommel of Mirakles's own sword. The brawny hero collapsed on the ground like a half-empty sack of lentils. "C'mon," cried Glorian, huffing, "let's get him out of here!"

"I don't believe it!" said Spike, picking up Mirakles's feet. "How did you do it?"

"Tell you later." It was obvious that the Supernatural Guide was too out of breath to do much talking as he and Spike carried the motionless form across the Plain of Constant Conflict and back to the ferry landing. They were alone there, and they waited patiently for Charon to arrive.

"Ha ha," laughed the ferryman. "Didn't think I'd see you so soon. It's going to cost you three oboli altogether." They paid their fares and took their choice of seats—no one or nothing rode back across the Acheron with them.

About halfway across, Mirakles began to regain consciousness. "Whack him again," said Spike.

"Oh yeah, always me," complained Glorian. "Well, I guess it's my responsibility." And he gave the mighty, broad-shouldered hero another clout, this time alongside the temple.

When they reached the vestibule shore of the river, Charon leaned on his pole and watched with interest as Glorian and Spike carried Mirakles up the bank, through the mob of waiting specters, and to the gate of Hades. Just as they were about to pass through and make good their escape, Spike lost his burlap sack and Glorian lost the non-magical sword. He did keep hold of Redthirst, however, and he noticed that Mirakles still wore the failed amulet. A few steps farther, and they all fell in a heap, safely beyond the precincts of dread Hades and awful Persephone.

"Let's rest, just a little bit," said Spike.

"Sure," said Glorian, "the hard part is over. We've got Mirakles back in the land of the living, but only because he's half-god. You can't bring mere mortals out that way without special arrangements with the Lords of the Underworld."

They rested for a quarter of an hour, and then they began bumping Mirakles up the dark staircase, caring not at all that the poor man's body would be a mass of bruises later.

CHAPTER SEVEN

Human life is mainly a process of filling in time until the arrival of death or Santa Claus . . .
—Eric Berne

"SURPRISE!"

Glorian and Spike had been sleeping—once again, they'd set no guard, and were thus caught unaware—and both sat up suddenly, staring at their visitors with anger and hatred.

"You're not deceiving me this time!" cried Glorian, grabbing Redthirst and leaping to his feet. "You're Morgrom, the File Restorer! And Narlinia, I recognize you even though you're made up like a member of a women's harmonic singing group! You both came to gloat, I suppose, but I'm afraid I have some bad news for you."

"Bully for you, Glorian!" roared Morgrom in a cheerful voice. "I wish we could get along better, so that you'd accept a compliment from me. I mean, truly, you're developing character at an alarming rate. I wish some of my minions could do the same. No, Narlinia, darling, I don't mean you. But you've pierced our disguises this time without a moment's hesitation."

Morgrom had transformed himself into a portly, florid-faced, sandy-haired man in his early 60s. He wasn't as fat as he'd been upstairs in the house, and the long, white, bristly mustache he'd given himself made him look almost grandfatherly. Narlinia had her auburn tresses tightly bound with hairpins that lifted them off her forehead and pinioned them tightly in a gather over her neck. It was not an attractive effect. Both villains wore military-looking uniforms of a heavy, dark blue material. Morgrom's was decorated with rows of battle ribbons and medals; Narlinia's severe jacket and long, tight skirt just made her look uncomfortable.

"Call me 'Major,' if you don't mind," said Morgrom. "And Narlinia is my driver. Isn't that the way it always is?"

Narlinia tugged angrily at her confining jacket. "I'm not half happy about these high heels now, either," she said. "The longer we spend in these Powers That Be-forsaken passages, the more I hunger for a warm bubble bath and a gossamer white negligée."

"All in due time, my sweet," said Morgrom, the Essence of Evil.

"Perhaps not," said Glorian, brandishing Redthirst, "remember that I have you at bay."

"Remember Shugreth the Unenviable?" said Morgrom simply.

There was no need for either Glorian or Spike to reply. They just nodded.

"Well, with a word I could summon something much less terrifying, but horrible and powerful enough to show up your threat for the puny, false bluff it really is. You know that's true, don't you, Glorian?"

Slowly, the supernatural sidekick lowered the point of the enchanted sword. He just stared at "The Major" and his "driver." The next move was up to the villains.

Morgrom twisted the ends of the bristly mustache, something that had apparently become a nervous habit. "He fought well in Hades, did he not?"

Glorian nodded. "I saw none who could defeat

him, although the Plain of Constant Conflict is populated by all the greatest warriors of myth and history. If Hades were at all bearable, if access to it were easier, I would visit it out of a foolish desire to see the great pairings of the imagination: Conan *versus* Achilles, for instance, or Siegfried barehanded against Jack Johnson."

Morgrom worked some more at his mustache. "You bring up a fascinating idea, young tool of The Powers That Be. Do you understand why those warriors of old fought so fiercely, so determinedly against this defeated hulk, Mirakles of the Elastic Tendon?"

"Only that he was in the highest rank of fighters," said Spike. "And the fighting relieved the boredom and terror of Hades for those on the Plain."

Morgrom gave a deep, hearty, red-faced laugh. "You probably noticed that they tried to block your way out of Hades."

Spike and Glorian exchanged looks. The Supernatural Guide shrugged. "I'm sure they would've responded the same way whomever we tried to steal away."

Thrag's Bane, in his blue officer's uniform, shook his head. He enjoyed lecturing those he believed to be his inferiors, which amounted to just about everyone. "All of them—from the first prehistoric stone-axe wielding battler through the latest arrival—hated Mirakles more than any other of the thousands and millions who strive daily on the Plain of Constant Conflict."

"Why?" asked Spike. "He hadn't even been in Hades long enough—"

"Listen and learn, human boy," said Morgrom in his evil villain's voice. "They hated Mirakles most because he was the son of Thrag, the Dogface God, the God of Smiting. It was Thrag's bloody hands that ended the happy lives of all the others and sent them before their time to Hades. They blame Thrag—and through him, Mirakles—for the years they did not spend with their wives and children, ruling their idyllic lands. They call Thrag the Well-Hated. Well, on the Plain of Constant Conflict at least, his belligerent son inherited that hate, and Thrag was not there to protect him."

"Looked to me like Mirakles didn't need much protection," said Glorian defiantly.

"No?" said he who'd last disguised himself as the rollicking Bardalf, the boon companion of John Falstaff. "He lies before us, dead, with no hope of resurrection in these damp, dark, and poisonous caves."

Glorian and Spike laughed aloud. "You err!" cried the Stewart Granger-looking guardian spirit. "Mirakles lives! We merely borrowed from him his consciousness with a couple of cracks across his princely jaw. Soon he will awaken, and he will return to his quest, and your foul life will once again be in danger of ending suddenly, bloodily, and with you, The Palindromic, on your knees begging mercy from this son of Desiphae. Your future is much darker than you think."

Morgrom didn't respond in the way that Glorian expected. He only shrugged. "Will Mirakles never cease?" he said. "This way, I won't have to hire and break in yet another hero. Come, Narlinia, we have business in better caverns than this."

The Essence of Evil and his female underling turned to leave through the westward winding passage. Spike, The Protector, jumped up and called out. "One question, Morgrom!" he cried.

Thrag's Bane turned and gave the young man a sneering look. "Not even a supernatural being, are you? The glowing part is nice, but it's just luminia, isn't it?"

"One question," said Spike in a lower voice. "If you met Mirakles in the white house, and gave him a ponderous mission—finding your Dipped Switch, if I have it right—then why did you attack him so soon with Shugreth the Unenviable? If the Switch means so much to you, why then did you kill Mirakles almost the next hour?"

Morgrom stopped and blinked for a few seconds. "Oh, that," he said, yawning. "Can't expect you humans and you bottom-of-the-barrel fantasy folk to understand everything you see with your own eyes and hear with your own ears. That Dipped Switch is somewhere in the Great Underground Empire, and Hades had to be examined. The person who stole the Switch may well have taken it to Hades and left it there. If it had been in Hades, the three of you would've found it, I'm sure. But it wasn't, it's sad to report—so what do you say, mates? Onward with the quest? All ready to pitch in and do our parts?"

"Um," said Glorian, "why don't you just get on with setting up your next trick or trap. Spike and I have some things to talk over, and we have to wait until Mirakles regains consciousness."

Narlinia patted at the tight roll of hair at the back of her head. "Do tell the Prince of the Sunless Grotto that we're truly sorry we missed him. Tell him I'm glad he got out of Hades all right."

With that, both Morgrom and Narlinia von Glech hurried off to the west and were soon out of sight.

As soon as they were gone, Glorian surprised The Protector by turning and putting the point of Redthirst against Spike's throat. "You've been a great help some of the time," said Glorian, "but I have one question to ask, and if I don't get a truthful answer, you will die within the next few seconds."

Spike just stared wide-eyed. He didn't even nod his understanding.

"You are the son of the thief," said Glorian. "I imagine that if Morgrom leaves any more of his low-brow treasures around, you'll take them, but I don't care anything about that. I just want to know one thing: Did you take the Dipped Switch in the first place? Do you know where it is?"

"I swear," croaked Spike, until Glorian dropped the point of the sword and the young man could speak more freely, "I swear that I know nothing about the Dipped Switch other than what I overheard you and Mirakles saying. I did not steal it from Morgrom, and I don't know where it is."

They stared deeply at each other for several long moments. Finally Glorian spoke. "I believe you," he said at last.

"Hooray," said Spike sourly. "I resent even being asked."

"You're the son of the thief!" cried Glorian. "You have your own light-fingered ways. I *had* to ask."

"I suppose so," said The Protector. Further discussion was interrupted by a groan from Mirakles, son of Thrag.

"He's coming around," said Spike. "And he's going to have a lot of questions."

"I know," said Glorian uncomfortably.

The Prince of the Sunless Grotto moaned some more, sat up and rubbed his cheek and temple where he'd been slugged by his two helpers, and looked around. "I got a question for you," he said in a grim voice.

"Yes, O Son of Thrag," said Glorian, standing with his head bowed.

"Look, those Maruts, whatever they called themselves. We spent a lot of time fighting together and they seemed like okay guys. Were they companions of Indra or Vajri?"

Glorian took a breath and let it out. It wasn't the kind of question he was expecting. "Indra and Vajri are aspects of the same god," he said.

"Ow," said Mirakles, "my head hurts."

Spike, The Protector, sat down beside Mirakles. "Do you want to know everything that happened?"

Mirakles thought about that for a few seconds. "Part of me doesn't want to know the details, but I guess I better hear it all."

"Where shall I start?"

Mirakles rubbed his aching temples and thought. "The last thing I remember . . ." He looked up, his face drained of blood, his eyes wide with horror. "The last thing I remember is being in the clutches of Shugreth the Unenviable."

"Right," said Spike, unable to suppress a shudder himself. "Your dead body soon disappeared, so we assumed that we'd have to go get you ourselves. The first thing we did—"

"You mean you boys, you more or less human young men, decided that you were going to force your way past the gate of Hades to rescue me?" Mirakles regarded both of them with astonishment.

"Well, I have a duty to my hero," said Glorian simply. "It goes with the territory. It's what we in the Supernatural and Fantastic Wayfarers Association are there for, what I've devoted my life to. I couldn't just give up on you because you seemed to be temporarily dead."

Mirakles stared for a long while at Glorian. "Who are you?" he asked at last.

"Oh," said Glorian, laughing, "you remember. The last time you saw me I looked like a big Nubian slave in harem pants."

"Ah, yes, Glorian. Well, keep this look. It suits you. More practical, too."

"And I," said Spike, "well, I promised that I'd protect you, and I didn't do a very good job. So Glorian and I figured out a way of getting into Hades—well, that was mostly his idea—"

"But it was Spike's idea about how to raise the silver oboli we needed to pay Charon, and that we'd need an extra coin for you," said Glorian.

They talked like that for ten minutes, filling in everything they had seen and learned since the encounter in the Dome Room with Morgrom's God of the Nameless Night.

By the time they finished, Mirakles had rubbed all the soreness from his muscles and was doing what appeared to be the Canadian Air Force setting up exercises. He said nothing for a few seconds as he huffed through his exertions, but at last he stood up and grasped each of the young men by the upper arm. "I owe you much, and by Thrag's deathly grin, you will receive your rewards. Although that all may have to wait until I return to my mother's domain in the Sunless Grotto. Her protection is uppermost in my mind."

"Sure," said Glorian, "we're not allowed to accept gratuities, anyway."

"I'm just a kid," said Spike. "I'm not even supernatural. I'd be happy to have a reward."

Mirakles laughed, a deep, booming, heroic sound. "That you shall, my Protector."

During the last few exchanges, Glorian had been Drawer Forwarding them a good, solid meal of meat and potato soup, sloppy joe sandwiches, and slices of apple pie that had been put on a grill so the filling caramelized a little, and topped with vanilla ice cream, melting down over the sides. He also had Cokes for all three of them.

"So let me get this straight," said the brawny hero, licking the last of the apple-ice cream mixture from his plate, "I was in Hades, but I was having a great time, and I wouldn't listen to you, and you had to knock me out and carry me bodily out of there? Out of Hades? I wanted to stay there?"

Glorian nodded solemnly. "That's about the way it was."

"That's not rational behavior, even for the son of Thrag, is it?" asked Mirakles. "I mean, given the chance between escaping back up here to the land of the living, or remaining in the joyless underworld through eternity, a sane person would get out of there like, well, a bat out of hell."

"You could look at it this way, O Prince," said The Protector. "You had finally achieved the full expression of your warlike nature, and that caused you a kind of joy, the closest a dead soul in Hades can come to joy."

For some reason, the warrior-prince wouldn't buy that easy answer. "Look, even if I grant you that business about the expression of my warlike nature," he said morosely, "what about the rest of me? Surely there's got to be more to Mirakles, son of Desiphae of the Sunless Grotto than whacking people with swords. There's got to be, right? Or am I supposed to go through the rest of my life believing that I'm worthless in any other capacity, that all I'm good for is combat? I mean, what happens when I become king of the Sunless Grotto? Does this Hades experience foretell that I can't possibly be a good and wise ruler to my people? That I can't find a loving wife and enjoy the comfort of beautiful children? Is that what it means?"

Neither Glorian nor Spike had anticipated this turn of mind, and had no idea how to deal with it. "Of course not," said Glorian in a falsely cheerful voice. "Who can say what the laws and customs of Hades are? Perhaps when one enters there, you're placed among the various regions according to one of your qualities, perhaps your most characteristic quality—but that doesn't mean that you don't have others almost as important to you."

"Exactly," said Spike. "I think, from a theological point of view, that it's impossible to give a rational explanation for anything one sees a dead soul doing beyond the gate of Hades. We just don't know enough about what the rules are down there."

Mirakles stared at the rock wall in distracted thought, and gave the arguments of Glorian and Spike a dismissing wave. "I really, really don't like what this says about me," he murmured. "This is all *very* depressing. I may have to re-examine my entire purpose, my reason for being. I mean, what's a hero? Maybe I should change professions now, while I'm young enough. Find something where I could help more people, more often. Killing a dragon that's ravaging a neighborhood is good and worthwhile work, but how often does that kind of thing come up? I'm lucky if it's twice a year. The rest of the time I admire my reflection in the Grotto. I mean, this Hades thing has really opened my eyes."

Now Glorian and Spike were beginning to panic. As they watched, Mirakles continued his monologue, and his voice got lower and lower until they couldn't hear him at all. He'd completely withdrawn inside himself.

"Uh oh," said Glorian. "Hero funk. It's a common-enough problem, but I didn't think it was something we'd have to worry about with Mirakles. He didn't seem the type. He didn't seem susceptible to it."

"Can we get him out of it?" asked Spike.

"With time, and with the right stimulus," said Glorian.

"You mean another Shugreth the Unenviable."

Glorian just stared, then nodded.

Together, the two young men led Mirakles out of the small cave and through a winding passage that eventually led north. "This is that Mirror Room I said we'd have to pass through," said Spike.

"It doesn't seem very special to me." The chamber was just like most of the other caves they'd visited. It was a large, square room with tall ceilings. Its single remarkable feature was that on the south was an enormous mirror which filled the entire wall. The exits to the east and west led back to the small cave the party had spent so much time in lately. As Glorian walked to the north to take a look at the third exit, Spike stopped him with a shout. "That just goes through a narrow passage back up to the Round Room."

Mirakles of the Elastic Tendon was staring at his reflection in the vast mirror at the southern end. "Do you know," he said with immense sadness in his voice, "if I hadn't been so battle-crazed, I might have spoken to my father, King Hyperenor, at the trench of blood." And then the prince's eyes squeezed tightly shut. It was obvious that he was in great emotional pain.

"Good," said Glorian impatiently, "great. Where are we going, and what do you have in mind?"

"Give me a break, okay? You're the official Supernatural Guide and I accept that, but I'm the expert on this warren of tunnels and passages. There are a few places where I think that Dipped Switch might be hidden—along with the Hot Key Mirakles needs to open the Scroll Lock on the message from his father. There are scores and scores of rooms and chambers and tunnels and passages and whatever else you want to call 'em down here, but I've got a shrewd suspicion, and I've narrowed down those possible locations to just a few. All I can say is, we're going to have to check them out, one at a time."

"And this Mirror Room was one of them?" asked Glorian.

Spike shrugged.

"What's so special about it, except the big mirror?"

The Protector laughed. "Come on, if you really

want to see what you're up against. Go touch that mirror. Be careful: Don't break it."

"Break it!" cried Glorian, walking to the end of the room. He reached out a hand. "My balance and poise are—" He was interrupted by a deep rumbling from within the earth, shaking the room. "Wow," said Glorian softly, "what was that?"

"That was one of the great engineering feats of the Great Underground Empire," said Spike.

"Uh huh," said Glorian dubiously. He looked around, but nothing appeared different in the least. He went and peered out into the western exit, but it still looked like the same twisting passage it had been before. He came back into the Mirror Room. He walked up carefully to the mirror, reached out one tentative finger, and touched it again.

Once more the earth rumbled and Glorian was disconcerted by the shaking of the room. "Don't tell me, I'll figure it out," said he of the Knowledge. He spent a quarter of an hour touching the mirror, feeling the deep grumbling of the earth, and getting no nearer to the solution of the puzzle. "All right," he said at last, "I give up."

"Good," said Spike, "because we've got more important things to do. We've got to get Mirakles back on his journey, first of all."

Glorian laughed. "You're not going to tell me what that mirror means, are you?" he said.

The Protector shrugged. "Maybe later, if you're respectful and well-behaved. Now, from here we continue north, through a cold and damp corridor that leads further west. From there we can go by slide to the cellar right under the house, but we still have the coal mine area to explore. Oh, by Morgrom's moldy mother! I forgot all about the garlic! We'll never get through there . . . unless you can Drawer Forward us garlic. One big clove for each of us."

"No problem about garlic," said Glorian. He turned around, and turned again almost immediately. He handed one large clove of garlic to Spike, another to Mirakles, and kept the third for himself.

"That's going to make things so much easier," said Spike. "Come on."

"Why garlic?"

The Protector led them through the cold passage and the slide room into the entrance to an old, abandoned coal mine. They followed the downward sloping tunnel westward, deeper into the mine. "Up ahead," said Spike. "Bats. Vampire bats."

Before Glorian could react to the proximity of vampires, there came a cry from Mirakles of the Elastic Tendon. "By all the Faithless Priests of Thrag!" cried the prince. "Look here!"

Glorian switched on his flashlight and aimed it where the mighty hero pointed. There was a carving in the stone wall—a weirder carving even than those in the Dome Room, because this figure's eyes moved.

"It's . . . it's an Embedded Character!" cried Spike. "I thought all of these had been removed long ago!"

"Is it alive?" asked Glorian with some trepidation.

"Yes, and it's suffering," replied Spike. "It must be another of Morgrom's works. We've got to set it free. Mirakles, please, I beg you, use your enchanted sword for this noble purpose."

Mirakles looked about himself as if he'd just awakened. He heard Spike's urgent plea. "Yes, of course," he said. "I'll do what I can to ease its pain."

The Prince of the Sunless Grotto carefully manipulated the very tip of Redthirst to pry loose the Embedded Character from its place of imprisonment on the wall of the coal mine. When the Embedded Character was free at last, it knelt before Mirakles. "I pledge thee loyalty and trust," it said.

It could hardly be called "he," although it was

clearly a male figure, because it wasn't in any way human. He existed only barely in three dimensions. He was as thin as a drawing on a piece of paper. He seemed to be a very old man, tall and straight, with bushy eyebrows and piercing eyes. He carried a stout, almost two-dimensional hardwood staff in one hand and was dressed in a garment of shining cloth of curious workmanship, a long gray cloak, a tall pointed blue hat, a silver scarf covered by his long, gray beard, and on his feet a pair of admirable black boots. In his other hand was a scroll of paper.

"Stand up," said Mirakles, shuddering at this fantastic product of someone's sorcerous art.

"You may also notice that he looks exactly as Morgrom the Malignant appeared at our confrontation in the Dome Room," said Glorian warily.

"Yes," said the Embedded Character, "he created me here on this wall, and then took my form as a model. I, of course, never learned his reason."

"No one who lives can put into words the reasons for Morgrom's actions," said Glorian. "We were about to search the coal mine area in the furtherance of our quest, and I believe wholeheartedly that you will be of great help to us. Would you consider accompanying us further, as we discover the new secrets of the Great Underground Empire?"

"I owe you that," said the Embedded Character, "and so much more."

Spike, The Protector, started forward, wielding his garlic, when he stopped suddenly. "That scroll you carry," he said to the Embedded Character. "May I read it?"

"Of course," said the Embedded Character, and he handed the extremely thin scroll to Spike.

The glowing young man read through the message quickly, then silently passed it along to Mirakles. He of the Elastic Tendon blinked stupidly for a few seconds, then took the scroll and read it. "By my mother's holy tresses!" he cried. "It's a second scroll from King Hyperenor. And it's the Second Secret of the Sword!"

"My goodness," was all Glorian could say in astonishment.

"What does it say?" asked Spike.

"Quite simply," said Mirakles, breathing heavily, "it warns me that using Redthirst creates a love of battle, and the better my opponents, the greater my desire for combat. It entirely explains my frame of mind and actions in Hades! This simple scroll relieves me of all the mental discomfort I endured today. It restores me entirely! It's as if—"

"A great weight," said Glorian.

"Yes," said the prince in wonder. "Thank you," he said to the Embedded Character.

"Do not thank me," said the Embedded Character. "It was not I who put that scroll on the wall of the coal mine. I was put there by the Essence of Evil."

"True," said Spike, "but I'd be willing to bet the scroll was added by someone else. Perhaps by King Hyperenor himself."

There was a pause as each member of the party gazed at each other, and there were quite a few embarrassed smiles. Finally, Glorian looked around. "Garlic at the ready?" he said. "Then let's press on!"

CHAPTER EIGHT

Dead? Dead? I have been dead many years.
—Greta Garbo

THERE WAS A LONG TUNnel that traveled eastward between the room of the vampire bat and the shaft down into the coal mine. The shaft room was large, and in the middle was a small shaft descending through the floor into darkness below. There was a metal framework constructed over the shaft, and it could be used to lower a basket on a heavy iron chain. Not even Spike could fit in the basket, so the party headed for the northern exit.

"I vaguely remember being down there once before," said Glorian thoughtfully. "Isn't there a strange machine that turns coal into diamonds?"

"Yes, there is," said Spike. "But surely you, as a Supernatural Guide, have little use for diamonds. And I live in this Great Underground Empire. All of its secrets are mine, as well as its remaining treasures. Perhaps the great Mirakles would be interested, though, in taking time off from searching for the Dipped Switch and the Hot Key to make a diamond or two to take back to the Sunless Grotto."

The brawny hero only sneered. "Do you think I care about treasure? Returning as soon as possible to my helpless mother is my only thought. As for treasure, well, there is a great treasure at the bottom of the Grotto itself, guarded by my sibling, the monster Smorma. So I have at least one more adventure to look forward to, even after we finish here. You may keep your diamond-making machine. But what about Ed here?" he said, indicating the Embedded Character.

"Thanks for thinking of me," said the thin image of a wizard, "but the life spans of Embedded Characters once released from captivity are very short. In a month or six weeks, I'll have eroded away into nothingness. When you think of me, I'll just be a handful of dust on the wind."

Glorian's eyes opened wider. "Why," he said with real pain in his voice, "that's the saddest thing I've ever heard!"

Ed shrugged. "You set me free of the rock wall, where I was in anguish every moment. Now I have a month or more to see what the world is like, to travel where I may . . . to *live!* Feel no grief for me, because you've given me the greatest gift an Embedded Character may receive: to be Unembedded."

There was a brief moment of quiet, and then Mirakles of the Elastic Tendon spoke up. "So I take it that we'll pass through this coal mine area, just to check if this is where King Hyperenor left the items we're looking for. What then? I mean, if they're not here?"

Glorian laughed. "My prince, you still have no idea of the vastness of this place! There are hundreds of places that remain to be searched. That's why it's not the Underground Empire, but the *Great* Underground Empire. Imagine it at the height of its civilization, or even in the days of decadence, during the Flathead Dynasty. Imagine this vast, sunless land populated with heroes and monsters of every description, as well as thousands or millions of average people. It must have been truly astonishing, for these are but its ruins, and they are astonishing."

"Glorian," said Mirakles, heaving a sigh, "I explained that I didn't want to use the diamond-making machine. Part of my reason was that I wanted to hurry home to see to Queen Desiphae's safety. But if you're going to stop and orate every time you get excited, then I could have gone below and done some diamond-making, and returned before you finished."

Glorian flushed a bright red. "Yes, my prince. I apologize, my prince. It won't happen again, my prince, because I thoroughly understand your situation, and I suppose I just needed to be reminded of our need for haste. I guess I'm still a little—"

There was the frightening aroma of freshly-baked bread, and someone said, "You cannot pass."

Everyone looked around to find the source of this great, deep voice. "Well," said Spike in disgust, "that's all we need. Over there, in the north doorway."

Blocking the exit rather effectively was a fearsome monster, fire coming from its nostrils. It was roughly of humanoid form, but it was surrounded by a darkness that swirled and stretched toward them, as if the darkness were a living extension of the monster. In its right hand it held a gigantic sword, laid flat across its massive chest.

Glorian turned to his companions and tried to give them a smile. It came out weak and crooked. "I know her," he said.

"Her?" said The Protector, cowering back from the searching wings of darkness.

"It's the great Glarbo," said the semi-mythical advisor. "She's a paid-up member of the Supernatural and Fantastic Wayfarers Association, but she never attends our banquets or other functions. She's pretty much the way you imagine she is. She doesn't socialize much. Mostly we just make fun of her because of her big feet. Look at 'em!"

"Not to mention the fire-out-of-the-nostrils bit,"

said Spike. "Jeez, how'd you like to sit in a nice restaurant with someone who did that?"

"This coming from a four-foot scarecrow who glows in the dark," said Mirakles sourly. He turned his attention to the huge monster, Glarbo. "I am Mirakles, son of Thrag, Prince of the Sunless Grotto. I am on a quest, and that quest takes me to the chamber beyond. If I must fight you to pass, then I will. First, however, I ask you to step aside."

Glarbo began to laugh, a slow, deeply-pitched laugh that sounded to Glorian like "Boom, boom."

"I think it sounds like 'groom, groom,' " said Mirakles.

"No," said Spike, "it's more like 'flume, flume.' "

"Hate to be a negative voice in this discussion," said Ed, "but it's definitely 'doom, doom.' "

"It's a foretelling," said Glarbo. "Whatever you hear, that's your destiny. Say, for instance, the short, glowing person heard 'flume, flume.' That means he'll next lead you back to the slide room."

"Groom, groom," said Mirakles. "I don't even want to think about that."

"And I've already explained that I'm doomed," said Ed.

"But what about Glorian?" asked Spike. " 'Boom, boom.' What does that mean?"

"After the awards banquet," asked the great Glarbo in an innocent tone, "how much time did you spend with that empty-headed Amitia?"

Glorian became furious. "Give me that sword," he shouted at the prince.

"No," said Mirakles, and slapped his Supernatural Guide across the face.

Glorian cooled down. "Forgive me once again, my prince," he said.

"Now, why don't all of you go away?" said Glarbo. "I want to be alone."

"We can't leave, and I've told you why," said Mirakles.

"Glorian," said Glarbo, "come here where I can give you something, something I don't want the others to see."

"Be careful, Glorian," cried Spike. "It's probably a trick."

Glorian just shook his head and hoped that Glarbo would stand by the Supernatural and Fantastic Wayfarers Association's mutual non-aggression pact. Members were not supposed to attack each other, although some were good mythical beings and some evil. For instance, Narlinia von Glech would not originate anything to harm Glorian, nor he her. Morgrom, however, had long disdained to join the Association. He felt that would demean him, and so he was free to cause misery to anyone of any description, human, supernatural, or divine.

"What is it, Glarbo?" asked Glorian as he drew near. The monster towered over him.

"I have this for you," she said, handing him a familiar Powers That Be envelope, sealed with a wax blob bearing the signet impression of the Autoexec.

"I don't even know why they bothered to send me on this trip," said Glorian, irritated. "I mean, with the amount of interference I'm getting, they should just have headed Mirakles in the right direction, and left him little clues along the way, like a treasure hunt."

"You will be needed for more," said Glarbo. "Read the note."

Glorian tore open the envelope and read the letter from the Autoexec:

> Glorian, listen to her. The Great Underground Empire is so huge, you and Mirakles could wander around down there until he dies of old age. I've

decided to make things easier for you. You can skip the rest of this portion of the Empire and proceed to the slide room, the Maze, and then outside to the Barrow. Still be careful of Spike, The Protector. He is not what he seems. Keep up the good work!

Good luck to you,
and may God bless.

"Uh huh," said Glorian. He felt a bitterness and an anger that he couldn't identify. His mission seemed to be progressing well enough. Why did he then feel so used and manipulated?

"Give me that letter back," said Glarbo, "and I'll destroy it for you." Glorian handed it to her, and she sneezed fire on both it and the envelope. "Now go, because what I said before was true."

"You want to be alone," said Ed.

"No," said the great Glarbo, "I want to be let alone."

"You definitely said 'I want to be alone,' " said Spike. "You just *said* you said 'I want to be let alone.' "

"Whatever," said Glarbo, and huffed fire at them.

"Back through the tunnel to the room with the vampire bat," said Glorian.

"You know," said Spike, "that monster reminded me of something. It was just like the one that faced Gandalf and his party in the mines of Moria. The what-you-call."

"Balrog," said Glorian. "Not a member of the Supernatural and Fantastic Wayfarers Association, either."

"I would expect not," said Ed. "Did you realize that Glarbo is an anagram of Balrog?"

Glorian, Spike, and Mirakles of the Elastic Tendon all looked at each other for a moment. "Could this be some more of Morgrom's cursed word play?" grumbled the prince.

"No," said Glorian, remembering the note from the Autoexec that indicated that Glarbo, however horrible in appearance, was actually on their side. "I think it's just a coincidence that the great Glarbo looks exactly like a Balrog and spoke the very line that Gandalf—to whom Ed here has more than a passing resemblance—used on it: 'You cannot pass.' Coincidences like this happen all the time in these adventures."

The Prince of the Sunless Grotto studied Glorian's face for a moment. "As long as you're not worried."

"Worried? No, she even gave me a hint about where to search next. We'll see the sun soon, but only briefly."

"Perhaps another hero would celebrate at that news," said Mirakles, "but you've got to remember that I lived my entire childhood in the land around the Sunless Grotto, where the Sacred River ran. I find the sun unnatural, even repellent."

"I've never been outside, of course," said Ed, the Unembedded Character, "but I have to say that from all I've heard, I agree." All this time, Glorian led them through the bat room and the chambers near the mine entrance to the slide room.

"Well," said Glorian, "this is the quickest way out of this part of the Great Underground Empire, I believe. This twisting metal slide will lead us back to the cellar, but no doubt Morgrom still has the trap door locked against us. Fortunately, there's another way to the outside world."

Mirakles stepped to the edge of the slide and drew Redthirst. He sniffed experimentally. "No bread-baking smell," he said. He held his enchanted sword tightly against his body, then gave his battle shout—"For Thrag and the Grotto!"—and launched himself down the slide. He was out of sight after a turn or two.

The remainder of the group waited a few seconds. Someone far below yelled something. "What was that?" asked Ed.

"Couldn't make it out," said Glorian. "The prince was telling us either that everything was all right down there, or else we'll all die as soon as we reach bottom." He glanced at his companions for a second, then grabbed Spike and shoved him roughly down the slide. "Mirakles is in the dark down there!" cried Glorian. "We forgot!"

"It's only been a few seconds," said Ed. "Maybe it wasn't enough time for the grues to arrive."

"You don't have the experience with grues that I do," said Glorian, shuddering. "All right, why don't you go next, Ed, and I'll bring up the rear."

Ed nodded. "I hope I don't land too roughly," he said, sadness in his eyes, "or I could shatter into a thousand pieces." He let go of the slide's edges and vanished from view.

At last, taking a deep breath, Glorian slid down to the cellar floor. It wasn't dangerous at all, and if he hadn't been involved in a life-and-death adventure, and if he were, say, a human of Spike's age, he would probably have enjoyed the slide immensely. In any event, when he reached the bottom, he jumped to his feet and looked around. His three friends all seemed uninjured and in good health.

"Forgot about the darkness, my prince," he said. "Again, I apologize."

"You apologize a lot, you know?" said Mirakles with a smile. "Is that a common trait among you supernatural types? It's all right, we all forgot. I heard the heavy pattering of grue feet approaching, but Spike arrived in the nick of time."

Glorian turned to Spike. "You haven't had much to say lately."

"Oh," said The Protector, "I've been playing with anagrams in my mind, ever since Ed noticed that Glarbo's name was an anagram. I've been working with yours, as a matter of fact."

"Really?" said Glorian, quite pleased. "Anything turn up yet?"

"Well, there are no real anagrams of Glorian. But if you let a wild-card character represent the 'n' then you get 'gorilla.' Glorian the Gorilla. It's a whole new image for you."

"Of course," said the Prince of the Sunless Grotto, "without the wild-card, you're Glorian the Gorilna. I kind of like that. No doubt, many members of your business association have run into gorillas in their time—by Thrag the Ultimate Conqueror, I wouldn't be surprised that some of your members *are* gorillas! But you must be the only gorilna in existence, and there's a certain value to being unique."

"I suppose so, my prince," said Glorian. He found little solace in being a gorilna. He just wanted to be liked, and he wanted to be welcome at the banquets, and popular but not too popular, and maybe win the Joseph Campbell Award sometime. He didn't think that was too much to ask. This was another example of the difference in thinking between a genuine hero and a fantasy mentor.

Mirakles turned to Spike, his expression all expectation. "Have you tried my name yet, my boy?" he asked.

"Well, you have to use the wild-card trick with the 'k' in your name," said Spike.

"Yes, yes?"

"And then you come up with several anagrams. " 'Miracles' first, of course. Also 'impalers,' 'reclaims,' and 'minerals.' "

He of the Elastic Tendon smiled broadly. "Bravely spoken, young man. It sounds as if Redthirst will have more work to do before it and I return to the Land of the Sunless Grotto, to reclaim what is now my throne and wrest the treasure from the ravenous Smorma."

Spike came up and whispered in Glorian's ear.

"Anagrams aren't prophetic," he said. "That was Glarbo and her laughter."

"*You* tell him then," murmured Glorian.

"There were other anagrams, too," Spike whispered. " 'Mislayer,' for one, and 'measlier.' " Glorian just laughed.

The last time they'd been in the cellar, they'd had only the illumination of Glorian's flashlight. Now, with Spike in their number, the stone blocks looked both stonier and blockier. Mirakles pointed to a crawlway to the south. "I want to explore in that direction," he said.

"Yes, but my advice from Glarbo said to leave this part of the Underground Empire through the Maze," said Glorian. "That's in the opposite direction."

"When we came down those stairs the first time," said the prince in a steely voice, "I chose readily to explore to the north. Now I wish to spend a little time—just a few minutes, perhaps—taking a look at what's to the south. Who in this party will stop me?" There was silence in reply.

They found themselves on the eastern edge of a chasm, perhaps the southern reaches of the same chasm they'd discovered north of the Round Room. Glorian peered over the side with his flashlight, but the light faded away before it reached the bottom. "Deep," said Ed.

"Yup," said Spike.

The path continued eastward until it opened up into a room, a gallery. Most of the paintings had been stolen by vandals and previous adventurers, if that isn't a redundancy. What was hanging on the walls was what's called in the trade "cover art."

"Part of Morgrom's restoration program," said Spike. "No comment on his taste in artwork."

There was a series of paintings that were all variations on a common theme: a gigantic monster threatening a sword-brandishing, heavily muscled hero, and a usually recumbent, beautiful young woman with certain of her body parts of an unnatural size and her limited clothing in a state of disarray.

Mirakles walked down the gallery and examined each painting in detail. "You know," he said, turning to Glorian and laughing, "if anyone ever wrote my wanderings, this is the kind of cover they'd put on it."

"No girl," said Glorian.

"What?" asked the prince.

"There's no girl in our party."

"Ah, but remember Glarbo's prophetic laughter: 'groom, groom'?" said Ed.

"I've had enough of this," said Mirakles. "It bores me. Let's go on."

"You know," said Spike confidentially to Glorian as they entered the artist's studio, "there's a way from this room upstairs into the house. But I don't think Ed would be able to follow and, besides, it wouldn't be wise to let Miracles confront his palindromic nemesis until the prince finds the key to the scroll."

"You're right, I guess," said Glorian thoughtfully. "Was that treasure chest there the last time you came by here?"

"Treasure chest? No!" The glowing young man ran to the treasure chest and worked at opening it for a few minutes. "Prince," he called, "there is a treasure here, but I cannot open this lock."

"Stand aside," said Mirakles of the Elastic Tendon, as he drew Redthirst. He raised the magic sword above his head and brought it down with all his strength, shattering the lock.

Spike kicked open the treasure chest and sighed.

"What is it?" asked Ed.

Spike stood up and scowled. "A year's supply of Frobozz Magic Tortle Wax. Anybody want it?"

They marched in silence back through the gallery, along the chasm, then north to the cellar and north again to the room with the bloodstains and deep scratches on the walls. "I remember this place," said the prince. "We went east last time. Where does your advice tell us to go now?"

"The Maze," said Glorian. "Through there." He pointed to the west, where there was a forbidding hole in the wall.

"The Maze it is, then," said Mirakles, "but you'd better know the way out of it, at the cost of your life."

Spike put his hand on Glorian's arm. "I could find my way through the Maze blindfolded," he said. "C'mon, follow me!" And he headed west into the first part of the great Maze.

Glorian hurried to walk beside the young man. "You know that I know that you're the son of the thief, right?"

Spike gave him a puzzled look. "Yeah, so?"

"So I know you're keeping secrets."

"Secrets? What secrets?"

Glorian shook his head. "I still haven't figured out if I can trust you or not. You never mentioned a word, while we were in the temple, about your father's treasure room."

The Protector came to an abrupt halt in the stone corridor. His expression was fierce. "Glorian, I *live* in my father's treasure room. Morgrom repaired the door that used to be smashed open between his living room and the Cyclops room, and he actually lets me live in peace in the old treasure room. You don't know what it means to me. I know that Morgrom is the Essence of Evil, but he's busy restocking the Great Underground Empire, and I guess he thinks I'll grow up to follow in my father's footsteps. Maybe I will."

"I'm sorry, Spike, if I—"

"Listen," The Protector continued, "you've got

the whole world to wander, and other worlds and other parallel universes, maybe. I've got one room that I call my own. I'm sorry if you wanted a peek at it, but it wasn't necessary, and I didn't make my bed the other morning. Okay?"

"Sure, Spike," said Glorian.

"And about trusting me: Well, that's something you're going to have to work out for yourself, because either you take my word that I'm on your side or you don't, and if you don't, there's nothing I can say that'll change your mind."

"What are you two talking about up there?" called the Prince of the Sunless Grotto.

"We're just chatting about how good it will be to feel the sun again," said Glorian. "It will be about three o'clock in the afternoon, unless the emanations I feel from Venus are actually those from Jupiter bouncing off a giant roc or dragon or something hovering above us in the upper world. The chances of that are very slim, of course."

"And I was saying that I'd have a chance to grab a fresh supply of luminia," said Spike.

"Tell me, one of you," said Mirakles, "how long will we be exposed to the sun's light. I swore an oath not to enjoy—"

"We come up through the grating," said Glorian, his forehead creased in thought, "which puts us in the forest north of the white house. It's very near where we first met. Then we'll slip through the woods west of the house, and into a stone barrow that leads to another part of the Empire."

"Fine," said the prince. "I won't have time to enjoy anything, and if we stay in the trees, we may not be discovered by Thrag's Bane."

"Exactly," said Spike. "Now, see, we can continue west, or we can turn south. Turning south brings us to the same room as the west passage, only the long way around."

"West," said Mirakles.

"I want you to feel included in the decision-making process," said Spike. "Even though you've never been here before. All right, here we are in that room. From here we can go any of three directions."

Glorian pointed, and Spike nodded in agreement. The party went off in that direction, and they traveled for some time confidently. "I don't know why," remarked the Prince of the Elastic Tendon, "but these passages seem even darker and danker than any of the others."

"It's an illusion," said Spike. "I've measured dankness all over the Underground Empire, and it's the same here as anywhere. South, Glorian?"

"That's the way I remember it," said the Supernatural Guide.

They turned south, but instead of another chamber of the Maze, they ran into a dead end. "Wait a minute," said Glorian.

"Something appears to be wrong," said Ed in a worried voice.

Glorian and Spike put their heads together and reviewed every turn they'd made. As far as both could tell, they had been entirely correct. Yet here was a dead end blank wall facing them, instead of the room with the grating and the way out. "You know what?" said Spike finally.

Glorian felt his throat go very dry. "What?" he said.

"I think Morgrom has been revising the Maze."

"Oh no."

"Anything wrong?" asked Mirakles, coming up to them. "To me, it seems like we're just in a maze of twisty little passages, all alike. I can't tell how you can find your way around. But why did we come here?"

"Rest stop," said Glorian.

"All right," called the prince in an authoritative voice, "everybody take five."

When Mirakles went away again, Glorian looked helplessly at The Protector. "What are we going to do?"

Spike shrugged. "Fake it, that's what. We'll just march around this Maze until winter comes if we have to, and sooner or later we'll stumble on the grating room. The hard way."

Glorian took a deep breath and let it out slowly. The hard way. He shrugged, too; there was no other way.

Mirakles got them up and walking soon, and eventually they came to a larger room, where there was a dry and fragile skeleton, probably that of a previous adventurer. The hapless explorer's useless lantern and rusty knife lay beside him.

"Here's a skeleton key," said Ed, picking it out of the dirt and mud on the chamber floor.

"Good," said Glorian, "we'll need that to escape through the grating."

"Hey, you guys," cried Spike, "aren't you excited about the treasure?"

"You mean the furniture?" asked the prince. "It doesn't look like treasure to me."

"Treasure is in the eye of the thief," said Spike. "Here's something I can come back and *steal!*" He was gazing covetously at a matching maroon sofa, loveseat, and wing chair. All three had fringe hanging down to about six inches above the floor. All three also had so much dust that they may have been in that room as long as the skeleton.

"Great," said Mirakles, "but let's remember why we're down here."

"Exactly, O Prince," said Glorian. "We just needed to stop by here and pick up the key."

The Supernatural Guide and the glowing young man looked at each other, but neither spoke. The party walked along for another half hour, until they began to smell the aroma of freshly baked bread.

"Uh oh," said Mirakles, drawing Redthirst.

They turned a corner, and before them, guarding the way into the grating room, was a gigantic Minotaur. "How are you, Glorian?" it said.

"Fine, Minotaur," said Glorian.

"Can't let your hero get by me, you know. That's my job."

"I understand," said Glorian. "The two of you will just have to work it out."

"I'm ready," said the Minotaur. "Who *is* your boss?"

"Prince Mirakles of the Sunless Grotto," said Glorian, "I'd like you to meet the Minotaur. You'll have to battle to the death if we're going to get out of here."

"That's *my* job," said Mirakles, moving closer to the Minotaur. "Nobody told me there'd be monsters down here, though."

"It's Morgrom's doing," said Spike.

"A prince, huh? I've met princes before," said the Minotaur. "Pansies, all of them."

"Typical braggart monster," said Mirakles, taking a huge swing at the Minotaur with Redthirst.

The Minotaur moved more quickly than its size seemed to allow, and the sword clanged off the stone wall. The Minotaur slammed its balled fists into Mirakles's belly, just under the breastbone.

The prince staggered back, all the wind knocked out of him. The Minotaur hit him again, and Mirakles fell. "Used to be locked up in another maze thing," said the monster reflectively. "You know what they fed me? Seven maidens and seven youths every nine years. That may sound like a lot to you, but believe me, it's not very much if it's got to last nine years."

Mirakles rolled to one side, still clutching his enchanted sword. He was ready to fight again, thanks to his semi-divine healing power. He feinted right and scored a hit on the Minotaur's lower left leg. "Aarrgh," it grunted.

"Must've been hard, huh?" said Spike.

"Hard?" The Minotaur waved a hand, temporarily calling off the fight, and sat down hard, rubbing his wounded leg. "I always promised myself that I'd pace myself, go slow, but a growing monster can't go nine years without something to gnaw on. So the very first day I had one of the princesses for lunch and then another for dinner and maybe a third for a snack that night. Before you know it, a week later I'm back where I started, with nine years left before the next delivery. And those well-fed Achaeans thought *they'd* been cursed!"

"Listen," said Glorian, seeing his opportunity, "if you let us by, I can promise there will be lots and lots of adventurers coming behind us. Adventurers all the time! Morgrom is renovating the entire Great Underground Empire, and you'll get your hands on your share of wayward explorers."

The Minotaur looked at him, wincing in pain. "I'm not as young as I used to be," it said.

"I ask this as a fellow Supernatural and Fantastic Wayfarers Association member. And if anybody questions me about it later, we got out another way, we never even saw you."

The Minotaur nodded. "Morgrom doesn't care that I had other plans. *You* know it's not my way to spread terror and dread. I can't help the way I look, can I? And Morgrom doesn't feed me, just the way Minos never sent me a little souvlaki, a little pastitsio now and then. I'll tell you what *I'd* like: I'd like Morgrom and onions, fried together on a bun the size of a coffin."

"You've earned your peace," said Glorian consolingly, signaling to his friends to slip past the morose monster. "There should be some more adventurers along, oh, within the next few hours, I'd say."

"With my luck," said the Minotaur with a moan, "it'll be some other swaggering hero out to make a name for himself. Go. You and your prince, just get out of here. Jeez, did you have to cut me this bad?"

Beyond the Minotaur, they found themselves in a small room. "Cute," said Mirakles, looking up. "The grating up there is fastened with a lock in the shape of a skull and crossbones. And we have a skeleton key. I'll tell you one thing: I *hate* cute. Of all Morgrom's crimes, this cuteness may be the worst."

He took the key from Ed and unlocked the grating. A shower of leaves fell down on the prince, but he brushed them all away. Cleaning and then sheathing Redthirst, he climbed out through the opening. He reached down and helped Glorian, Spike, and Ed escape as well.

"Well," said Glorian cheerfully, "here we are, exactly where I planned, although it's a couple of hours later than I thought."

"And the barrow?" asked the Prince of the Sunless Grotto.

"We'll just amble through the woods," said Glorian, looking around and listening for any suspicious noises. "This way."

CHAPTER NINE

The only thing necessary for the triumph of evil is for good men to do nothing.
—Edmund Burke

MIRAKLES WAS IRRITATed. "I tell you, before I walked under your tree, I searched this forest north, south, east, and west for *miles.* I'm *sure* this barrow wasn't here. I'd be willing to stake my honor on it, maybe even my life."

Glorian only shrugged. "This is another part of the forest."

"It couldn't be!" insisted the well-tanned hero. "I must have searched around every tree within a two-mile radius of the white house. I know I couldn't have missed this barrow. It's as big as the house is!"

They had entered the open door of the stone barrow, and Glorian had reassured them when the door closed inexorably and permanently behind them. "Morgrom's doing!" cried Mirakles. "Just like the trap door in the house!"

Glorian tried to soothe him by patting the air. "No, no," he said, "nothing like that. As your official Supernatural Guide, I advise you pay no attention to the fact that our line of retreat has been cut, and we have no choice but to go on to greater and stranger dangers below. Trust me, O Prince. All is happening as it is meant to happen."

"Right, sure," grumbled he of the Elastic Tendon. "Another part of the forest. Bah!"

Glorian led them forward, to a brightly lighted cavern. "You know how in old plays, if some mysterious or magical things were to happen, the scene would begin in 'another part of the forest'? The barrow is in *another part of the forest.*"

"Ah," said Mirakles, understanding at last. "All right, I get it. Let's move along, then. It looks more pleasant than the other part of the Empire."

A wide stream ran through the center of the cavern. There was a small wooden footbridge spanning the stream, but on the farther side a path led into a dark tunnel. Above the bridge, floating in the air, was a sign that read: "All ye who stand before this bridge have completed a great and perilous adventure which has tested your wit and courage. Those who pass over this bridge must be prepared to undertake an even greater adventure that will severely test your skill and bravery!"

Mirakles stood at the beginning of the footbridge and stared up at the floating sign. He read it once, twice, maybe three times slowly to himself. Then he laughed aloud. He turned to his companions. "Either Morgrom put that there," he said, "or it's left over from the old days of the Great Underground Empire. In either case, somebody hadn't reckoned on dealing with Mirakles, son of Thrag, son of Queen Desiphae of the Sunless Grotto. We'll waste no more time."

Glorian and Spike, The Protector, just looked at each other and shrugged. They followed Mirakles across the wooden bridge. Ed, the Embedded Character, followed silently behind, as usual.

They headed southward, into the center of the great cavern. Stalactites and stalagmites of many sizes were everywhere. The vast chamber glowed with the dim light provided by a phosphorescent moss, and the feeling of eeriness in the cave was intensified by the weird shadows that seemed to stalk them along the rocky walls on all sides.

Spike cleared his throat. "You may well notice that the rock of which this cavern is formed is limestone." The young man still had an unfortunate tendency to lapse into his overbearing tour-guide persona at times like this. "As you will remember, the tunnels in the portion of the Great Underground Empire we previously visited were chiefly granite. Here we have limestone. Perhaps a geologist would be better able to explain this situation, but I'm better able to get you through it alive. Let's move along now to the southwest. I warn you, for a brief time we'll pass through a dark tunnel. I assure you, you're all quite safe. No grues have ever killed a traveler in that tunnel, unless he was foolish enough to dawdle too long."

"Say, Spike," said Glorian, staring up at the high, vaulted ceiling, "is that the luminia you use to make yourself glow?"

Spike maintained his lecturish tone. "No, the luminia I depend on grows above ground. I've taken the liberty of naming my species 'Luminia spikea.' This phosphorescent moss is related, I believe, but I've never been able to study a sample of it. Therefore I've not classified it. I leave it to some future botanist to examine the moss. He or she may have all the credit. I'm not the jealous type."

Glorian heard a stifled chuckle from Mirakles as they crossed a shallow ford and crept into the dark tunnel. As small as it was, it appeared to have been enlarged at one time, and the inner walls had been smoothed.

They emerged at the north end of a formal garden. "Remarkable," said the prince, wandering about the grounds for a few moments. "The style of this part of the Underground Empire is so different from the other. It's so much more pleasant here."

"Take that as an ominous warning," said Glorian. "This area is every bit as deadly."

"I think it all reflects the tastes and preferences of the particular Flathead king who was in power during the building of each section," said Spike with a yawn. "Confidentially, no one seems to have made any records concerning who did what, and certainly no one today cares at all."

Mirakles pulled at his lower lip in thought. "The cavern's walls are hidden here by hedges—recently trimmed hedges. That means that Morgrom has his workers making renovations here, too, turning this place into his twisted vision of what it once was. Look, there's a break in the hedge here." He drew Redthirst and hacked away some underbrush.

"And there's a carefully manicured path leading south," said Ed.

"You're not going to believe this," said Spike.

Everyone turned to see what he'd discovered. In a bed of roses was a lovely, white-painted gazebo. On the far side of it, a unicorn—a *true* unicorn—was grazing on the grass.

"Now," said Mirakles, "there's something you don't see every day. And it's a very handsome unicorn, too. I believe it's the first innocent creature I've come across in this entire adventure. It's the first I won't have to defeat in battle or deal with in some other way."

"Don't be too sure," said Glorian. "You are not out of the testing phase of your quest, so it's unlikely that you'll meet anything here that you won't have to deal with."

They all sat on white-painted iron chairs around a white iron-lace table in the gazebo. It was cool and restful there, and they silently regarded the unicorn, which showed no signs of panic. On the table were place mats and a teapot. There were no cups or saucers, or tea in the teapot.

"Well," said the prince, "what now?"

"I'm not exactly sure," said Spike, "but if we sit here long enough, sooner or later the denizens of this part of the Empire will make themselves known and demand some response. In the meantime, we deserve a little rest, anyway."

"Well," said Mirakles, "I don't want to rest. Every moment I sit here, Morgrom the Malignant moves nearer to possessing my mother, the queen. I can just picture her, blissfully unaware of the approaching evil, gazing at her lovely reflection in the waters of the Sunless Grotto, her two small, transparent wings beating slowly and creating the breath of air that supports all life in the kingdom."

"All right," said Glorian, "why don't you go explore the south end of the garden. As I recall, we may need this teapot filled with water. I'll go back to the shallow ford and fill it."

"Right," said Mirakles. "You know, Glorian, I have come to realize you are not the Weasel Spirit I once called you. We are all friends now. We are a party of adventurers with common goals. Somehow that makes my burden lighter."

"Thank you," said Glorian humbly. He knew he was blushing, so he took the teapot, crawled back through the dark tunnel, and filled it up at the stream. Then he carefully made his way back to his seat in the gazebo.

"While you were gone," said the son of Thrag, "I approached the unicorn experimentally. It bounded away. When I went into the south part of the garden, the unicorn returned. It doesn't seem to be concerned about us at all now."

"It's a beautiful animal," said Ed. "Like a horse with a horn."

Glorian and Mirakles just looked at each other. The prince muttered, "That Embedded Character sure has an artist's eye."

"What did you discover to the south?" asked Glorian.

Mirakles of the Elastic Tendon thought for a moment. "What do you call it when you take a bush or a shrub and trim it into the shape of something?"

"Topiary," said Ed.

"Thank you," said the prince. "Topiary. *Weird* topiary."

Glorian leaned back in his iron-lance chair. "As I recall, the topiary was in the shape of a dragon, a unicorn, a huge snake, a huge dog that wasn't right somehow, and some human figures. You always got the feeling that the topiary was moving and changing positions when you weren't looking, but when you looked back, it all seemed the same."

Mirakles nodded. "That's the same creepy feeling it gave me, all right," he said. "Except the shapes of the bushes are all different. It must be Morgrom's doing. Now they're things that could be used as weapons: a knife, a revolver, a coil of rope ending in a noose, something that looks like a bent pipe, a wrench, and a candlestick."

"This is not a place I'd want to bring my kids," said Ed. Everyone stared at him for a few seconds. The Embedded Character just spread his hands. "Well, *you* know what I mean. As if it should be filled with sweet little old blue-haired ladies in tennis shoes whom no one can stand anymore."

They passed through another tunnel and came to a circular room whose high ceiling was lost in gloom far overhead. Eight identical passages led out of the room.

"This is the central room of this part of the Great Underground Empire," said Spike, "just as the Round Room was in the previous section. This room is the Carousel Room, and it could be made to rotate rather quickly, so that the average tourist lost his bearings and had a difficult time finding the exit passage of his choice. The famous adventurer who finally conquered the mysteries of the Empire turned off the machinery of the Carousel Room, and I am happy in the extreme that Morgrom hasn't turned it back on yet."

"From here," said Glorian, "we can travel to the eight rather separate areas of this district of the Empire. The exit to the east goes back the way we came, to the garden and back to the closed stone door of the barrow. The exit to the northeast meets the same path farther along. Beyond that, the choice is yours, O Prince."

Mirakles spread his hands. "Is this the area where the new dragon is supposed to be endangering wayfarers?" he asked.

"The kimono dragon," said Spike. "Yes. The passage to the northwest."

"Well," said the son of Thrag, "I feel obliged to eliminate that dragon. That's part of my hero's nature, and I consider it a sacred trust."

Glorian felt uneasy, because dragons always overwhelmed his somewhat limited mythological weapons. Dragons tended to overwhelm *everything*. "I suggest we search elsewhere before we tackle the dragon," he said glumly. "If we find the Dipped Switch and the Hot Key first, we might not have to face the dragon at all."

"By Thrag's pierced palms!" cried Mirakles. "I'm disappointed in you, Glorian. After all, didn't The Protector offer to murmur in my ear the single stratagem that would defeat the kimono dragon?"

Spike stared down at the ground and pushed some pebbles around with his foot. "I lied," he said in a quiet voice.

"That was when he was still pretending that he, too, was a member of the Supernatural and Fantastic Wayfarers Association," said Glorian.

They all stood around and looked into each other's faces for a few moments. Then Mirakles shrugged and said, "Well, let's go do it anyway."

"Right," said Spike hesitantly.

"Sure," said Glorian diffidently.

"Hey," said Ed, "while I was still Embedded, I heard the Control Character himself was in this part of the Empire. Maybe we'll get some help when we least expect it."

Spike led the party northwest, into a room that was cool and damp. "I've never even heard of the Control Character," he said.

"Above The Powers That Be is the Autoexec," explained Glorian. "Above the Autoexec is the Control Character. No one I know has ever seen the Control Character. A lot of us Association members even think he's a myth. I mean, a non-existent myth, not like the real myths the rest of us are."

The air was filled with mist. The path began to curve back on itself again and again, and soon led them to a wide stone bridge. They paused there for a few seconds to catch their breath.

"Still carrying that teapot of water, Glorian?" said Spike.

"Yes."

"Going to put out the dragon's fire with it?" asked Mirakles with a laugh.

Glorian shook his head. "It'll come in useful if we have to search to the southeast of the Carousel Room. You'll see. Maybe."

The stone bridge was partially ruined, but it was still impressive. Far below in a deep chasm, water rushed along with a murmurous voice. From the north end of the bridge, a paved path led into a large open space, a huge cavern full of broken stone. The walls were scorched and there were deep scratches on the floor. There was a sooty, dry smell in the air. "This is where that other dragon dwelt," said Spike. "The one killed by the adventurer.'

Mirakles nodded. "All dragons' lairs are pretty much the same. I would have recognized this place as such."

Glorian turned to Spike. "Yet didn't you say that a new dragon had taken up residence here?" he said.

"Yes," said the glowing young man. "Can you see, far in the rear of the cavern, to the left, a small structure? It's made of bamboo and rice paper. That's the home of the kimono dragon. She knows we're here. If we wait a little longer, she'll take it as a challenge and come out. Then she'll invite us into her home."

"Invite?" said Mirakles. "I've never been invited by a dragon to do anything. Usually, you just run across a dragon and it kills you or you kill it."

"As I tried to explain earlier," said Spike, "the kimono dragon is unlike any you've ever seen or heard of. And more dangerous, too."

"We could just pass on by," suggested Ed. "There's a nice, wide passage to the west, or we could go back across the bridge."

"By Thrag!" said Mirakles. "The Prince of the Sunless Grotto is not afraid to face any creature!"

"In addition," said Glorian, "you probably wouldn't be allowed to by The Powers That Be. My experience tells me that this is probably your ultimate test. I don't think you could avoid it, even if you wanted to."

He was correct; even as he spoke, a small figure made its way from the small house at the back of the cave, toward them across the broken stone of the floor.

"Here she comes," said Spike. There was great fear in his voice.

"What?" exclaimed Mirakles. "She can't be any bigger than you! She's tiny! Does she breathe fire or anything?"

"No," said Glorian. "You've passed all your physical challenges. This is an intellectual test. You see, on a quest of this nature, brute strength is not enough. You must demonstrate that your mind is worthy, as well. I'm sure the kimono dragon will present you with some kind of riddle or puzzle to solve, and your life—all our lives, perhaps—will depend on your native wit."

"Hey," said he of the Elastic Tendon, backing away and raising his hands, "nobody said there was going to be a written part to this. I understood that I'd just have to hack and hew my way to the goal, and I was perfectly prepared to do that. Springing surprise quizzes on me isn't fair. That wasn't part of the original bargain."

"I'm sorry, Prince," said Glorian. "You agreed only to find the Dipped Switch for Morgrom. Nothing was said about the nature of the dangers along the way. You agreed implicitly to face them all, whatever they were."

Before Mirakles could speak again, the kimono dragon arrived. She was, as the prince had said, only about four feet tall. She was dressed in a formal Japanese kimono, which was made of a lovely, purple and cream-colored floral brocade. She also wore an obi, the traditional sash, around her minuscule waist.

Her head was not much larger than a grown man's hand, and covered with bright, beautiful yellow scales. Her eyes were red, and cast down modestly toward the ground. The scales shaded from yellow to orange and then to red at her throat. Her wrists and hands were a brilliant emerald green, and her lower legs and tiny bare feet were of the deepest violet color.

"Makes you wonder how anything so beautiful could be so deadly," whispered The Protector.

"I still don't see how she's deadly," said Glorian.

"Just wait."

The kimono dragon bowed to them, and spoke in

a low, humble voice. "Please, honored travelers," she said, "I summon the courage to beg you all to honor me in sharing tea in my wretched abode, there in the back of this miserable cavern."

Glorian and Spike looked at Mirakles, but said nothing. The prince was very definitely not pleased, and his expression was gravely troubled, but at last he spoke. "We would be the honored ones," he said. "We thank you for your generous invitation."

"Please, then," said the dragon, "follow me, and beware the footing."

Mirakles nodded and followed closely behind her. Then came Spike. Glorian transformed himself again, this time into an elderly Japanese gentleman in traditional Japanese clothing. Ed brought up the rear, being more careful than ever about where he stepped. He was in serious danger of falling and breaking off an important appendage or two.

They removed their shoes or sandals and placed them neatly together facing the dragon's door. Then they entered the flimsy-looking structure. There was a front room which was furnished formally and sparsely in the Japanese manner, with only a small table in the middle of the room, surrounded by tatami mats. There were sliding rice-paper doors that indicated other rooms, but nothing could be guessed about what they contained.

The dragon indicated the mats and bowed. "Please," she said.

Glorian and Spike returned the bow and took their places, sitting cross-legged at the table. Ed followed, and then Mirakles reluctantly did the same.

The kimono dragon began the ancient Japanese tea ceremony, interrupting the ritual procedure only once to comment on Glorian's teapot. "Ah," she murmured, her eyes on the table before her, "a white Hall Airflow, no decoration. Twenty-two dollars, book price. Very nice, guide-san."

"It's not mine," said Glorian uncomfortably. "It's the one from the gazebo."

"Yes, guide-san, I know." Then the dragon returned to her mixing, whisking, and serving. She prepared the tea by boiling water in an iron kettle over a charcoal brazier. There was not much else on the table except for the bowls from which they'd drink, and a small lacquered box.

The kimono dragon deposited a small quantity of tea in Mirakles's bowl, then added some boiling water, and began whipping it with a bamboo whisk. The prince looked questioningly at Glorian, who only held a finger to his lips. The dragon whisked the tea for a very long time, then handed the bowl to the brawny hero with a bow.

"You must drink it in three sips and a half," murmured Glorian.

"Why?" said Mirakles.

"Local custom," whispered Spike. "And observe the polite silence."

Mirakles did as he was instructed. He lifted the bowl suspiciously to his lips and drank it. He returned the bowl to the table.

The kimono dragon smiled. "Now, hero-san," she said softly, "are you fortified to consider my most unworthy yet vexing problem?"

Spike leaned toward Glorian. "Don't *we* get any?" he asked.

Glorian's expression did not change. "If our prince screws up here, we'll get plenty. I can feel it."

Mirakles looked at Glorian for help, but the old Japanese gentleman sitting across from him averted his eyes and said nothing. "Yes, by Thrag's eternal fury!" the prince swore. "What is this riddle, then?"

Glorian thought he saw the little kimono dragon blanch a bit at the prince's tone, but it must have been his imagination. Scales don't blanch, he realized.

The dragon reached forward and opened the beautifully painted and lacquered box. Just then, there was the very audible cry of a young woman, as if removing the lid of the black box had been a signal.

Mirakles got quickly to his feet, drawing Redthirst, which was giving off its strong bread aroma. "Who do you have back there? Some captive princess or something?"

The dragon still studied the tabletop. "Yes, exactly," she said in her low voice. "A captive princess. If you solve my puzzle correctly—"

The Prince of the Sunless Grotto did not wait any longer to hear the kimono dragon's explanation. He crossed the room of the tea ceremony and threw back the sliding door.

Beyond was another room, smaller than the first. In it was a rather gorgeous young woman, wearing a dirty and bedraggled gown, sitting on a rock in the corner. There was a manacle around her left wrist, and she was chained to the rock. She didn't actually seem to be conscious, but as Mirakles gazed at her, she heaved another mournful cry.

"By Thrag and by the Grotto!" said the prince loudly. "She is the most beautiful woman I've ever seen, except of course for Queen Desiphae, my mother. If I had not taken an oath to forswear all pleasure until I completed the task Morgrom set before me, I would waken her now and take her to wife."

Glorian had left his seat at the tea table and come up behind the prince. "Great hero-san," he said, "you may win this princess only by solving the problem the kimono dragon will give you."

"And what if I refuse?" cried Mirakles. "What if I simply free this lovely princess and carry her out of here? Who will stop me?"

"The Powers That Be will stop you," said Glorian sadly. "This I know for certain. It will not be allowed."

Glorian watched the prince's expression change, from defiance to wrath to resentment. Finally, Mirakles said, "I've learned enough in the last few days to know that you speak the truth. Then I must conquer the dragon and her puzzle, for though the princess knows it not, I have already pledged her my heart." He turned and went back to the tea table.

"You are most wise, hero-san," said Glorian, taking his seat across from Mirakles.

"And what becomes of those who fail?" asked Spike.

The kimono dragon kept her eyes on the lacquered box, but she permitted herself a small smile. "I have several rooms filled with modern art of my own creation. My chosen form of expression is free-form sculpture, which I weld together from the armor of failed heroes. It is, no doubt, of no artistic merit as critics judge such things, but it gives me pleasure. I would be honored to show you the remains of your predecessors before you view the contents of this box."

Mirakles gave a grim laugh. "I don't care a worm's whisker for the failures. Let's get on with it."

"As you wish, hero-san," said the kimono dragon. She lifted one graceful hand and put it into the lacquered box. When she removed it, she held a golden ball. This she gave to Mirakles.

Mirakles turned the ball over in his hands and studied it, his brow furrowed. Then he passed it to Glorian. "What must I do?" he asked.

The kimono dragon answered. "You must take it and tell me to whom you wish it delivered. If your decision is correct, if you choose the proper person, you may claim the princess. If you choose wrongly, then you and all your companions will die, I will not say how. And that marvelous, fragrant sword of yours will be added to a work-in-progress I am tentatively calling *Adagio in Steel £3.*"

The prince looked at Glorian. "I still don't see why I can't just cut her puny head off and get out of here."

Glorian's voice was as sad as death. "As I've told you, The Powers That Be require you to make a decision. But I could not have foreseen this." He held the golden ball up. "This is a golden apple," he said. "On it is inscribed *For the Fairest.* On the other side it says *Frobozz Magic Golden Apple Company.* It's the Judgment of Paris all over again. It appears you are doomed, hero-san."

"Why?" asked Mirakles. "I've never been to Paris."

"No, no," said Glorian. "In ancient Greek mythology, the Trojan War was caused by a golden apple just like this one. It was given to a youth named Paris to decide who deserved it among Aphrodite, Hera, and Athena. Each of the goddesses promised him vast rewards if he chose her. He gave it to Aphrodite because she promised him Helen, the most beautiful woman in the world. The trouble was, Helen was married to a powerful king, who got all his allies together to help get his wife back. Paris was the son of the king of Troy. You know the rest. It's a puzzle with a no-win solution."

"Well," said Spike, "actually I don't know what happened at Troy, but how does that affect us here? Where is the peril?"

Glorian rubbed his forehead wearily. "After Paris's decision, the two goddesses who lost were very jealous and angry, of course. If our hero-san doesn't choose correctly, he'll incur the wrath of a large part of the super-pantheon that the Supernatural and Fantastic Wayfarers Association serves. He—and we—would probably be blasted to dust in minutes."

"I could give this to my mother, the Queen of the Sunless Grotto," said Mirakles thoughtfully, "but somehow I feel that's not the correct solution."

"I don't know what the right answer is, either," said Glorian helplessly. "I could create some more golden apples that said things like *For the Barest, For the Rarest, For the Sparest,* and so on. That might appease some of the other goddesses. Or I just might be able to change the wording on this apple to read *For the Forest,* and you could leave it in the woods in the upper world." He placed the golden apple back on the table.

"Choose now," said the kimono dragon in a sibilant whisper. "I need to hear but one name from your lips."

"No, Glorian," said Mirakles decisively, "yours are all transparent tricks, and would surely result in our sudden deaths. That is not how I wish to die. I prefer meeting death with Redthirst in my hand, like this!" And he drew the sword back and brought it down in a mighty stroke, splitting the golden apple into two parts.

"The apple!" cried the kimono dragon. She gave a high-pitched cry and fell limply to the tatami mat.

Glorian laughed. "The Gordian Apple," he said approvingly.

"Look," cried Spike, "one half says *For the Fair,* and the other half says *est.*"

Mirakles looked around at his companions with grim determination. "The first portion I will give to the princess whom this creature keeps prisoner, as soon as I rescue her."

"*Est* is Latin for 'he is,' " said Ed in an offhand kind of way. "I would surmise that it belongs to the Control Character."

"If there *is* such a being," said Spike.

"No more talk," said Mirakles. "Glorian, get out of that shape and pick up the apple pieces. I've got hero work to do."

Spike just shook his head admiringly. "He's great to watch, isn't he?"

Glorian didn't answer. He'd transformed himself into a middle-aged woman, a tough Katharine Hepburn-type wearing a female version of the rugged khaki outfit he'd worn as a man, with a long skirt and sensible shoes. He grabbed up the two halves of the golden apple and put them in a pocket of his skirt. Then he hurried to see what Mirakles was up to.

The mighty hero had gone to the princess's cell. Once again he lifted his enchanted sword and brought it down, severing the chain that bound the princess to the rock. The lovely young woman didn't respond. "Is it a spell?" asked Mirakles.

"More of a trance," said Glorian. Mirakles heard the difference in his voice, turned, and looked at his Supernatural Guide. He was quite evidently shocked. "Do you honestly think you're going to be as useful to me in that form?" he said.

Glorian gave him a Hepburn glare and said in a husky voice, "I'll match you mile for mile. Just because I'm a woman now—"

"All right, all right," said the prince. "We don't have time for this. How do I get her out of the trance?"

"You kiss her, of course," said Spike.

Mirakles raised his eyebrows, then turned back to the princess. He leaned forward and gave her a chaste kiss. She shook herself awake, then noticed the prince and the rest of the party. "Thank you for rescuing me from that horrid creature," she said in a voice like a silver bell. "I must leave now."

"Apple," said Mirakles impatiently.

Glorian looked at the two pieces, and handed the *For the Fair* half to the prince, who knelt and offered it to the princess.

The young woman took it and sighed. "I see you've found a way around the hopeless riddle," she said. The more she spoke, the more delightful her voice seemed. "No goddess could be jealous of me, for it says only *For the Fair,* and does not imply that I am in any way more attractive than anyone else. But I cannot accept this from you, sir. I was betrothed at birth, and I must remain faithful to my intended husband."

Mirakles looked crushed. "And who is this man? By Thrag, he and I'll discuss this matter most thoroughly!"

The princess shrugged her pretty shoulders. "I do not know his name," she said. "I know only that he is a prince whom some call 'The Unhamstringable.' Beyond that, he is a mystery to me, and I languish here between dragons, waiting for him to come to me."

Mirakles laughed. "Then know that I am he, for I am Mirakles of the Elastic Tendon, which is but an alternate translation of your betrothed's epithet."

The princess' eyes opened wider. "And you are a prince?"

"I am of the house of King Hyperenor and Queen Desiphae of the Sunless Grotto. The king is now dead, and the realm is mine to claim when my quest is ended."

The princess cried aloud with joy. "Then you are indeed he!" And she threw her arms around Mirakles's neck.

Glorian stepped closer and said urgently, "Let's get out of here before the kimono dragon recovers."

"Yes," said the prince, "you're right. We must escape while we may." The brawny hero, the glowing young man, the beautiful young woman, the tough older woman, and the Embedded Character hurried out of the cell and through the dragon's ceremonial chamber.

"Which way now?" asked Spike.

"West," said Glorian. "We may as well search

that way next, as long as we're in this part of the Great Underground Empire."

Mirakles paid little attention to Spike and Glorian's discussion. He and the princess walked along, holding each other around the waist, and gazing longingly into each other's eyes.

Spike shook his head. "You know, this is going to slow us down," he said.

"I never anticipated it," said Glorian. "We're just going to have to keep prodding them forward, or separate them somehow."

Spike laughed. "Sure. I'll leave the job of separating them to you. I think it would take semi-divine powers."

Glorian sighed and looked up toward the high, vaulted ceiling. "Why me, O Autoexec?" he exclaimed. "Why me?"

CHAPTER TEN

Money can't buy friends but you can get
a better class of enemy.
—Spike Milligan

THE MEMBERS OF THE party were still congratulating themselves on their escape from the kimono dragon. "Well," said Mirakles, turning to his new-found love, "I know you're a princess, but I don't even know your name."

She blushed and cast her eyes down. "I am Princess Melithiel," she said, "of the House of Fourth."

"Melithiel," said the prince in a soft voice. "That's the most beautiful name I've ever heard."

It was clear to Glorian, Spike, and Ed that the two royals were going to go on like that for some time. They were all hungry, so Glorian Drawer Forwarded a sumptuous celebratory meal of thick, charcoal-grilled bear steaks, sturgeon filets, a farmer salad of mixed greens and aronica, potatoes bryant, cherryhs jubilee for dessert, and great tankards of stout.

"You know," said Mirakles, as Glorian refilled the muscular hero's tankard, "I've never eaten this well in my life. I almost hope we don't find the Dipped Switch for a little while longer, because despite the battles and the illogical aspects of this place, moments like this almost make it all worthwhile." He turned and gave Melithiel a fond smile.

Glorian raised his own tankard in a toast. "My friends," he said, "it doesn't get any better than this."

"Sure, it does," said Spike. "I can think of six things I'd rather be doing right now, and that's not even including sex or winning the Campbell Award."

"Well," said Ed, "this is the best time *I've* ever had, and I'm grateful to you all for letting me accompany you."

They all sat in silence for a few moments, gazing into the upward-pointing beam of Glorian's flashlight, which had to stand in for a campfire. "We'll sleep here," decided the prince, "and when we wake, we'll continue our journey westward."

"You know I must leave soon, my darling," said Melithiel sadly. "I have to be sure that my unicorn is all right. I haven't seen it in absolutely *ages*."

"We saw it earlier today," said Spike, "and it seemed perfectly well. It was grazing on the lawn near the gazebo."

The princess nodded. "Thank you, but I have my responsibilities, too."

The son of Thrag frowned. "How and where will we meet again?" he asked.

Melithiel leaned over and gave him a kiss on his well-rounded shoulder. "Very little happens in these caverns that I don't hear about," she said. "As soon as I've attended to my duties, I will hasten to rejoin you."

"In the meantime," said Mirakles, removing a golden ring from his finger, "I give this to you as a remembrance."

The princess took the ring, but it was too large to wear on any of her fingers. She tore a narrow strip from the hem of her gown, threaded the ring onto it, and tied the piece of cloth around her neck. "I love you, my prince," she said sadly, "but I have no such token to give to you."

He laughed. "Tear another strip of cloth, and I will wear it tied above the elbow of my sword-arm." She did as he suggested, and bound the material around his bulging biceps. "There, now," he said. "In every battle, whenever I raise my enchanted sword, Redthirst, your strip of cloth will be like a banner to me, a martial flag to remind me that I am fighting for more than merely myself, or even the safety of the gentle Queen Desiphae. I will be fighting for you, and for our future together."

A tear fell softly from Melithiel's eye, and she stood up. "I'll go now," she said, "because if you say another such thing, I'll not be able to leave you, ever."

"May that soon be true, my love," said the Prince of the Elastic Tendon. She turned, sobbing, and hurried back toward the large cavern from which they'd just escaped.

"Do you think she'll be able to sneak past the kimono dragon's house?" asked Ed.

"I think the kimono dragon is dead," said Mirakles. "That's the way these riddle sequences usually work."

"Good," said Spike, "because after we explore the northwestern corner of this part of the Empire, we have to pass through that cavern ourselves. It's the only way back to the Carousel Room and the rest of the area."

"You know," murmured Mirakles, "she didn't take any light source with her. I've noticed that certain dwellers in this Great Underground Empire don't carry torches or anything, and never seem to be concerned about grues."

"Maybe they've signed special pacts with the beasts or something," said Ed.

The hero just shook his head. "Just more illogicality."

They talked for a while longer, and then stretched out on the cold stone floor to sleep. Glorian provided them with blankets and pillows by Drawer Forwarding, and in the end they were all fairly comfortable. They each slept until he could sleep no more, and Glorian served a light but nourishing breakfast. He returned the dirty dishes, the blankets, and the pillows to his room in the Valhalla Hilton, and then they started the day's march.

The first chamber they came to was decorated with beautiful frescoes of someone battling dragons and rescuing fair maidens. "Hey," said Mirakles, "I've done these things!"

"So have many other heroes, my prince," said Glorian reprovingly in his Kate Hepburn voice.

Unfortunately, the frescoes had been blackened and cracked by intense heat, and so it was impossible to determine who the hero actually was. "Evidently," said Mirakles, "this damage was done by the great fire-breathing dragon, before it was killed by the legendary adventurer who solved the puzzles and sacked the Empire of its riches. No doubt Morgrom will get around to restoring the paintings, and he'll probably insert his own ugly face for the hero's."

That brought laughter from the rest of the party. They took one final look at the scorched frescoes, and continued on the west-leading path.

"Know what you forgot, Glorian?" said The Protector after a little while.

"Forgot?" said Glorian dubiously. *"Me?* We Supernatural Guides are trained never to forget."

"You left your teapot in the kimono dragon's house."

Glorian looked at Spike. "Oops," he said. "Well, I suppose I can get a pot of tea from the hotel and throw the tea away and fill the pot with water, if I have to. No problem." It was clear that he was shaken more than a little by this lapse, though.

"We're headed for the bank area now," said Spike.

"I can't imagine that we'll run into any trouble there. There never used to be any ogres or trolls or other unpleasant creatures in the bank. It was more of a problem than a danger. There was treasure there once, and the adventurer had to be particularly clever to make off with it."

"So let me get this straight," said Mirakles. "The kimono dragon was my final test. Does that mean we're going to find the Golden Dipped Switch and the Hot Key soon? No more monsters to fight or anything like that? I find the Switch, I take it back to Morgrom, I use the Hot Key to open my father's scroll and learn the Third Secret of the Sword, I meet my princess and take her home to meet my mother. Then the rest of you all go your separate ways and we write to each other for a year or two and then never hear from each other again. Is that how it goes?"

Glorian considered how best to explain things to the prince. "I'm really not allowed to tell you too much about how the universe works," he said. "You've heard me mention the Campbell Award."

"Only about a million times," said Spike.

"Well," said Glorian, ignoring Spike's sarcastic tone, "Joseph Campbell formulated a circular mythic pattern. He was able to relate this pattern to myths from all over the world, from every century and every culture. At first, the Hero gets a Call to Adventure, which may or may not be refused."

"Yes," said Mirakles, "I remember that. I refused until Thrag's Bane offered me my father's scroll in return for a service."

"Exactly," said Glorian. "The Hero usually finds supernatural aid in one form or another."

"That's you all over, ain't it?" laughed The Protector. "One form or another?"

Glorian continued to ignore him. "Then the Hero crosses the first threshold and begins the succession of trials. Some heroes reveal themselves to be unworthy, and are killed or prevented from achieving their goals. These trials are more than merely tests to see if you're strong and fit enough to be a Hero. They function as a psychological exercise program that will change your outlook without your even knowing it. You must be made ready to pluck the fruit of victory—in your case, recovering the Switch and Key. After that comes the mystical union with the Great Goddess."

Mirakles backed away. "The Great Goddess? Who is the Great Goddess? Which of the many in your super-pantheon is greatest?"

Glorian spread his hands. "In a Hero's case, a special woman may represent the Goddess, may even be the Goddess herself in human form. There are many different ways that it can go. I believe you've already met this woman, but you have yet to consummate the mystical marriage."

"Melithiel!" cried Mirakles.

"Yes. That's probably why she departed before we slept last night. You won't see her again until you've achieved your material goal."

"And then I take her home to meet Mother," said the prince, his eyes wide and shining with tears of joy.

Glorian frowned. "Well," he said slowly, "I shouldn't tell you this—technically, I'm breaking a big rule here—but the Hero generally faces a new series of tests on his way back to the Real World. You haven't sniffed your last loaf of freshly-baked bread, and you haven't slain your last monster, either."

The Prince of the Sunless Grotto only let his head fall back, and he laughed heartily. "Bring 'em on, Glorian! I'm ready for anything! For the rewards you promise, I'll hack my way knee-deep through an army of trolls and ghouls."

"You may have to," said Spike.

"Let's go on," said Mirakles enthusiastically. "We

have to search the bank area. Which way? Straight ahead?"

"Yes," said Spike.

The entrance hall to the former Bank of Zork was not far away. At one time it had been the largest banking institution in the entire Great Underground Empire, and owed its magnificence to the ornate and ostentatious tastes of the late, fabulously wealthy J. Pierpont Flathead, who pursued the unusual hobby of giving away, anonymously, the sum of one million zorkmids—to persons he had never even met. He did this twice, as a matter of fact, and then suddenly realized how stupid he was being. So he sent his four largest and most persuasive henchmen to visit the beneficiaries, and thereby recovered most of what he'd given away. From then on, his motto became "A penny earned is *mine*."

The floor of the entrance hall was covered with a layer of rock and brick dust, and there were paths of footprints leading to the northwest and northeast corners. Spike knelt and put a forefinger in the dust, then tasted it. "Just as I thought," he said, standing again. "This is fresh. Some of these footprints are only hours old."

"What do you make of it?" asked Glorian.

"I have an idea," said Spike, "but I don't want to say anything until we take a look for ourselves."

"Which way?" asked Ed. There didn't seem to be much to choose between the northwest and northeast paths.

"That way," said Mirakles, pointing to the northeast. He gave no reason for his choice, but as the designated hero of the party, he didn't need to. The others followed him and found themselves in a small teller's room, which had been used by a bank officer who retrieved safety deposit boxes for the bank's customers long ago. On the north side of the room was a sign which read "Viewing Room." On the east side of the room, above an open door, was a sign reading "Bank Personnel Only."

"Safety deposit boxes!" said Spike excitedly. "If the Dipped Switch and Hot Key are hidden anywhere in the whole Empire, a safety deposit box here seems like a very possible choice. We may be only a few yards away from success!"

"We'll see," said Mirakles in a grim voice. "I have a hero's tendency to doubt simple solutions. Still, we have to examine every room here." He strode across the dusty floor to the open door to the east.

"Wait, my prince," called Glorian. "It might be safer to look into the Viewing Room first."

"He's right," said Spike. "After all, we're certainly not Bank Personnel. There will surely be all sorts of tricks and traps beyond that door to keep out the uninitiated. Like us."

"Safer, Glorian?" sneered Mirakles. "Your Weasel Spirit showing its beady-eyed little head again? Just follow me and you'll be safe. I'll take all the risks." As he spoke, he slowly withdrew Redthirst from its scabbard across his broad back. He turned again and passed through the east door.

Glorian, Spike, and Ed all looked at each other briefly and hurried after the prince. They followed him down a very long hallway to a large rectangular room. The east and west walls of the chamber had been used in the heyday of the bank to store the safety deposit boxes, but every single one had been removed, dashing Spike's hope of finding the Switch and Key in one of them. There was another large doorway, just like the one they'd come through, on the west side of the Safety Depository, and a smaller door to the south.

"What's that?" asked Ed, pointing to the north "wall."

Glorian looked and saw a shimmering curtain of light. "I don't know," he said worriedly.

"I'll tell you what it is," said Spike. "It's part of the strange transportation network set up within the bank. That curtain can transport you to several different places. I don't know how it's done, but it wasn't working the last time I was here. This is part of Morgrom's renovation, and those footprints mean his workmen are around here somewhere, restoring the inner chambers of the bank, I suppose."

"What do you do?" asked Mirakles.

"You walk through the curtain of light," said Spike, "but there's a trick to it."

"Forget it for now," said the Prince of the Sunless Grotto. "Let's see what's through that door to the south."

What they found was the office of the former chairman of the Bank of Zork. They also found twelve white-faced creatures who moved stiffly around the room performing various chores. They lurched, actually, and it didn't take Glorian long to realize they were zombies. Zombie carpenters. One turned to face them, his face a ghastly mask of horror. "Mmmm," he said in a dead voice, "fresh bread."

Mirakles stood there, holding Redthirst cocked back over his shoulder, ready to strike, but the zombie carpenters offered them no threat. They went about their various tasks, which included laying expensive, deep-pile carpeting on the floor, staining newly fitted mahogany paneling, and installing lighting fixtures on the ceiling.

After a long while, the prince relaxed a little and put down his sword. He looked at Glorian, who only shrugged. It was very quiet in the room, except for a faint sound of moans, groans, and heartrending weeping coming softly from the zombies as they fixed up the chairman's office. They may have been captured forever in a terrible undeath, but they put in an honest day's work nonetheless.

"Good grief," said Spike, indicating a small sign that had been thumbtacked in place where the portrait of the bank's founder once hung. The sign read *All renovations by Frobozz Magic Contracting Company.*

"Where to now?" asked Mirakles.

"Let's go back into the depository," said Glorian, "and through the curtain of light, if we can."

The prince nodded. As the party passed through the door of the chairman's office, one of the zombies called after them, "Have a nice day!"

The safety depository was exactly as they'd left it. "I'll bet Morgrom will have that work crew out here next," said Spike.

Mirakles gave a wry smile. "I can see him as a tycoon," he said. "J. P. Morgrom, financier."

They stood before the curtain of light. As they stared at it, it gave them an uncomfortable, disorienting feeling. Once more, Redthirst began to give off its warning fragrance. "Me first," said Mirakles with a growl. And he disappeared through the curtain of light.

Glorian, Spike, and Ed followed immediately. The feeling of disorientation increased as they passed through, but then they found themselves in a very small room. There was nothing in the room. Not even exits.

"Oops," said Ed.

They looked around for a few seconds, but the room was absolutely bare, just stone walls, a stone ceiling, and a stone floor. There were no secret panels or other discoveries to hold their interest.

"I wonder what this tiny room was for," asked Spike.

Glorian gave the young man a slow wink. "Maybe J. Pierpont Flathead explained his policies here to his secretary in intimate detail. If you know what I mean."

Spike shrugged. "Maybe."

"Oops again," said the Embedded Character.

"What do you mean, Ed?" said Glorian.

"I mean that I turned to go back through the curtain of light, and there's no curtain of light there now. Just a blank wall."

"Hmm," said Mirakles, "it appears that we're trapped in a small, square, stone room with no way out."

"Yeah," said Spike, laughing, "but appearances can be deceiving. Follow me, and ask no questions, because I can't answer 'em." He walked resolutely toward the stone wall, and then stunningly he was gone. Somehow, he passed right through it.

"Good enough," said Mirakles, and he followed. Glorian went next, and Ed brought up the rear. They all found themselves back in the safety depository.

"Diffusion," said Mirakles. "Refraction. The Coriolis Effect. I understand now."

Spike danced from one foot to the other. "Now here's the real surprise!" he said, grinning. "Follow me back through the curtain of light."

"Why?" asked the Prince of the Elastic Tendon. "There wasn't much to do in that little stone room."

Before he finished speaking, Spike ran through the curtain of light. Glorian spread his hands and said, "He's lived down here all his life," and disappeared through the light barrier. Mirakles and Ed did the same.

This time, they didn't end up in the small stone room. After the feeling of disorientation passed, they found themselves in the main vault of the Bank of Zork. There were no doors here, either. There were, however, another couple of dozen workmen, many large stacks of newly-printed zorkmid bills—with Morgrom the Malignant's face on each one—piled against one wall, and Morgrom himself, accompanied as usual by Narlinia von Glech, this time wearing her Princess Dawn des Malalondes outfit.

"Prince Mirakles!" cried the Essence of Evil in a jovial tone. He'd changed his appearance again. Now he looked about thirty or forty years younger, like a fairly recent graduate of some high-power business college, young and handsome with abundant blond hair parted on the left side. He was wearing a good, expensive blue suit with a yellow power tie, and shiny wingtips that must have been imported from someplace where gnomes and elves stay up all night making the world's best footwear.

The Prince of the Sunless Grotto pointed at Morgrom with Redthirst. "You fool me not in this guise, Thrag's Bane!" he cried.

"You don't understand!" said Narlinia breathlessly. "You must realize that we're all working on the same side, that we're all one team, and we have to cooperate." She was wearing her long, Dorothy Lamour hair and the tight, red-sequined gown.

Mirakles turned on her and snarled, "Why should I believe anything you tell me?"

"Because you're a prince," she said, "and I'm a princess! I don't think you've ever seen me in my true identity before, the Princess Dawn des Malalondes. You and I share a sensitivity, a duty that only the well-born can comprehend. You and I have more in common with each other than with any of these other people, including Morgrom." As she spoke, she came closer and closer to Mirakles, until with her last words she had clutched his strong right arm with both of hers, preventing him from using his sword.

He looked down into her beautiful face, and for a

moment his expression wavered. Glorian was afraid that Mirakles would fail at this late stage of the adventure and fall victim to Narlinia's temptation, but the prince shook his head a couple of times, as if to clear it, and then he flung Narlinia away. She landed in a heap at the feet of Morgrom the Palindromic. "I have met a true princess, worthy of my devotion," he said to her harshly. "Take whatever shape you will, I have looked into your heart and I know what lurks there."

Narlinia did not get up. Her lip curled in a sneer. "Do you mean Melithiel?" she said. "Ha! She may be your first princess, but I can assure you that you're not her first prince! Ask Glorian if you don't believe me!"

"Bah!" said Mirakles.

"Friends, friends!" said Morgrom. "Let's leave these lovers' quarrels until later, until our mutual quest has ended. There will be time enough to sort all the rest of it out when the Dipped Switch has been recovered. Who knows? The answer to our hero's destiny probably lies in his father's scroll, so all our efforts should be in one direction: finding those missing items. Every other distraction should be put out of our minds."

"In this instance, Thrag's Bane speaks with an undeniable wisdom," said the prince. It was clear that he found it disconcerting to agree with Morgrom about anything. "Yet I find myself thinking that I've struggled and fought my way from the white house to this Bank of Zork, facing grues and Glarbo and Shugreth the Unenviable, gone to Hades and back, outwitted a dragon, and done deeds that will someday make a great saga. I've done all this in pursuit of something I promised you I'd find. Yet now I discover that you're doing nothing to help me. You're here in your bank instead, overseeing construction work. Morgrom, I wonder if I'm risking my life in a sane cause."

Morgrom came nearer and clapped Mirakles on his broad back. "Prince, prince," said the Essence of Evil, "try to see things from my perspective. I explained that I need the Golden Dipped Switch to use the time machine to restore this Empire more quickly, more efficiently, and more completely than my limited resources now permit. You've no doubt run across some of the meager treasures I've left in these caverns."

"Tortle Wax," snorted Spike.

Morgrom paid no attention. "I have a huge amount of work to do, Mirakles, my friend. I have to oversee the reconstruction of this bank, yes. It may not mean anything to you, but it is a vital part of the Great Underground Empire. At the same time, I'm responsible for work going on all over this vast subterranean area, most of which you haven't even visited yet. And all I asked of you was to locate one little switch. From my point of view, *I'm* the one doing all the difficult labor, and *you're* the one who's failed again and again in the single simple task I asked of you."

Mirakles's outraged bellow could probably have been heard all the way back to the Round Room.

Morgrom the Malignant only shrugged. Even though he now looked like a bright, ambitious young MBA, he was still the Essence of Evil. "To be brutally honest with you, son of Thrag," he said, "I can no longer afford the investment in time and slain underlings that you represent. I think perhaps it's time to dispense with your services entirely and seek out the assistance of a new hero. There are always plenty of new heroes coming along, right, Glorian?"

Glorian stepped forward, regretting that he was in a female form at the moment. Still, he drew himself up to his full height and glowered, hoping that he'd create the proper psychological effect. "Morgrom," he said fiercely, "if by your words you are threatening the life of Prince Mirakles, or any in our party, I have to warn you that—"

Morgrom raised one hand and a cold blue light surrounded it. He pointed his glowing blue forefinger at the prince, who deflected the strange energy with the flat of Redthirst's blade. "For Thrag and the Grotto!" cried the hero, and he flung aside his enchanted sword and leaped at his enemy.

They fell to the dusty floor and wrestled there, seemingly so equally matched that for a long time neither could win an advantage. It was a bizarre sight, as the Prince of the Sunless Grotto was dressed in his bare-chested, semi-barbarian manner, and the Essence of Evil wore a tidy, well-tailored banker's suit. Another odd aspect of their combat was the silence. Neither so much as grunted or gasped for breath.

They rolled over and over in the thick dust of the vault's floor. Finally, using a wrestling trick well-known to heroes but obviously a surprise to the villain, Mirakles ended up sitting on Morgrom's chest, pinning the evil one helplessly to the paving stones.

"I could kill you, you know," said the prince in triumph, "and for the depredations you devised against my innocent mother, perhaps I should dispatch you to a netherworld where your powers will not avail you."

Morgrom, however, didn't seem in the least bit worried. He only raised his voice in a high, screeching wail.

Mirakles looked over his shoulder at Glorian, an unspoken question on his face.

"I don't know," said Glorian warily, "but I'd guess he just summoned aid."

Slowly, the Prince of the Elastic Tendon stood, freeing Morgrom. "My oath still binds me," said the great hero, "even though I know you have no such scruples." Mirakles hurried to where he'd flung Redthirst and retrieved his weapon.

"Let's get out of here before we're trapped by Shugreth the Unenviable," said Spike. "Or by something even worse." He shuddered.

"Lead on," said Mirakles, his eyes still upon the supine form of his arch-foe.

Spike led them through one of the walls, which seemed to be made of solid stone, but that proved to be an illusion. "I've got to come back here later," he said. "I owe it to my heritage to steal the new money Morgrom's printed up."

"That should be the least of your current worries," said Glorian. "Look."

Coming out of the vault into the safety depository, they found themselves facing a dozen of the zombie workmen, only these zombies were neither oblivious nor strangely friendly. They were murderously angry, and armed with their work tools, two-by-fours, and chunks of stone, they blocked the party's escape.

"Get behind me, all of you," said Mirakles.

"There's twelve of them," said Spike fearfully, "and only one of you!"

The prince only laughed and leaped forward to the attack. With one slash of Redthirst, he cut the head off the nearest zombie, and with the backstroke he beheaded another. The two decapitated undead began wandering around helplessly in the large depository room.

Then the remaining ten zombies closed in. The greatest weakness of fighting with a broadsword is that its wielder is helpless if the enemy somehow gets too near. Mirakles found himself unable to take a good swing at any of the ten zombies, and he began kicking and shoving them out of range, but it appeared that soon they'd overpower him.

Glorian entered the battle, having first transformed himself into a tall, hooded masculine figure with strong arms and legs. He looked like an executioner, and the headsman's axe he carried complemented his outfit. He wore black trousers held up by a wide black leather belt. He was as bare-chested as the prince, but he wore one black leather gauntlet on his right hand.

There was a sharp spike at the top of the poleaxe, and Glorian reached forward and stabbed and cut at the zombies, driving them back far enough for Mirakles to lop off their heads. "I don't think," said Glorian, slightly out of breath, "that there's . . . any real way. . . of killing 'em."

"They're already dead," said the prince, who seemed to be enjoying himself immensely. "Without their heads, though, they can't find us. All right, we've got most of them. Let's get out of here and on to the next part of our search!"

Spike led the way again, through the east door that led back to the teller's room. "Oh, no," muttered The Protector, when he realized that the teller's room, too, was filled with blood-lusting, armed zombies. "Glorian," he cried frantically, "Drawer Forward me a weapon!"

A few moments later, while Mirakles was separating a few undead bodies from their puzzled heads, Glorian gave Spike something that looked like a Roman short sword. "Watch me now!" shouted The Protector, as he waded into the crowd of zombies.

More and more zombies appeared through the room's north portal, but the three fighters never found themselves in danger of being overwhelmed. They fought back-to-back, shoulder-to-shoulder, holding off the undead with heartening ease. The zombies did little more than shuffle around stupidly, even with their heads firmly attached. They made only the most clumsy of attacks with their hammers and wooden clubs, but the problem was that there appeared to be endless numbers of them.

"I want to see if some of Morgrom's power rubbed off on me," said Ed. The other three warriors had forgotten he was even there, standing safely behind them. He was much too fragile to get into a fistfight with a zombie, but he had a brave heart. That came from the Autoexec only knew where, because Ed had been created by Morgrom, after all. Ed's personality was entirely different from the Essence of Evil. Ed had proved to be a warm, friendly, courageous companion.

Now he threw back his silver scarf and raised his paper-thin hardwood staff. He muttered a few words, and all together the zombies stopped what they were doing and stared at him. "Go back!" cried Ed. "Go back to work! Finish your chores! This bank must be ready for business, and you have a firm deadline!"

"*Dead*line is right," muttered Spike.

To their amazement, the zombies turned and staggered out of the teller's room, leaving Mirakles, Glorian, Spike, and Ed all alone.

"That, gentlemen," said Glorian, shivering with relief, "is our cue." He led his friends through the south exit, into the bank's main entrance, then east through the fresco room.

"We'll have to sneak through the great chamber where the kimono dragon dwells," said Spike. "But if the Princess Melithiel could do it, I think we can, too. After all, the dragon's house was in the far rear. We won't go anywhere near it, and we won't make a sound."

"My friends," said the prince, "and you are all indeed my friends, I thank you for your aid. I think it's safe to say that, by Thrag! we kicked some zombie butt in there! I was prepared to do all the fighting myself, but your courageous help made it much less of a trial. I'm sure Morgrom won't underestimate us again."

"We'll see," said Glorian. He didn't sound confident.

"Where do we go next?" asked Mirakles.

Glorian looked through the eye-holes of his black hood at Spike, who only shrugged. "My prince," said the semi-mythical being, turning to Mirakles, "have you ever climbed down into a deep, dark volcano?"

CHAPTER ELEVEN

All you need in this world is ignorance
and confidence, and then success is sure.
—Mark Twain

NONE OF THE ZOMBIES or any of the Palindromic Enemy's other nefarious allies followed them as they hurried back through the dragon room and then south across the great, ruined stone bridge. "What are the odds now?" asked Mirakles.

Glorian raised his eyebrows. "The odds that we'll find what we're looking for before Morgrom destroys us?" he asked.

The prince nodded.

"Well," said Glorian from within his executioner's garb, "I can't help feeling that Morgrom isn't making as good an effort to kill us as he could be."

"Right," said Spike, "setting aside for the moment the fact that he actually, truly *did* kill Prince Mirakles here, and we had to go to Hades to fetch him back. I mean, the prince was *dead,* as dead as you can possibly be. Doesn't that count in your estimation?"

They were in the cool room just northwest of the Carousel Room. "I thought he explained that to you before," said the Supernatural Guide. "Morgrom had to kill Prince Mirakles *but not us,* so that we could go to Hades and rescue him, and in the meantime, see if the Dipped Switch and the Hot Key might have been hidden down there. It was a gamble, but evidently Morgrom felt the odds were on his side."

The others thought about this for a few seconds. "But we've been attacked since then," said Spike.

"Just now, as a matter of fact," said he of the Sunless Grotto.

Glorian laughed wryly. "If you can call that stumbling around by those death-wimps an attack. I don't. I never actually felt that we were in true danger."

"Yeah," said Spike, "but what about the kimono dragon?"

"What about her?" asked Glorian. "The prince is a true hero, not an impostor. Any true hero would have solved the problem the same way—and that's always been true. A lesser adventurer would have just sat there drinking tea and playing her deadly guessing games until he was just another notch on the kimono dragon's obi. That's not the fate that's in store for the son of Thrag, however."

The prince laughed. "What is my fate, O Guide?"

"Well," said Glorian thoughtfully, "there are three separate areas or neighborhoods of the Great Underground Empire, which once formed part of the greater nation of Quendor. We've visited all of the first third and about half of this one. Yet you've completed all your initiation tests—"

Mirakles turned to look at Glorian. "I meant to ask you about that," he said. "I did think that I'd passed all those tests. So that's why I was caught off-guard for a moment in the bank. What was that? Another test for extra credit?"

"That wasn't a test," said Spike. "That was just good, old-fashioned meaningless violence."

"Ah," said the prince, "I'd let myself think that everything down here had to mean something."

"No way," said Spike. "Lots of stuff here not only

doesn't mean anything, it takes meaning away from anything meaningful that comes near it."

Mirakles shook his head. "Sometimes, young man, I like it better when you're silent and merely attending to your glowing. I don't understand you at all." Spike just grinned.

"We don't need to go on to the Carousel Room," decided Glorian. "We'll head west from here." He led them into a large hall of ancient lava. The igneous rock had long ago been worn smooth by the movement of a glacier. The great, fire-breathing dragon of long ago had melted the glacier and opened a way to the chamber beyond, but already the glacier was creeping back into place. It would not be many months before the way west would be sealed once more.

"Are we going to have to squeeze past that wall of ice?" asked Mirakles.

"That's the idea, O Prince," said Glorian. "Beyond it is another room hollowed out of this ancient lava flow. Perhaps these lava caverns were excavated by the Flatheads, or perhaps they were natural bubbles that solidified in the cooling lava."

They went quickly through the ice room, because the cold was so intense that it was actually numbing. Ed, the Embedded Character, had the easiest time fitting through the opening where the glacier blocked most of the exit into the lava room beyond. Spike, who was very thin, also had no trouble; he merely turned sideways and scooted past the diamond-like surface of the ice wall. Glorian passed his poleaxe through to Spike, then sucked in his stomach and inched his way, scraping and scratching himself painfully on the sharp, hard edges of the ice. Finally came Mirakles, the largest of them all, and for a while it seemed as if he wouldn't be able to make it, that he'd be trapped on the eastern side, while the others went on to explore the volcano area. Then, grimacing, the hero drew his sword and began to hack at the ice as if it were some hideous, monstrous enemy. Slowly he hewed a path for himself, and in about an hour he joined the rest of the party in the lava room.

"Come back a year from now," said Spike, "and you'll need a flamethrower to get through there."

"I don't intend to come back a year from now," said the Prince of the Sunless Grotto. "I don't intend ever to see this nightmarish Empire again. My realm is a land of peace and plenty, of gloom perhaps, but also of gentle warmth. And there is only one monster in all the kingdom—Smorma, whose acquaintance you may make only if you work very hard at it, because you must seek Smorma out at the bottom of the Grotto itself. We have no wandering trolls or grues or zombies."

"It sounds like an idyllic land," said Ed.

"That it is, my unembedded friend. I invite you to accompany me back there, after we complete our mission here."

"Perhaps I'll accept," said Ed. "I have only a few weeks to live, and the more you speak of it, the more I'd like to see the Sunless Grotto for myself."

There was only one other exit from the small lava room, to the south. Glorian let Mirakles take the lead again. Soon the tunnel opened up, and the explorers realized that they were at the bottom of a large dormant volcano. High above them, they could see light filtering down through the vent of the volcano.

They wandered about the floor of the volcano for some time, wondering what they would discover next. There were no tunnels or caverns leading away, except for the one to the north from which they'd just come. There was a pool of clear water, surrounded by small shrubs and ferns. There was only a handful of trees, tall, arching palms. On one of them Glorian spotted an envelope stuck about eye-level with a green thumbtack. He went to the tree and pulled the envelope free. He tore it open to read the message:

From the Desk Of:
The Autoexec
Glorian, everyone here is saying that you're doing a superhuman job. Of course, you *are* superhuman, but what they mean is that you have already overcome obstacles that have stumped some of the best talents in the Supernatural and Fantastic Wayfarers Association. We've had reports on your progress, and frankly I'm amazed. It makes it even more difficult to understand how a semi-actual persona as gifted as you could have finished behind Narlinia von Glech for the Campbell.

Be that as it may, I have good news for you. It will probably not be long before our assignment, this shirtless prince of yours, achieves his goal. Your adventures will all make for wonderful conversation over lunch when you get back. My treat, of course.

Finally, I do want to remind you to be careful where Spike, The Protector, is concerned. He *is* the son of the thief, of course. Once Mirakles finds what he's looking for, keep your eyes glued on Spike, or else you may find that the young man has stolen the prince's treasures and that you've made your entire journey in vain. I cannot say it enough: After the Dipped Switch is found, *watch Spike closely,* even if you must do without sleep.

In any event, as I said, it will all be over soon, most likely. We'll talk more later.

Good luck to you,
and may God bless.

Glorian put the note back in the envelope and Drawer Forwarded them away.

"Good news?" asked Spike.

Glorian jumped as if he'd been stuck with a pin. "I hadn't realized you were watching me," he said.

Spike shrugged. "Not much else to watch down here," he said, "No dinosaurs or anything. Not even monkeys in the palm trees. Who was the letter from? Your supervisor?"

"Yes," said Glorian.

"What did he have to say?"

Glorian looked down at the glowing young man for a few seconds. "What's the meaning of all these questions, Spike?" he asked.

Spike shrugged again and walked off to join Mirakles, who was sitting beside the pool, admiring his reflection.

"I've found it!" came Ed's voice after a short while. Even at its loudest, Ed's shout was not very startling. The three other members of the party looked toward him. He was standing and waving both arms. It was only when they made their way closer that they could see what he'd discovered.

What Ed had stumbled upon was a true relic of the old, great adventurer. It was a large and extremely heavy wicker basket. An enormous cloth bag draped over its side and was firmly attached to the basket. A metal receptacle was fastened to the center of the basket. Dangling from the basket was a long piece of braided wire.

"This," said Glorian in a respectful tone, "is the very lighter-than-air balloon the adventurer used to explore the upper reaches of the volcano. There are chambers up there, and as I recall, the adventurer found a few treasures. They must be searched. Morgrom may have hidden new treasures in the library and the small, dusty room, but more importantly, the Dipped Switch and Hot Key may have been left there, as well."

"Excellent," said Mirakles. "Now, how does this contraption work?"

Glorian walked around and around the deflated balloon, stroking his chin in thought. "It's not only helium and hydrogen that will lift such a device," he said at last. "Many balloons are carried aloft by hot air. My guess is that metal receptacle is where the fuel is put. The fuel is then set alight, and the hot air from the fire fills the bag and lifts that ponderous wicker basket off the ground."

Spike shook his head. "It's hard for me to believe that the small amount of fuel burning in that metal box could generate enough hot air to lift the weight of the whole thing, plus occupants."

"That leads to the next question," said Glorian. "How many of us are necessary to make the ascent?"

"I, of course," said the son of Thrag, God of Smiting.

"Of course," said Glorian. "And I, as well, because speaking as your official Supernatural Guide, I am pretty much required to stay by your side through all these adventures."

"And I'll go," said Spike. "No doubt Morgrom has restocked those two remote rooms with treasures."

The prince gave the wicker basket an experimental kick. "I'm not sure this balloon can carry all four of us," he said.

"I'd just as soon stay here on the ground," said Ed. "I have an inordinate fear of heights. I guess it stems from my fear of falling in general."

Glorian laid his hand gently on the Embedded Character's shoulder. "That's all right, Ed," he said. "You can stay here."

Spike opened the metal receptacle and pointed to its contents. "I think I made a pretty good point before," he said. "Do you think this is going to be enough fuel to lift us off the ground?"

Glorian examined the half-burned copy of *U. S. News and Dungeon Report* that still rested in the metal container. "Well," he said, shrugging, "this is probably the very same newspaper that the great adventurer used to make his ascent. Of course, no doubt his weight was somewhat less than the weight of the three of us put together."

"That still hasn't answered my question," said The Protector.

"Our advantage," said Glorian, "is that this is a fantasy-tinged adventure, and this also happens to be a fantasy-tinged balloon. All that remains is for me to Drawer Forward some fantasy-tinged newspaper, and we're all set." He picked up the semi-destroyed copy of *U. S. News and Dungeon Report* and turned some of the brittle pages, but they were unreadable. It was impossible to discover how old the copy of the newspaper was by examining it; indeed, after a few seconds, it began to crumble into dust and blow away on the light breeze. Glorian dropped the remainder of the newspaper to the ground.

"I'll tell you one thing," said the Prince of the Elastic Tendon, "we don't allow littering of that nature in the Sunless Grotto. We have stiff fines, jail terms, and rehabilitation dungeons to deal with litterers and every other sort of scofflaw."

"Forgive me, my prince." Glorian was getting tired of talking through his black hood, because it muffled his voice and often spoiled the effect of what he tried to say, and because it was getting all soggy and unpleasant from his saliva. He looked forward to the next moment of peace, when he could again change form.

In the meantime. Glorian brought forth a thick edition of *The Satyrday Evening Post*, which was still published in Valhalla, and which the Hilton there still presented free of charge, along with complimentary nectar and ambrosia for the guests in the suites.

"Pretty nifty," said Spike with grudging admiration.

"Well," said Glorian, "I have to admit that it's not my copy. I can't afford a suite in that hotel! I sort of more or less picked this paper up from someone else's tray, in a manner of speaking, the evening after the ceremony. I didn't feel up to making the rounds of award losers' parties, and I planned to spend a quiet night reading. That was before I found the first note addressed to me from the Autoexec, assigning me to Prince Mirakles."

"Well, my friend," said the brawny hero, "they always say that stolen newspapers are sweeter, or something very much like that sentiment. It's a good, thick, solid, heavy, dry newspaper, too. I'm sure it will make excellent fuel. Now, Ed, stand you well back. Glorian, enter the basket first and examine it closely, and assure us that there are no small monsters waiting to leap upon our throats, ruining our joy to be airborne."

Glorian lifted one leg over the edge of the wicker basket, and then the other. He saw no small monsters, and so informed the prince.

"Spike," said Mirakles, "have you thoroughly checked the integrity of the cloth bag? It must be without holes or punctures, as I understand this science, so that we may in all confidence entrust our safety to it."

"First thing I looked for, my prince," said The Protector, "were just the kind of little rips and tears that might spoil our afternoon. The bag is in remarkably good shape, though, considering how long it's just been sitting here."

Mirakles seemed pleased. "Then you enter the basket, too. We may need your glowing light to examine those high rooms you mentioned, carved from the cone of the volcano."

Spike joined Glorian in the wicker basket, and both non-heroes waited impatiently for the prince to join them. He, however, showed a rather distinct hesitation, as if air travel were a new idea to him, and he hadn't completely come to terms with it as yet. Finally, though, he took a deep, calming breath and let it out again, and swung his massively muscled legs over the rim of the wicker basket.

"Look," said Spike, "directions!" He picked up a blue label.

"!! FROBOZZ MAGIC BALLOON COMPANY !!
Hello, Aviator!
To land your balloon, say LAND.
Otherwise, you're on your own!
No warranty expressed or implied."

"That's enough to give you a world of confidence, isn't it?" asked Glorian.

The prince crammed the special double-issue of *The Satyrday Evening Post* into the metal receptacle. Then he turned to Glorian and said, "Match."

Glorian looked at Spike, and Spike looked at Glorian. Finally, The Protector said, "Hey, *I'm* not going to tell him."

"Tell me what, my boon companions?" said Mirakles.

"We have no matches, my prince," said Glorian.

"Well," said the hero reasonably, "just Drawer Forward some from your room in the Valhalla Hilton."

Glorian gulped. "I've been through this before, at the gate of Hades," he said. "I have no matches in my room, either."

At first, the prince didn't like the sound of that, but he didn't panic. He had too much royal and divine blood in his veins to panic like a mere adventurer. "What you are telling me," he said at last, after studying the problem from all angles, "is that we have no actual source of fire."

"That's it in a nutshell, O clever prince," said Glorian.

"Right," said the Prince, lifting one leg as if to disembark from the wicker basket. In the right light, one might even get the idea that his expression was just a trifle relieved.

"May I make a suggestion, my friends?" said Ed, who was leaning against one of the arching palm trees.

"Certainly," said Mirakles.

"I have this itchy patch of flint where a normal person has his left knee. Now, if we carefully gather tinder, I'm sure that my knee and the mighty prince's miraculous blade might go a long way toward providing the very ignition you're looking for."

Mirakles stared at Ed with new-found admiration and respect. "Wonderful, Embedded One," he said at last. "Will the striking of your knee with my mighty sword hurt you?"

"Well, of course it will," said Ed, "but I see no other solution."

The prince hopped out of the basket and began building a small pile of tinder, first with teeny, tiny twigs, then with less teeny twigs, and then with small branches. "Forgive me, Ed," he said regretfully. The Embedded Character had knelt near the mound of tinder, and Mirakles gave his left knee a sharp thwack with Redthirst. Ed grimaced and sparks flew, but none caught fire in the tinder. "Please, brave laminar mage, one more stroke," said the prince. Again he raised his enchanted blade and brought it down, and this time sparks ignited the tinder. Both Ed and Mirakles leaned forward and blew on the hesitant point of red until it was undeniably fire. "Ed," said the prince, "you will have my eternal gratitude."

"I will have a permanent limp now, too," said their wizard-shaped companion.

"I will see that you are properly rewarded when the time comes," said Mirakles, hurrying with his blazing bundle of sticks to the metal receptacle. He thrust his hard-won fire into the pages of the newspaper and hopped lithely back into the basket. Within seconds, the cloth bag was inflating robustly over their heads.

"Here we go!" cried Spike.

"Don't look down," Glorian advised the prince.

"Thank you," said Mirakles, who, although they had yet to actually leave the ground, was already beginning to look a little green.

Glorian could see that the prince's bouquet of twigs was no longer alight, but that the blazing newspaper was supplying the hot air to lift the vast bulk of the balloon into the clear, still air above the volcano bottom.

"We're about a hundred feet up!" cried Spike. He was having the time of his life. Mirakles, on the other hand, had wedged himself into a corner of the wicker basket and was clinging to the ropes with both huge hands. Looking up, Glorian could clearly see the round opening of the volcano's mouth.

"Two hundred feet!" shouted Spike. As the balloon ascended, there was actually nothing for the passengers to do. It wasn't like sailing in small boats or any other such form of transportation, and at least Glorian and the prince seemed glad of it. Glorian looked out at the wall of the volcano and saw that they were approaching a small ledge on the west side.

"Let's stop here for a little while," said Spike. "There's that ledge, see? And beyond it used to be a library. I thought maybe we could take a look, to see if the File Restorer has been up this way yet. And who knows? There might be some odd little treasure, something that nobody else wants. . . ."

The Prince of the Sunless Grotto nodded. "Of course we'll stop here, Spike, if you want. And any treasure you find, you may keep. You've proven your worth to our venture time and time again, and as I've said before, I didn't get into this hero business for the treasure."

"Land," declaimed Glorian in an unusually deep voice. It made him feel even more semi-mythical to give orders to a Frobozz Magic Something-or-Other.

The hot-air balloon obeyed, pausing beside the small ledge. Spike climbed out first and made sure the balloon would still be there when he got back. "Wish me luck," he called.

"I'll come with you, too," said Glorian. "I don't care about the treasure. You've just made me curious about what Morgrom may have done with this area."

"In that case," said Mirakles, scrambling from the dangerously rocking wicker basket, "I think I ought to see these rooms first-hand, as well."

The ledge was about halfway between the volcano floor far below and the rim above. "Look," said Spike, "more of those ancient Zorker glyphs."

"Not little Shugreths and things, I hope," said Glorian.

"No," said Spike, getting down on his hands and knees to read the ancient writing. "There's only one line at the very bottom of this large empty wall. It says *This space intentionally left blank.*" They all looked at each other and nodded, as if they'd known that's what it would say.

There was a small doorway to the south, in terrible disrepair. The door itself hung from only one hinge, and Spike pushed it open, out of their way. The prince went first, Redthirst clutched in his great hands, but there was no aroma of freshly-baked bread. The room was dusty and deserted. At one time, it must have been a large library, probably for the royal family.

"That tells you even more about the Flathead Dynasty," said Spike, shaking his head in disbelief. "I mean, who else on Earth has built his official, royal library in a carved-out cave inside a volcano?"

"Well," said Glorian, in a generous mood, "I can think of a few world leaders who might, except they don't have volcanoes where they live."

"Hmm," said Mirakles. "I am a man of action, not a man of learning. Yet I well know the value of knowledge and wisdom. Perhaps these books could form the beginning of a library in the Kingdom of the Sunless Grotto, something that might grow with time into a center of learning. With them, I could give my loyal subjects yet another great gift."

"Noble sentiments, my prince," said Glorian. "The only difficulty is that all these books are written in Zorkish."

Spike picked up one book from a shelf, glanced at it for a moment, then dropped it again with a look of distaste. "The other problem," he said, "is that most of the books have been destroyed over the years by rats and other vermin."

They searched the abandoned Flathead library and found five books in readable condition, two purple, one white, one blue, and one green. The son of Thrag claimed them, although neither he nor anyone in the area around the Sunless Grotto could read them. "Take these, my Supernatural Guide," he said, handing them to Glorian, "and Drawer Forward them for the time being. That way, we won't have to carry them around with us. Perhaps, when I return to my mother and my kingdom, I will devote myself to puzzling out their meanings. They may be worthless, or they may be of great value."

"Indeed," said Glorian, sending the five volumes back to the Valhalla Hilton. His estimation and admiration for Prince Mirakles went up still another notch.

"Well," said Spike in disappointment, "that's all that's here."

"Back to the balloon," said the heavily muscled hero.

The three explorers trooped back through the library and out onto the narrow ledge. It was even more difficult to get into the wicker basket now, because it was swinging around in the air, rather than sitting in a compliant, stationary way on the ground. Mirakles watched Spike hop in. He wasn't happy about it, but he *was* a hero, and he had a sufficient supply of courage to quell his queasiness at crossing from the ledge into the balloon's basket. Glorian brought up the rear, and in a moment they were on their way again.

They ascended even further, high above the floor. The mouth of the volcano looked very narrow, and the balloon had nearly reached it. "I don't think this thing would even fit through the opening," said the prince.

"Well," said Glorian, "we have to go back the way we came, anyway. We left Ed down there."

"That's right," said Mirakles. "Good. I've had just about enough of this unnatural flying experience."

Still, they continued to rise, up and up. At last they were very near the rim, and they could see the clean blue sky through the open mouth of the volcano. On the same side of the volcano's vent as the narrow ledge they'd previously visited was another ledge. It was wider, and it was obvious that it had been shaped as a place to land.

"Land," cried Glorian again, in his most authoritative voice.

Spike gave him a sarcastic grin. "You have a natural aptitude for ordering inanimate objects around," he said. Glorian ignored him.

When they'd finished the landing routine and were all standing on the ledge, Mirakles turned to Glorian. He kept his eyes directly on a level with his Supernatural Guide's, not daring to look down. "How high do you think we are now?" asked the prince.

"I'd hate to venture a guess," said Glorian. "I'd say it's about two hundred feet up to the rim of the volcano, and the floor is many times that distance below. Straight down."

"Yup," said Spike, "one false step and you'd be seedless raspberry jelly all over the landscape at the bottom of the volcano. Exciting, huh? Invigorating?"

He of the Elastic Tendon turned, but kept his eyes at the same level, somewhat above Spike's head. "I hate being invigorated," he said in a tightly controlled voice. "I consider invigoration an unasked-for intrusion into my mood and feelings."

"Right, mighty prince," said Spike. "This way." The glowing young man led them into a dusty room that had obviously—and rather clumsily—been hewn from the living lava rock of the volcano. "This chamber," he explained, "once housed the Crown Jewels of the Flathead kings, but our predecessor, the fabled adventurer, looted them long ago."

Glorian pointed to a large hole in the far wall. "This must have been where they were kept. All that's here now is a rusty box whose door has been forcibly removed."

The floor was still cluttered with debris, but the walls had been shored up with wood and metal scaffolding. "This construction work is recent," said

Mirakles. "Perhaps Thrag's Bane intends to restore this room to its former purpose, and keep here the choicest of all his stolen treasures."

Spike laughed. "Well," he said, "if that's the case, then I'll just lie low until he finishes the restoration. There's plenty of time later to find out what valuables he brings to this remote cave, and how he guards them."

"Here's something for you now, Spike," said Glorian. He was poking around in the dark in the southwest corner.

"One of his new treasures?" said Spike hopefully. He hurried to join Glorian. When he arrived, the glowing effect of the luminia he'd rubbed on himself revealed a long, wide, waist-high freezer.

"If you keep real quiet," said Glorian, "I can hear the hum of its electric motor."

"That means it's working," said Spike excitedly. "That means it *is* one of Morgrom's treasures. I hope it's worth all the trouble it takes to get up here." Spike lifted the lid of the large freezer and peered inside. There was a sign that said: *Freezer not included with treasure.*

"What is it?" asked Glorian.

"Boxes," said Spike, his voice dead. "Boxes of Inuit Pies. A year's supply, no doubt."

The prince came over to satisfy his own curiosity. "What's an Inuit Pie?" he asked.

"Seal fat and walrus blubber," said Spike in disgust, "dipped in chocolate, on a stick. There must be hundreds of boxes here."

"Well," said Mirakles, shrugging, "they're edible. A hero soon learns to make do with whatever sustenance nature and good fortune put in his path." He took a box of Inuit Pies, ripped it open, and took one out. He tore off the paper wrapper and bit into it.

"What do you think?" asked Glorian.

Mirakles did not reply. He carefully replaced the opened box of Inuit Pies in the freezer and let Spike lower the lid. Then the prince walked determinedly to the room's exit, and out onto the wide ledge. From there he flung the Inuit Pie he'd tasted as far as he could throw it. After that, he turned to Glorian and Spike. "Let's agree never to mention this," he said.

"All right," said Glorian.

"Fine," said Spike.

After they all got back in the balloon, Mirakles turned to them. "I would like to return now to the volcano bottom," he said. "Unless either of you know why we should continue upward?"

"I think it would be dangerous to do that, in any event," said Glorian.

"Then down it is," said Spike. He closed the lid of the metal receptacle. In a short amount of time, the cloth bag over their heads began to deflate slowly, and the balloon sank slowly back down through the cone of the volcano to the overgrown floor below.

"There were two other items in that last room," said the prince thoughtfully. He held them out on the palm of his hand. One was an amulet that looked exactly like the one around Mirakles' neck, the one he'd gotten from the Tortle. The second item was a very small Phillips-head screwdriver.

"Are the amulets identical?" asked Glorian.

"In every way that I can see," said the prince. "This one doesn't glow, either." He turned it over in his hand. "There's some small lettering here, the same as on the amulet around my neck. It says Frobozz Magic Amulet Company."

Time passed slowly as the balloon made its graceful descent. The prince worked with the small screwdriver on the back of the new amulet. "Didn't the

Tortle mention something about a secret compartment?" he asked.

"I think so," said Glorian. "It bragged about a built-in pencil sharpener, compass, secret compartment, decoder, and a special whistle that only grues can hear."

"Uh huh," said the prince, removing the last of the four tiny Phillips-head screws. He lifted the back off the amulet, revealing the secret compartment. "There's a piece of paper inside!" he said excitedly.

"Well," cried Spike breathlessly, "what does it say?"

The son of Thrag took out the piece of paper and read it. "It says 'Inspected by Number 13,' " he said in a disappointed voice.

"We're down to a hundred feet now," said Spike. "I hope Ed has enough sense not to be standing under us when we land."

"This whole volcano thing has been one long wild-goose chase," said Mirakles grumpily.

"I'm sorry you feel that way, my prince," said Glorian. "As I've said several times, these areas of the Great Underground Empire are almost unimaginably vast, and we have to do a thorough job of searching them. The two items we're looking for could be anywhere. They could've been in that Hall Airflow teapot I left in the kimono dragon's house—I don't know, I never looked."

The prince dropped the second amulet to the floor of the wicker basket without bothering to reassemble it. "What you're saying now is that this is probably a hopeless task," he said.

Glorian pulled himself up to his full, rather imposing executioner's height. "I would *never* say hopeless," he said.

The prince shrugged and peered over the edge of the wicker basket. They were making good progress down the vent of the volcano, and the Prince of the Sunless Grotto had long since gotten over his trepidations. He idly toyed with the amulet around his neck, humming to himself and working on the four tiny screws that held the backplate on the device.

"Where next, Glorian?" asked Spike.

Glorian looked thoughtfully over the tops of the palm trees, which were no longer so far beneath them. "There's that whole 'Alice' area," he said, "but truthfully I was holding that off until last. That part of the caverns gives even me the creeps."

"The wizard's workshop?" asked the glowing young man.

"That's definitely a possibility," said Glorian. "And it's only a few rooms from the volcano bottom back to the Carousel Room, and then a straight shot southwest to the wizard's quarters and workshop. Yes, Spike, that's where we'll go. Unless you have something better to suggest?"

"Why, no, I was only wondering if—"

"Hold on," said Mirakles, son of Desiphae, Queen of the Sunless Grotto. And he uttered the words "Hold on" in a firm command voice more arresting than any he'd ever used before.

"What is it, my prince?" asked Glorian. "If you don't wish to search the former wizard's quarters—"

"Behold," he said, holding the amulet he'd taken from the Tortle, now disassembled on the palm of his right hand. Both Glorian and Spike could see into the secret compartment. Nestled within were two small metal objects.

"The Golden Dipped Switch," murmured Glorian in awe.

"And the Hot Key to release King Hyperenor's magic Scroll Lock," said the prince. "I've been carrying them with me all this time. Ever since the encounter with the Tortle."

Just then, with a bone-jarring bump, the hot-air balloon came to rest on the floor of the volcano.

"Well," said Spike, shrugging, "it just goes to show, huh?"

CHAPTER TWELVE

Treason in our time is a proof of genius.
—Antoine de Saint-Exupéry

AFTER THEY GOT OUT OF the hot-air balloon, each of the three of them and Ed reacted in a different way. Ed, who had waited on the ground, just stood to one side and laughed delightedly. Spike stared in astonishment, as if unwilling to believe what he was seeing. Glorian leaned against the balloon's wicker basket and nodded, realizing the extracosmic sense it all made. But it was Mirakles, the hero, who was especially having trouble accepting the truth.

He stalked back and forth across the volcano floor, holding the amulet in one hand and gesturing wildly with the other. "You mean to tell me," he cried, "that I've been wearing this *the whole time?* And the Switch and the Key have been bouncing on my chest since we bargained with that ridiculous Tortle? And who knows, that blasted, blistered beast may have known the Switch and Key were in the amulet all along!"

"Put your mind at ease, my prince," said Glorian. He'd used the moment of excitement and confusion to transform himself again. Instead of the tall, ominous executioner, Glorian was now in his favorite form: a cheerful young man, tall and slender, with darkly tanned skin over a well-muscled frame. He was wearing a white silken pullover shirt with bloused sleeves, comfortable old blue jeans, sturdy black leather boots, and a sleeveless, many-pocketed canvas vest in camouflage colors. His hair was blond and cut very short, and his eyes were the color of a river after an evening's rain. Now they radiated calmness and confidence.

Mirakles turned to face him, and the prince flinched as he always did when Glorian changed from one physique to another behind Mirakles' back. "I'm glad you got rid of that black hood over your face," said the son of Thrag. "Now do me a favor? Unless we're overwhelmingly attacked and you must transform yourself into a warrior—one that is necessarily a bit inferior to my incomparable size and strength—just stay like that, all right? Don't pull any more surprise transformations."

"Yes, my prince," said Glorian, "if that is indeed your wish."

"You bet," said Mirakles. He stood there, gazing off into the distance for a few seconds. Then his eyes focused again on Glorian's handsome young face. "Well," he said at last, "I've just realized that I hold in my hand the Hot Key that will unlock the Scroll Lock, and when I do that I'll be able to read the final message from my step-father, King Hyperenor. If I'm not mistaken, the scroll will unfold to me the mystery of my destiny, and also tell me the Third Secret of the Sword."

"So this is what all the shouting and fleeing and fighting and dying were about, right?" said Spike, giving a disparaging look at the Switch and the Key in Mirakles' hand. "I don't know, they hardly seem worth it. I mean, if you'd relaxed a little more in the kimono dragon's house, she might have relayed to you three fabulous offers from three mutually-antagonistic goddesses. If you'd accepted one of those offers, who knows where you'd be sleeping tonight—or with whom? But instead, you may or may not have killed the dragon, you split the apple so that it's worthless as a bribe to any goddess *I've* ever heard about, and you gave the good half to a princess you may never actually see again."

Mirakles's expression softened as he thought of Melithiel. "Even if our paths never cross again," he said in a melancholy tone, "my life's been made more complete by my brief acquaintance with her. Yet I feel in my illustrious bones that Melithiel and I *do* have a life together, somewhere, somehow."

Glorian had done a lot of deep thinking while the other two conversed. Now he turned to the Prince of the Elastic Tendon. "Mighty Mirakles," he said, "if my help to you during the long trek has been of any value at all, I beg that you grant me now one exceptional boon."

Something in Glorian's voice turned the prince's expression to concern. "What is it?" he asked.

Glorian nodded toward the opened amulet in Mirakles' hand. "I'd like to examine the two small items for only a moment. They'll be perfectly safe."

Again the prince looked troubled. "What do you suspect? Do you think they may not be the real Switch and Key? That they may be counterfeits, manufactured by someone—Morgrom the Malignant—for some unguessable reason?"

Glorian's reply was more insistent. "Please, my prince. I'll let you know the truth. If my honor and trustworthiness have been proven to your satisfaction, allow me to make my examination."

Mirakles muttered something under his breath; not even Glorian's acute, not-of-this-plane-of-existence hearing could make out the prince's words. Slowly, carefully, the son of Thrag placed the Golden Dipped Switch and the Hot Key in Glorian's hand.

The Supernatural Guide brought first the Switch,

then the Key nearer to his eagle-sharp eyes. There were no details worth noting on the Switch, but on the Key were the words *Frobozz Magic Lock and Key Company*. Beneath that were letters too tiny for anyone in the party but Glorian to read: *If it isn't a Frobozz, it's probably something else.*

"Well?" demanded the prince. "What's your evaluation?"

Glorian nodded. "So far, they seem like the genuine articles. Of course, they may just be spare parts scrounged by the Essence of Evil. It wouldn't be difficult for him to plate any cheap toggle switch with gold, and then include a miscellaneous key made by the correct company."

"Yes, that's obvious," said Mirakles. "And those deeds would also be in keeping with the character of the Wretch of Wordplay. What more can I do to help you?"

"If you so order it, my prince, I'll give you a more satisfactory answer; but you must lend me the tightly-coiled steel scroll we received from Morgrom. I won't open or read it, because those acts are your honor and privilege. I merely wish to ascertain that this key is indeed the single, unique key that will give you access to all that you desire."

This was asking quite a bit more, of course, and Mirakles had to pause for a few seconds to weigh the alternatives. Glorian was certain that he'd come far in winning the respect of the prince; but even so, it was entirely within Mirakles's rights to refuse.

"Let us travel to the end of the road we've chosen," said the heir to the Realm of the Sunless Grotto at last. "I put the scroll, which is made of steel harder than any in my experience, either in my wallet or girdle." In olden days, among the heroes who came along but rarely even during the Golden Age, wallets and girdles were quite different from the items that go by those names today. It was not out of place for an able-bodied athlete such as Mirakles to carry both, and to use them for storing away food and other supplies and sometimes objects such as severed heads.

Nevertheless, after the prince made a thorough search of both his girdle and his wallet, he failed to come up with the vital scroll. He seemed to be on the verge of panic. "Where is it?" he cried. "What could I have done with it?"

"Perhaps you set it down on the kimono dragon's table," suggested Ed.

"Perhaps you lost it in the heat of the zombie battle in the bank," suggested Glorian.

"That was never a heated battle," complained Mirakles, driven now almost to distraction by the loss of his father's final message.

"Well," said Spike, "you can't find the scroll because you no longer have it. *I* have it. I stole it from you quite some time ago, almost immediately after we met, as a matter of fact. I'm heartily sorry to cause you so much anxiety and worry, O Prince Mirakles. I didn't do it out of malice. It's only that on this journey, there've been so few opportunities to do any stealing at all. Now that I realize the extent of my crime, I must abide by your judgment."

Spike reached under his black sweater and withdrew the missing locked scroll, which he dropped into the hand of the hero from the Sunless Grotto. Then the glowing young man gradually seemed to lose every bit of his customary cocksureness, and he stood waiting for Mirakles' verdict, his eyes cast miserably down toward the rough-bladed growth of grass on the volcano floor.

Glorian recalled the warnings he'd received time and again concerning Spike from the Autoexec. He blamed himself, in a way, for permitting Spike the opportunity to steal the scroll in the first place. Then

Glorian watched the prince's expression change. At first, of course, there was anger. More than anger, really, it was pure rage. Yet during the moments of his fury, Mirakles did not speak. Slowly, the rage passed and became something like sadness or disappointment. Then that, too, changed. When he of the Elastic Tendon spoke at last, his voice was steady and firm, but without a trace of unreasoning wrath; and his expression was solemn, but there was no sign of cruelty in it.

"Spike," said Mirakles, "you've committed a grave crime. As you recognized, you also caused me several moments of severe anguish, when I thought my late step-father's ultimate communication to me had been lost in this immense maze of caverns and tunnels. Now, even when my mind argued that I should give up and turn back, I've proceeded with this adventure because of who I am. I am a hero, and heroes are expected to do certain things. I hope that after the day of my death, I'll be remembered as a man who was born to certain duties and responsibilities, and who fulfilled them all to the best of his ability. If they also wish to recall my individual acts of greatness, that will be additional honor; but that will be of no meaning if I do not first successfully embody the role into which I was born."

The prince paused and waited in silence until Spike looked up. The hero and the resident of the Great Underground Empire looked into each other's eyes for moment. Then Mirakles went on. "Even as I was born to fill a role," he said, "so were you. You are the son of the thief. The thief may have been the undoing of many unwary adventurers down here, but he was put here by The Powers That Be for a purpose. I've given it much thought, and I believe I'm beginning to understand what that purpose was. I also believe that you were born to follow where your late father led. Granted that difficult insight, I can no more hold you accountable for stealing than I can punish Glorian for changing his shape when the situation calls for it."

Spike stared at Mirakles, and then he gave the son of Thrag a small, respectful smile. He said nothing, apparently overcome by the generosity of the prince's sentiments.

Mirakles looked around at Glorian and Ed. "Let me make this perfectly clear, however," he said in a tone that sent a chill up Glorian's spine. "If anyone but Spike had stolen King Hyperenor's scroll, the penalty would have been severe, *exceedingly* severe. And Spike, this does not give you license to steal from me or from Glorian or from Ed in the future. One more such theft from your friends, and you'll quickly experience that grievous punishment at which I just hinted. Does everyone understand?"

"Yes, and a thousand thanks, O Prince," said Spike. He sounded wholly sincere.

"Indeed, O Prince," said Ed.

"You have grown and learned much about justice and mercy on this journey," said Glorian.

Mirakles shrugged off his Supernatural Guide's remark. "Here is the scroll," he said, passing it to Glorian. "I must know now: Does the key fit the lock?"

Glorian pursed his semi-mythical lips as he fitted the Frobozz Magic Hot Key into the Frobozz Magic Scroll Lock. After a very few seconds, he was sure that he knew the answer. "Son of Thrag," he announced, handing back the tightly-wound steel scroll, "I'm positive that I hold the correct key. You may unlock your step-father's final message whenever you wish."

"Then give the key back to me immediately!" cried Mirakles, greatly agitated. "I must unlock this scroll!"

And that's when the horror struck. At first, it seemed as if the day had suddenly become overcast. Glorian tried to look up toward the mouth of the volcano, expecting to see some sudden black cloud high above them, but he couldn't even tilt his head. Then he realized that what he'd mistaken for the shadow of a thunderhead was really an ever-darkening blue fog that surrounded him and prevented him from moving so much as a single muscle.

This was not the first time such a thing had happened to him. It was the third time, in a career that spanned many decades. Some enemy had learned of Glorian's single weakness, and was now exploiting it. Many members of the Supernatural and Fantastic Wayfarers Association had such an Achilles' heel. Glorian's was that he was powerless within blue glass. Someone had bent the rules of the physical universe just enough to imprison Glorian within a slab of the stuff.

His three companions ran to him and rapped on the smooth-sided block of cobalt blue glass. They could barely see him within, enclosed like carrot slaw in a bowl of lime-flavored gelatin. He, on the other hand, could see and hear perfectly what was happening on the outside. It was only that he couldn't move or communicate with his friends. If he could, he would have warned them that what had happened was only the prelude to something much worse that might strike at any moment.

There *was* an exceptionally bright light coming from the north, the lava room. It grew brighter by the second until neither Mirakles nor Spike nor Ed could bear to look at it. They covered their eyes with their hands. They stood like that for a few seconds more. Then they heard someone clear his throat.

Glorian saw Spike experimentally peek through his fingers. Another person had joined them on the floor of the volcano. "That glacier sure is starting to make this place inaccessible again," said the newcomer. He was wearing an open-necked white shirt, white duck shorts, white socks, and low-cut white sneakers. His shirt had the initials of the Association embroidered around a large A on the pocket of his white shirt.

"Are you . . . are you the *Autoexec?*" asked Spike in a tremulous voice.

The newcomer nodded pleasantly. He didn't seem much older than Prince Mirakles, although Glorian knew for a fact that he had been around since the universe had been created the second or third time. The Autoexec, along with The Powers That Be, had founded the Supernatural and Fantastic Wayfarers Association, and that organization was tens of thousands of years old, at least.

Both Spike and Ed seemed awed to be in the Autoexec's presence. Mirakles, however, was a hero, and he had an entirely different psychology. Anyone who could fight a monster like Shugreth the Unenviable and hope to prevail would not be put off by a smiling young man in a tennis outfit.

"I don't know if Glorian has been keeping you posted," said the Autoexec, "but I've been following your party's progress through the Great Underground Empire with keen interest. I know that you've finally discovered the whereabouts of both the Dipped Switch and the Hot Key."

There was the most intense aroma yet of freshly-baked bread coming from Redthirst. Glorian uttered a prayer that Mirakles would soon realize that the fragrance appeared only in the presence of those the prince might consider a supernatural enemy. If that person—such as Glorian—proved not to be an enemy, after all, the bread-baking aroma disappeared.

It was clear to Glorian now that the Autoexec, who ruled The Powers That Be Themselves, had become corrupt. He had probably thrown in with Morgrom the Multi-Faced, and the two villains had dogged Glorian and Prince Mirakles' tracks through the Empire, just waiting for the chance to pounce on the Dipped Switch. The owner of the Switch could use the time machine in the white house, and not even Glorian could imagine the full extent of the havoc that could then be wreaked. The very notion made Glorian angrier than he had ever before been.

"Perhaps you can help me, then," said the Prince of the Sunless Grotto. "I have, as you must know, King Hyperenor's last testament, but the scroll is useless without the Key. And the Key is currently in Glorian's possession, there within the slab of blue glass. If you are indeed the Autoexec, you can surely dissolve the imprisoning material. Then I can regain the Hot Key, and I can fulfill my oath and return the Dipped Switch to Morgrom."

The Autoexec laughed, a pleasant, heartening sound. "You know," he said, "I can't remember all these non-Newtonian solutions to life's little problems. I have a file that's nothing more than a batch of such useful procedures, but I swear by the photo of me in the 'Doer's Profile' ad on Page 154 of the issue of *The Satyrday Evening Post* within the closed metal receptacle of this hot-air balloon, I neglected to bring the file with me."

"What do you mean?" said Spike, working up his courage to address the Autoexec. "That Glorian's stuck in that blue glass until you go home or to your office and find your batch of files?"

"Not exactly, Spike," said the Autoexec, staring at his own right hand until it began to glow with a fierce white light that made the others turn away. Glorian saw the Autoexec reach into the slab of blue glass and take the Dipped Switch and the Hot Key from his open hand; and then the Autoexec removed his own brilliantly gleaming fist. Before the others could bear to look, the Autoexec put the Switch and Key in the pockets of his shorts.

"What should we do next, then?" asked Mirakles. It was apparent to Glorian that the prince hadn't yet figured out that the Autoexec was as much their enemy as Morgrom himself. More so, because the Autoexec had taken possession of the Golden Dipped Switch. Now the entire Empire was in danger, perhaps even the entire world. And the Supernatural Guide was helpless.

The Autoexec's radiant hand returned to normal. "I'll go on from here," he said in what was supposed to be a good-guy's thoughtful voice. "I think with the aid of Redthirst you'll be able to chip Glorian out of there in a few hours. If the Essence of Evil shows up, deliver a message for me, please. Tell him that he was a fool ever to believe that he was a match for the Autoexec."

"I'll do that," said Spike.

"Oh, yes," said the white-garbed Autoexec, "let me give you all my congratulations once again. An excellent job, a pat on the back for each of you. A truly excellent job." Then he headed back northward into the lava room. Glorian watched, his unblinking eyes filled with unshed tears, as the Prince of the Sunless Grotto set to work freeing him from the slab of blue glass.

Redthirst first hacked away huge chunks of glass, but as Mirakles succeeded in chopping through the great block, quite near to Glorian's trapped body in several places, the prince had to proceed more cautiously. Even Spike joined in with his short sword, sometimes cracking the blue glass, sometimes prying away loose shards.

And as they worked there on the floor of the volcano, one terrible thought ran many times through

Glorian's mind: If the Autoexec himself could be so corrupt, what now was the value of the Supernatural and Fantastic Wayfarers Association? Could it be that other of its members had also been twisted and ruined by greed and ambition? What could be done to save the organization, which, after all, was for the most part a benevolent, even holy Association? What would happen if the Association disbanded because of this horrible crime and scandal? What would become of future heroes like Mirakles, left to their own inadequate devices—without supernatural aid—as they faced the many physical, intellectual, and spiritual trials of their various quests?

At last, seemingly several hours after they began, Spike and the prince removed the last bit of blue glass from Glorian. He went to the pool on the floor of the volcano, removed his clothing, and immersed himself in the cold water, washing all the sharp fragments of dust from his hair and rinsing away the last debilitating particles. When he stepped naked from the pool, he Drawer Forwarded his clothing back to the hotel and got an identical outfit—it was his favorite traveling clothes, and he'd brought three complete sets to the Valhalla Hilton.

No one, not even Spike, made any crude jokes about Glorian in his nakedness, not even about the pearl-gray cloud that hovered about his genital region. Once again dressed in clean, dry clothes, he felt a great deal better. "I have to thank you for saving my life," he said simply. "If I'd been left to languish much longer in that blue glass, I would have died a semi-mythical death, beyond resurrection. I owe you all a great deal."

Mirakles just spread his hands. "Seems to me that we've all done the same for each other, at one time or another. No one's keeping score anymore."

"Wonderful," said Glorian. "Now, of course, our

mission is to catch up to the Autoexec and recover the Dipped Switch and the Hot Key. I don't know if the Autoexec is in league with Morgrom, or if he manipulated the Malignant One just as he manipulated us, in order to have one of us find the Switch and give him access to the corridors of time. To be frank with you, now that I know that the Autoexec is our enemy, I'm more frightened that he has the Dipped Switch than if it had gotten back to Morgrom. And my sense of outrage is immense. The feeling of betrayal—"

"Why are you frightened?" asked Mirakles. "I thought the Autoexec was on the side of right and justice."

"The Autoexec *used* to be a good guy," said Glorian. "Now, however, it looks like he's been seduced by the dark side of the Switch."

"You said we'd seen only about half of this Great Underground Empire," said the prince worriedly. "The Autoexec could be going anywhere in the rest of it."

Glorian shook his head. "Some areas would be useless to him, such as the 'Alice' area in this section of the Empire. I'm convinced that he's continuing southward and downward, heading for the third and last part of these subterranean lands. Let's get on his trail."

"I'm hungry," complained Spike.

"Too bad," said Glorian. At some moment in the recent past, the Supernatural Guide had taken charge of the party, had silently and without a struggle wrested control away from Prince Mirakles. The prince, too, followed behind Glorian as they made their way back to the Carousel Room and then headed due south, passing many strange rooms and wonders. Glorian seemed so intent on closing the gap between himself and the Autoexec, that he ignored the chambers he passed through, and gave no explanations at all to the son of Thrag. Spike, who knew these rooms as well as, if not better than, Glorian, filled in the details as they jogged along.

Glorian interrupted suddenly. "An important meeting was supposed to take place in the wizard's workshop. No doubt our progress is being noted, and that meeting will be rescheduled for somewhere along the path ahead of us. You need not worry, my prince. We will take back from the Autoexec that which is yours, you will face your final trials, and you will meet those who will influence your future life even as it was written that you should. Only the times and places will be changed. Now, let's stop dawdling and make some *real* time."

Glorian led them at top speed past a group of odd-angled rooms in which Mirakles and Ed became terribly disoriented. "This way!" Glorian shouted angrily. "This way!" They followed him. They followed him past a room where Cerberus, the three-headed dog that should have been protecting the gate of Hades, was chained up.

"This is how we got out of Hades so easily," said Spike. "This is where Hermes must have kenneled Cerberus."

"Blast it!" cried Glorian in frustration. "How can we get by him now? Who would've expected to find this three-headed hellhound here, instead of at his usual station?"

"There will be no problem," said Mirakles gently. He stepped forward and Cerberus began hopping about, wagging his tail, and acting like a delighted puppy. "He loves me," explained the Prince of the Sunless Grotto. "Because my father is Thrag the Commonly Detested, who sends so many customers down to Hades, Cerberus and I have a wonderful relationship."

"You send your own share of customers down to Hades," said Ed.

"I guess that's true," said Mirakles thoughtfully. "Anyway, we'll be able to slip right by him, as long as the three of you go first. I'll keep Cerberus busy here. Hey, boy! How ya doin'? Roll over, that's it! Let me scratch your belly!"

"A boy and his many-headed mongrel," murmured Spike, shaking his head. He ran past the horrible monster, not far behind Glorian. Ed put on his best show of speed. Then, bringing up the rear, came the Prince of the Elastic Tendon.

They entered an anteroom to the crypt area, which was large, empty, and full of echoes. There were marble bas reliefs depicting probably untrue incidents in the lives—and occasionally afterlives—of the Flathead kings. A huge marble door stood at the south end of the room. The marble door was closed, and above it was the inscription *Feel free.*

"Do you?" asked Glorian at last.

"Do I what?" said Mirakles.

"Feel free."

The prince growled his hatred. "Not until I get the Autoexec's neck in one hand, and the Hot Key in the other."

"In the meantime," said Spike, swinging open the noisy marble door, "let's keep moving."

"First, let me try something," said Glorian, suddenly inspired. He wrote out a note on Valhalla Hilton note paper, describing all that had happened to them, and the Autoexec's part in it. His colleagues in the Association would be as shocked to learn of the Autoexec's treachery as he'd been. Then he Drawer Forwarded it back to the hotel, and silently supplicated The Powers That Be that the message would reach sympathetic eyes.

Beyond the anteroom was the crypt itself. The room contained the earthly remains of the mighty Flatheads, twelve somewhat flat heads mounted securely on poles. "You might think that the crypt would have other things in it," said Mirakles, shuddering despite his well-publicized courage.

"Like what?" asked Ed.

"Oh, funerary urns or other things the Zorkers used in their ritual practices."

"Nope," said Spike casually, "it's empty of anything at all like that. And believe me, you don't want to get up close to any of these heads mounted on the poles. They don't bear close inspection. I know."

At first, there didn't seem to be any other way out of the room except the way they'd entered, but Spike urged them all toward a secret doorway. There was a faintly glowing letter in the center of this area. "Is that an F?" asked Mirakles.

"It looks like an F," said Ed. "What does it stand for?"

"Maybe it's our grade."

Glorian opened the secret door. It didn't make a sound, not even the noise of heavy marble rubbing against the grit on the floor. Beyond the door was a roughly hewn staircase leading down into darkness. The landing the explorers found themselves on was covered with carefully drawn magical runes that meant nothing to them. Strange green lines of enormous power began to sweep and undulate across the landing, making each member feel as if he had no will of his own, but that he must continue forward.

"I don't like this," said Mirakles.

"There's . . . nothing . . . I . . . can . . . do," said Glorian from between clenched teeth. He felt himself compelled downward. At last he yielded, as did the others, and they stepped onto the long, dark staircase.

As they passed, the green lines flared and disappeared in a burst of light, and Glorian, Spike, Prince Mirakles, and Ed tumbled down the staircase.

At the bottom, a vast hall illuminated in red light

stretched off into the distance. Sinister statues guarded the entrance to the next chamber far ahead. "Uh oh," said Mirakles. "I get the feeling that things aren't going to get any easier down here."

"I can pretty much assure you that you've summed up the situation precisely," said Spike.

"By all that's holy, look!" cried Glorian. There were tears in his voice. He pointed to a small pile of stone shards and rock dust.

"What is that, another magical threat?" asked the prince.

"It's Ed, or all that remains of him," said Glorian, rocking back and forth in grief. "He didn't survive the fall down the staircase."

"By Thrag!" shouted Mirakles in helpless frustration. "He was a good companion. He knew he didn't have long to live, but he never even made it out of this unholy realm of caverns! He told me often how much he wished to see the land about the Sunless Grotto."

"Let us see if we can scoop him up and fill a rucksack with his remains," said Glorian, Drawer Forwarding a fresh pack from his room in the Valhalla Hilton. They all spent many wordless minutes trying to sweep up every last fragment of Ed, and when they were all put in the rucksack, Mirakles took it. "I will carry him with me and remember his good humor," said the prince. "And I will lay him to rest in a place of honor in my mother's realm."

They rested there, and Glorian Drawer Forwarded them all sufficient but unambitious food. He was not in a mood to worry about "cuisine." They still had too far to travel, and too many other battles to fight.

CHAPTER THIRTEEN

Women, as some witty Frenchman once put it,
inspire us with the desire to do masterpieces,
and always prevent us from carrying them out.
—Oscar Wilde

THEY HADN'T PROCEEDED far before Mirakles called a halt. They were at the junction of a passage leading south from the great, endless staircase down which they'd fallen, and an east-west passage. The ways east and south were narrow tunnels, but a wider trail led to the west. In the center of the junction was a great rock, in which a mythical sword was once stuck. The sword was long gone, but the monolith still stood, dividing the chamber.

"Why are we stopping?" asked Spike. "We had a decent meal and we rested, and since then we've come only a little way."

The prince didn't seem to have heard the young man's question. He just spread his hands and shook his head. "I blame myself," said the son of Thrag. "I take all responsibility."

"Blame yourself for what, my prince?" asked Glorian.

Mirakles looked at his two remaining companions with an expression of almost utter despair. "Why," he said, "for the death and destruction of our friend, Ed, the Embedded Character. It was my fault, and I'll never be able to forgive myself. I kept pushing us onward, I kept urging us to hasten. Maybe if I hadn't demanded so much of you lesser folk, Ed would still be alive this moment."

"There, there," said Glorian. This was one of the more frustrating occasions that every Supernatural Guide had to face. Sooner or later, on every quest, something would happen to shatter the hero's seemingly invincible self-confidence, and the appointed quasi-real assistant was powerless to do anything but say "There, there," and try to make the hero feel better. Sometimes heroes were just like little children.

So Glorian had been through this all many times, and he knew what to do. It was just so tedious! It was exactly like when a friend calls you up at three in the morning, collect, in a hysterical and usually besotted condition, and wails on and on about some series of horrible problems that don't strike *you* as particularly horrible, but your friend is determined to be miserable, and eventually he starts making vague references about all sorts of totally irrational solutions to these horrible problems, and you realize that you're going to have to spend the next half-hour talking your friend back into coherence and non-violence, usually at long-distance rates. What do you do first? You say, "There, there." Then you have to agree with everything your friend says, and not anger or upset him, and eventually you succeed in making him see that life is, indeed, worth living, at least until the sun comes up. In professional circles, this is called "talking him down."

Glorian knew he had to talk Mirakles down, or none of them would ever see the happy solution to their varying sets of problems. After the obligatory commiseration, he told the hero, "It wasn't your fault. Don't you remember those bizarre green lines of force? They more or less *pushed* us down the staircase. We didn't have any choice in the matter."

Mirakles nodded glumly. "Yes, I know but—"

Glorian would've bet the farm that those would be the son of Thrag's next words. "But nothing," he replied. "It could be that Morgrom put those lines of force there for his own nefarious purposes. Perhaps he intended that we *all* should perish in that long, bruising fall."

"Well, actually," said Spike, "those lines of force have always been there, even before Morgrom's arrival on the scene."

Glorian glared at the glowing young man. "Spike," he said, "don't you think it was the lines of force that caused Ed's death, and not the insuperable Mirakles, Prince of the Sunless Grotto? Don't you think so, Spike?"

Spike read Glorian's expression correctly. "Oh, why, yes, of course. There's no doubt in my mind that the lines of force were responsible, and that the mighty Mirakles shouldn't give another moment's thought to any feelings of obligation or liability."

"Exactly," said Glorian. He turned back to the prince. "You're indulging yourself with these thoughts, O Mirakles of the Elastic Tendon. You're wallowing in unearned guilt, which is the worst kind. Now, come along, we have places to go and people to meet."

"Those green lines of force would prevent the Autoexec from going back the way we all came," said Spike. "He's trapped in this area along with us. South of here is a lake, and east the passage comes to a dead end. To the west is a barren area above the Flathead Ocean, and the Land of Shadow."

The son of Thrag looked as if he were waking from a dream. He glanced about himself and muttered something. "Right, then," he said, "west. The way is easier, and since we have no information about where the Autoexec went, one way is as good as another. We have to believe, however, that with the Dipped Switch in his possession, he is most likely in a hurry to return to the white house, where the time machine is."

Glorian nodded his head in agreement. "Morgrom may be in that house, too," he said. "I wish I knew more about their relationship."

"Enough talk," said Mirakles impatiently. He led the way to the west, into a barren area. It was a large plain entirely devoid of vegetation. Ahead, though, there were more signs of life, at least in the form of trees. The barren area had been cut off from the south by a mighty wall of stone, which now was in a sad state of disrepair. The intelligent explorer would not even attempt scaling the wall, except in the southwest, where it had crumbled and fallen enough to allow passage. Mirakles, however, was not interested in what lay in the southwest. He kept traveling in a straight line, toward the trees.

Soon they saw that they were at the top of a high cliff. Perhaps two hundred feet above them was a gaping hole in the earth's surface, and bright sunlight poured in. "This is a rather unique location in this subterranean world," said Spike. "A few seedlings from the world above, nurtured by the sunlight and occasional rain, have grown into giant trees, making this a virtual oasis in the desert of the Great Underground Empire. Except for the volcano area, I can't think of anywhere else in this part of the ancient Empire where the sky is visible, and where aboveground trees grow in such abundance."

"Thank you, Mr. Tour Guide," said Glorian. "That's what Ed would've said."

Mirakles was already peering over the edge of the cliff. It was a sheer precipice, dropping a long, *long* way to jagged rocks below.

"The rope's still here," said Spike.

The prince turned and looked at the young man. "Huh?" he said.

"There, tied to that tree. There's a rope knotted around the trunk, and the other end is dangling over the edge of the cliff. Either it's been here a very long time, or else the File Restorer has replaced the original."

Glorian noticed there was something else on the tree: an envelope. He retrieved the envelope and examined it. The note inside was written on official Supernatural and Fantastic Wayfarers Association stationery, and signed by Savitri, the East Indian golden god of the sun, the current president of the organization. It said:

> Glorian:
> Shocking news about the Autoexec, but your report has been independently corroborated by several other sources. Steps are being taken. Do not worry. Step One is for you to meet Phretys. She'll be waiting for you beside the ocean. Best that you leave the others behind for a time and meet her alone. Know that the Supernatural and Fantastic Wayfarers Association is behind you one hundred percent. I can tell you that I voted for you for the Campbell Award, and was very sorry that you lost. But, of course, it's an honor just to be nominated.
>
> Good luck to you,
> and may God bless.

"From the Autoexec?" asked Spike.

"He wouldn't have the brass-bound nerve," said Mirakles.

Glorian put the paper inside his shirt and Drawer Forwarded it away. "No," he said, "Just some advice from the president of the Association. I'm supposed to meet someone named Phretys. The name rings a bell with me, but I can't quite place her."

"I've never heard it before," said the prince.

"Where do we go, then?" asked Spike.

"I meet her alone," said Glorian. He pointed over the edge of the cliff. "Down there."

"Ah," said Mirakles. He looked relieved that he wasn't going to have to make the descent as well.

Glorian grabbed the rope and tested it by pulling as hard as he could. It seemed trustworthy. "The two of you can just wait for me here," he said. "I don't know how long this meeting will last, but I don't want to lose track of you."

"That will be just fine," said the prince.

"Glorian," said Spike, "you won't be able to climb back up the cliff, will you?"

"No, I don't think so. But if I remember correctly—"

"You'll have to pass through the Land of Shadow," Spike interrupted, "then through the narrow tunnel north to the junction room, then west until you find us. Don't worry about Mirakles and me, we'll just be alternating between boredom and worrying ourselves sick over you."

Mirakles came forward and clasped Glorian's arm. "Glorian of the Knowledge," he said. "Good fortune attend your journey. May you come away from the meeting with useful tidings."

"I hope so, O son of Thrag," said Glorian.

"What about light in the Land of Shadow?" asked Spike. "I won't be with you."

"Flashlight," said Glorian simply, and then he began the difficult climb down the sheer face of the cliff. He made slow progress, seeking for footholds and inching his way toward the rocks below. Part of the time, he thought of quitting the Supernatural-Guide business, because it had just gotten too aggravating. Then, the next moment, he told himself that belonging to the Supernatural and Fantastic Wayfarers Association was something he was inordinately proud of, and he couldn't imagine giving that up.

Of course, it wasn't the same now as it had been in the Good Old Days. These kids nowadays . . . what would they have thought of the Hanged Frog back in the early years of Glorian's career? On the other hand, there had always been fools and tricksters and downright villains in the Association—take Narlinia von Glech, for one. She'd been around as long as Glorian himself had.

There'd never before been even a hint that the Upper Echelons were tainted with wrongdoing, though. The revelation of the Autoexec's true nature was still too startling for Glorian to accept completely. He wondered about The Powers That Be—what authority could they exert, if everyone suspected them of hidden motives? It was as if there were a cancer on the Association, and Glorian had gotten himself into the middle of the battle to excise that cancer and keep it from spreading.

It was not long after that morbid thought that Glorian reached a rock-strewn ledge near the base of the high cliff. The very bottom of the cliff was perhaps fifteen feet farther. Unfortunately, the Campbell Award nominee had quite literally come to the end of his rope. He dangled there for a few seconds considering his options.

They all boiled down to one: He'd have to scramble down the rest of the cliff the hard and dirty way, and when he got to the bottom, he probably wouldn't be able to climb back up to the end of the rope. Not that Glorian seriously believed that he could haul himself back up to where Spike and Mirakles waited. The glowing young man had been right in saying that Glorian would have to return the long way.

Well, there was no profit in standing at the cliff base and cursing his luck, so Glorian retrieved his flashlight via Drawer Forwarding, clicked it on, and looked around. He saw that he wasn't far away from the sandy beach of the Flathead Ocean.

Of course, it was a *big* ocean, and this Phretys person could be almost anywhere. The ocean itself was an amazing feature of the subterranean world. It was a huge underground sea, and rumors and legends of it had made their way to the surface world over the centuries. Just now there was a heavy surf, and a fresh breeze blowing onshore.

The land rose steeply in the east, into the Land of Shadow, Glorian knew. He also knew that he couldn't walk much farther south, because the seaside terrain became impassable quicksand. He gazed out over the water, into a thick fog that was rolling toward the shore. Soon Glorian would be enveloped in that heavy mist, and his travels would become that much more difficult. He took a deep breath and let it out slowly. He decided to search the beach area as far south as he could go. Phretys had to be around here somewhere.

He'd walked about a hundred yards when he heard a woman's husky voice call his name. He stopped and looked around, turning the beam of his flashlight this way and that, but he couldn't see anyone. Then, unexpectedly, a hand touched his shoulder, and Glorian gave a little yelp of surprise and dropped his flashlight. He bent down to pick it up where it lay beside a woman's delicate, shell-pink, sandal-shod foot.

"Sorry," said the woman. "This whole place is too spooky. I'm sorry already that I agreed to do this."

"Are you Phretys?" asked Glorian.

"Sure," she said. "I can't imagine there are very many other goddesses like me, just strolling along beside this awful ocean. Let me explain my business, and then I can get out of here."

"Whatever you like," said Glorian.

"What I'd like first is a cigarette." She opened a black designer handbag and rummaged around in it, coming up at last with a crumpled pack of cigarettes. "Got any matches?" she asked.

"No, sorry."

"A lighter? I lost my lighter somewhere down here, and I know I'll never find it."

"No fire-making capabilities at all," said Glorian. "That's caused a certain amount of trouble in the recent past."

"All right," said Phretys, "forget it." She dropped the pack of cigarettes back into her handbag and closed it. She was tall and willowy, with very patrician features. She had long, wavy blonde hair and pale gray eyes. She wore a long, white garment with a Grecian border in purple. Glorian recognized it as a *stola,* the sort of thing rich women in ancient Greece used to wear. "Bloomingdale's," she said.

Glorian nodded. He had no idea why he had been instructed to meet her, so he waited for her to give him an explanation.

"My name is Phretys," she said. "I'm a Muse, a daughter of Zeus and Mnemosyne."

Of course, most people had heard of the nine big-time Muses—Thalia, Clio, those ladies. The original nine ethereal beauties had been enough in ancient Greece, when nine could cover just about every aspect of mankind's artistic endeavors. A lot of time had passed since then; and what with progress and civilization, there came to be a need for supplementary Muses. Nowadays, Glorian estimated, there were about twenty-two hundred of them, and it was impossible to keep up with every one. Most, if not all, were members of the Association, and it may well have been that Glorian had seen Phretys before, at one function or another.

"May I ask what you're the Muse of?" he said.

She looked around herself and shook her head. "I'm the Muse of Modern Science Fiction," she said.

"Uh huh," said Glorian.

"My sister, Threnia, was supposed to speak with you. She's the Muse of Modern Fantasy Novels. Unfortunately, she couldn't make it, and she asked me to cover for her. So here I am."

"Uh huh," said Glorian.

"I've come to deliver a message, to give you a valuable piece of information, and then to sort of bless you and send you on your way. The message is that when you recover the Golden Dipped Switch—and we all expect that you *will* recover it, or rather that Mirakles will recover it with your guidance—you must guard it as if it were the very World-Egg itself.

"You cannot begin to imagine the horrors that would be unleashed, should either the Autoexec or Morgrom replace the Switch in the time machine, and then go about their nefarious plans. I'm sure you've already begun imagining what they could do; but, believe me, you don't know the half of it, and I don't have the time to go into detail.

"All right, the second thing is, we know what the Autoexec's weakness is. Darkness. He's powerless in total darkness. And I don't mean like walking into a closet and not turning the light on. I don't mean like going up into the attic when you were a kid, or down into the basement. I don't mean darkness because all the lights are off. The Autoexec can create light, you've seen him do it. I'm talking about absolute darkness, the utter blackness that is the total absence of light, or any possibility of light. It's a quality that's rather difficult to achieve, and so the Autoexec feels he's perfectly safe from attack on that front. He may be right, but I had to give you the information. I hope it will be useful to you.

"Third, bless you, go forth and be victorious, you

know what I mean. I just want to go home and take a nice, hot, soaky bath and have a little chablis and smoke a cigarette. I don't like it here."

Glorian was almost overwhelmed by the Muse's personality, but that's the effect they have on some people. "How can I thank you for all you've told me?" he asked.

"Just get the Switch and deliver it only to the Control Character," she said.

Glorian's eyes grew larger. "Then there *is* such a being?"

"You bet," said Phretys. "One thing about Threnia's job that I like—in a science fiction novel, I'd have to explain and rationalize everything, but in a fantasy novel, people will believe just about anything. She has it a lot easier than I do, you can believe me. Now, listen, this is a piece of advice from me, because I was sorry you lost the Campbell Award."

"It's an honor just to be nominated," said Glorian in a dull, dead voice.

"Yeah, sure," said the Muse. "I'll tell you this, then I'm leaving. When you get the Dipped Switch back, and the Hot Key, your adventure still won't be over. Do you understand?"

Glorian blinked a few times. "No?" he said. "What else is there?"

Phretys looked up, as if Zeus were hovering overhead, ready to give the poor Muse sustaining strength. "If you haven't figured it out already, Glorian of the Knowledge," she said in a low voice, "this isn't Mirakles's story."

"It's not?"

"No, dummy, it's *yours*. You've explained a great deal to that hefty hunk of hero about how the mythic cycle works, and yet you haven't tumbled to the fact that everything that is true for him is also true for you. Don't you recognize this conversation as the mystical meeting with the Goddess? Mirakles had Melithiel, you get me in Threnia's place. And the next stage—"

"The reconciliation with the father-creator," whispered Glorian.

"—as I was saying, is when you finally meet the Control Character. Glorian, my sweet, you're still pretty naive for someone who's been in this game as long as you have."

"I never guessed," said Glorian in awe. "Does that mean—"

"See ya," said Phretys, the Muse of Modern Science Fiction, and then she was gone.

Glorian just stared at the place where she'd been. "You know," he thought, "I'll just bet that this strange, mixed-up feeling I have now is exactly how all the heroes of the past have felt when I guided them near the end of their own epics. The tables *have* been turned." He gave a weak laugh, rubbed his face with weary hands, and headed east, into the Land of Shadow.

This was an eerie place, a land of eternal night. It was a magical place, a fantastic place, and Glorian could understand why Phretys wanted to leave so quickly. The Land of Shadow intimidated even Glorian, who had been hardened over the centuries to most normal, everyday horrors. This was not a part of the Great Underground Empire that he ever visited voluntarily. In fact, it was only the second time that he'd been through it. Generally speaking, Glorian preferred to avoid this part of the Empire altogether.

"Well," he thought, "I suppose I can cross this entire region from my list of places where the Autoexec might be." There was a terrible, enchanted darkness here, and Phretys' bit of advice suggested that the Autoexec would avoid the Land of Shadow and all chambers, tunnels, passages, and dangling ropes that forced one to pass through it.

The darkness seemed to eat the light from Glorian's flashlight greedily. The flashlight's brilliant beam was reduced to a faint yellow glimmer that served only to warn him of stones, holes, and other hazards of the way. He knew the path out of the Land of Shadow, and he tried to keep his mind on other things until he emerged.

He thought about what Phretys had told him. First, that this whole adventure was for his benefit, and not Mirakles'. How would the hero feel about that? Glorian decided that it wasn't in the basic agreement that he'd have to inform the prince himself. Let Phretys or Threnia do it. Or Narlinia. Narlinia always enjoyed delivering bad news to someone.

And what did it all mean? Had Phretys been trying to tell him that if he recovered the Dipped Switch from the Autoexec—and kept it safely out of the hands of Morgrom the Malignant—that Glorian would end up apotheosized? That was something he'd rarely even dreamed of. It would take him out of the rank of mere Supernatural Guide, and raise him up at least one whole echelon. He'd be a hemi-semi-demigod or something. He could feel his mythological pulse race, just considering the possibilities.

He had almost reached the farthest limits of the Land of Shadow. He wondered how mere mortals reacted to the place. After all, he was a member of the Supernatural and Fantastic Wayfarers Association, and he was afraid. Well, if not exactly afraid, then at least deeply concerned. And he was a non-real entity, unlike a human being. Glorian didn't have to worry about being killed in the Land of Shadow, unless there were open vats of molten blue glass lying around, which he doubted. Yet if this place caused such shuddery feelings in him, then it must work its evil that much more on human beings. They could and did fear the darkness because they imagined that it concealed death-dealing monsters. Glorian promised himself that he'd no longer find that trait amusing in his future clients.

Finally, at long last, Glorian arrived at the edge of the Land of Shadow. He entered a dark crawlway that was pretty frightening in its own right. He made his way slowly, inching forward on his stomach. The greatest hero in the world, who would face a dozen Shugreths, might quake at the claustrophobic tightness of this passage.

It didn't bother Glorian, of course. He kept going until he rolled out of the crawlway's mouth into the junction room. Then he just followed the same path he'd traced with his two companions not long before. He hurried over the barren area to the cliff top, and found Mirakles and Spike pretty much as he'd left them.

"Glorian!" cried Spike. He seemed genuinely glad to see him.

"Well?" said Mirakles, showing some concern.

"There's good news and there's bad news," said Glorian.

"I hate it when people say that," said the prince.

Glorian shrugged. "The good news is that I know exactly where the Autoexec isn't. The bad news is that pretty much everything we thought we knew about where we were going and why is wrong."

CHAPTER FOURTEEN

Man is a credulous animal and must believe something.
In the absence of good grounds for belief,
he will be satisfied with bad ones.
—Bertrand Russell

THE FIRST IMPORTANT thing was a hearty meal. Glorian conscientiously believed in hearty meals. Although they had far to travel and many difficult feats to attempt, he made all three of them pause and relax a little, and enjoy a hearty, nutritious, stick-to-the-ribs meal.

"I don't want anything stuck to my ribs," said Mirakles angrily. "I want to go after that Autoexec guy of yours. I can do it on pure hatred, Glorian! I don't need a blasted meal!"

"Now, now," said the Supernatural Guide, "you're just fooling yourself. Everyone needs a proper diet. How would you feel if you finally caught up to both the Autoexec and Morgrom, and the two of you—well, the three of us, actually, but we're counting heavily on you and Redthirst carrying most of the load—if you suddenly felt all weak and washed-out and unable to continue because you'd skipped an important meal? How would you feel? How do you think that would fit into the grand song they're going to write about you after you die or sail off to some mystic isle or something? 'And then the great Mirakles/Prince of the Sunless Grotto/ felt faint from lack of proper nourishment/ and was cut into a million pieces by his evil enemy.' How does *that* sound in your saga?"

Mirakles looked at Spike, and Spike looked back at Mirakles. "It would be quicker to let him serve the condemnation-deserving meal than for us to argue about it anymore." The prince looked at Glorian. "Fine," he said, "feed us. You're right. I'm sorry if I hurt your feelings."

"It's not a matter of my feelings," said Glorian. "It's a matter of good, common sense. You can't function at your best on an empty stomach. It's a proven fact. I could show you statistics."

"Don't, please," said he of the Elastic Tendon. "Just let's eat."

So Glorian served up to his companions Roast Elk à la Jefferson, steamed Okeanos endymions in *comus* sauce, and Zulu coconut cream pie. He apologized for the brevity of the menu; but he reminded them that they were, in effect, in a state of war, and therefore they didn't have much time to kill.

After they'd eaten just enough to replenish their energy, yet not so much that they couldn't effectively pursue the Autoexec, they got up and continued their march. Spike led them away from the edge of the cliff, back across the barren ground to the Junction Room. There they turned south through the tiny crawlway. Glorian was proud of Mirakles, because he displayed no fear of closed-in spaces that other, less formidable heroes had shown.

The three of them made their way on their bellies southward, from the crawlway into a misty room. That chamber was a dank passage filled with a wispy fog seeping in from the Land of Shadow, which was not far to the west.

"Say, Glorian," said Mirakles, shivering, "isn't there another way we can go? We're covering some pretty strange territory here—first that crawlway, and now this rocky chamber filled with foul-smelling fog. Although my enchanted blade, Redthirst, has not begun throwing off its warning aroma, I have a feeling deep down that we're heading into trouble."

"*Of course* we're heading into trouble," cried Glorian in exasperation. "Isn't that what we're *here* for?"

"I suppose," said Mirakles. He sounded less enthusiastic than before. Glorian blamed that on the *comus* sauce.

The way led due south, along a path that became wide and easy to tread. Soon the prince was his former confident self, and Spike was entertaining them with long, boring descriptions of where they'd been and where they were and what they'd see next. It warmed Glorian's fabulous heart. This was what a *real* quest was supposed to be like.

They followed the path for quite a long while—so long, in fact, that Spike eventually ran out of interesting yet tedious things to say about it. They hurried on in blessed silence for almost a quarter of an hour, until the path widened, and they realized they were now in a very large cavern, on the north shore of a small lake. Some polished stone steps led down to the southeast, and a sheer rock face prevented any progress around the lake to the southwest.

"Well," said Glorian, "we have two choices, my prince."

"Any suggestions?" said Mirakles.

"Those steps take you to a dead end," said Spike. "They go down to a place where you can look out and see the busted aqueduct."

"Can you swim?" asked the son of Thrag.

"You bet," said Spike. "It's a survival skill here in the Great Underground Empire."

"What about you?" said Mirakles to Glorian.

"I'm disappointed that you even had to ask," replied the Supernatural Guide. It seemed that no matter how much he did for the hero, it was never enough. "Of course I can swim."

"Then it's into the lake and onward," decided the prince.

"Wait," said Glorian. "Before we rashly jump into the cold water at our feet, we ought to be aware of a few things."

"Like what?" asked Spike.

"Well," said the Campbell Award-nominee, "if you go into the lake, it will wash off all the luminia on your body. From then on, we'll be dependent on my poor flashlight."

"Ah, good thinking," said Spike. He gave Glorian his remaining supply of luminia, which the guide then Drawer Forwarded back to his room in the Valhalla Hilton for protection.

"And the rucksack," said the prince. "If I swam across the lake with it, the remains of poor Ed would turn to mud. He deserves better." So Glorian Forwarded the rucksack, too.

"Are we ready now?" asked Spike.

"I think so," said Mirakles. He looked at Glorian for confirmation.

"Let's do it, then," said the leader of their party. All three of them jumped into the lake and began swimming toward the western shore. The water was icy, and at first Glorian thought he'd made a dreadful mistake. They had so far to swim, and the lake was so cold, that he feared their muscles would cramp, they'd suffer hypothermia, and they'd drown. There was a brief instant when Glorian believed that he'd condemned them all to varying degrees of death, thanks to his lack of foresight.

But then, just when he thought he could swim no farther, the shore came into view. They crawled out of the water and fell exhausted on the hard, rocky ground. There were a few sickly reeds managing to push their way up around the water's edge, but otherwise there were no signs of life. There was only one path, and it led into a narrow passage to the south.

"Let's rest a little," said Glorian. "I'll get us all dry clothing." They took some time to send and receive towels and new outfits, and Glorian returned Spike's supply of luminia to him, as well as the rucksack to Mirakles. After a short while, they got up and followed the path.

"Oh," said Spike, "this is the way to the Scenic Vista."

"Scenic Vista?" said the prince with some vehemence. "We don't have time for Scenic Vistas. That's why we didn't take the side-trip to look at your busted aqueduct."

Spike shook his head. "It's not that kind of Scenic Vista," he said. "You'll see."

They came finally to a small chamber carved in the rock, with no other exit. Mounted on one wall was a table labelled "Scenic Vista," whose featureless surface was angled toward them. One might think that the table was used to indicate points of interest in the view from this spot, like those found in so many parks. Mirakles discovered the flaw in that logic at once.

"Hey," he said, "there's nothing at all to look at here!" He was right about that. There was only the somewhat confined cavern, and by no stretch of the imagination could it be considered scenic. There was an indicator above the table, and it now read "II."

"This room," said Glorian, "is a cleverly-disguised transportation device. It can materialize us in places we've seen already, or places we didn't visit, or places we've yet to come to. We have only a strictly limited amount of time to spend at our stopping place, however, and then the room brings us back here."

"How does it work?" asked Mirakles.

"The table lists destinations," said Spike. "If you watch long enough, you'll see the indicator change." Even as he spoke those words, the "II" became "III."

"Yes," said the prince most agreeably, "but how does it *work?*"

Glorian waved a finger in admonishment. "In my business," he told the son of Thrag, "we have a saying: Any sufficiently advanced technology is indistinguishable from doubletalk."

Spike nodded agreement. "It's not important how it works," he said. "It's only important that we know how to use it."

Mirakles smiled. "And do you?"

Glorian looked at Spike, and The Protector looked back. For a moment, they were speechless. "Of course we do," they said loudly in unison.

"If we didn't know how to use such things," Glorian continued, "what possible use would we be to you?"

"You're not the only one to ask that question," said the Prince of the Sunless Grotto.

Spike took offense. "Are you suggesting—"

Mirakles laughed out loud. It was a good, solid, hearty laugh. "You can dish it out, Spike," he said, "but you can't take it! You can't stand someone else having a bit of fun with you!"

"A bit of fun!" cried Spike. "Here, where we're in the uttermost peril of our lives, sanity, and the continuation of normal existence as we've come to know it, you talk about *a bit of fun?*"

The prince was about to respond when he was interrupted by the arrival in the Scenic Vista room of another party. Another rather large party.

"How are you all feeling?" asked the Autoexec. He stood at the head of an army of shambling, senseless creatures.

"Just fine, thank you," said Mirakles, slowly drawing Redthirst from its scabbard across his brawny back. The mighty blade was wafting the bread fragrance so strongly in the small, enclosed chamber that it was almost enough to make one ill.

"You!" cried Glorian. "You, in whom I'd placed so much trust and faith!"

The Autoexec still looked like a young, upwardly-mobile citizen of some suburban town. He was still dressed in his tennis whites, and his pleasant, suntanned face was still as handsome and friendly as ever. "Trust," he said, shaking his head, "and faith. Glorian, do you honestly expect me to put any value in such concepts? After all these ages, eons, epochs? From your point of view, the future opens broadly into an ever-expanding universe of greater success, one legendary exploit to be piled on top of another. But what about me, Glorian? What about *me?* Where is there for *me* to go?"

"I could give you a hint or two," said Spike in a vicious tone.

The Autoexec paid no attention, and neither did Glorian. "Were you not in command, even over The Powers That Be?" asked the latter. "Wasn't that enough?"

The Autoexec shrugged his moderately-muscled shoulders. "It was at first," he admitted. "But after a few thousand years passed, I began to think about advancement. I looked up the corporate ladder, and above me was only the Control Character himself. What was I supposed to do? Just go on, putting in a good day's work millennium after millennium, until the Control Character patted me on the back and gave me his desk in the Home Office?"

"We all do what we have to," said Mirakles. "Those of us who can't do even that, we do what we can."

The Autoexec nodded. "A fine philosophy, my friend," he said sadly. "Here, do battle with my army of mundanes. If you don't perish horribly, maybe we'll continue this conversation later. I've grown terribly weary over the centuries, you know, and I take my entertainment where I find it." He turned his back on the prince, Glorian, and Spike. A way opened for him through the ranks of the army he'd brought with him, and he walked slowly to the rear.

It was obvious now to Glorian that the Autoexec meant to use the Scenic Vista room to travel back to the white house, where he could fit the Dipped Switch in place in the time machine. Glorian didn't know precisely what the Autoexec planned beyond that, but he didn't need to know the details. "It's the three of us against this army of mundanes," he said to Mirakles.

"All right," said the prince. "No problem. What are mundanes?"

Glorian gritted his teeth. "They're just like zombies," he said, "except they're not dead. They're merely living human beings who chose to pursue this numbing lifestyle. They're the degenerate descendants of a tribe founded by Ascius, the mortal enemy of the legendary military leader, Caius Julius Flathead. The Ascii aren't really very good at this sort of thing anymore."

"Then they'll be easier to deal with than zombies," said the son of Thrag. "I can actually *kill* these empty-eyed soldiers."

"Yes," said Spike, "but they're here in overwhelming numbers, in case you haven't noticed. Glorian, don't you have some supernatural power that you've been holding back? Something you've saved for a hopeless situation like this?"

Glorian considered Spike's question. "Well, yes, I have, as a matter of fact. Several neat tricks, actually. For one, I can spin straw into molybdenum."

Mirakles feinted toward the mundane army with his enchanted sword. Collectively, they didn't flinch a single muscle. "Right," called the prince over his shoulder. "And what's a heaping lot of molybdenum going to do for us?"

"Some people might hide behind it," said Spike, stepping up beside the son of Thrag, his short sword in his hand.

The blank-faced legions of the Autoexec pressed forward. "For Thrag and the Grotto!" shouted Mirakles, wading into the front line of the enemy.

"For . . . for my Dad!" cried Spike, following the prince's lead.

"I'm right here, too," said Glorian. "I'm keeping an eye on the Autoexec."

Mirakles grunted. "Spike," he said, between decapitating one mundane and slitting open the belly of another, "we must hold this doorway. We cannot let them into the room, or they'll crush us to the floor; nor can we go out among them for the same reason. Here in the doorway, only a dozen or so can reach us at once. I can handle ten of them, I think, if you'll get the other two."

Spike laughed fiercely. "I'm starting to enjoy this," he said, hacking and hewing at every mundane who came within reach.

"Chemicals in your brain," said Glorian. "That's why."

Mirakles glanced briefly at The Protector. "The Knowledge," said Spike. "He knows these things."

"Uh huh," said the prince, getting back to the business of slaughtering the Autoexec's dull-witted forces.

When the bodies of the mundanes had piled up so high that he could barely see over them, the Autoexec decided that things were not going as he'd expected. That's when he stepped in to lend a hand.

"Mirakles!" shouted the former Lord of The Powers That Be. He was making his way forward through the ranks of his army. "Where do your loyalties lie?"

The prince answered while he lopped, chopped, cleaved, and cut. "My loyalty is first to my father, Thrag the Rarely Invited, then to my mother, Queen Desiphae of the Sunless Grotto. Next, I recognize ties to the people of my kingdom. Finally, I am bound by an oath to Morgrom, the Essence of Evil, Thrag's Bane, the Malignant."

The Autoexec laughed cheerfully. "You did not mention your companions," he said.

"Watch him," said Glorian warily. "His hand is beginning to glow."

"I see it," said Mirakles. He and Spike were still eliminating whole platoons of mundanes. The prince glared at the Autoexec. "What foul thing are you preparing now, O treacherous one?"

"Nothing you haven't seen before," said the Autoexec. He raised his hand and blazed a blue-white bolt of force at Glorian.

"You're trying to kill my Guide again," growled Mirakles. He leaped high to his right and deflected the bolt of force with the flat blade of Redthirst.

"Nice move, my prince," said Spike admiringly.

"Thank you. By Thrag, I love doing this!"

"The Second Secret of the Sword," said Glorian.

There were still many mundanes trying to get into the Scenic Vista room. Mirakles went on with his bloody work without the least sign of fatigue, but Spike was already beginning to falter.

"You did not answer me before," the Autoexec called. "How strong are the bonds between you and your companions? Have you examined them, prince? Have you noticed that bonds can be broken, even stronger bonds than those that bind mother and child?"

"There are no stronger bonds," said Mirakles.

"You wouldn't know about that," said the Autoexec.

"I would. Believe me, *any* bonds can be broken, if one feels he has reason enough." He loosed another bolt of force.

This time, Mirakles had to make a saving dive to defend Glorian. "I will not debate with you, Master of Perfidy."

The Autoexec was about to say something, but he stopped himself. "Where do these epithets come from all the time?" he said. "Master of Perfidy?"

"Just made it up," said Mirakles.

"All right," said the Autoexec. A third time, he hurled a lightning-like bolt of energy.

A third time, the son of Thrag fought it off with the agile use of his mighty sword.

"I'll tell you what his problem is," said Spike, decapitating one of the Ascii un-undead. "He has no playground moves. You can figure out his style in two minutes. He should be giving you head-fakes and stuff."

Mirakles did not reply. Redthirst drank deeply of the mundane blood.

"Watch the bonds break!" shouted the Autoexec, in a curiously triumphant tone. He hurled something small and shiny at the prince.

At first, Mirakles began to swing his sword like a great, flat cricket bat, to swat the shiny thing into the next county. Then he stopped himself. "The Key!" he cried. "The Hot Key!" Suddenly, it seemed as if he completely forgot the battle and his friends. He held Redthirst in one hand, and stooped to pick up the Frobozz Magic Hot Key with the other.

The Autoexec took advantage of Mirakles' distraction to launch another ball of white fire at Glorian. The Supernatural Guide ducked it easily and gave a quiet laugh. "My turn," he said. He raised his hand, and a pearl-gray cloud formed around it. The cloud got darker and darker, until Glorian's hand was completely hidden. Suddenly, a stream of absolute blackness blasted through the cavern entrance, from Glorian's hand toward the Autoexec.

"Wow," cried Spike, "pumping darkness!"

"Not darkness," said Glorian. "*Darkness*. With a capital D."

The Autoexec was stunned by the attack, and fell back weakly. The mundanes, seeing him retreat a little, followed him, moving away from the door. The Autoexec recovered quickly, however. "Caught me by surprise with that one, Glorian," he said. He turned up his brightness and returned to the attack.

Glorian and the Autoexec struggled for a long while, until Mirakles and Spike lowered their swords to watch in amazement, and the mundanes turned away in horror. The Autoexec aimed his bright, fiery force at Glorian, and Glorian directed his impenetrable Darkness in return.

"A contest of will," said Mirakles. He nodded approvingly. "This is as it should be."

"I don't know," said Spike, shaking his head. "I don't fully understand the symbolic nature of this battle. I mean, we seem to be cheering for the Force of Darkness, and the guy over there is all white and bright and clean-looking."

The prince put his arm around Spike's shoulders. "And what does that tell you about symbols?" he asked.

Spike thought for a moment. "That they don't mean anything?"

"Or that they mean everything. Whatever you need at the moment."

Spike nodded. "I didn't even know Glorian could create Darkness like that."

"I can't," said their virtual companion.

"But—" Spike began. Mirakles put his finger to his lips, and The Protector was silent.

First the Darkness turned the chambers into deepest, most terrifying midnight, then came the impossibly brilliant dawn of light. Neither Glorian nor the Autoexec seemed able to overcome the other. They were quite equally matched, because sometimes the Darkness and the light met in the middle of the area and dissolved each other.

The Autoexec held something in his other hand. "Glorian, I prepared this specially for you!" And he threw the physical object with one hand at the same time that he hurled another bolt of light with the other.

Glorian chose to worry first about the Autoexec's blast of force. Unfortunately, that left him open to injury by the weapon. It was a cobalt blue grass knife, and it wounded Glorian in the thigh. He gave a faint cry and fell to the stone-paved floor.

"By Thrag!" bellowed Mirakles. "I did well in naming you Master of Perfidy!" He stood between Glorian and the Autoexec, ready to deflect any energy balls.

Spike hurried to Glorian's aid. "It's just a flesh wound," he said.

"I don't have actual flesh," said Glorian.

"Whatever," said Spike.

Glorian's breathing became more shallow. "Here," he said, obviously in great pain, "I've Drawer Forwarded these medical supplies."

"Right," said Spike. First, he removed the knife from Glorian's thigh. Then he quickly slathered on a great gob of Byelbog's Balm and bound up the wound.

By that time, the Supernatural Guide had recovered his strength enough to continue the battle. "Just help me to my feet," he said. There was still a little strain in his voice.

Standing once again, he began pouring Darkness at the Autoexec at a furious rate. "You made me angry with that knife," he said. "I rarely get angry. I may seem like a nice, easy-going guy, but now feel *my* wrath for a change. This is for The Powers That Be, the Implementors, and all the members of the Supernatural and Fantastic Wayfarers Association you let down." And the Darkness came stronger and deeper and faster.

"Give it to him, Glorian!" cheered Spike.

The Autoexec turned up his brightness a notch, and then a notch more. Glorian matched him, until the Darkness was so all-pervasive that neither Mirakles nor Spike could see what was happening any longer.

"Are you all right, Glorian?" called the prince worriedly.

There was no reply. Then the Darkness slowly began to lessen, as it diffused into the other chambers and caverns and passages. After a while, they could see Glorian, kneeling on the floor of the Scenic Vista room. He was vomiting wretchedly.

"Behold!" cried Mirakles, pointing in the other direction.

"What?" said Spike, no doubt expecting to see something a thousand times more terrible than a mere Shugreth the Unenviable.

"What is it?" said Glorian, standing weakly and joining his friends. He looked where the prince was pointing. He saw that the Autoexec had been blasted and blasted again, that he'd staggered and stumbled backward along the path toward the western shore of the subterranean lake, where he'd fallen at last and died. Or discorporated. Or whatever verb applies to the death of a godlet.

"Glorian the Victorious!" said Mirakles proudly. He beamed at his Supernatural Guide.

"Way to go, Glorian!" said Spike. "Now tell me how you suddenly learned that Darkness trick."

"The mundanes?" asked Glorian.

"All gone home," said the son of Thrag, beginning the cleaning and resheathing of Redthirst, which had served them all so well.

"Good," said Glorian.

"Answer my question," Spike demanded.

Glorian just shrugged. "It was simple. After I got the information from Phretys, I had to travel through the Land of Shadow to rejoin the two of you. I remembered what she'd said, that the Autoexec's weakness was ultimate darkness. I imagine she'd been sent by the Control Character to relay that fact to me. He must have realized that I'd have to pass through the Land of Shadow."

"So you stored up the Darkness somehow?" asked Mirakles.

Glorian nodded. "I Drawer Forwarded it. I packed my hotel room with it. I stuffed in as much as I could, praying that no one would open the hotel room's door before I had to face the Autoexec. Then I just acted as a quasi-human siphon in battle."

Spike laughed with delight. "There's just one more thing I don't understand," he said. "Why didn't Phretys or the Control Character or *somebody* just come right out and tell you to use the Darkness? They were taking the chance that you wouldn't think of it, and then the Autoexec might have defeated us again."

Glorian looked very uncomfortable. "I didn't want to get into this yet," he said, casting his eyes toward the floor, "but Phretys told me something else. She told me that although this journey began as Mirakles' quest, it was mine as well. It seems that we both have the credentials for eventual apotheosization. Apparently, I have every bit as much right to think of myself as a hero as any I've ever guided. But," he hurried to add, "just because this was also my quest, it takes nothing away from the great son of Thrag's achievements."

"Of course not," said Mirakles, his smile wavering just a little. "We're not competing in any way. We're like classmates in school who both reach graduation. There's no winning or losing between us. Of course, your quest was much harder than mine. I didn't have to destroy the second-most powerful being in the universe. And I failed you when the Autoexec threw the Key."

Glorian's heart sank. He could tell from Mirakles' tone that the prince was feeling tremendously guilty about his single lapse. It seemed likely to Glorian that he'd have to talk the prince down all over again. "Come on," he said gruffly, "you were only distracted for a moment. Your faith never wavered. Now we have to search the Autoexec's pockets for the Dipped Switch. And then the Prince of the Sunless Grotto has an appointment to keep in the Wizard's Workroom."

CHAPTER FIFTEEN

Father should neither be seen nor heard.
That is the only proper basis for family life.
—Oscar Wilde

GLORIAN STOOD BACK and allowed Mirakles to get the Golden Dipped Switch, because after all, the Switch was the prince's goal.

"Here it is," said the son of Thrag at last, standing and holding up the Switch for his companions to see. With the kind of timing that occurs so charmingly in fantasy epics, not an instant passed between Mirakles' taking of the Switch and the sizzling, smoking, sparking disappearance of the Autoexec's body.

"What happened?" cried Spike in alarm. "Was he just faking? Did he escape?"

"No, he's good and dead," Glorian explained. "That body was only a form he'd taken, and without his consciousness to motivate it and hold it together, it merely reduced itself to its constituent atoms. Much as those dead mundanes will, only much faster."

The mighty-thewed hero looked at the hundreds of dead mundanes that littered the area around the entrance to the Scenic Vista room. "I wonder if anyone's going to be angry with us for leaving so many dead bodies all over their nice, clean Empire."

"Morgrom, you mean?" asked Glorian.

"I sure wouldn't want to have to clean it all up now," said Spike.

Mirakles looked down at the little object that had caused so much death and destruction. "It may well be that the Switch will cause even more hardship and violence in the future. Yet I am compelled by my oath to deliver this into the very hands of Thrag's Bane himself! O, irony of ironies!"

"We'll be with you," said Spike confidently.

Mirakles turned a fond gaze on the glowing young man. "Spike," he said, "in addition to your duties as The Protector, I hereby appoint you Royal Bearer of the Dipped Switch." And he gave the Switch to Spike to carry.

The young man gulped. "You'd trust me with this?"

"With that and more still," said the prince. "Now, let's make haste to end this little drama."

Glorian led them back to the Scenic Vista room. He was deeply troubled. He wondered how he could accomplish the double task that he had accepted: On the one hand, according to the basic agreement between heroes and their Supernatural Guides, Glorian was honor-bound to accompany Mirakles and watch him hand over the Dipped Switch to the very Essence of Evil. On the other hand, the Control Character, Phretys, and his own intelligence forbade him from doing just that. It was the worst dilemma of Glorian's long and marginally distinguished career, because the fate of the Great Underground Empire hung upon it—and from there, perhaps the fate of the entire world. For the moment, he said nothing. He hoped and prayed that an answer would come to him before that final meeting in the white house.

Back in the Scenic Vista room, the prince asked, "Where do we go from here? You said something about the Wizard's Workshop. Where is that? I've had sore trials because of wizards, and I don't much like them."

"You needn't worry on that score," said Glorian. "There is no wizard there now, unless Morgrom has paid some poor fool to dress up in a pointy hat and a cloak with stars and planets all over it, and sit around the Workshop waiting for an adventurer."

Spike snorted. "He'd be a wizard the way Morgrom's treasures are treasures. That is, not very."

"Well, all right then," said Mirakles.

"We have to wait for the indicator to cycle around," said Glorian. At the moment, it said "IV."

"What number do we want?" asked the prince.

"We're waiting for 'II,' " said Glorian. "Great prince, clasp Spike's right hand. Spike, give me your left. Just a little while longer. . . ."

As he spoke, the "IV" changed to "I." It was very quiet in the room, but the air was filled with foul and reeking odors from the aftermath of the battle, and Glorian was glad to be leaving it, even if for only a few minutes.

His supernaturally-sharp eyes detected the very nanosecond when the indicator began to change to "II." He touched the table of destinations, there was a brief flicker of colored light, a moment of disorientation, and then they'd arrived in the Wizard's Workroom.

It was a dark, evil-smelling place, lined with empty shelves and racks that Morgrom hadn't yet gotten around to re-stocking. The Workshop was dominated by the former wizard's workbench, however. It was made of dark, heavy wood bound with iron. It was stained from many years of use and deeply gouged, as though some huge, clawed animal had been imprisoned on it. There were burn marks and even notes written in a crabbed hand, and other items scattered around, the sort of things one might expect in such a place: alembics, mortar and pestle, odd scraps of vellum, wax candles.

"Remember," Glorian told the prince, "you must open the Scroll here, and we can remain only a brief time. Then we'll find ourselves back in the Scenic Vista room."

"Right," said Mirakles, "then let's get down to business." He took the tightly-wound steel scroll in one hand, and the Hot Key in the other. "By Thrag!" he muttered. "I've faced many a horrifying, dreadful danger in my career, but I've never been so anxious about an outcome."

"There is nothing to fear here, O Prince," said Glorian gently.

Mirakles nodded, then turned the Key in the Frobozz Magic Scroll Lock.

At first, nothing happened. The prince looked toward Glorian for an explanation. Then, very slowly, the steel scroll began to unwind. As it did so, the air in the Workshop hummed with an energetic mixture of high and low tones, too random to be called music, too harmonic to be called random. Then came the visual signs that something unusual was happening. There were brilliant, tiny skyrockets and great pulsing glows that filled the entire room. At last, the special effects settled down to a repeated four-bar figure played on a whispery, tinkly keyboard sort of instrument, and a certain organization in the fireworks that lit up even the far corners of the Workshop.

These fireworks began to solidify into an image of Prince Mirakles' step-father, the late King Hyperenor of the Sunless Grotto. Phretys, the Muse of Modern Science Fiction, would have called it a hologram. Threnia, the Muse of Fantasy, would use terms like "accumulation of aura" or "trans-death resubstantialization." They all meant the same thing, really. What stood before Mirakles now was a vibrant, life-filled, moving, speaking replication of the man who had loved him and taught him and fostered in him everything that was good and noble. The prince stared blankly for a few seconds. He raised his hand to wipe away tears.

"My son," murmured the hollow voice of King Hyperenor, "and you *are* my son in many important respects, although by now I guess you know the truth about your lineage, I will give this scroll into the safe-keeping of those whom I think will serve you best. Perhaps I'm wrong to do this. Your mother, the queen, thinks I'm wrong. She doesn't trust Morgrom at all. If I'm wrong, it won't be the first time, although it may well be the last."

"Father!" cried Mirakles, trying to grasp the immaterial image of the dead king.

The blazing illustriousness could not be silenced or interrupted. Hyperenor went on. "You will soon be given a mission, a quest, on which you will prove yourself, or die trying. You are a hero born, my son. I am merely a king. This quest will be of vital importance to you, to your mother and me, to he who is the enemy of your true father, and possibly to many other people and beings of our world.

"Listen, then, my son, because I have little time. I don't know how much I can get on this scroll, but I was told I had only a minute or three. When you complete your mission, you will have two choices. You can return to the Sunless Grotto and rule in my place—I have no doubt that by that time I will be gone. Or, instead, you can remain in the land where you find yourself, as the guardian and overseer, to protect all who live there against the sort of depredation, ignominy, and virtual slavery that your mother feels Morgrom will surely introduce.

"I have a secret, Mirakles, my most beloved. I have a secret that even your beautiful mother, the queen, knows not of. It is the Third Secret of the Sword. It is that the river that runs down to the Sunless Grotto has its origin in the Frigid River of the Great Underground Empire, a mighty stream that you may or may not view along your quest. The significance of this secret is that the Empire and my realm are connected through certain narrow, water-filled passages. Therefore the Sword is dedicated to protecting both these lands, and thus the monarch of the Sunless Grotto can keep an eye on what occurs in the Empire, and this I've been doing. I'm not certain of the significance of what I've witnessed over the last few years. I tend to think that Morgrom is indeed the beneficent ruler who will do what he proposes; that is, he will restore the Underground Empire to its former greatness. Your mother firmly disagrees.

"I can feel and hear that my time is almost up, my son. Therefore, these last words. Make your choices carefully, select your companions with even greater care, and beware of false friendship. The fact that you're viewing this scroll indicates that I failed in that last item somewhere along the line. Now, when you finish the quest, you must choose between returning to your mother's side, or staying behind in the land in which you find yourself. I cannot be more specific. Perhaps you'll find a way to do both, although I've thought long and hard about the matter, and I've not discovered that elegant solution. You may well choose to remain in that other Empire; I've always suspected that you have Flathead blood in you somewhere. On your mother's side, of course.

"Remember always that I love you, Mirakles, as though you were the child of my loins your mother still pretends you are. I pray that your decisions will be wise and fair and just, and that you will give to our people, to the subjects of the Sunless Grotto, the leadership, protection, and honor they deserve."

That was the end. The skyrockets imploded, falling back into the projected figure of King Hyperenor until it grew brighter and brighter, and then gradually dimmer and dimmer, until he'd quite faded away.

"Father?" shouted Mirakles, moving forward and waving his arms through the empty, dim space where the image had been.

The prince turned helplessly to Glorian, who grasped the hero firmly by the shoulder. "There, there," said Glorian.

"I don't know if I can bear this," said Spike mournfully. "It reminds me too much of my own . . . Dad. Now in Hades. Forever."

"Hades?" said Mirakles sadly. "If I hadn't been so overwhelmed by the sensual grandeur of battling those legendary heroes, I might have met with my father, as you did yours."

"Do not reproach yourself, my prince," said Spike. "I didn't give my father the love and respect he deserved while he was still alive. Yet I'm sure that, beyond the grave, he knows how I came too late to love and appreciate the sacrifices he made for me."

"It's that way with everyone," said Glorian. "Or most people, anyway. That knowledge too often comes too late. Do not demean yourself, do not punish yourself the rest of your life. You must have seen the love in your step-father's eyes. He forgave you. You must forgive yourself."

Mirakles nodded sadly. "If you were the least bit human, Glorian," he said, "you'd know how impossible that can be."

Glorian frowned. "I'm not as—"

Suddenly, they all found themselves back in the Scenic Vista room.

"—inhuman as you think," Glorian finished. "Merely unhuman. There's a difference."

Mirakles and Spike exchanged glances. "Where do we go now?" asked the prince.

"Well," said Spike, "I don't think you can get anywhere from here. I mean, I think we have to swim the lake again."

Mirakles shuddered. "That is not a pleasant thing to look forward to."

"I think Spike is right, though," said Glorian. He began walking out of the small chamber. The dead mundanes were still stacked up shoulder-high near the entrance. "I think we ought to make our way toward the Technology Museum. It's where the time machine came from. Morgrom had it dragged to the house. Maybe something there can help us."

He'd walked past the spot where the Autoexec had fallen, and nearly to the place where they'd crawled out of the lake after their swim, when a woman's breathy voice said, "Here's your last chance at treasure! It's . . . *a new chariot!*"

Glorian went "Yipe!" and jumped about ten feet sideways.

"Who's that?" demanded Spike, drawing his short sword.

Mirakles alone had not been startled. "Hold," he said in a quiet voice, "there's no bread-baking aroma coming from Redthirst. There are no enemies here."

"No supernatural enemies," reminded Spike. "There could be plenty of ugly-tempered people with guns and knives and things."

"I don't think so," said Mirakles. "I remember that voice so well. Melithiel, what game are you playing at?"

The princess stepped out from behind some tumbled boulders that bordered the lake. She had changed into a lovely, long white gown. She'd run a comb through her hair and washed her face, and in other ways made herself absolutely entrancing. She was, very possibly, the most beautiful woman in the world. "I'm sorry if I upset your companions, my betrothed!" she said.

Mirakles went to her and clasped her in chaste fondness. "How did you get here, my love?" he asked at last. "Surely you didn't swim the lake."

"I wasn't kidding about the new chariot," she said. Glorian recalled that at the kimono dragon's house, he'd thought Melithiel's voice had sounded like a silver bell. Now he realized that he vastly underrated her. She was a perfect fantasy princess.

They walked a little farther, and Glorian saw a chariot large enough to haul the four of them. Harnessed to it was the unicorn they'd seen idly munching grass near the gazebo so many days before.

"Okay," said Spike, "I'm willing to be the one to ask. How did the unicorn get you across the lake?"

"Why," said Melithiel, turning her long eyelashes on the glowing young man, "he flies!"

"Of course," said Spike.

The princess gave him a petulant frown. In a certain light, Glorian felt, the young woman would begin to remind him more of certain of Jimmy Stewart's romantic comedy co-stars. He'd never liked any of those films. Except, of course, for the ones with June Allyson. She was all right in his book.

"He can fly in this form," she explained. "He's actually a were-unicorn. He serves many functions in the Great Underground Empire. In five minutes, he can change from his unicorn-self into a cute elf maiden who speaks in couplets or a winged vampire or anything. And he has a crystal horn that *glows in the dark*!"

"I don't suppose you can get it loose," said Spike. It was the thief's blood in him that made him say that.

"No," said Melithiel, a little bit offended, "I don't suppose."

"Please forgive me, O Princess," said Spike, recovering his manners.

The princess smiled at him. It was like the sun

breaking loose of a cloudy sky. "That's all right," she said. "Now, we must be on our way. We have far to travel, and you all have much yet to accomplish."

The prince let her enter the chariot first, then he stepped beside her. Glorian and Spike followed. "I'll drive," she said. "Rex the Wonder Unicorn knows my hand on the reins."

Glorian was surprised that the unicorn, which didn't seem any larger or stronger than an average-sized horse, could pull a chariot carrying one massive hero, one pretty good-sized Supernatural Guide, a lithe princess, and a young man who also glowed in the dark. And not only did the unicorn pull them, he lifted them as he climbed steadily into the air. The ceiling above the lake was comfortably high; and it, like the region farther below, was studded and riddled with passages, gaps, holes, tunnels, and clefts. Rex flew unerringly into one of these openings.

"I never knew these routes were up here," said Spike.

"Of course not," said Melithiel sweetly. "They're inaccessible to non-flying creatures."

The way led northwestward, angling over the lake and, Glorian surmised, the Land of Shadow. A tiny bit of the Darkness had seeped in here, and for a while it began to remind him of his recent battle with the Autoexec. He was saved from a fit of nausea as the chariot emerged high above the sheer cliff. Sunlight poured down from the opening overhead. The unicorn climbed higher and higher, and finally escaped the subterranean world.

"We're out!" cried Mirakles. "We're free! Ah, how good it feels to feel the fresh breeze on my face."

"We're out, my prince," said Glorian, "but we're not yet free."

The son of Thrag turned and nodded. Glorian knew he understood the seriousness of what would happen when the unicorn and chariot touched land again.

They flew over the dense forest for what seemed to Glorian like many miles. The sun began to climb down the sky toward the western horizon, and then Glorian's fantasy-character eyesight picked out a clearing far ahead. In the clearing, isolated from the rest of the world by distance and enchantment, was the white house.

"We're almost there," he said.

"Good," said Mirakles.

"What are we going to do?" asked Spike.

"I'm not sure yet," said Glorian. "I'm still thinking."

Mirakles wore a regretful expression. "I know what I'm going to do," he said. "I'm going to give Thrag's Bane the Switch. Then I will separate his head from his body."

Glorian shook his head. "That won't work. It's exceedingly rare for a hero to defeat a semi-actual supernatural figure like Morgrom."

Princess Melithiel put her hands on Mirakles' right biceps. "The prince is an exceedingly rare hero," she said.

"Yes," agreed Glorian, "that's true, but Morgrom is one of the most powerful of us."

Mirakles considered that. "As powerful as the Autoexec was?" he said.

"I don't know," said Glorian. "Perhaps."

"All right," said the prince, "then *you'll* have to defeat him."

"I suppose I'll have to give it a try," said the Supernatural Guide. He was not looking forward to the confrontation. The Autoexec, after all, had only recently been corrupted. Morgrom had been evil for thousands of years, and had refined that quality so far that one had to have a grudging admiration for his skill and dedication. He hadn't earned the epithet of Essence of Evil for nothing. In some ways, Glorian feared him more than he'd feared the Autoexec.

Melithiel guided Rex down to a soft landing in the clearing. Glorian looked around and noticed that all the workmen had apparently finished their jobs and left. He really had no idea how long they'd been on the quest, how much time they'd spent exploring the Great Underground Empire. "My prince," he said, "what do you suggest?"

"The proper thing now is to gather information. We must reconnoiter, just as we did when we first came here. We're not going to charge in there blindly, because Morgrom might have a whole legion of monsters arrayed in his protection."

"We'll be cautious," said Glorian, "but only because I'm not in a great hurry to go in there. Morgrom doesn't need a whole legion of monsters."

Mirakles nodded. "Melithiel, please wait for us in the chariot. There's no need for you to go inside, and we may need to make a fast getaway. Keep the unicorn warm."

The princess' eyes grew larger. "But my betrothed!" she objected. "I wish to face the danger by your side!"

The son of Thrag gazed at her adoringly. "That's very heroic of you to say, my beloved, but truly you may do us more good by staying here."

It was clear that Melithiel didn't agree, but at last she nodded. A gentle tear fell slowly down her cheek, and Mirakles stooped to kiss her. Then he looked at Glorian and Spike. "All right, then," he said in his marvelous hero's voice. "Are we all ready?"

"Yes," said Spike. He looked more frightened than Glorian had ever seen him. He carried his short sword in his right hand, at the ready.

"Let's do it," said Glorian with a sigh. The three companions left the chariot and walked slowly around the house. It was quiet—*too* quiet. They peered in the windows, but there were only vague shapes inside, dim outlines of furniture and appliances, and no movement.

When they reached the front door, Mirakles grasped the handle. "On three," he said. "One. Two. Three!" Then he threw open the door and charged in, yelling "For Thrag and the Grotto!" at the top of his lungs.

Glorian ran in next, followed by Spike. The inside of the house was as quiet as the outside had been. There were no monsters. They fanned out and searched all the rooms; Morgrom had changed the floor-plan considerably. They saved the living room for last, because that's where he was surely waiting for them.

As indeed he was.

The room was more of an office or study now. Morgrom sat in a huge chair with tapestry arms, idly pushing a beer bottle cap around with one fat finger. He was in the same physical form as during their previous meeting in the white house: tall but carrying around about one-seventh of a ton, rather good-looking if you liked plump men, brown hair that had begun to go to gray, very nicely dressed in a dark suit and vest. He smiled at them, and his teeth were brilliantly white. "Welcome," he said. "Prince Mirakles, may I ask you to leave your enchanted sword in the hall? That stench coming from it is unbearable. I assure you, you'll have no need for it."

"I think I'll just hang on to it for now," said the son of Thrag.

Morgrom lifted his shoulders a fraction of an inch and let them fall. That passed for a shrug in this incarnation. "As you wish. Then may I invite you to sit here, in this red leather chair by my desk, so that we may get on with this interview?"

"Interview!" exclaimed Spike.

Glorian indicated that the prince should do as the Malignant One had asked. Mirakles sat in the leather chair, and Glorian sat on a yellow chair nearby. "Where's Narlinia?" Glorian asked Morgrom.

"I told her to take the afternoon off. Now, shall we get down to business?"

"Is this it?" asked Spike. "Is this the famous time machine?"

Morgrom looked up in annoyance. "Who is this boy? Spike, the thief's son, whom I permit to abide in peace below this very house?"

"He's The Protector," said Mirakles, his voice daring Morgrom to say anything more about the young man.

"Yes, fine. Please make him sit down and be quiet."

Mirakles nodded to Spike, who sat in a yellow chair beside Glorian.

"Now, then," said Morgrom, turning a little to face the prince, "do you have the Golden Dipped Switch?"

Mirakles looked him directly in the eye. "No," he said, "I do not."

A slight hint of an emotion began to cross Morgrom's face, but he got himself properly under control almost instantly. "Then you must forgive me for asking, why are you here? You swore an oath to bring me the Switch."

A little of the starch went out of the prince at those words. His meager stratagem had failed, as he'd no doubt known it would. "Spike, bring me the Switch. The young man is carrying it for me."

Morgrom only waited patiently. Spike stood and went to Mirakles. He gave him the Golden Switch and returned to his yellow chair.

"Excellent," said Morgrom with a slight hiss.

"Hold!" said Mirakles fiercely. He clutched the Switch tightly in his fist.

"You must give it to him," said Glorian sadly.

The prince shook his head. "After all the terrors I passed through, the nightmarish things I witnessed, the horror I bore all in the name of fulfilling my oath, now at the ultimate moment I cannot give the Switch into your possession, Thrag's Bane!"

"You *have* to," said Spike. "You swore—"

"Silence!" roared Morgrom. "The Switch!"

"Do it," said Glorian, "and then move away from the desk."

"Yes," said Spike, "do it."

Morgrom looked at Glorian, a wholly evil look of pleasure on his face. "Do you intend to interfere, Glorian? After I have the Switch, you plan to do battle with me? How wonderful! This is more than I could've hoped for."

"I must make my attempt, Morgrom," said Glorian. "I have a mission of my own. I must keep intact the cycle of history."

"Yes, yes, of course," said the Essence of Evil impatiently, "but I still don't have the confounded Switch!"

Slowly, Mirakles' fist opened. The Golden Dipped Switch tumbled onto the blotter on Morgrom's desk. It looked like such a tiny, worthless thing there.

"Ah!" said Morgrom, his attention firmly focused on the glittering object.

Spike leaned toward Glorian. "Let's just get out of here!" he muttered.

"Yes, go," Glorian replied. "You and the prince, go."

"You too," urged Spike. He dragged Glorian to his feet. The prince left the red leather chair and joined them. Glorian struggled, but Mirakles and Spike together hauled him out of the living room, toward the door.

"I can't!" said Glorian with an angry growl. "Let me go! I've got to—"

"Stop!" screamed Morgrom in a furious rage.

Glorian came to a sudden halt and shook himself free of the other two. The adventurers turned to look, to understand the murderous tone of Morgrom's voice. Glorian saw him standing at the time machine.

"What foolish trick is this?" said Morgrom, his voice now quivering with suppressed wrath.

"Trick?" asked Glorian. "If it's a trick, then it's a trick of the late Autoexec. I promise you on my honor as a member of the Supernatural and Fantastic Wayfarers Association, that is the very Golden Dipped Switch we recovered from his body."

"Yes," exclaimed Morgrom, "I have no doubt that it is. What I want to know, Glorian, is where are the other two? The Copper and Silver Switches. They were here on this machine not more than half an hour ago. Now they are missing. That's such a pitiful attempt, Glorian. It does your name and reputation no credit."

Glorian stared at him in shocked silence for a few seconds. Then he turned to Spike and held out his hand.

"I told you we should've gotten out of here fast," said The Protector. Reluctantly, he dropped the Copper and Silver Dipped Switches into Glorian's hand.

"Wait, Morgrom," said Glorian. "We had no arrangement at all about the other two Switches. If you can't protect your property any better than this, that's no fault of Prince Mirakles. He fulfilled his oath, you have the Golden Switch. I don't see why I should give these two back to you now."

The Malignant One's expression turned hard. "I can make you see why you should," he said in a low tone.

"I suggest you give it—" Glorian was interrupted by a strange, mechanical, clanking sound.

Morgrom, too, looked surprised. He stepped toward the door of the office. "My new elevator! Someone's in it, coming down! What, have you surrounded the house with reinforcements? Do you think you can sneak in warriors from the roof? Is that your next empty scheme?"

Glorian shook his head, his face a picture of innocence. "I know nothing about your elevator. I didn't even know you'd had one installed."

Further speech was prevented by the arrival of a blur in the office. Certainly, to Mirakles and Spike it must have been just a mysterious blur. To the trans-dimensionally-enhanced eyesight of Glorian and Morgrom, however, it was an even weirder sight. It was a figure that was in constant change—a lion, a bluebird, a tulip, an old woman, a reindeer, an oak sapling, a slime mold, a teenage boy, a grey squirrel, a lobster, a salamander. The figure was changing so rapidly and so constantly that it didn't hold the same form long enough to be visible to human eyes as other than a blur. A talking blur.

"Glorian, I congratulate you and Prince Mirakles and Spike on your success." The voice more or less filled the room, coming from everywhere. It was a kind, patient, and absolutely authoritative voice. Although Glorian had never seen this strange being before, he knew immediately that it was the Control Character.

Morgrom fell back a few steps in dismay. "Why are you taking a hand in this?" he cried. It was clear that the Essence of Evil suddenly realized that his plans had been completely ruined by the arrival of the Control Character.

"It is my business," said the Control Character.

"Sir," said Glorian, "are you taking an active or passive role in this struggle?"

"Why," said the Control Character, "active of course."

"No!" screamed Morgrom. "I demand—"

Suddenly, Morgrom was absent. He was gone. He wasn't there so much, it was almost as if he'd *never* been there.

"Someone explain what is going on," demanded a puzzled Prince Mirakles. "Who is this?"

"I'm what is called the deus ex machina," said the Control Character in a good-humored tone. "In this case, I think the term is more appropriate than ever, considering how I arrived in this room. In Greek and Roman dramas, actors playing gods were sometimes lowered to the stage by machinery. I know you can't see me. I am the Control Character."

Mirakles and Spike were almost stunned by the revelation. "In the Sunless Grotto," said the prince, "many of our wisest people argue about your existence."

"Yes, of course," said the Control Character. "Tell them hello for me when you get back. Now, Glorian, if you please, give the two Dipped Switches you hold to Spike, who will replace them in the time machine, making it ready for your journey. The leaflet you need is there, in that safe. Please get it."

"Yes, sir," said Glorian. He went to the safe and tried to open it, but it was locked. He began slowly turning the dial, using his hypernormal senses to discover the combination.

"Sir," said Spike, "if you don't mind my asking, you'd be the only one who could answer the one question I have about this adventure."

"Then ask."

"Why didn't you step in sooner? Why didn't you tell Glorian exactly how to defeat the Autoexec? Why did you risk the ruin of our universe, and put the responsibility for its safety on our shoulders?"

The blur . . . shrugged. Only Glorian might have seen it, but he wasn't looking. He was still having trouble with the safe.

"Listen to me and try to understand," said the Control Character. "There is not one universe, but an uncountable infinity of them. I seem to have had an active hand in creating this one, but of the others I can say nothing. There are uncountable universes and uncountable Control Characters and uncountable Spikes in them. What is the loss of one universe? Nothing. Not even a tiny dent in the reality of the multiverse."

"The multiverse?" asked Mirakles. "What does that mean?"

Glorian rattled and shook the safe's door, but it wouldn't budge. "Sir," he said, "I can't seem—"

The Control Character explained. "There is a universe like this, in which the adventurer came to this house. But in that universe, the adventurer never even discovered how to enter the Great Underground Empire, grew restless and bored after half an hour, and went back outside, never to return. There is a universe in which he climbed down the stairs, but was killed almost immediately by a troll. Every time the adventurer starts out on his quest, he creates a new universe, with new arrangements of people and treasures and monsters and outcomes."

"Perhaps so, Sir," said Spike, "but this is the only universe I have. From your point of view, it would've been no great loss for this reality to be ruined, or to disappear entirely. I just don't see it that way."

"Sir?" called Glorian plaintively.

Spike glanced at him and then went to the safe. "Please, Glorian," he said, "give me a crack at it." He wiggled his nimble fingers, and then quickly, deftly opened the safe.

"Ah," said Glorian, "thank you, Spike, I appreciate it." He looked inside the safe and took out the leaflet. "I've got it now, Sir."

"Good, Glorian," said the Control Character. "It's time now for rewards for our three heroes. Or two of them, anyway. Glorian, your reward must wait a bit. Prince Mirakles and Spike, your rewards will be determined by your score on Lord Raglan's point system, which I will explain briefly. Raglan studied many of the myths and legends familiar to him from his Latin and Greek studies, as well as European folklore, and determined that heroes tend to have twenty-two common characteristics."

"Sir?" said Spike. "Forgive me for interrupting, but Glorian and Prince Mirakles are the only heroes. I don't recall doing much to deserve a reward, and I surely don't share any of those twenty-two characteristics."

A brief laugh came from the blur. "Let me go on, and we'll see. First, the hero's father is a king, but he's also rumored to be the son of a god. And his mother is a royal virgin. Are these items not true in your case, Mirakles?"

"Why, yes, Sir," said the prince. "Of course."

"My father was a mortal," said Spike. "The thief. And I don't even know who my mother was."

"Well, Spike, it's very possible that your mother was a goddess. That would give you two out of three points."

"Do you know who my mother was?" asked Spike excitedly.

"Yes, Spike. Your mother was Threnia, the Muse of Modern Fantasy. Muses are allowed to raise families these days. We've tried to update our standards and keep abreast of the times."

Spike looked stunned. "My mother? A Muse?"

"I think so," said the Control Character.

Spike just fell into a chair and stared at the blur.

"Further," said the Control Character, "you must realize that just as Glorian was acting as the prince's Supernatural Guide, you were acting as Glorian's."

"It never even occurred to me," said Spike wonderingly.

"Yes, of course!" said Glorian.

Mirakles came up and put his hand on the boy's shoulder. "I'm happy for you, Spike," he said. "It appears that your future is brightening considerably here."

"Indeed so," said the Control Character.

He went through the remainder of Lord Raglan's list, and when he finished, Mirakles had scored eleven of twenty-two. The remaining points might yet be earned, as they concerned events that would happen after he became King of the Sunless Grotto. His reward was first, Melithiel, and second the Warm Boots, which the Control Character made appear on the prince's feet. As long as he wore those boots, Mirakles would be impervious to neuritis, neuralgia, and muscular aches and pains.

Spike, being much younger, scored only six points, but he had a long and wonderful career ahead of him. His reward was admission as a Neophyte Probationary in the Supernatural and Fantastic Wayfarers Association. "I must be dreaming," said the young man. "I don't know what to say."

Sudden understanding dawned in Glorian's eyes. "This is what Phretys meant when she told me that even after we returned here, our adventure wouldn't be over."

"Exactly, Glorian," said the Control Character. "Now, each of you must attend to your separate business. Glorian, you must take the time machine and use it to place the leaflet in the mailbox, so that the adventurer may find it there. That act is usually one of the first that he tries. You will be here at this house, and the thief will still be alive, and all the treasures and monsters and ruins and hazards of the Great Underground Empire will be in their pristine condition, awaiting the arrival of the adventurer."

"I've never seen the Empire in its pristine condition," said Glorian, awed despite his determination not to be.

"And you must disturb nothing then, either."

"I know, Sir," said Glorian.

The Control Character next addressed Mirakles. "You must return to your mother and assure her of her safety. Then you must build a tomb or cairn for the remains of the Embedded Character beside the Sunless Grotto, as you said you'd do. You must rule your future kingdom wisely and well, with your queen, Melithiel, beside you. And if you choose, you may assume the guardianship of the Great Underground Empire."

"I do so choose," said Mirakles, his voice choked with emotion.

"Then you three must now say farewell to each other." The Control Character disappeared as suddenly as he'd made Morgrom disappear.

"He's gone?" asked Spike sadly.

"Yes," said Glorian. "He no doubt has business elsewhere."

They stood around in the living room of the white house, unwilling to look at each other, in an uncomfortable silence for some time. Then Glorian went to Spike. "I will be your sponsor," he said. "I'll give you the benefit of my experiences in the Supernatural and Fantastic Wayfarers Association, if you wish. You'll make an outstanding guide."

"Thank you, Glorian," said Spike. "I'll always have your example before me."

Next, Glorian went to Prince Mirakles and clasped his arm. "Farewell, my prince. My thanks to you. We've come to the end at last."

"It is I who owe you thanks, Glorian. I thought I was a hero when I left the Sunless Grotto. Since then, I've learned how hard and how wonderful it is to become a hero. I hope I achieve that goal someday."

"Soon, my prince, if not already," said Glorian.

Mirakles nodded. Then he went to Spike and put his hand on the young man's head. "Be well, Spike, son of a Muse and a thief. You'll always be welcome in the Kingdom of the Sunless Grotto."

"Yes," said Spike, "I hope to see it soon."

Mirakles glanced from Spike to Glorian. Then, unwilling to bear the pain of the farewells any longer, he turned and left. Glorian heard the front door open and close.

"I guess I've got to go below and get my things together," said Spike. "I'll meet you back here when your mission is done."

"You bet," said Glorian. He watched as the young man threw back the Oriental rug and opened the trap door.

"Lock this after me, will you?" Spike called from below.

"Yes," replied Glorian. He closed the trap door and closed the bolt. Then he spread the rug over it. He was alone in the white house. It was very, very quiet. It felt as if marvelous sights were just hovering at the edges of his vision. Then he turned to the time machine. He had an important leaflet to deliver. The mail must go through.

EPILOGUE

Die Göttercocktailpartei II: The Return

THIS YEAR, THINGS GOT off to a suspiciously good start. That made Glorian wary right from the beginning. He wasn't used to things going well without a fight, and it made him a trifle uneasy, as if he were waiting for the obligatory catastrophe to thunder down upon him. For one thing, this year the acolytes showed up—*on time*—and fought each other for the privilege of carrying his well-stuffed bags. Spike followed along, awed, and carried his own single suitcase.

There was very little trouble getting to the Hyatt Regency Elysian Fields, except that one of the acolytes spent the entire trip pointing out all the palm trees and pastel pink and aqua architecture that littered the ungodly pleasant landscape and the famous restaurants and the famous theaters and the famous expensive shops and the famous Hangouts of the Gods. One of the other acolytes leaned over and told the first, "He's Glorian of the Knowledge. He's been here before. He *knows* these things."

"Things have changed since the last time he was here," said the first acolyte. He went on and on until Spike told him to shut up.

"What are you?" cried the no-longer-glowing young man. "Some kind of semi-immortal tour guide?" Glorian gave The Protector a long, sage look, but it seemed to him that Spike missed all the significance in it.

They arrived at the hotel, and an acolyte said he'd watch the bags while Glorian and Spike checked in. This year, Glorian felt he deserved to reward himself, and he'd reserved a suite for the two of them. "Glorian of the Knowledge and Spike, The Protector," he said to the desk clerk in a firm, clear voice. "Reservations under 'Glorian.' Here for the Supernatural and Fantastic Wayfarers Association awards banquet."

The desk clerk nodded absently and rummaged through his plastic box of forms. "Glorian, you say? Sorry, I see nothing here for Glorian. Could you have given Reservations a different name?"

Glorian was about to point out that he only had the one name, but that wouldn't have cut any ice with the desk clerk. Desk clerks are trained from Day One not to cut ice. And, anyway, Glorian felt rather relieved. This was how things were *supposed* to happen.

Finally, of course, the reservations mess was all sorted out. "Here you are, Mr. Florian, Room 1026." Glorian nodded, took the room keys, and led Spike toward the elevators. A terrible, booming voice called out the new Implementor's name from across the lobby. It was a voice that could shatter worlds, and it had done just that on a number of occasions. Glorian turned around and saw Shiva the Destroyer stalking toward him. "That's Shiva the Destroyer," he told Spike.

"Jeez," said Spike. His mouth opened and closed and then fell open again in a kind of sickly, oddly wobbly grin.

"Things are much different from last year, aren't they?" said Shiva, slapping Glorian on the back in a comradely fashion. "A lot of blood has passed under the dam, or over the bridge, or whatever. You've moved up in the world, haven't you?"

"Not so's you'd notice," said Glorian, in what he hoped sounded truly humble. "Shiva, let me introduce Spike—"

"I know all about this young man." The Destroyer shook hands with The Protector, who looked as if he wouldn't be able to stand upright much longer.

"As far as everything else goes," said Glorian, "I'm an Implementor now, but I'm glad to be on the Campbell Award ballot again. I still feel the same."

"Well," said Shiva, "I voted for you. Good luck tonight. I truly hope you win."

"Thank you," said Glorian, "but it's an honor just to be nominated."

Shiva gave him a sideways look and squinted just a little. "Sure," he said. Then he turned and went back the way he'd come.

Upstairs, the suite was plush and luxurious, quite a change from the spartan, cold elegance of the Valhalla Hilton. Glorian took the bedroom to the left, and Spike carried his bag into the bedroom to the right. They shared a living room that was comfortably furnished with a wet bar. The drapes were pulled back, and unlike the view from last year's room, this view was actually viewable. There were vibrant, green meadows there, and warm, rich sunlight, and probably the best dead heroes who'd ever lived. Here were the heroes who'd also been good-hearted law-givers. The ones who could only kill people were in Hades.

Spike came into Glorian's room and sat on the edge of the bed. He watched in silent amazement as the Implementor transferred the contents of his voluminous bags to the bureau and closet. "This suite come with Drawer Forwarding?" he asked.

Glorian nodded. "Of course," he said. "I don't go

anywhere now without it. We wouldn't even *be* here now without it."

"I know. I just wanted to be sure. Will you show me how it works?"

Glorian nodded again. He had *a lot* of stuff to put away, and Spike wasn't helping.

"You know there are three TV's in this suite?" said the young man.

"Well," said Glorian, looking up from his task, "you wouldn't want to miss a moment of 'My Three Suns' if you had to step out into another room."

"Uh huh," said Spike dubiously. "Say, how long is it going to take you to finish that?"

"I'll be done in ten minutes. The cocktail party before the awards ceremony doesn't start for another hour. We have plenty of time."

"Oh," said Spike. ""I just thought I'd go down to the lobby or sit in the bar."

Glorian stood up straight and stretched. He smiled at his friend. "Go on down," he said, "but do me one favor. Don't ask for autographs. Everyone knows I'm sponsoring you as a neopro. Don't embarrass me."

"You don't have to treat me like a kid. I hate that. Just because you're a million and a half years older than I am or something." Spike got up from the bed and left the room. A moment later, Glorian heard the suite's front door open and close.

As a matter of fact, he was glad that Spike had left. He was having a tough time concealing how anxious he was about the awards ceremony. This was the eleventh time he'd come to one of these banquets as a nominee, and so far all he had to show for it were the tiny memories of twenty free drinks.

Glorian completed his unpacking, switched on the television, and stretched out on his bed. He couldn't seem to relax. He also couldn't seem to keep his attention fixed on the movie, which was about a gigantic humanoid being who breathed fire, who rose up out of the sea and crushed a vast cardboard city populated by terrified kimono dragons who shrieked in close-ups. Glorian could see the wires on the little model kimono dragon fighter planes. When the giant humanoid stepped on high-rise apartment buildings and office towers, they collapsed instantly, and there didn't seem to be anything inside them, not even floors or walls.

He looked at the clock beside the bed and guessed it was time to go downstairs. He'd decided that he'd try to make an impression tonight, so he'd had an acolyte get him a tuxedo for the occasion. It was an Elysian Fields tux, which meant that it was pastel pink with matching aqua tie and cummerbund. He'd been shocked for a few moments when he'd opened the box, but then he shrugged his pseudo-human shoulders and put it on. He changed his body to fit the tuxedo. When he finished dressing, he was an extremely handsome man. He walked out of the suite looking like Cary Grant, but with James Mason's voice. He knew it was a killer combination.

He found Spike in the bar. The neopro was drinking expensive bottled water and staring around at all the famous non-people nearby. When Glorian sat down across the table from him, Spike's eyes opened wide. "Jeez," he said. "You look great."

"Thanks," said Glorian. "I don't feel great."

"Nervous?"

Glorian just nodded. A waitress in a very revealing Wicked Temptress outfit came over, and Glorian gave her his two free-drink chits. "Gin and bingara," he said.

"You want that with some lime?"

"That's disgusting," said Glorian.

"All right, no lime." The Wicked Temptress took her tray and pad away.

The two companions talked for a few minutes. "I wish Mirakles was here," said Spike wistfully.

"Heroes have their own association," said Glorian.

"I wonder if we'll ever see him again."

"I'm sure we will. I'm sure that you'll guide someone through the Great Underground Empire again someday, and Mirakles will be there somewhere to greet you."

"You think so?" asked Spike hopefully.

"I'm almost sure of it," said Glorian. The waitress returned with his two drinks and set them down on sodden cocktail napkins.

Spike watched her walk away again. "Jeez," he said, more wistfully than ever.

"Glorian, is that you?" said a croaking voice nearby in the gloomily-lighted bar.

The Implementor looked up and saw the Hanged Frog and Amitia standing there. He was delighted. "Hi, how are you? Sit down!"

They pulled chairs over to the table, set down their drinks, and seated themselves. Glorian made introductions. Spike was impressed all over again. "If you don't mind me getting personal," he said to the Frog, "you don't look the least bit Hanged. I kind of expected that you'd be walking around with your head at some bizarre angle, with a black, swollen tongue lolling out of your mouth."

The Hanged Frog laughed. He was a frog, all right, a tall, green frog built along roughly human lines. He stood on two sturdy legs, with his large webbed feet crammed into green leather boots. He wore green tights and a green short-sleeved tunic that displayed his well-muscled arms. His hands were huge and webbed. He had a froggy human face, and Spike was correct, he didn't look the least bit Hanged. "Actually," the Frog explained, "my name comes from a play written by a little-read Magyar playwright, Sandor

Courane, a contemporary of Shakespeare. 'The Hanged Frog' is actually a slight mistranslation of the title of the play, which more accurately was printed in English once in 1604 as *Thee Frogge welle-Hunge*. You'd have to read the play to understand the reference."

There was silence around the table for a moment after that. Glorian gave Amitia a smile. "It's good to see you again," he said.

She seemed even younger than she had at the awards ceremony in Valhalla. Of course, she could change her body just as Glorian had, so that didn't really mean anything. Last year she'd been a blonde. This year, she had thick, raven tresses tumbled down over her shoulders. It contrasted with her skin, which was as white and perfect as a bowl of milk. She wore a long gown with about ten pounds of rhinestones and sequins, all sewn on by hand. "Glorian," she said, her eyes shining, "we all owe you so much."

He shrugged modestly. "I couldn't have done it without Spike here."

"Jeez," said Spike, "don't believe him. I was only helpful in the extreme. I wasn't indispensable."

Amitia smiled. "By the time you've been around as long as the three of us have, you'll have learned indispensability. It's one of our chief commodities."

Spike just nodded dumbly. He was In Love.

The Hanged Frog took a sip from his drink and put the glass back down. "So, Glorian," he said, "how do you feel about being up against Narlinia von Glech for the Campbell again?"

Glorian considered how best to answer that. "Well, of course, it's an honor—"

"Don't you dare say it," said the Frog. "I learned all about that last year."

Savitri, who was still serving his millennium-long term as president of the Supernatural and Fantastic

Wayfarers Association, tested the microphone at the podium. "Is this thing turned on?" he asked.

Glorian glanced at Spike. "Here we go," he said.

Amitia reached across and squeezed Glorian's hand.

"We had such good response to the non-appearance of our guest speaker last year," said Savitri, "that we decided to try it again this year. Therefore, we'll dive directly into tonight's important business, and then we can get back to the even more important business of partying."

There was applause from the crowd at the news that they wouldn't have to wait through a dull and boring speech before they could learn who'd won this year's Joseph Campbell Award for Best Semi-Actual Persona.

"I want to go home now," Glorian murmured. "I don't want to sit through this."

"Shh," said Spike, "he's opening the envelope."

"And the winner is . . . Glorian of the Knowledge! Congratulations, Glorian, it's about time!"

Glorian realized he'd been holding his breath. He let it out now and took another. He was literally dumbstruck. It only lasted a second or two. Then he looked at Amitia. "I've won a Campbell Award," he said in an amazed voice.

Amitia nodded. "Then go up there and *get* it!"

"Way to go, Glorian!" cried Spike proudly

"Congratulations!" said the Hanged Frog.

"Right," said Glorian. He pushed his chair back. His ears were ringing very loudly, and his heart was beating so fast he thought he could hear it shift into a new gear that had never been used before. He walked dreamily to the podium where Savitri was standing, beaming at him, holding the Campbell Award.

Glorian accepted it graciously. It was the Cary Grant in him. He turned to the microphone, and in James Mason's wonderful voice he said, "I suppose everyone knows how much I've wanted one of these. I want to thank everyone who voted for me. I also want to thank my friend, Spike, who's just joined our Association. And, of course, I owe a lot to the Control Character. We *all* do. Good luck to you, and may God bless."

He was startled to see that he was getting a standing ovation from his friends and colleagues. He posed for a few photographs, holding the award over his head and grinning.

The first person to come up to congratulate him was Narlinia von Glech. She was doing her tired beauty-queen number again. "I'm so happy for you, darling," she said in a breathy voice. "I'm so glad you finally won. You needed it more than I did."

Glorian gave her a sour stare. "I wanted it, Narlinia," he said. ""I didn't need it."

She laughed. "Believe that if you like," she said.

Glorian was too busy looking at the Campbell Award, the beautiful bronze mask, to pay any more attention to her. There was a shiny rectangular brass plate fixed to the front of the award's base. At first, the plate looked completely blank. Only Glorian's supernatural eyesight could have found the tiny letters inscribed in the lower right corner. They read:

This space intentionally left blank.

It was probably meaningful, in a symbolic way.

GEORGE ALEC EFFINGER is a writer whose imaginative and innovative short stories and novels have made his name an important one in the science fiction field for nearly twenty years. Author of such novels as *When Gravity Fails* and *A Fire in the Sun,* his works consistently garner nominations for the field's highest awards, and he recently received the Hugo and Nebula awards for his novelette "Schrödinger's Kitten." He lives with his aquatic dwarf frogs in New Orleans, Louisiana.